D0534045

TOWER OF SILENCE

Also by Sarah Rayne

A Dark Dividing
Roots of Evil
Spider Light
The Death Chamber

TOWER OF SILENCE

Sarah Rayne

POCKET
BOOKS

LONDON · SYDNEY · NEW YORK · TOKYO · TORONTO

First published in Great Britain by Simon & Schuster UK Ltd, 2003
This paperback edition published by Pocket Books, 2008
An imprint of Simon & Schuster UK Ltd
A CBS COMPANY

1 3 5 7 9 10 8 6 4 2

Simon & Schuster UK Ltd
Africa House
64–78 Kingsway
London WC2B 6AH

www.simonsays.co.uk

Simon & Schuster Australia
Sydney

A CIP catalogue record for this book is
available from the British Library

ISBN 978-1-84739-349-4

Printed and bound in Great Britain by
Cox & Wyman Ltd, Reading, Berks

TOWER OF SILENCE

CHAPTER ONE

'If you're as broke as all that,' said Gillian Campbell to her godmother, 'why on earth don't you sell Teind House?'

'Oh, I couldn't do that,' said Selina at once.

'Why not? You'd probably make enough on the sale to live anywhere you liked. You could leave Inchcape altogether if you wanted. Buy a little bungalow.'

'Oh, no,' said Selina, and instantly felt the words take on a menacing reality. Leave-Inchcape, *leave-Inchcape* . . . She shivered and said, 'No, that's out of the question.'

'Why not?' said Gillian again.

But it was impossible to explain to Gillian, who lived a crowded modern life in London, that there were things at Teind that strangers must never find: things that must be kept concealed from the prying outside world at all costs . . . No, she could never leave Inchcape.

And so she said, 'You see, Gillian, I've always lived here.

Since I was seven years old – dear goodness, forty-eight years ago! The aunts and Great-uncle Matthew left me Teind House. They wouldn't like to think of it going out of the family. I wouldn't like to think of it, either. I – I feel *safe* here.'

Gillian looked at Selina, for whom life seemed to have stopped somewhere in the 1940s, and about whom people smiled sadly and indulgently and said, Oh, she's just like a Victorian pressed flower in somebody's old album, and tried very hard not to feel exasperated. Selina was not Victorian, of course, she was nowhere near old enough, but she did seem to have been stuck in a past age – a dim, cobwebby past – ever since Gillian could remember. All the fault of those finicky old women who had brought her up, and the even more finicky old man who had been their brother. 'OK, if you won't sell up, why don't you make the place work for you?'

'How?'

'Well, there's only you rattling around here and you don't use much more than a quarter of it. You could let the top floor – turn the attics into a flat. There're always wildlife students at the bird sanctuary in Stornforth who want summer accommodation.'

'Oh, not students. I couldn't have students – so noisy, so irresponsible. Parties and drugs—'

Gillian pounced. 'Then how about offering bed and breakfast?'

'You mean – charge people for giving them hospitality?'

Dear, twittery Selina was plainly shocked to her toes.

Gillian grinned and said, 'Why not? It needn't be anything high-powered; you'd get retired couples motoring through Scotland, or little groups of two or three ladies. Stop-over accommodation, that's what they call it. The Black Boar does lunches and nice evening bar meals, so all you'd need provide would be tea or coffee and orange juice, with scrambled eggs and ham or kedgeree and toast.'

'And a room.'

'Selina, darling, even without the attics you've got four bedrooms you never use, and three sitting rooms!'

'But there'd be laundry,' said Selina, rather desperately. 'Bathrooms – gentlemen using the lavatory—'

For pity's sake! thought Gillian, but she said, 'There's a perfectly good second loo on the half-landing. And a wash basin in two of the bedrooms to my knowledge. There's even a laundry in Stornforth who still collects and delivers. You could do it easily. Look on it as an adventure.'

'But would people want to come?'

'I don't see why not. There're always tourists driving through and stopping for lunch at the Black Boar. The bird sanctuary gets masses of visitors. And there's a lot of history scattered about this part of Scotland. I bet you'd get loads of people wanting to stay. You could charge thirty or forty quid a night, and you wouldn't need to take more than two couples at a time if you didn't want to – in fact you'd probably only need to do it between April and October anyway. If you averaged two couples for two nights a week, that would bring in between a hundred and twenty and a hundred and sixty pounds each week.' She grinned. 'Truly, Selina darling, it'd be money for old rope.'

Gillian's words reminded Selina sharply of her father, even after so many years. It was odd how an expression could trigger a memory.

Money for old rope, father used to say when Selina was small and somebody commissioned him to write an article about a politician or a statesman. He had said it when the family sailed for India all that time ago. After years of reporting about the warlords of Europe, he had said it would be money for jam to write about the birth-struggles of Indian independence, and to focus on Mr Nehru's determination to modernise his country. Father always gave his articles what the newspapers called human interest, which was why he was commissioned to write so many things. And he liked travelling around and meeting people. ('Nothing but a gypsy,' Great-aunt Rosa had once said, lips pursed.)

Father had not been a gypsy, of course; it was just that he was good at making friends in new places, and at finding out what was going on and shaping it into the kind of story people liked to read. He would have discovered everything that went on in Inchcape, except that nothing much ever did, and father would probably have been bored very quickly.

Selina was not bored by Inchcape, and the tourists who drove through the place did not seem to be bored by it either. They were usually bound for the bird sanctuary at Stornforth, of course, but they often stopped to have lunch at the Black Boar, and they almost always walked up to see the eleventh-century church, and the remains of the monastery which had been abandoned somewhere around the ninth century when the monks of Columba decamped to Ireland.

Teind House itself had a history, as well: it took its name from the old Gael word *teind* meaning tithe, because the house had once been a tithe barn where the laird of Inchcape – when Inchcape had a laird – had gathered tithes from his tenants every quarter day. The whole village would come along and there would be a party in the evening after all the tithes had been paid.

Great-uncle Matthew had told Selina all this when she came to live with him and his two sisters, who were Great-aunt Flora and Great-aunt Rosa. It was nice to know about the place where you lived, wasn't it? said Great-uncle Matthew, who studied local history, and always smelt of bay rum and ink. The aunts smelt of Yardley's lavender water, and the little sachets Aunt Flora made to put in clothes cupboards.

Selina, considering Gillian's wild suggestion from all angles, thought that the aunts and Great-uncle Matthew would have been horrified at the thought of their great-niece taking in paying guests; they would have seen it as a lowering of standards. Standards, they had always said, were very important. To be sure it was very sad that Selina's mother and father had died – the implication was that John March ought not to have taken his wife and small daughter to such an outlandish country as India in the first place – but it was important not to make any scenes. Certainly not to sob and weep and make an exhibition of yourself. The good Lord had seen fit to take John and Poor Elspeth to His bosom – although it was a great pity He had done so in such a very unpleasant and unChristian fashion – but it was His will and Selina must accept it. There would be a memorial of some kind, naturally: a tablet in the church, perhaps – they would ask the vicar. Memorials were important. You had to honour the dead, said Great-aunt Rosa. Great-aunt Flora thought Selina might plant rosemary or a little lavender bush in a corner of the garden as a private little memorial, how would that be?

In Scotland, death and your parents' memories apparently smelt of lavender and rosemary, but in India, where John and Elspeth March had died, they had smelt of sandalwood and frankincense, which the people burned to prevent the spread of disease from decaying flesh, and to help speed the departing soul on its way to heaven.

But on the day that Selina's parents had died, there had been no sandalwood or burning oil. There had only been the dreadful stench of blood and fear, spilled entrails and burst eyes.

'I've thought of a problem,' said Selina.

'Darling, there aren't any problems. We've worked it all out—'

'Moy,' said Selina. 'It's one thing for tourists to drive through Inchcape and stop for lunch and walk round the church and so on. But they won't want to stay in a place

6

where there's an asylum for the criminally insane on the doorstep.'

Gillian said, 'Moy isn't really on the doorstep. It's four miles away. And I think you're wrong, anyway. People go to Dartmoor in positive droves.'

'Butterflies and Sherlock Holmes,' said Selina.

'Well, Inchcape's got birds and monks – OK, the ghosts of monks and the remains of a monastery. But listen, Moy's so high-security it squeaks. When was the last time the alarm bell was rung? 1920? 1910? The place is famous for only having had about one break-out in the last hundred years!'

And then Selina said, 'There was a bulletin on the television news last evening. Moy's head of psychiatry – Dr Irvine – made a statement. It's been decided to transfer Mary Maskelyne to Moy.'

'Oh,' said Gillian rather blankly. 'Oh, yes, I see what you mean.'

Opinions among the staff at Moy were divided as to whether Patrick Irvine had angled to get Mary Maskelyne here in order to help with his research into the criminal mind, or whether he had done everything he could to avoid it.

Donald Frost, who was D wing's head, and would therefore be Maskelyne's wing governor, God help him, said non-committally that Maskelyne was a very interesting case; Dr Irvine would find it very valuable to study the lady. In private, he reminded his team that observation of Maskelyne would need to be covert but extremely high.

Dr Irvine might put her on suicide watch after he had carried out an initial assessment; they would have to wait to see about that.

The original case, in the mid Sixties, had been very high-profile indeed, of course, and most people remembered it, even those who had not been there at the time, in the way that people remembered things like President Kennedy's assassination, or the day war broke out, even though those things might have happened before they were born. It was not surprising, of course; the tabloids had gone to town on the Maskelyne story and even the broadsheets had given a fair degree of coverage. The television stations had trampled over one another in the rush to get interviews and opinions, and court coverage. And the letters! Sackfuls of them Maskelyne had had, from all the usual weirdos who wrote to murderesses, including the customary sprinkling of peculiar men who wanted to marry her.

Over lunch in the mess room, somebody referred to that, and somebody else made a coarse prophecy as to the possible fate of any man foolhardy enough to get into bed with Maskelyne. The first speaker demanded to know if there was to be a free issue of jockstraps for that wing, which raised a rather uneasy chuckle because you had to keep hold of a sense of humour in this place – never mind how black it was – or you would not be able to cope with these shut-away, closed-minded people who were sometimes dangerous and frequently disgusting.

Mary Maskelyne had been fourteen at the time of the first murders. *Fourteen*, for God's sake! The age at which most girls were thinking of nothing but pop music, make-up, clothes and boys, and, if you were lucky, their GCSEs. Don Frost, whose own daughter had just turned twenty-one, said with feeling that there was no doing anything with a fourteen-year-old, didn't he just know it. They metamorphosed into some peculiar things at that age, although fortunately the metamorphosis was usually temporary, and, to be fair, did not normally include a spell as a serial killer.

One of the younger warders wanted to know about the letters: had they been hate mail?

'There was a lot of hate mail,' said Patrick Irvine, who had just come in. He sat down at the end of the table, next to Donald. 'But they kept those letters from her. They let her have the mad ones – the sycophantic ones. I-hate-my-father, and I-would-like-to-kill-him-like you-killed-yours. In fact— Oh, thanks.' He broke off as one of the waitresses handed him a plate of food. Several of the younger men noticed wistfully that bread rolls, butter, and a fresh carafe of water were all brought to the table without Dr Irvine's having to ask for them. He fascinated the waitresses, of course, just as he fascinated most people.

'Those kinds of letters die a death, though, don't they?' asked someone. 'They trickle away after the first few months.'

'They do, and that was Maskelyne's trouble,' said Patrick. 'Once she had to shake down to a routine in that Young Offenders place, she missed the attention.'

'And killed again,' said Donald Frost, softly.

'Yes. That was when they began to realise that she was genuinely psychotic.'

'Mad,' said somebody.

'Oh, yes. Don't be fooled by the doe eyes and the soft voice,' said Patrick. 'She's very severely deranged indeed.'

There was a rather uncomfortable silence, and then the young warder who had asked about the hate mail, whose name was Robbie Glennon, said, 'Are we in for trouble with her, sir?' He had been carefully brought up to call older men 'sir', and he thought it polite to do so when it was Moy's chief psychiatrist he was addressing.

'She'll most likely behave reasonably for a while because she'll have been enjoying this new wave of attention after the transfer,' said Irvine, and Robbie Glennon absorbed this fact solemnly because he tried to absorb most things Dr Irvine said. Dr Irvine was just about the most brilliant man he had ever encountered in his life. He was an absolutely dedicated doctor, although to look at him now, eating cottage pie with industrious enjoyment, you would never think it. Detachment, that was what it was. Detachment was very important in this job; it was something Robbie was still struggling to achieve. But Dr Irvine never seemed fazed by the behaviour of Moy's inmates; he never seemed to mind about the vomit, the seizures, the blood-flecked foam or voided urine, and he was known to be carrying out privately funded research into the various treatments of the cracked or dislocated minds that made up Moy's inmates.

Patrick poured himself a glass of water. 'If I could tell

you what Maskelyne would be likely to do next time she gets bored, or next time the psychosis kicks in,' he said, 'I wouldn't be slaving away out here with you lazy sods; I'd be making a million telling the fortunes of the rich and idle.'

The inevitable joke about crystal balls followed, lightening the atmosphere, as Patrick had intended. The most effective way of imparting unwelcome information was often to wrap it up inside a bit of a joke.

But he hoped that none of the men would forget Mary Maskelyne's reputation. Or that her vicious intelligence had outwitted prison warders and killed four people.

As the years slid past, it had become easier for Mary to look back to the start: to see her life since she was fourteen, almost as if it were a tapestry she could unroll at will. For long stretches the pattern was plain and dull and flat, but here and there were sudden exciting splashes of life and colour.

One of the earliest splashes of colour, one of the milestones, had been the juvenile court, of course. Mary could see it as a vivid jigsawing of colours on the tapestry, and she could remember it very clearly indeed. She could remember how a distant aunt had come to be with her, and how there had been a social worker, and she could remember how she had deliberately chosen to wear her most grown-up clothes. Dress *young*, the aunt and the social worker had said beforehand. As young as possible. Wear your school uniform. The younger you look, the more sympathy you'll get from the court. But Mary had worn the tangerine mini-skirt and the dark brown figure-hugging sweater that went with it. Clumpy-heeled 'moddy' shoes and diamond-patterned tights. She had washed her hair the night before the trial started and smoothed it into two shining wings on each side of her face, and she had applied black eye-liner in the Cleopatra fashion of the day. This was going to be pretty boring; she knew what the verdict would be before it was given, which meant it would be utterly tedious to have to sit through days of people talking and giving evidence and arguing as to whether she was sane or mad, and whether she understood what she had done or not. At least if she could dress up, people would look at her, and there might be articles in the newspapers and bits on TV.

She was not mad, she was completely sane, and she understood perfectly well what she had done. Her parents had deserved to die, and when they had heard the evidence the judge and the people on the jury would think so as well.

When the jury foreman had given the verdict Mary had not believed it. At first she had thought she must have heard wrongly, and then that they were playing a sick joke on her. After all the attention they had accorded her, all those letters sent to her – twenty-seven men wanted to marry her the minute she reached sixteen, and at least as many girls had written asking her to tell them how she got her hair to look like that – after all that, the single, cold word *Guilty* had been like a blow across the eyes, and she had had to put up a hand to shield her face.

And then, almost instantly, she had understood that

this had been the only possible verdict. You had to see the thing in a broader context: you had to understand about sending out signals, warning evil people who could have seen an acquittal as a sign that murder was permissible. Yes, it was right that the jury should give a guilty verdict.

But she had known, with absolute conviction, that when the judge pronounced sentence it would be the very lightest of punishments. They would not send her to prison, she knew that, because girls of fourteen did not go to prison. It would most probably be probation. The judge would say that what Mary had done was justifiable and understandable, and he would set her free, just as a judge last year had set free a woman who, having endured years of cruelty and sexual abuse from an alcoholic father, had eventually lost control and killed him.

Waiting for the judge's sentencing, the courtroom hushed and solemn, she had stared disdainfully over the heads of the people in the court. She had known that they were all watching her, and she had known they were awed at what she had done. She had ignored them, fixing her eyes on the judge, her face already half-arranged in a gracious little smile of acceptance. He would understand, this wise old man, about dispensing justice and about vindication of wrongs. He would know that only the strong and the honourable dared take the law into their own hands, as Mary had done. He would admire her, so young, so brave, so cruelly treated by the world.

The courtroom was charged with anticipation. They

were all waiting to hear that she was to be set free – Mary could feel it.

The judge laid his hands, palms downwards, on the polished surface of the bench, and said that after consideration and after studying the psychiatric reports he could reach only one decision.

Mary Maskelyne was to be incarcerated at Her Majesty's pleasure in an institution for young offenders. After four years she was to be reassessed, and, if thought appropriate, transferred to an institution for the criminally insane.

It had taken three prison officers to restrain Mary and carry her back to the cells below the court.

CHAPTER TWO

Gillian had meant well, talking about buying a little bungalow if Teind House were sold, but Selina did not actually want to live in a little bungalow; she did not want to live anywhere that might mean neighbours and people calling on her to borrow lawn-mowers or invite her to coffee mornings or Tupperware parties.

('Selina, darling, people don't have Tupperware parties any more,' Gillian had said, and Selina had said, well, she knew that of course, but still.)

She liked the remoteness of Teind, and she liked living with the bricks and timbers and windows that had belonged to her mother's family for so many generations. As a child she had helped the aunts to look after the house, because that was what girls did. Some people went away to school, and for a long time after she came to Scotland this had worried Selina quite a lot, because she had not known

15

if she might have to go away, but Aunt Rosa had said, and Aunt Flora had agreed, that going away to school was not necessary. Boys had to go away to school – Matthew had done so – but that was because boys had to work. They had to support wives and families – although Matthew had not, in the event, done either – but girls did not have to worry about that. Girls got married and became housewives and mothers.

Selina would attend the village school each day, which was just a few minutes' walk from Teind House, they said. She could learn all she needed there, and be home in time for tea. After the first few days, Selina discovered that most of the other pupils took a packed lunch; they all sat together in the gymnasium and ate their sandwiches and in the winter they took a flask of hot soup. It was rather friendly and nice, and in the half-hour before afternoon classes started all kinds of things went on. Little unofficial clubs and groups to which you belonged depending on the kind of thing you found interesting. There were domino tournaments and hopscotch contests. There was much scoffing by the boys at the girls, and much head-tossing by the girls towards the boys.

The older girls talked about clothes, which came off rationing that spring, and giggled over furtive copies of *Forever Amber*. Transistor radios were still a thing of the future, but somebody smuggled in a portable gramophone so that everyone could listen to Johnnie Ray singing about Hernando's Hideaway, and Frankie Laine and the Mule Train. Frankie Laine was a dreamboat, all the older girls said so.

In the aunts' youth people had liked songs from musicals: *Rosemarie* and *The Desert Song*, or sentimental ballads
like 'Night and Day'. Great-uncle Matthew had once
shocked their parents by singing 'Minnie the Moocher'
at a Christmas party, but that had been when he was
much younger of course.

Aunt Flora and Aunt Rosa did not approve of domino
tournaments at lunchtime or of dreamboats who sang the
blues. They did not approve of sandwiches and flasks of
soup either, most unwholesome, said Aunt Flora. Selina
would do better to come home each day and have a proper
nourishing meal.

At weekends and holidays there were always things
to be done in the house. There was furniture to polish
and flowers to arrange, and there was a proper routine.
Friday was polishing day, just as Monday was wash day
when Jeannie from the village came up to deal with the
laundry, and the wash-house behind Teind smelt of steam
and soap. Tuesday was ironing day and Thursday was
baking day. You had to have orderliness, the aunts said
firmly. And baking on Thursday and polishing on Friday
meant that the house smelt of lavender and beeswax for
the weekend and there were cakes in the tin for visitors.
The vicar sometimes called on Saturday, and there might
be guests to afternoon tea on Sunday before evensong. If
it was after evensong or before Sunday lunch, it had to
be sherry or Madeira and wine biscuits.

Great-uncle Matthew never helped with the polishing
or the baking, of course. He made notes about local
history and wrote letters to people, and had a stamp

collection. He saw to incomprehensible things called annuities and insurances and had luncheon in Stornforth with the hospital governors on the third Wednesday of every month. He enjoyed these meetings: he always came back looking quite spry, although it did not take him long to sink back into his usual disapproving humourlessness.

Once, when Aunt Flora had to have a thyroid operation and Aunt Rosa sprained her ankle the very same week, there had been a great to-do over the preparing of Matthew's meals. Somebody had asked why Matthew could not prepare his own meals, which Aunt Rosa said just went to show. In the end Aunt Rosa had managed to hire a temporary cook from an agency in Stornforth, but it had not been very successful. The woman had not known how to make egg sauce for the baked ham that was Great-uncle Matthew's favourite Saturday evening supper, and after she left Aunt Rosa had had to hobble into the scullery to put everything back in the right place, and discovered that garlic had been used in the omelette pan.

'Nasty foreign stuff,' said Aunt Rosa and Aunt Flora shuddered, and they went on a shopping trip to Stornforth to buy a new omelette pan and to replace all the tea towels.

Gillian had suggested that a suitable letter be sent to Stornforth Bird Sanctuary and to the nearest Tourist Information offices, advertising the bed-and-breakfast facility at Teind House, and had even discovered some-one in Inchcape who would come to help with the extra housework and cooking when people were staying.

'She doesn't need much in the way of cash,' said Gillian. 'It's one of the warder's daughters at Moy. Lorna Laughlin from the school suggested her. She's only about twenty – I think she dropped out of university last summer, and she just wants something to do. Her name's Emily Frost.'

'Shouldn't I see her – interview her or something?' Selina knew people did this. The aunts had always interviewed the daily cleaners who came to Teind House, even though it was generally somebody from the village whose family they had known all their lives. And in India, before Selina and mother went to live in the Alwar village which father thought was safer for them than Delhi, they had had houseboys and Selina had had an ayah, but mother had always interviewed them before agreeing to give them work. You could not be too careful, she had said. There were such dreadful stories these days and India was a simmering cauldron, father had said so only that week, and then had jotted the expression down in his notebook to use in an article sometime or other.

But the little English settlement just outside Alwar, with its wonderful smudgy purple backdrop of hills in the distance, was perfectly safe. 'Your father would not have sent us here if it had not been,' mother had said, patting her hair complacently.

But John March, writing of India's unrestful state, writing of Gandhi's hunger strikes, and of the dark cloud of partition that was to hover for years in the aftermath of India's independence, had not known that in sending his wife and his small daughter into the little colony at Alwar – consisting mostly of English wives and families of the doctors and teachers and lawyers who had come out here in the aftermath of World War II – he was sending the one to her death, the other to a nightmare from which she was never fully to emerge.

It had been the end of the afternoon when it happened: the time when people had got up from after-lunch naps, and the scents of sandalwood and jasmine lay drowsily on the country air. Servants and houseboys had begun preparing their employers' evening meals, and there was a faint drift of the spices the Indian people used for their cooking – tamarind and cumin and ginger.

'But the spices,' Selina's mother always said unhappily, 'are too often used to conceal the fact that the meat is not as fresh as one would like.'

But on that afternoon, playing in a group of children – five English, one Canadian – Selina had cared nothing for her mother's fastidious discontent. She had been absorbed in that day's game, which was a new one called the Maiden Tower. Christabel Maskelyne's father had told them the tale of the princess who had been imprisoned in the doorless tower in a place called Baku because she would not marry her father. This had been interesting, although nobody had properly understood the bit about marrying her father, because everyone knew you did not marry your father. Still, it was a good story, and it was going to make a good game. Christabel had thought they could pretend that a maharajah, which meant a prince, came to rescue the princess, and so there was going to be a journey through the mountains, with the maharajah riding on an elephant, and servants bearing gifts of gold and ivory.

Selina was the princess, in one of mother's evening scarves and a dab of Max Factor lipstick on her forehead, and Douglas, the boy from Toronto, was the maharajah because his Canadian accent made him sound a bit foreign. Christabel, wearing a discarded curtain for a cloak, with a kitchen knife for a sword, was the princess's wicked father, and everybody else was a servant. They had put a ladder against a tree for the doorless tower, and Selina was going to look down and say, 'Oh, who is this handsome prince,' and then Douglas had to climb up the ladder for the rescue while Christabel waved her arms in the air to indicate impotent fury. After this everybody would say things like, 'We bring you gold from the east, princess,' and, 'Let us flee to the shining palace in the mountains.'

They had just reached the part where Selina was saying, 'Oh, who is this—' when somebody said, 'What's that?'

This was not in the script, but Christabel thought you should improvise in games, and so Selina said, 'Oh, do you hear my father's men coming?' And then stopped and looked across the gardens, because she had heard it as well.

The sound of something clanging and banging – something that went on and on clanging, and made your heart jump in fear, because you knew deep inside that something bad was going to happen, and something very fearsome indeed was coming to get you.

And then one of the others said, 'It's a bell,' and another said, 'It's the alarm bell in the old tower. It means there's a raid or something—'

For a moment they had stood looking at one another, none of them quite knowing what to do, the smallest ones not even sure what a raid was. Then Douglas said, 'Listen – I can hear horses coming. And men shouting,' and Selina, who was still in the tree and therefore higher up than the others, saw a group of men running towards them, shouting as they came. The shouts echoed through the sleepy squares, and the men's feet churned up the dust as they ran, so that they seemed to be coming out of a vast whirling cloud of smoke. They were wearing turbans and raggedy cotton gowns, and brandishing knives, and as they came hurtling across the quiet English garden she saw that the ones at the front had guns and she clutched at a branch of the tree, because her legs had suddenly gone trembly. Something bad was about to happen – the alarm bell was still ringing, on and on, and that meant something frightening and terrible was going on . . .

Other people were screaming by now, and several of the children's mothers were running towards the March house. Selina could hear her own mother and she could hear Christabel's mother as well. Somebody was shouting something about Sikh dissidents, and somebody else was shouting about Muslim spies, and the garden with its pleasing scents of jasmine and spices, and the huge splashes of colour from the rhododendrons, was suddenly becoming a place filled with anger and fear; it was turning into a dust-storm because the rioters were beating huge whirling clouds out of the hot, dry ground. And all the while came the insistent clamour of the alarm, and you felt that if it did not stop you would go mad or your ears would burst from it . . .

Selina half fell, half slid down from the tree, dry-burning her hands on the ladder's frame because she came down too fast, landing on the ground with a thump. The others were clustering together, no one quite knowing what they should do, the two smallest children beginning to cry.

The dust-shrouded, knife-wielding men erupted into the garden, and surrounded the little group of children. Selina saw Christabel kick out at one of the men who snatched her up in his arms and Douglas swing a punch at another. Yes, they must fight these men, they must be very brave and beat them off until their parents reached them— The rest of the thought was cut abruptly off as Selina was grabbed from behind and swung into the fierce grip of a dark-eyed man, his cotton garments streaked with dirt and caked in mud, his teeth showing in a grin so frightening that Selina forgot about being brave and fighting, and squealed with panic and terror.

'Quiet, little girl! You stay quiet and no one hurt, understand?'

But no one else was being quiet; everyone else was screaming, and people were stampeding everywhere, trampling over the jasmine and the leopard lilies and crushing them underfoot – mother was going to be furious about that when all this was over . . .

Selina was yelling and crying with the rest by this time, her face half jammed against the man's shoulder, so that the smell of his body was thrust into her nose. It was a horrid smell – unwashed skin and stale sweat – and his breath was horrid as well: sour and clotted with the spicy food he ate. Selina started to feel sick, but she tried to take in deep breaths because she absolutely must not be sick all over him.

By the time she had taken enough deep breaths, and had managed to wriggle around a bit so that the man was not huffing his smelly breath all over her, the other men had carried the children out of the trampled-on garden and were running along the road. Several of them were screeching in triumph, but the children were screaming just as loudly. Douglas was yelling at the men to set them free, and Christabel – dear brave Christy – was hammering with her little fists on the shoulders of the man who was carrying her. Selina felt better just seeing Christy do that; it encouraged her to inflict a few blows on her own account, but her captor instantly said, 'You not do that. You not strike me. You keep quiet or we kill.'

And then they were all being tumbled into a kind of cart drawn by a small pony. Before they could even think about scrambling out and running off, two of the men climbed in after them, and the pony started off at a smart trot, jolting them out of Alwar, and along the bare, dusty road that wound up to the northern hills.

The children clung to the sides of the horrid bouncing

cart, watching not the road ahead but the road behind, because surely they would see people coming after them at any minute. But there was only the long dusty road unwinding behind them like a dry, dark-brown ribbon, and there was no welcome sight of cars racing after them, or even of people running to catch them up. For what felt like miles upon miles they saw only thin starveling dogs and no people at all, except two or three pitiful little groups of beggars by the roadside, ragged and bony, their eyes looking as if they were filled with milk. Selina thought it was this kind of thing her father might be trying to write about, but Douglas said he had heard his father say you would never cure the poverty in India, not if you tried for a thousand years.

The cart took them towards the huge sweep of the mountains. India was bakingly hot almost everywhere, but as they got closer to the mountains it was starting to be dark, and it felt very nearly cold. Selina had on a cardigan, but most of the others had only been wearing cotton sundresses or thin shirts and shorts for playing in the garden.

And then they were being thrust into a horrid little stone hut-place on the side of the road; there were more men with guns waiting, and they were all grinning, displaying brown-stained teeth, and nodding at Selina and the other children, and looking as if something very clever indeed had been done.

Inside the hut there was an overpowering smell that made you think of lavatories that nobody had cleaned for years, and there was nowhere to sit except on the floor which was hard, dry, red earth, and when the door was slammed it was horridly dark. Selina felt sick again. She was more frightened than she could ever remember being in her whole life.

The smaller ones were still crying, and Douglas was saying loudly that his father would get them out, because he worked at the embassy in Delhi, and he would not stand for Douglas and his friends being dragged out of their homes and shut into a bad old hut like this. Selina felt a bit better then; she remembered that her own father worked for newspapers and that people did not like bad things written about them in newspapers. She added this to what Douglas had said, and the children began to look more hopeful.

But it was Christy who said, 'Shush – we ought to try hearing what the men are saying. Then we'll know what they're going to do to us.'

So everybody was quiet, and Douglas crawled across to the door and pressed his ear against it to listen. The men talked in their own language, but Douglas and one of the other boys had been here since they were very small, and they knew some of the words the Indian people used. After a moment Douglas crawled back, looking white and a bit sick.

Hostages, that was the word being used by the men, he said. They had marked out six men who had influential jobs and positions, and they had made a plot to kidnap those six men's children and hold them to ransom.

The plot had been thought up a long time ago; all the

kidnappers had had to do was wait until the six children were together in one garden.

There was a garden at Teind House, of course: Selina had been pleased about that when she came to live with the aunts and Great-uncle Matthew. It was quite large and there were nice things in it.

'It's an English garden,' said Aunt Rosa firmly. 'So it will be very different from what you have been used to. There are lawns and herbaceous borders and an orchard and a rockery. You must learn the names of the flowers and the plants.'

Aunt Flora wanted to give Selina a corner of the garden for her own. 'A distraction from her bereavement,' she said in the kind of voice grown-ups used when they did not mean you to hear. Aunt Rosa had frowned and said in a loud, clear voice that *of course* Selina should have a little patch of the garden. She could plant snapdragons and sunflowers, and they must not forget the idea of a memorial for John and Poor Elspeth. In the normal way there would have been graves: bodies could be brought back to England in lead-lined caskets, and proper Christian burials arranged. But in this case . . .

And lavender, said Aunt Flora, a bit hastily. Selina should grow a little lavender bush so that muslin sachets could be made for wardrobes and dressing-table drawers. They would go outside now to choose where it should be. 'Gumboots and a woollen scarf first, though,' said Aunt Rosa. 'For you aren't in that heathen place now, Selina, and September can be quite chilly.'

The garden felt very chilly indeed. There was a faint scent of bonfires and of apples from the orchard which Selina quite liked, and there were crisp golden leaves on the ground between the trees: you could stomp on them and hear them crackle under your gumboots. It had not been possible to stomp on things in India like that.

It had been while they were plodding round the garden that Selina had looked between the laden apple trees, and the damson trees with their clusters of velvet-skinned fruit, and seen, just beyond Teind's grounds, the towering structure like a huge brick chimney against the sky.

'Aunt Rosa, what is that?'

'Don't point,' said Aunt Rosa automatically. 'It's rude to point. Oh, you mean the Round Tower. That is one of Inchcape's little pieces of history, Selina. Once there were monks here and a monastery, and the monks built the tower so that they could watch for enemies. Or perhaps so that they could hide valuable possessions that people wanted to steal.' Her tone said that if you must needs be a monk, you must expect to encounter problems like that.

It was stupid to suddenly think that the apple-scented garden was dissolving in places, like when you held a candle to thin fabric and the fabric shrivelled, and that the hot, blood-smelling nightmare was showing through the shrivelled bits. Selina listened to what Aunt Rosa was saying, because it was very interesting: all about how people in Inchcape were quite proud of the Round Tower, especially since there were very few such structures left in Scotland, and those that were left were mostly so tumbledown as to be dangerous. But Inchcape's tower was in very good condition, said Aunt Rosa; students of archaeology and early Christian customs frequently came here especially to see it.

'Forty feet high,' added Aunt Flora. 'And with a stair-case inside going all the way up to the top.'

Aunt Rosa pointed out to Selina the tiny slit-like windows set high up in the circular brick structure – twenty or thirty feet from the ground at least, could Selina see them clearly? – and Aunt Flora described how the monks would have used the windows to look out for foes creeping towards them.

Selina said, How interesting, and, Thank you for telling me, and tried not to look at the parts of the garden that had dissolved. By this time if you looked directly at them – only Selina was trying not to – you could see through them quite clearly. You could see into the trampled jasmine of mother's garden, and you could see Christy and the others scratching and kicking to escape from the men who had snatched them up . . .

'Once there would have been a conical roof on the tower's very top,' Aunt Rosa was saying. 'It would have looked like a little pointy hat, but it crumbled away years ago, so now there is just a layer of lead to keep the inside weatherproof.'

The hut in Alwar had not been weatherproof; the thick choking dust had blown in from outside, making their throats raw and dry. Selina's eyes had stung and watered a lot.

'You must never go inside the tower, Selina.' This was

29

Aunt Flora. 'You might fall over and hurt yourself, and in any case the stairs aren't likely to be very safe.'

Selina was staring up at the top of the tower. She said, in a strained little voice, 'There're birds on the top, aren't there? Large birds,' and Aunt Rosa said briskly that certainly there were large birds; they would be from the bird sanctuary at Stornforth where all kinds of different birds were kept. A very interesting place, the bird sanctuary: they would go along there one day soon, would Selina like that?

Selina said politely, 'Oh yes, thank you very much,' but as she watched the birds soaring up to the tip of the sinister tower the nightmare, which had gradually been receding since she left India and came to Inchcape, was trickling back through the shrivelled fabric of Teind House's garden.

They had been kept in the bad-smelling hut for nearly two days. Christy and Selina had marked the hours off carefully, not because it made a lot of difference to the situation, but because it was something to do. Douglas said that when this was all over they would have a good tale to tell, and so it was important that they knew how long they were kept prisoners.

The men brought them some food: cornmeal mush and dry bread, and a pitcher of water. It was not very nice, but Christy said they should eat it because of keeping up their strength. It was what you had to do in an adventure, Christy said, her eyes glowing. You had to keep up your strength, so that when you saw a way of outwitting your captors you were strong enough to take the chance.

Most of the children found the cornmeal mush horrid. Selina managed to choke down a few mouthfuls, but it made Douglas sick. He did it in the corner, but it splashed onto his shoes, and the smell of it in the hot enclosed space made two of the smallest girls sick as well. Christy and Selina cleaned them up with the water from the jug as well as they could, but it was not very good really.

There was no lavatory in the hut, and after a while they had to use the corner farthest from the door. Normally Selina would have found this embarrassing beyond belief, but that kind of thing had stopped mattering by then.

It was not money that the men wanted from the children's parents; it was free pardons for some of their number who were in gaol. The children understood this after a while – Douglas had tried to overhear as much as he could, but in the end the man who was in charge of the plot told them about it. His English was not very good, and they had not understood very much of what he said about Hindus fighting Muslims – they had not actually been very sure which their captors were – but they had understood enough.

It did not matter whether these men were Hindus or Muslims, because the outcome was going to be the same as far as the children were concerned. If the free pardons were not given by sunset that day the children were going to be taken out of the hut and shot.

CHAPTER THREE

Sunset came gradually into the room Mary had been given at Moy, and she hated it, because it was not the gentle beautiful thing that people painted or wrote poems about: it was a slow, inexorable clotting of daylight, the dying sun smearing the sky with blood, and the blood oozing down onto the world and dripping into this cell . . .

'It's a nice room,' the stupid young warder had said when he brought her here. He was baby-faced and earnest. He looked about sixteen, although he must be older, and his name badge said he was called Robert Glennon. Robbie. Mary had thought, Well, Master Robert or Robbie Glennon, if you like it so much, you live in it, but she had not said it because it was better to seem submissive and quiet until she had these people's measure.

In the house where she had lived until she was fourteen, sunset had been gentle and warm, creeping softly over the garden, turning the windows to melted gold. It ought to have been lovely, but in that house sunset was not something to admire or enjoy.

'I hate sunset,' Mary's mother always said, not once, but over and over again.

'Sunset is the hour your sister was taken from us,' Mary's father always added, regarding his wife anxiously.

'Sunset on the twelfth of September 1948,' said Mary's mother, her face taking on the remote pinched look. Stupid, thought Mary. She looks so stupid. 'Seven years old and three months, she was on that day, your lovely sister.'

There was always a memorial service at the local church on 12 September, and then there was another one on 8 June. 'Her birthday,' said Mary's mother reverently, counting off the years. In 1957, when Mary was six, and old enough to understand, her sister would have been coming up to her sixteenth birthday.

'Sixteen,' said Mary's mother wistfully. 'Just starting to go to dances.'

'The belle of the ball she would have been as well.'

They talked like this, even though the era of *Rock Around the Clock* and *Blue Suede Shoes* had started, and people of sixteen were jiving and rocking and rolling, wearing flirtily wide skirts, or tight jeans with ballet-pump shoes for bopping.

'Show Mary the photographs, William. You see, Mary, what a very beautiful sister you had.'

33

'Beautiful,' said Mary obediently, although the black-and-white photograph really showed a bunchy-faced child with her hair tied up in silly spanielly ringlets on each side of her head.

When Mary was six she was allowed to accompany her parents to the memorial service, and afterwards they walked around the garden, hand-in-hand, talking quietly just as they always did. Mary had thought she would walk with them this year: she thought she could walk in the middle holding her father's hand on the left and her mother's on the right. She thought that even though she had not been born until two years after this wonderful sister died, she could join in the If-she-had-lived game, because she had listened to her parents and she knew all the things that had to be said. Things like, If she had lived, she would have been learning to play the piano now. If she had lived, she would have been a wonderful musician.

'She loved music,' said Leila Maskelyne.

'I like music as well.' Surely mother knew this from school concerts, when Mary sang in the junior school choir?

'Yes, dear.'

And English. If Mary's sister had lived she would have been studying at the grammar school by now. She might even have been clever enough to go on to university.

'I'm clever,' said Mary. 'Miss Finch thinks I'm very good at sums and writing. I could go to grammar school if I pass the eleven plus.'

'That will be very nice, dear.'

A year later, 8 June fell on a Sunday, and Mary's mother started to say 'Seventeen come Sunday' months ahead, and arranged for that year's memorial service to include the Vaughan Williams arrangement of the old English folk song.

'A very nice sentiment, Mrs Maskelyne,' said the vicar. 'Yes, the organist can certainly play that for the service. My word, you do keep your girl's memory green, don't you?'

Mother said, 'She is never out of my thoughts for a moment. Not for one moment.' After supper that evening she said, 'Seventeen, William, only think of it. If she had lived she'd have been seventeen. We'd have had a party. There'd have been young men taking her out, by now.'

Mary was almost eight and it was half-term so she was allowed to stay up a little later. She listened to the conversation, wondering what year her parents thought they were living in, because life seemed to have stopped for them in 1948.

'That child who escaped,' said Leila Maskelyne, and Mary heard with a shock that her mother's voice was different as well. It was harder, colder. 'She is so much in my thoughts lately. I hate that child, William.'

Mary's father said, 'Hush now, my dear, no good ever came of hating anyone.'

'I can't help it. I hate her so much.' Mary had always thought of her mother as very pretty, but now, for the first time, she saw how the prettiness could change, and become thin and cruel and spiteful. 'She is enjoying the life that our dear girl should have enjoyed,' said Leila.

'Seventeen this year. I know how old she is, that girl, I marked her age at the time, William. She is our dear one's age almost exactly, and so today, this summer, all these lovely sunny afternoons, she will be doing all the things that girls of seventeen do. Out there in the world. *Alive! Living!* Walking and breathing and laughing and buying new clothes and listening to music . . .' The pretty hands that sometimes played the piano in the front sitting room – hands that must have taught that other child how to pick out some of the notes – and were always protected from gardening and cooking by household gloves, curled into claws – there was no other word for it. Mary watched. 'If there was to be one who escaped,' said Leila, 'why couldn't it have been our dear, lovely girl?'

Mary had wanted to say, But you've got me now, but mother was already starting the harsh dry sobbing that made her feel so uncomfortable, and father was kneeling in front of her chair, giving her his handkerchief, saying, There, there, my poor dear, you always feel like this after the birthday memorial, and putting his arms round her and saying she would soon pluck up.

Plucking up meant that father would lead mother up to bed and bring her a cup of tea and her supper on a tray. Mary and father would have their supper together, and later on when mother had stopped crying into the pillow, after Mary was in bed herself, mother would say the thing she almost always said, and Mary almost always heard through the wall: 'Come into the bed with me, William.'

Mother and father slept in two beds, side by side in the

same room, with a little cabinet between them, but when mother said, Come into the bed with me, there was the creak of bedsprings, and the sound of father getting into mother's bed with her. Then the bedsprings bounced for quite a long time in a kind of rhythm, and father panted as if he had been running very fast. Then he groaned, and said, 'Better stop for a moment – better let me get something – I'm very near to—'

'No, don't use those horrid things, William! I want another child! Tonight we could make one!'

There was the sound of father going h'rm, h'rm, in the way he sometimes did when he felt embarrassed.

'Yes, *please*, William. Because supposing she's waiting to be re-born to us. Only think of it! Our lovely girl!'

The bedsprings bounced more violently, and then father gave another long groan, and the sounds stopped. There was the creak of a floorboard as father got out of the bed, and then a chink as he poured himself a glass of water from the washstand. He said, in a sad, rather defeated kind of voice, 'You believed she would come back when Mary was born.'

'Mary could never replace Christabel. Oh, William, I miss her so much . . .'

Some nights Mary put her hands over her ears so that she would not hear, but after a while she stopped doing that because it was far more interesting to listen – to spy on mother and father and know their secrets, even though some of the secrets were not very easy to understand. One day I will understand, though. One day I'll understand what it is that father does, and all that thing about babies.

There was no need to feel in the least guilty about listening through the wall, because Mary's parents deserved to be spied on. It served them right for always wanting Mary's sister to come back, and for not letting Mary take her sister's place.

In the event, having people staying overnight at Teind House in twos and threes was not as bad as Selina had feared. In the main they were nice, usually retired couples who were touring Scotland. Once or twice there were groups of three or four ladies who had been widowed or divorced, and who had got together to share little holidays. They did not in the least mind doubling up in the two big twin-bedded rooms at the front of the house.

And it was rather pleasant to serve dainty little breakfasts in the square morning room at the back of the house. Selina wore a crisp white apron over a navy frock, and always spoke softly because the aunts had considered that hearty breakfast conversation was slightly ill-mannered. Gentlemen especially did not like loud voices at the breakfast table.

Gillian had helped Selina to find and buy two large coffee pots with matching cups and sugar bowls. They were rejects, but they were rejects from a good pottery manufacturer, and they looked nice. Selina had also hunted out some of Great-aunt Rosa's cut-glass jam dishes, and always put the marmalade and the honey on the end of the table that caught the morning sun so that the honey turned transparent. She had found Great-aunt Flora's recipe for Orkney pancakes as well, and offered them to guests as an alternative to toast. It was unexpectedly gratifying when some of the ladies asked for the recipe for the pancakes.

'You ought to bake a large batch and freeze them,' said Emily Frost, who came down from the warders' little community at Moy each morning to help cook breakfasts when there were people staying. 'If you got a microwave you could have them ready in minutes.'

But Selina was not sure about freezers and microwave ovens, which she found bewildering. She was not actually sure about Emily, either. Emily had come as a shock that first day. She had a face that reminded Selina of a wayward pixie, and hair so red it was practically crimson, four earrings in each ear, and probably a tongue stud as well if you looked closely. Surely Gillian had not considered that a child with crimson hair and eight earrings would be suitable to help with the guests?

'Don't underestimate her,' said Gillian.

And in fact Emily was cheerful and willing, and except when she made suggestions that frightened Selina to death, like this newest one about a microwave, she was quite easy to have in the house. Neither of the great-aunts would have countenanced her clothes or her hair, of course, and they would have thrown up their hands in horror at her method of transport, which was a huge black motorbike, surely the noisiest machine ever invented. Emily wore a shiny black crash helmet whilst riding the motorbike, but once inside Teind House the helmet was left in the scullery, and her hair subjected to a variety of arrangements. At the moment she was gluing it into spikes all over her head, which made her look like a modern-day elf.

'I've had a request from someone who wants to stay here for a couple of weeks,' said Selina to Gillian on the phone.

'Well, that's great, isn't it? What's the problem?'

The problem was that Selina had not really visualised long stays when she had embarked on this project.

'But think of the dosh,' said Gillian promptly. 'Three or four hundred pounds in the bank, just for cooking an extra breakfast each morning.'

'But – she's a writer,' said Selina worriedly.

'So? What kind of writer is she? Because unless she writes hardcore porn or something—'

'Novels,' said Selina hastily. 'She writes novels. And she said she wants a bit of solitude to assemble some research.'

'Well, she'll certainly get solitude at Inchcape.'

'Oh, yes. She says she'll be quite happy to have her lunch and supper at the pub. So I suppose,' said Selina doubtfully, 'it would be all right.'

'Of course it would be all right. What's her name?'

'Joanna Savile.'

'I think I've heard of her,' said Gillian. 'She's not a bestseller, but she's quite well known. She writes modern whodunnits, I think – very pure and moral.'

'Yes, that's what she said. And she wants to gather some background about institutions for the criminally insane, which is why she thought of Inchcape. Because of Moy, you know. She's trying to set up interviews with the governor and the doctors there.'

'Sounds fine to me. What is it that's really worrying you?'

'Well, noise for one thing.'

'Oh, she'll probably bring a laptop,' said Gillian. 'So you needn't be worrying about typewriters being bashed into the small hours. In any case, if you give her that big L-shaped attic on the second floor you'll hardly know she's there.'

Selina supposed this would be a reasonable arrangement.

'Perfectly reasonable,' said Gillian.

'I'd better get a couple of her books to read beforehand,' said Selina.

Contrary to all her expectations, Selina liked Joanna Savile.

She arrived more or less when she had said she would, which was at around seven o'clock in the evening, driving a big estate car with careless expertise. She had long, rather untidy, hair the colour of autumn leaves, and hazel eyes and a skin that reminded Selina of buttermilk. She wore an ordinary tweedy-looking jacket, a silk shirt and dark trousers, and she had brought Selina a huge bunch of the most beautiful bronze chrysanthemums.

'There was a farm a few miles back selling them on a roadside stall, and I couldn't resist them. You said that Teind House was very old, so I thought they'd be bound to look good somewhere. They smell wonderful, don't they?'

She carried her suitcases cheerfully up to the second floor, refusing offers of help, and Selina, rather anxiously leading the way, noticed that both the cases were very good ones. Great-aunt Rosa had always said you could tell a lady by her accessories, and Joanna Savile's suitcases and also her handbag and shoes were leather and expensive-looking.

The second-floor room was not really much more than a half-attic, with sloping ceilings and casement windows, but Gillian, who presumably knew about these things, had told Selina at the start of this bed-and-breakfast project that it could be made very comfortable. When Selina said there was not really any money to be doing rooms over, Gillian had said, 'Oh, phooey, all it needs are some new curtains and a new cover on the window seat. Chintz, or something William Morrisy. I'll splash some paint around while I'm here – that'll freshen it up no end. And aren't there some odds and ends of furniture in the junk room? I'll help you sort a few pieces out and we'll polish them up and move them in.'

The room, its walls and ceiling newly emulsioned by Gillian, was, Selina had to admit, now rather charming. The glazed chintz for the curtains and chair covers had been bought in Stornforth market – 'for a fraction of the price you'd pay in a shop', Gillian had pointed out, and Selina had not dared say she had never been to a market stall in her life.

There was a wash hand basin in the corner, and Gillian

had unearthed a porcelain soap dish that matched it, and also a huge blue and white Chinese bowl for the dried lavender that Selina still collected and scattered about the house. In the junk room they had found a small gateleg table, too narrow to use as a dining table, too large for what Aunt Rosa had termed an occasional table, but which Gillian, appealed to for guidance by phone, said would be just right for a laptop.

'I've put it under the windows so that there's a view over the orchard.'

'And straight across to the Round Tower,' said Gillian. And then, because Selina was clearly in a bit of a stew, she said, 'That'll be fine. If this Joanna Savile is any kind of writer, she'll probably see the place as the inspiration for a plot. *Murder in the Tower*, or something.'

'It's been done,' said Selina with one of her rare flashes of dry humour, and Gillian had laughed and said, Nothing new under the sun, and the view from up there was great anyway, because you could not see the ramshackle little road that hardly anyone ever used and Matthew McAvoy had tried to have closed.

And now, here was Joanna Savile looking delightedly around the room, admiring the gateleg table and the little Victorian bookshelf in one corner, and the Victorian patchwork quilt that had been made by Selina's great-grandmother, and whose colours had faded to gentle muted blues and lilacs. And the view was simply *so* beautiful, said Joanna, standing at the window look-ing out, and how clever it had been of Miss March to give her a room high up; it meant she would be able to work up here quietly without disturbing anyone.

Selina, who had decided on a rule of non-involvement with everyone who came to Teind House, and had vowed to keep firmly to serving breakfast only, heard herself saying, 'Would you like a cup of tea after your long drive? And I don't suppose you've had supper yet?'

Over one of the curious, unfamiliar meals that Emily Frost had prepared and left in the freezer ('because you don't know when you might find yourself caught out with a guest wanting an evening meal') Joanna said, 'I've managed to fix a visit to Moy for tomorrow.'

Selina had been worrying about whether the food was properly thawed and heated. You could not really go by taste because Emily seemed to have added some rather fierce seasoning. Now she hesitated, and then said, 'For – for research, is it?'

'Yes. I've been in touch with Patrick Irvine – the head of the psychiatric wing. He thinks he can probably arrange for me to talk to some of the inmates.'

'Won't that – forgive me, Miss Savile – won't you find that distressing?'

'Yes, possibly. But I'll have to try to switch off afterwards. Listen, do call me Joanna. Actually, to be absolutely correct, it's Mrs Kent not Miss Savile.'

'Oh—'

'It doesn't matter at all. It's easier to keep being known as Savile because of the books, and my husband's working abroad at the moment, so I feel more like "Miss" again anyway.' She smiled. Her upper lip creased when she smiled, so that it was as if a mischievous schoolboy invited you to share an amusing secret. She had taken off her travelling things to eat the hastily prepared supper, and she was wearing an ankle-length skirt and what Selina thought was a chenille jacket, the colour of horse chestnuts. The aunts used to have a tablecloth of the exact same material, only in crimson with bobbles round the edges. It seemed odd to see someone wearing the material as a jacket. Joanna said, 'Krzystof – my husband – is due back in three weeks' time. If I'm still here it would be all right if he joined me for a night or two, wouldn't it? We'd eat at the pub, so you wouldn't be put out at all. And he could share my room.'

Selina was instantly thrown into confusion at the thought of this lovely girl's husband sharing a room with her after several weeks' absence. The bed was quite large enough for two to sleep in, but there was the thing. Beds and married people, and a reunion ... And she had called him Krzystof, which meant he was foreign – middle-European from the sound of it. Hungarian or Romanian or something.

And they would have sex, of course, there in the second-floor room that used to be the cook's when the aunts had a live-in cook; there in the bed that had been in the guest room; there between the sheets that went religiously to the Stornforth laundry after each guest. Selina might even find she was lying in her own room, wondering about them – perhaps hearing them ...

Joanna said, 'I did think it might not be possible, of

course. For Krzystof to stay here, I mean. I thought you might have other bookings . . .'

Other bookings. I'm being given a polite way out, thought Selina. Is she seeing me as a prim old maid who can't cope with married people in bed together? This was so unpleasant a thought that she said firmly, 'I don't believe there are any other bookings that would cause a problem. I'll need to look in the diary, but I'm sure it will be *quite* all right.'

There was the curved smile again. 'I'm so glad,' said Joanna. 'It would have meant going back to London just for a couple of nights to see him before he sets off again.' She speared another forkful of Emily's peculiar dish, whatever it was, and said, 'He works for the Rosendale Institute in London; he's one of their translators. They specialise in religious artefacts, so he has a terrific life swanning around the globe, negotiating with archivists and curators while the field workers scrabble around trying to find Tibetan prayer wheels and Russian icons and pagan masks.'

'How very interesting. Have you been married long?' She'll say, oh ages, thought Selina. She's easily twenty-eight and probably a bit more than that, so they could have been married for quite a few years, and surely that means they aren't likely to be quite so *passionate* about being reunited—

Joanna said, 'Eight months. I do miss him.' And then, as if pushing away an unwanted emotion, 'This chili con carne is absolutely delicious, Miss March. I'd love a spoonful more if it wouldn't be greedy.'

'But of course,' said Selina, thankful that she had apparently done the thawing and reheating properly, and relieved to find out what Emily's peculiar concoction was called.

CHAPTER FOUR

Emily Frost was coming to the conclusion that Selina March – Miss March she preferred to be called, wouldn't you just know she would? – was a bit of a weirdo.

Emily had not much wanted to come to Inchcape at all, but dad had said it was a good posting for him as well as a promotion. He would be third-in-command: a wing governor in his own right, so it was not to be sneezed at. Still, if Emily absolutely hated it after – well – say three months, they would see about her setting up somewhere on her own. Providing, he said sternly, that she got a job at least for the duration. Stornforth was not very far, and there was a cottage hospital there and a bird sanctuary; she might find something quite interesting. Or there might even be something at Moy itself. Something in one of the offices, maybe.

There had not been anything at Stornforth, but after

they had been at Inchcape for a few weeks Emily had begun helping out at the village school. Two afternoons a week it was, and only helping to supervise the tinies, the five- and six-year-olds, painting and playdough and things, but Lorna Laughlin was pleased with what Emily was doing and the kids were great. Lorna was the schoolmistress. Anywhere else she would have been called head teacher or something, but in Inchcape she was the schoolmistress, as if she was something out of Dickens for heaven's sake!

But Inchcape itself was like something out of Dickens – Emily had never been to such a backwater in her life. It was a good thing that there were staff cottages, all of them about ten minutes' walk from the main prison buildings, because otherwise they would never have found anywhere to live, because it did not look as if anyone had moved from Inchcape for about a hundred years.

Selina March did not look as if she had moved for about a hundred years, either. She looked as if she had been born here in Queen Victoria's time, and had stayed here getting more and more twittery and faded every year. When Emily first went to help at Teind House she had avoided looking in any of the mirrors, because she had a horrid suspicion that, if she did, there would not be a reflection of Selina in any of them.

Patrick Irvine said he would like to study Selina March sometime. He said she sounded like something that had reached the chrysalis stage, died, and become fossilised, like a fly in amber. Emily thought she would not be at all surprised if that were the case because living at Inchcape was like living inside a time-warp. If she stayed here for any length of time she would probably become fossilised herself.

Teind House was very old indeed. The downstairs rooms had thick oak beams and on warm days there was a dry powdery scent of old timbers and woodsmoke. The furniture shone with age and beeswax but it was dark and gloomy; it seemed to watch you all the time. In the hall was a large grandfather clock with a face that looked as if it disapproved of just about everything. It ticked crossly to itself and just before it was going to strike the hour it wheezed and creaked, like an old man with lung disease clearing his throat before a revolting coughing spasm.

Emily hated the clock, which Miss March reverently said had been Great-uncle Matthew's. It had to be wound every Saturday night at exactly six o'clock – Emily had not liked to question this practice in case there turned out to be a ghost story attached. Like Great-uncle Matthew rising up from the churchyard and tottering into Teind House in his shroud, and winding the clock with his fleshless fingers, and then stumping sulkily back to his grave. Selina March did not seem the kind of person who would tell a story like that, never mind believe in it, but you never knew. From what Emily could make out, Great-uncle Matthew had been a selfish, finnicky old fart whose ghost would enjoy haunting poor old Selina, and making her feel guilty about forgetting to wind up a creaky old clock for God's sake!

Miss March clung to the past. Her bedroom had silver-framed photographs of the aunts who had brought her up, and on a low table were more silver-framed photographs of a man and a woman. They were black-and-white photos and a bit faded, but you could see a resemblance between the woman and Selina March. The man did not especially resemble anyone: he had nice eyes, and crinkly hair, cut the way men used to have their hair cut at least fifty years ago. Next to the photos, neatly folded, was a really beautiful black lace stole – the kind of thing ladies had once worn over evening dresses in the summer. It was cobwebby with age, but when Emily touched it a faint, wistful perfume stirred from its folds.

Alongside the two photographs was a small oblong frame with a cutting from an old newspaper. One day, when Emily had been asked to 'just run up to my room and fetch my cardigan', she had rather guiltily read the cutting.

It said, *The deaths, in tragic circumstances, were announced in Alwar, India, of John Mallory March, and his wife, Elspeth March, on 12 September 1948 . . . A Memorial Service was held at the Anglican Church in Alwar . . .*

Next to it, protected by two small pieces of glass, was an article from an old, yellowing newspaper. It was quite hard to read the newsprint, but Emily made out the heading, which said, *Partition in India stirs up unrest again. Nehru and Mountbatten in talks . . .* The date was August 1948, and the journalist's name at the bottom was John Mallory March. Selina's father? Yes, of course.

On the lower shelf of the little table were several old books, carefully arranged. They had battered covers and the brown age-spots that were called foxing. The titles were printed in large, easy-to-read letters. Children's books. Emily picked them up, wary in case they fell apart. They did not fall apart but they were very brittle, and touching them made Emily feel all over again that she was brushing against the past – not a very long-ago past, but certainly a past that had existed before she had been born.

Two of the books were by Enid Blyton, and three were by somebody called Frances Hodgson Burnett. Another was a book about a girl called *Heidi*, written by a Johanna Spyri. Emily had heard of Enid Blyton, but she had never heard of the other two. The *Heidi* book had an inscription in the front: 'To Selina who loves mountains. On her seventh birthday, with love from daddy'. There was a date – June 1948. And three months later he had been dead, this unknown man who had chosen this book for his small daughter who liked mountains, and had written a message that Selina had kept ever since. The book looked a bit advanced for a seven-year-old, but Emily could see the man with crinkly hair and the woman who had worn the black lace stole reading the book to Selina when she was in bed, a page or two a night. Afterwards Selina would probably not have had anyone to read books to her, because those fearsome great-aunts and dried-up old Great-uncle Matthew would not have done so, that was for sure!

It was doubtless reading the blurred newsprint about that far-away time, and the deaths of Selina's parents in tragic circumstances, that made Emily shiver. She had a sudden vision of Selina sitting up here on her own, poring over the sad little mementoes of her dead parents, although as well as being touching it was a bit macabre. It was one thing to mourn for your parents and want to remember them and have photos and stuff, but to do it for fifty years?

Still, it would be dreadful to lose both parents when you were so tiny: you would probably never get completely over it. Emily was still not getting over mum's dying last year. She wondered if that long-ago Selina had attended the memorial service for her parents, and if she had been tearful, or if she would have been told by somebody that she must be brave, and not cry. Emily had not cried at mum's funeral, but that was because of knowing that if she cried, dad would cry as well, which was not to be be borne, not in front of everybody. They had held one another's hands all through the service, as if they were clinging on to the last bit of life left in the world. Later, Emily had found dad crying bitterly over a batch of biscuits mum had baked a week ago, which were still in the airtight biscuit tin. She had not known, until then, that grief got at you through silly, everyday things. Somehow you coped, though, and life went on. But she could not begin to imagine how Selina, at six or seven, had coped.

The photographs and the death notice were sad and somehow rather lonely, and Emily had gone quickly back downstairs with the cardigan. She thought Selina had not realised that she had seen the things or read the newspaper cuttings.

The other thing that Emily hated about Teind was the

old brick tower just beyond the orchard. It was supposed to have been some kind of look-out for a gang of monks in the year dot, and it was about forty feet high and just about the most sinister thing Emily had ever seen. It made Great-uncle Matthew and his clock seem harmless by comparison.

Miss March did not like the Round Tower much, either. She only said it was a rather nasty place, and that Emily must be careful not to go near it because it was dangerous, but her voice sounded different when she said it. False. Like a bad actor in a film.

Of course, said Miss March, still in the same unconvincing voice, the authorities ought really to have pulled the tower down long ago. Great-uncle Matthew had written to various people about it any number of times and various promises had been made, but nothing had ever been done. He had even tried to buy the piece of land surrounding it, so that people did not make use of the little roadway, but the authorities had not been permitted to sell because it was some kind of ancient right of way that had to be kept open. Nobody used the road much, these days, though, just as nobody ever went into the tower. Birds went in there sometimes, said Miss March, and Emily, who had been stirring a pan of rice intended as a base for kedgeree, looked up in surprise.

'Birds?'

'From the sanctuary at Stornforth,' said Selina. 'They fly up there and perch on the top. I see them quite often. They always look as if they're waiting. But what are they waiting for, I wonder? That's the thing, you see.'

After a moment Emily said that the tower probably made a good stopping-off place for the birds.

'They stand on the rim and keep watch,' said Selina, and this sounded so peculiar that Emily turned round to look properly at Miss March. She had been chopping hard-boiled eggs to add to the kedgeree, but she seemed to have forgotten what she was doing; Emily thought she almost looked as if she had forgotten where she was as well. She was holding the knife out in front of her, and she was staring at nothing. Emily began to feel uncomfortable.

And then Selina said, in a rather horrid, whispery voice, 'They're so very patient, you see. Large birds are very patient. But they're cunning. They wait and wait, and then just as you think it's going to be all right they come swooping down.'

There was an awkward silence, because this time Emily had no idea what to say at all. Miss March was still staring straight in front of her, and Emily felt a shiver trickle down her spine.

And then the moment passed, and Miss March said, in a brisk voice, 'But of course, I believe they do not allow flesh-eating birds at the Stornforth sanctuary,' and went back to chopping the eggs. In her ordinary, familiar voice, she said, 'I'm not awfully fond of birds, Emily.'

'Oh, I see,' said Emily, not seeing at all, wondering if they could have fallen into an old Hitchcock film without her noticing it. She went on with her cooking, but she was left with the strong feeling that for a few moments another person had looked out of Miss March's eyes –

a person who was quite different from the Miss March that Emily and everyone else knew.

But this was so shivery an idea that she pushed it well down in her mind, and asked whether she should add any more salt to the kedgeree.

CHAPTER FIVE

It was curious and rather unexpected of the crimson-haired child, Emily Frost, to have asked about the Round Tower. As far as Selina could remember people in Inchcape hardly ever talked about it. But Emily, being new to Inchcape, had probably found it interesting.

Great-uncle Matthew had not thought the Round Tower interesting. He had thought it an eyesore, and a danger to inquisitive people. It would be an honourable thing to get it demolished, he said, and after he had failed to buy the piece of land with the disused road he had begun writing letters to local newspapers and church commissions and parish councils, most of which were not answered.

Honour was an odd thing. It meant different things to different people. To Great-uncle Matthew, honour meant doing good, and talking loudly about it, so that people knew how much good you were doing. To the aunts it meant being polite and obedient. 'Honour thy father and thy mother,' Great-aunt Rosa often said.

In India, honour had been all mixed up with dead people, and with the respect you had to give to them. The ayah who had looked after Selina had said that if you did not honour the dead properly, they would not be able to rest, and that was very bad indeed. When Selina's parents died she said Selina would have to honour their memories always, especially since the poor master and his lady had not been able to pronounce the *patet*, the repentance-prayer, at the end of their lives. That meant they might still be *tanu-peretha* – sinful – said the ayah, her dark-liquid eyes inward-looking and solemn. To honour their memories might help them to rest; it might help them take the first of the three steps of Humata, Hukhta, and Hvarshta, and then cross the old and holy Bridge that would lead them into paradise. Selina must promise to always remember and revere her father and mother, and honour their memories, or their ghosts would not be able to rest or reach paradise, said the ayah.

Selina had promised because by that time she was frightened to do anything that might make people angry with her. When she was sent to live with Great-uncle Matthew and the aunts she had been afraid to go to sleep in the strange bedroom because that was where her parents came to her. She had not dared to tell the aunts, because they might think it was all her fault. 'There was nothing like that here before *you* came to live in the house,' Aunt Rosa would say. Aunt Flora would be at a loss to understand about Selina's parents' needing to be helped across to paradise, because once you died you went straight to heaven. Both of them would say that of course people did not come back after they died, the very idea.

But Selina's parents came back; they came back almost every night, right into her bedroom in Teind House. They hid in the corners – usually they crouched down in the lumpy shadows at the side of the washstand, drawing their knees up to their chests and hugging their legs so that they could not easily be seen, so that you might start to believe they were not there after all. But Selina always knew they were there. She watched them for hours and hours, forcing herself to stay awake. And gradually she saw that what looked like bars of moonlight were their hands, and what looked like the rubbed silvery bits of the looking glass reflecting the light were their faces . . .

They always waited until the house was dark and quiet, and then they moved out of hiding: they unfolded their hunched-over bodies until they were standing upright, and then they came creeping and fumbling across the floor, their hands outstretched. They no longer looked as they had looked when they were alive: they were no longer happy and smiling – mother wearing pretty clothes and with her hair shiny; father smart and neat. They looked as they had done when they died.

So the ayah had been right, and a way would have to be found to honour them and send them on their way across the old and holy Bridge. Selina had no idea how this could be done until the day Great-uncle Matthew started to talk about the tower, using the word *honourable*. That had been when she had suddenly seen how she could stop her parents coming into her bedroom every night, their flesh hanging in red tatters from their bodies, their hands reaching out beseechingly to her . . .

'Help us, Selina . . . Help us . . .'

They needed her to help them because they could not see any longer, because their eyes were hanging out on their cheeks.

Even on a bright late-October day, the Round Tower was frightening. Selina walked determinedly through the orchard and scrambled through the gap in the bramble hedge, being careful not to tear her frock so as not to annoy the aunts.

The little old road that wound along to the tower was not a road you would want to drive a car over because it was horridly rutted and bouncy and you had to be careful not to turn your ankle in the ruts. Great-uncle Matthew said it was scandalous neglect and a good cartload of gravel ought to be put down. But hardly anyone ever used the road, so the authorities who owned it had never bothered.

Selina thought it was the kind of road you read about in story books: a road that might take you into strange lands. The grass all around was overgrown and there was rosebay willowherb everywhere and puffy-headed thistles – the sort you blew on and watched the seeds float away. Father had told her that really the seed-heads were fairies in hiding, and blowing on them made the fairies scurry off in a hurry, back to their own world. Selina liked this story – she liked remembering how father had looked when he told her about it – but the aunts and Great-uncle Matthew had not seemed to believe in fairies in disguise, and Great-aunt Rosa had said that thistles were nothing but nasty weeds, fit only for pulling up by the roots.

The scents of apples and damsons from Teind House's orchard lay heavily on the air. Aunt Flora would be making jam quite soon. She liked to serve jam with her home-made scones when the vicar came to tea or the doctor called. Aunt Rosa said Flora made a show of herself with the vicar and it was not dignified, but Aunt Flora still made the jam and the scones.

Selina concentrated on Great-aunt Flora and the jam because it was a homely, ordinary thing, and it took away some of the horror of the looming tower. The trouble was that the nearer you got to it, the taller it looked, and the more it seemed to be leaning forward, as if it might be about to topple over.

Like the tower at Alwar . . . ? said a sneaky little voice inside Selina's mind.

Yes. That was the thing. The Round Tower of Inchcape looked exactly like the tower at Alwar.

Walking cautiously through the raggedy grass, sending frequent glances back at Teind House in case anyone saw her, Selina was remembering how, on that first night here, the orchard and the gardens had seemed to get thinner in places, so that you could nearly look through and see other worlds. People said that magic did not exist and only babies believed in it, and Selina was nearly eight, practically grown-up, and so she knew that there was no magic.

But there might once have been magic. You read about it. People in stories had magic boxes or they fell down enchanted rabbit-holes. So Selina thought it was just possible that there might still be little bits of magic left lying around the world, and that if you stood very still and said the right words – if you knew the right words – you might set the magic working for you. And then you might even find that there were holes in the world, where you could look back into the past.

As she drew nearer to the black tower, she saw several large birds settle on the far-away top, and fold their wings around their bodies, like a man folding a cloak around his shoulders.

The tower at Alwar was where the children had been taken as sunset approached. They had tried not to watch the slow fiery dying of the sun through the horrid mean little windows of the hut, because they were trying not to think about the men shooting them at sunset.

Christabel said it did not matter whether they thought about it or not, because it would not happen. It was absolutely impossible that their parents would let them be shot. They would arrange for those men to be let out of gaol, she said fiercely. Her father would arrange it because he loved her very very much, and he would find a way to do what the kidnappers wanted. She was not quite crying when she said this, but she nearly was.

Douglas said that probably his father was already talking to ambassadors and people about the kidnappers' friends being let out of prison. He did not think the kidnappers would shoot any of the children, either. People did not shoot children.

It was not sunset when the men came to take them out of the hut, but it was not far off. It was dreadfully frightening to be herded into the cart again, but Christy said that probably they were being taken home. Probably it was all over by now.

But the cart had only jolted a few miles along the road when Douglas said suddenly, 'This isn't the way back to Alwar.'

'Are you sure?' asked someone, and one of the boys said, a bit uncertainly, that they were still on the mountain road.

'Well, not absolutely,' said Douglas. 'But we're going north, aren't we? And Alwar's south.'

'Is it?' But no one was quite sure how you told north from south.

And then Christy said, 'What's that?' and they all looked to where she was pointing.

And there it was, straight ahead of them. A great rearing tower, at least fifty feet high, jutting up into the blood-splashed, dying-sun sky like a huge decaying tooth or a monstrous chimney. It was round and windowless and it looked as if it might be doorless as well, and it was *old*, it was so old that it might have been here for a thousand years, and as Selina stared up at it she felt cold and sick inside, and she thought: *now* I'm frightened. I was frightened quite a lot before, but now I'm *really* frightened. Looking at the tower gave you the same sickening pain you got if you wrenched your ankle while running fast, or the wincing feeling you got in your teeth if someone drew a nail across a slaty surface.

After what felt like a long time, Christy said in a whisper, 'It's like something out of a nightmare,' and Selina instantly thought – yes, *of course*! That's why it's so familiar! It's the giant's tower from the nightmares and the fairy tales. It's the place where the ogre lives – where he eats children for breakfast. It's the castle where the floors are strewn with the bones of dead men, and with their hearts and livers as well, because the ogre likes human hearts, he eats them with pepper and vinegar for tea . . .

And if the ogre sees us or hears us approach, thought Selina in panic, he'll come stomping down the thousand stairs inside the tower, and he'll catch us and eat us up.

One of the boys said fearfully, 'What is it?'

'I think it's a Tower of Silence,' said Douglas, still staring up at the black tower. 'It's a place where the people of India bring their dead.'

'To bury them?'

'No. They put them on the ledge near the top,' said Douglas. 'The – um – the dead bodies, I mean.' In the livid glare from the dying sky, his face was pinched and scared and he looked much younger than he had done before. This upset Selina quite a lot, because Douglas had been very brave until now.

'I can see the ledge,' said Christy, after a moment, shading her eyes and staring upwards.

Selina could see it as well. It was like a thick lip, near the very top of the tower. After a few moments, during which her eyes were adjusting to the brilliance of the sunset, she was able to make out other things on the ledge. Black shapes with beating wings against the sky.

'Birds,' said one of the smaller children, with a shiver. 'Large birds.'

'Birds of prey,' said Douglas, half to himself, and then Selina understood what happened to the dead people who were brought out here.

They were left on the ledge near the tower's top so that the birds of prey could eat them. It was the ogre's castle after all, and the birds were really ogres.

And inside the tower were the tattered remains of all the humans that the birds had torn apart with their beaks and claws in order to eat them.

The birds gathering on the Round Tower at Inchcape were not the same as the birds in Alwar, of course. Selina knew that. She knew that this was not a tower where dead people were brought so that they could be eaten.

But there was the feeling here that there had been in Alwar: the feeling that inside the tower there might be an ogre who liked the taste of humans, and who chanted the rhyme that went Fee-fi-fo-fum, I-smell-the-blood-of-an-Englishman, and the part about grinding people's bones to make bread.

When Selina came to Teind House, the aunts had

looked out some of their own childhood story books for Poor Elspeth's girl, and among these had been the fairy tales of Jacob and Wilhelm Grimm and Hans Andersen, most of them illustrated with the brilliant grisly perception of Arthur Rackham, or Doré. As Selina walked towards the tower on that autumn afternoon, she was remembering the books so vividly that she could feel the thick linen of the old paper and smell the mustiness of the pages . . .

Selina was allowed to look at the books on Sundays as a special treat after tea. They had to be treated very carefully because they were old and valuable, and Selina had to say thank you, and pretend to enjoy them. She did say thank you, and she took the books into the dining room which still smelt of Sunday dinner. The dining room was not very comfortable, but at least the aunts could not see how slowly Selina turned the pages when she was coming to the story about the giant and Jack who killed him, because she hated seeing the picture of the castle which looked exactly like the tower at Alwar, and reading the rhyme about fee-fi-fo-fum. In Great-aunt Rosa's book the giant added a bit about having liver and lights for supper tonight. It was difficult to know if it would be worse to have your bones ground up for bread, or to have your liver eaten for supper.

But stories about ogres and giants were for babies; it was important to remember they did not really exist, and so Selina, her heart beating uncomfortably fast, went across the grass and right up to the tower.

*   *   *

Close to, it was not as bad as she had feared. It was actually quite sad, as if people had once used it for quite ordinary things, and it had liked that. But now that it was just an old ruin nobody took any notice of it, and it had got sadder and sadder with the years. Forlorn. Yes, that was the word.

The tower at Alwar had not been forlorn. It had been frightening and greedy, and there had been a bad smell from it – a smell that made you think of squelched bones and chewed-up bits of flesh, where the birds of prey had spat out the bits of bone and gristle that they did not like.

But Inchcape's Round Tower smelt of dust and dirt, and loneliness. There was a neat little door set into the bricks. Selina thought it would be locked, but when she pushed it it gave at her touch, scraping on the stone floor, the hinges screeching loudly, but opening quite easily. It was dark inside, but there was a trickle of light where the bricks had crumbled, and she could see a little round room, the floor thickly covered in dust, with a stone stairway at the centre that wound up and up into the blackness of the tower's top.

The floor was strewn with small bones, and for a truly dreadful moment Selina thought that it was the ogre's castle after all, just as it had been in Alwar, and these were the remains of the people he had eaten. But she waited for her eyes to get used to the dimness, which was something you had to do in dark places, and she saw that the bones were too small to be people: they were tiny, pitiful remnants, and she understood that they were the bones of birds who had become trapped in here and died from fear at not being able to get out.

Selina stepped inside. The smell of dirt and decay closed round her, and the bones crunched under her feet. She did not mind about the bones, because she could pretend that they were the bones of the birds who had been in the tower at Alwar. She could pretend she was killing them for what they had done to her mother and father. She stomped about a bit, feeling the light dried-out skeletons splinter like glass under her shoes. Good. Horrid greedy things, they deserved to be crunched.

It would not be very difficult to make a shrine here. It would not be necessary to go up the stairs, but this little round room would have to be swept out and dusted a bit: you could not have a dusty floor when you were making a shrine. Anyone knew that. Selina thought she could smuggle out a dustpan and brush and a bucket of water and some washing soda.

The room had a little ledge where photographs could be put, and flowers. Yes, it would make a good shrine, this room, and once it had been made mother and father would rest and Selina would not have to force herself to stay awake so as not to see them hiding in her bedroom.

The best part was that nobody would find the shrine, because nobody ever came to the tower. People looked at it from outside because it was interesting and historic, but most of them avoided it. Children thought it was haunted and grown-ups thought it was dangerous. It was a pity that the door could not be locked, but it might be wedged shut. And Selina could save some of the birds' bone-dust and sprinkle it just inside the door. She would jump over it when she came here herself, but anyone else coming here would not know to do that and they would leave footprints in the dust. So if there were ever footprints there, it would mean the shrine had been desecrated.

In Alwar people who desecrated shrines were called outcasts. Quite often they were killed, and everyone said it served them right because shrine desecrators deserved to die.

CHAPTER SIX

Stupid people who made their lives shrines to the dead deserved to be killed.

Mary could not remember when the idea of killing her parents had first come to her: all she knew was that one day she had looked down into the deepest part of her mind and seen the idea of murder lying curled up in a corner. It was an ugly idea to have in your mind – it was a wizened, hunched-over shape. But once you had seen it, it was no longer possible to ignore it. Sometimes Mary thought the dark ugly idea had been quietly growing there for years – ever since she could think thoughts and dream dreams – but at other times she thought it had only come there when she was much older.

For a long time she tried to pretend it did not exist, but really she knew it was there, getting stronger and bigger, tenaciously clinging on to her mind. When she finally looked at it properly she was surprised to find that it no longer seemed ugly at all. It seemed familiar and sensible and comforting. Kill mother and father. Send them to where they wanted to be most of all, which was with the child who had died all those years ago and whose memory had stopped them from loving Mary.

Thinking these thoughts made the idea uncurl a little, so that Mary could see down into its heart. She could see that killing her parents would be an excellent punishment for all the years of making her feel second best. If they were dead, Mary would be an orphan. Pitied. Poor child, people would say; both her parents gone. What a tragedy. It would be very good to have all that sympathy and attention. Her sister had had it for years and years and it was time Mary had a turn. Yes, killing them was the right thing to do. But how should it be done?

Lying on her bed, the faded photograph of her sister watching her from the dressing table – 'So *sweet* that Mary wants Christabel's likeness in her room,' Leila Maskelyne had said – Mary considered the matter carefully. It ought to be an appropriate murder. Something that would show her mother and father what she thought of them. Something to do with the years they had spent in Alwar? The murder-embryo unfolded a little more; it flexed its claws, and the plan slid into Mary's mind, neat and whole, the edges buffed smooth.

When you have been forced all your life to listen to tales of India; when you have had stories of violence and rioting, and sagas of religious quarrels, drummed into you since you were old enough to understand; and when you have absorbed the customs of Muslims and Hindus and Sikhs, you do not have to look far for a murder method.

If William and Leila were so bound up with the dark sub-continent that was India, they should die in a way that would be understood – and approved – by its people.

In India, Mary's father had worked for a government department, dealing with something called auditing of public services. It sounded utterly boring to Mary, but it meant that William knew about things like how much the government was spending on the development of the country, and on hospitals and schools. It meant he had been quite important and that he was paid quite a lot of money.

'Your father was a very important man in India,' Mary's mother sometimes said. 'But after the Tragedy I had to come home – the doctors said so; they said I couldn't possibly stay in that place – and of course your father came back with me, there was never any question of his staying on alone. They gave him a pension. An insult to offer us money – and the money was hardly more than a pittance – but we took it out of politeness.'

What the pittance had meant, in practical terms, was that when Mary was born her parents had been able to buy a house in the country – not a huge house, but a nice old redbrick with ivy on its walls, and shady gardens, in a village in Berkshire. William did some work from home, which was called consultancy, or sometimes worked for a few weeks in offices whose books had to be audited, and Leila helped with one or two local charities. It was something to do. There were WI committees and modest dinner or lunch parties. Mary went to a small private school for girls in the next village. Life went on, said Mary's mother, bravely.

(But there were still all those nights when Mary could hear, through the bedroom wall, her parents trying to make another baby. 'One day, William, we'll have her back, our lovely girl. Come into the bed with me, William . . .')

The house was quite old, and there were some rather tumbledown outbuildings – what had been a small stable block and an old buttery. Leila said, oh dear, wouldn't they have made splendid hide-and-seek places for children, but William said they were an eyesore and he would see about getting them pulled down one of these days.

One of the outhouses had been a wash-house, in the days when people did not have automatic washing machines and dryers, and washing was done separately. It was a stone-floored room with a deep, square, old-fashioned sink and a huge copper boiler, nastily crusted with green verdigris around the waste pipes. The sink smelt of clogged-up drains and sour dish cloths, and there were black beetles and spiders inside the boiler. It was not a place where people wanted to go, but it was far enough from the house and far enough from neighbours for sounds not to carry. Mary inspected it carefully, walking all round it, examining the door and the window and the floor. She took a transistor radio in there one day and tested the range to see how much sound carried. With the door shut, hardly at all.

Yes, this should be the Murder House.

Leila Maskelyne regularly took sleeping pills, which the local doctor prescribed for her. It had been years since she had been able to fall asleep naturally. 'Without my pills I should never get a good night's sleep,' she said.

The pills were kept in her bedside cabinet, along with aspirin and indigestion mixture and the contraceptives that father sometimes used. Mary knew about those by now; some of the girls at school had started experimenting with boyfriends, and the upper fourth, most of whom were fourteen, had been given a sex talk by a nursing sister from the local women's clinic. Most of the class had scuffled and giggled embarrassedly, but Mary had listened carefully because of understanding about what her parents were doing to get her sister reborn. It was actually a bit revolting to think of father doing that.

She waited until mother got a new bottle of sleeping pills, and then tipped out a dozen and crushed them between two sheets of baking paper in the bathroom with the door locked. Six each. Would it be enough? Or too much? The label said you could take two, with a third one four hours later. So six each ought to be about right.

It was easy to tip the white powder into father's mid-evening cup of coffee and mother's mid-evening cup of tea, half quantities each. Making the night-time drink was one of Mary's weekend tasks when there was no school the next day and she could stay up until ten o'clock. Usually she hated doing it, but tonight she made properly filtered coffee for father and mother's favourite Earl Grey tea, and even set the cups on a little tray with a plate of biscuits.

'That's my good girl,' said father, looking up from the evening paper, which he was reading. Mother looked up approvingly from her knitting and smiled.

The pills did not take long to work. It was barely fifteen minutes before Mary, pretending to listen to Radio Luxembourg in her room, heard a crash of china – one of them dropping a cup, that would be. She waited a little longer and then went tiptoeing down to the sitting room, her heart beating furiously with nervous excitement.

But it was all right; they were both knocked out by the pills. Mother had fallen sideways in her chair, her legs sprawling so that you could see her underwear. Pink petticoat and knickers, for God's sake! She looked stupid and ugly and a dribble of saliva ran out of the corner of her mouth. Horrid!

Father's head had fallen back and his glasses had slipped to one side. His mouth was open so that you could see the fillings in his teeth, and he was snoring. Mary stood looking at them both for a long time, not because she was afraid of the next part, but because this was starting to be so violently exciting that she wanted to hold on to the feeling. Remember it. Remember how this feels. Curiously, she had the feeling that Christabel was with her now, and that Christabel was urging her on.

Do it, Christabel was saying in Mary's ear. *Stupid selfish creatures, both of them . . . Kill them, Mary, and you'll be free, and I'll be free as well . . .*

Christabel needed to be free? For a moment Mary had not understood this, but then the whispery voice had said, *Of course I need to be free! I'm the prisoner of those stupid maudlin memories just as much as you are! I'm the angel-child, the virtuous perfect prodigy . . .* Was there a note of impatience in Christabel's voice there? *I'm the one who should be set free, you silly bitch . . .* said Christabel in Mary's ear. Yes, the impatience and the scorn were unquestionably there, and Christabel's strength was filling her up, and she could do it, she could do anything . . .

Moving slowly, like a swimmer moving through water, Mary reached for one of mother's knitting needles. They were steel needles because mother had been knitting a thick winter jumper and they would not break or bend under the weight of the heavy wool.

They did not break or bend when Mary stood behind father's chair and pushed his head forward a little, and then drove the point of the needle hard into his neck, at the place where it joined the skull. There was a bad moment when the needle hit something hard – bone? gristle? – and Mary was afraid she would have to take it out and try it a bit higher up. But it only stuck for a second or two and then it slid deep in – deep, deep into father's skull, mushing up his brain and stabbing through all the nerves in the spinal cord. There was another bad moment when she thought he was going to wake up – he seemed to grunt and his whole body jerked as if he were a puppet and strings had been pulled. His hands flailed, and a wet sound came from his throat, and then he flopped forward and Mary came round the chair to look at him from the front, to see what he looked like now that he was dead.

He did not look much different, but he was definitely dead. People said you could always tell, instantly, if somebody was dead, and Mary saw what they meant. It was as if a light had been switched off inside. There was some blood on his neck where the steel needle had gone in, and he had dribbled some sick out of his mouth – that would have been the wet choking sound.

Getting him out to the wash-house might have been awkward, but there was a small, lightweight wheelbarrow in the potting shed, and it was the easiest thing in the world to tip father forward out of his chair so that he fell into it. His hands flopped over the sides, and his legs splayed out. Mary saw that his trousers were wet at the crotch, which was pretty disgusting. It had run down the inside of his leg and puddled into his shoe. It was a small indignity, but it pleased Mary to see it, because when his body was found, people would know what he had done while he was dying.

Christabel was with her as she trundled the wheel-barrow through the house and across the little paved area at the back, and round to the wash-house. It was quite heavy, but it was not very difficult. Christabel watched from the shadows, and when Mary glanced up she could see that Christabel was smiling.

Do it, Mary, do it, DO IT . . .

Without Christabel's strength Mary might not have

been able to tip father's body out, and prop it up against the rusting boiler, and then make the return journey for mother. But it was all right. She managed it, and the strength was still coursing through her body and firing her mind and it was all going to work out exactly as she had planned.

The next part was a bit tricky, because the essence of the murder – the echoing of an Indian wife's death – was that mother must not be dead. She must die with William's body, just as the widows in India died, flinging themselves onto the burning funeral pyres of their dead husbands. And so Mary had to work quietly now, in case Leila roused from her drugged slumber. It was a bit disconcerting to see the rim of white under her mother's eyelids, but Mary thought that drugged people did look like that.

First she tied William to one of the rusting pipes protruding from the copper boiler, and then positioned him so that he was leaning back against it. After this she twisted her mother's hands behind her back and bound them tightly with thin tough nylon rope. She bound her ankles in the same way and stood, considering. Enough? No, she could wind the rope around Leila's upper arms as well, so that they were clamped to her body. It was absolutely vital that her mother did not manage to loosen the ropes. She bent over, tightening a knot. Yes, that was better. The bitch would never be able to work free of those cords. Now for the next part.

Working with care, testing the strength of each section of rope and the toughness of each knot she made, she bound her mother's body to that of her father, so that they were face to face. It amused her to position her father's arms around his wife, in the travesty of an embrace. She thought she heard Christabel laughing as this was done, and then she realised it was her own laughter. It sounded faintly eerie in the dank enclosed space, and there was a faint echo. Mary thought she had better remember not to laugh like that again.

It was lucky that William's body had not yet stiffened in *rigor mortis*, because it was easy to tie his arms into place, and turn his head so that the dead eyes stared straight into his wife's, and so that the sick-crusted lips were only inches from his wife's lips.

It was lucky, as well, that Leila Maskelyne was thin, because it made it easier to manipulate her. 'Grief,' Leila often said, ordering a smaller size skirt or dress. 'Grief strips the flesh from one's bones, I am afraid.'

It would not be grief that would strip the flesh from Leila's bones now. It would be the embrace of her dead and decomposing husband.

Mary thought it would take about a week for Leila to die. She was going to enjoy watching it happen.

Emily was going to Teind House every day at the moment, on account of Miss March's having a writer staying there for two whole weeks. Miss March had seemed a bit jumpy about it; Emily thought she probably had an image either of a frumpy scholarly person with scragged-back hair and lisle stockings, or a husky-voiced female with draped scarves and a pink feather boa and too-elaborate make-up from the 1950s. Barbara Cartland, maybe, or that woman who wrote those books about girls from poor homes becoming millionairesses and heads of industry, and marrying gorgeous hunky men along the way. Emily did not think Joanna Savile was likely to fall into either of these categories, which was just as well, because if she had done Selina would never have coped.

Joanna Savile was neither frumpy nor elaborate, of course. Her hair was great, but although she was quite nice-looking you would probably not have crossed the road to look at her a second time. Her clothes were great, as well. She wore jackets like velvet patchwork quilts and she had a Chinese-red silk skirt you would die to own. Emily wondered whether, if she saved up her Teind House and Inchcape School wages for about six months, she would be able to afford a skirt like that. It made the idea she had had about having a butterfly tattoo on her shoulder seem a bit tacky.

Joanna – she had told Emily to call her that, because she said breakfast-time was not a time for being formal – was going to Moy to get some background for a new book. She was meeting Patrick Irvine: she asked if Emily knew him, and Emily said, carefully, that she did. She thought it would be better not to say that most of the female staff at Moy fancied Dr Irvine rotten. If he had not been so old Emily might have fancied him herself, but he was at least forty so it was out of the question.

'Is he good-looking?' asked Joanna. 'I could do with seeing a good-looking man at the moment; my husband's working abroad.' She grinned when she said this, and quite suddenly she was not merely vaguely nice-looking, she was absolutely beautiful. Emily stared at her.

'He's in Spain,' Joanna went on, eating toast and honey with industrious pleasure. She could probably scoff food all day and never put on an ounce. 'He's in the northern part, near the Pyrenees. The people he works for are mounting a display of western versus eastern religion, which means northern Spain and then across to the Czech Republic and as far east as possible. I don't think they've got much further than chasing Inquisition thumbscrews in Spain yet, but Krzystof's probably having a wonderful time, the rat. Have you ever been to that part of Spain, Emily?'

But Emily had only been to a couple of eastern Spanish resorts on package holidays and they had not been all that different from Blackpool except the weather was better and the food unfamiliar. And although the Spanish boys she had met talked a lot about making beautiful love all night, the one she had finally gone to bed with had suffered from premature ejaculation, which had been embarrassing for both Emily and the boy. But clearly she could not say any of this to Joanna Savile, so she said, 'Um, no, I haven't,' and asked should she bring fresh toast or more coffee.

She wondered what sort of man somebody like Joanna would have married. People married the most surprising partners. Emily hoped Joanna's husband matched her. The name Krzystof sounded Romanian or Russian, or something equally dark and romantic and passionate.

Emily hoped Krzystof was drop-dead gorgeous and nice into the bargain.

Patrick Irvine was not really surprised when the governor asked him to talk to Joanna Savile.

'You deal with her, will you, Patrick?' the governor had said. 'It's more your territory than mine, this business of creative writing workshops.' He added that in any case Patrick had more experience at handling women, and took himself off to a finance meeting to consider orderly reports and quarterly budget reviews, which were the things he understood best.

Patrick, in fact, was perfectly agreeable to setting up some kind of gathering so that Ms Savile could study a few of the more intelligent of Moy's inmates. It often worked both ways, that kind of arrangement: the inmates liked to see a new face, especially a nice-looking one, Moy got an outside speaker without having to trawl the lists, and on this occasion their image might be boosted by having an acknowledgement in whatever work was in the melting pot. Joanna Savile was not a bestseller, but she wrote good mystery books that you saw in libraries and bookshops, usually with the sub-heading 'A Jack Tallent Mystery'. Patrick was always curious to see the effect that visitors had on the patients, and he would be intrigued to see how they coped with a writer of popular thrillers.

His first impression of Joanna Savile was very similar to Emily's: nice-looking, but not outstanding. She explained about wanting to study a handful of Moy's more seriously disturbed inmates, and said it did not matter which ones;

she simply wanted an all-round view of life inside a mental institution if that was possible.

'I'd make sure there was a proper acknowledgement to Moy in the preface when the book comes out, of course,' she said, seated in Patrick's office, her face alight with enthusiasm. 'And one to you as well, Dr Irvine, if medical etiquette doesn't ban it – I'm never sure about things like that.'

She smiled, and Patrick instantly revised his first opinion. It was the smile that did it. It was extraordinary. In the space of a single heartbeat, Joanna Savile switched from being an unremarkable young woman to a confiding and rather sexy gamine. Patrick said, 'If it turns out that I've been of any help, I'd be rather honoured to be acknowledged, Ms Savile.'

'Joanna.'

'Joanna. Good. I'm Patrick.'

'Irish?' she said, putting her head on one side as if assessing him.

'On my mother's side.'

'I thought you might be. It's the eyes. And there's a trace of accent as well.'

'My father was Scottish, though. Hence the Irvine part. Not the easiest of mixes, Scots and Irish.'

'My husband's half Hungarian. But mostly the English half has the upper hand.' The smile showed again, briefly. 'But the Hungarian's there just often enough to keep people on their toes. You're not very happy about one-to-one interviews with inmates, are you?'

'I'm not.'

'I thought you wouldn't be. Well then, how about this for a deal? I could give a talk to your more literate people – any of them you think might be interested in creative writing. I could even set up a couple of workshops for them, if that would be allowed – say three or four sessions, giving them some writing projects. I don't mean "What I did in the hols", or "My pet parrot", but things they might find interesting, or even helpful. I'd discuss it with you first, of course, in case I was trespassing on any therapy.'

'Most forms of writing are therapy anyway,' said Patrick.

'That's true.' Her eyes flickered as if something – some unpleasant memory perhaps? – had stirred. But she only said, 'You see, simply by meeting some of the inmates and talking to them I'd get a fair idea of their lives in here and the routines of their days.' Before he could break in, she went on, 'I do know I could get that from your warders, but it's the prisoners' point of view I want. Working it this way would give me that, and it would also give you an outside speaker. I'm not the world's greatest lecturer, but I've talked to quite a number of writers' groups and adult learning set-ups over the years, and I'm not bad.'

'It sounds a reasonable *quid pro quo*,' said Patrick. He studied her. 'Tell me how you'd approach it when the audience was a clutch of mentally disturbed murderers and rapists.'

He had used these words deliberately to see if she could be thrown off balance. But she was not. She leaned forward, her thin hands moving expressively, and said, 'I don't know that I'd approach it very differently. Presumably they aren't murdering or raping twenty-four hours a day. And what I've done with potentially awkward groups before is to start them off with music. Play a few pieces to them, and then see what word-pictures they conjure up.' Again the grin. 'I expect that's first-year psychiatry-course stuff, isn't it?'

'We do use music in therapy, sometimes,' said Patrick.

'Are you being tactful?'

'Not really. I'm interested. Go on.'

Joanna paused, frowning slightly as if assembling her thoughts. She said, 'Do they watch much television, your patients?'

'Yes. Too much, most of them.'

'I've got a tape of some of the great classic pieces used in TV commercials. The Bach *Air in G* for Hamlet cigars, of course, and Delibes' *Flower Duet* for British Airways. Dvorak's *New World Symphony*—'

'Hovis bread?'

'Yes. *Yes.* Well, all right, I know it's probably a bit obvious, but it works quite well. To start with – mostly to break the ice – I'd make a little quiz for them. Playing the pieces and seeing if they could match the TV advert to them. It needn't be very competitive – just a fun thing. After that we'd discuss why which music was chosen for which product: what emotions did the ad-makers hope to inspire? And from there, with luck, it'd be a fairly easy step to playing other pieces – deeper stuff – and asking them to write down their reactions. Some of them might want to drop out at that point, but there might be enough

85

who'd want to go on to a second or even a third session, perhaps with a bit more advanced stuff. Then I could set them exercises to write on specific subjects, or ask for suggestions for short stories, and have group criticism.' She regarded him. 'What do you think? Any good?'

'Yes, certainly.' Patrick thought about it for a moment, and then said, 'I'd have to choose the participants carefully. Off the top of my head I can think of about six or eight who would be genuinely interested, and whom you'd probably find very worthwhile.' He glanced up at her. 'The thing is that with any kind of outside speaker we always have the problem of time-wasters. Life in here gets monotonous for most of them, and there's an element that will sign up for anything going, regardless of whether they're interested in it.' He did not say that there was an element that might get a sexual kick out of sitting in Moy's small lecture room with a female talking to them.

'I wouldn't necessarily mind opportunists being in the group,' said Joanna.

'No, but I would. It might lead to a difficult situation,' said Patrick. 'They might start barracking – they aren't here purely because they're mentally sick, these people; they're also here because they've committed serious crimes. Moy isn't a place for charming rogues or Ealing-film bank robbers. You'd be in amongst the murderers and the child-molesters. It'd be important that you didn't forget that, not for a minute.'

'I do know that,' said Joanna, after a moment. 'You've just had Mary Maskelyne transferred here, haven't you?'

86

There was an odd little silence. Patrick, no slouch when it came to gauging another's emotion, thought: you've been waiting to plant that, my girl. Now why, I wonder? Is it Maskelyne you're really after? Is all this stuff about background just a blind? But he said, equably, 'Yes, Maskelyne is one of my people. I'm still assessing her, but I think she might be included in your group. She's an intelligent girl.'

'"Girl"? She must be well over forty by now.'

'She's forty-five, in fact. According to her file, she's kept a diary at various times. That indicates a fair degree of literacy. Yes, I think we could include her.' He made a note, and added a few other names.

'Thank you very much,' said Joanna. 'I won't take up any more of your time: I expect you're fiendishly busy. But – would you phone me at Teind House with a possible day? Here's the number. Teind House, care of Miss March. I'm in Inchcape for at least two weeks and I could fit in with any day you wanted.'

'I'll sound out the wing governors,' said Patrick. 'But let's provisionally say Thursday afternoon, shall we? At two o'clock? That would mean their lunch would be over and the half-hour recreation would just have finished.' He considered briefly the idea of inviting her to lunch beforehand. No, she would probably be too taken up with the preparations.

'Thursday at two would be fine,' said Joanna, standing up and holding out her hand. As Patrick Irvine took it, he thought it was rather a pity about the Hungarian husband.

CHAPTER SEVEN

———————❖———————

Mary did not especially want to attend some crappy talk by some even crappier female writer, but Dr Irvine had sounded as if he would like her to go, and for the moment it was probably a good idea to play along with him. They had had several discussions now: it was actually quite stimulating to find ways to dodge Dr Irvine's calculatedly worded questions. Mary could see through most of them, of course, because she knew by this time how these doctors worked. They tried to set snares for you, and sometimes they placed depth-charges deep inside your mind, so that you would find yourself reacting or responding when you least expected it. Mary was not going to fall into any stupid doctor's traps.

At best, being at the talk might give her a chance to spy out Moy's possibilities. So far, these had been non-existent. Moy was famous for its extremely high security: the word had even passed into the language. 'As safe as Moy,' people said, in the same way that they said, 'As impenetrable as Fort Knox.' But that meant that it was going to be extremely difficult to find a chink in Moy's armour and burrow beneath it, and turn things to her advantage.

The years inside the different prisons had melted into one another, and time had sometimes blurred a bit. Mary often felt there were huge gaps in her life – black pits of incredible tedium in which she had become trapped and during which absolutely nothing of any interest had happened. The thing to do was to recognise these pits for what they were, and to climb out of them by making something happen. There were any number of ways that could be done – she had tried several – but the result was almost always the same. Public interest in the original double murder was revived, and articles were written by people who thought they understood what had motivated it, sometimes comparing Mary with Myra Hindley or Rosemary West. And practically overnight Mary became a Somebody all over again. A person to be treated with respect. Warders and fellow inmates who had more or less forgotten what she had done looked at her through different eyes, often with awed curiosity. Mary could feel their thoughts clearly. Did she really do those things? they were wondering. She looks quite normal now, but how must she have looked when she committed those murders? She always made a point of looking her best at these times because of everyone's interest.

And always, after these articles appeared, people began

writing to Mary all over again. New generations of angry teenagers grew up, and wrote to Mary saying they absolutely identified with what she had done all those years ago: they hated their parents who did not understand them, and they wished they had Mary's courage. Some said they were going to leave home because their parents would not let them go clubbing all night, but some wrote how they had been abused – how fathers or uncles had been secretly screwing them since they were eleven – and how they were one day going to kill them, just as Mary had killed her father. These teenagers – who were not all girls – did not always just use the word 'screwed'.

Mary would have liked to reply to these letters, especially to the girls, urging them to go ahead, not to be afraid, telling them that their evil selfish fathers and uncles deserved to die writhing in agony. But the first time she tried it, the letters were intercepted, and she was told curtly that they were regarded as incitement to murder and could not be sent. Years later, at Broadacre, when she met Ingrid, she found out that if it had not been for those letters she might have been allowed a phone card so that she could make calls from one of the hooded phone boxes that smelt of stale sweat and halitosis. Mary said, 'But who would I ring up? I don't know anybody,' and Ingrid had laughed and said, You know me. Mary had regarded her, and thought: yes, I do, because you're easy to know. But you'll never really know me, not if I can help it . . .

Some of the letters asked how Mary had managed for so many years without having sex. Mary thought they were probably try-ons to see if she would start up a titillating correspondence with boys of fifteen and sixteen, who wanted to be turned on by reading about masturbation or lesbianism. She did not bother to reply to these, even though it was a joke for people to think she had to manage without sex. She had not had to manage without sex at all; she had had all the sex she had wanted, and she could probably have had more if she could have been bothered.

The prospect of the talk by this Joanna Savile started Mary wondering about writing a book: the story of her life it would be, telling about the years in the Young Offenders' Hostel, and then, later, in Broadacre. (And Ingrid? said her mind. Would you tell what really happened between you and Ingrid in Broadacre? How Ingrid seduced you . . . ? How you let Ingrid do all those things to you . . . ?) She might not tell everything about Ingrid, but she would tell how her parents' murder had been the fault of the child in Alwar who had escaped instead of Christabel.

Dr Irvine would be pleased if Mary said she wanted to write a book. She would not tell them it was to be a sensational book, an exposé, in case they forbade her to write it; she would say it was a confession – what Roman Catholics called an absolving. Yes, she would use that very word; it was a good one. Dr Irvine would think she was repenting or finding Jesus or something, and she might even be allowed to use a computer – Moy had quite good education facilities. There was a computer room here where you could learn about word-processing.

Broadacre and the Young Offenders' Hostel had had neither word-processing classes nor a computer room. Mary had had to attend lessons at the Young Offenders place, because she was still not quite fifteen, and they said that schooling was important. So there had been English and history and maths; later there had been current affairs and social economics. Most of it had been useless, and nearly all of it had been boring, except occasionally the English lessons. But she had learned how to compose letters and talk politely on the telephone, and how to operate a typewriter and prepare a CV. All these things would be necessary when she went back into the world.

And then in the end the bastards had not let her go; when she was eighteen she had been reassessed and even though she had been confidently expecting to be released, she was not. She was talked to by a great many doctors, and in the end they told her that they were transferring her to Broadacre. They pretended to be sad about it, but Mary had known they were not sad at all, only triumphant because their stupid tests and their childish traps had caught her. The matron at the YOH had folded her lips like a drawstring purse and looked pleased at the decision.

That was when Mary had screamed at them: not just a single angry scream, but long, furious screechings that went on and on, bouncing off the walls of her room, letting all of the pent-up agony and bitterness stream out, because it was not fair, it was *not fair* that they should do this to her, not when she had allowed them to shut her away for all these years, not when killing her parents had been the logical culmination of years and years of neglect and disinterest.

After a while one of the doctors had come, and there had been the jabbing needle of a hypodermic, and she had sunk, spinning and helpless, into a stupor that might have lasted for an hour or for days, she had never known which.

When she came out of the stupor she felt sick and blurry, and for a while her mind felt as if it was wrapped in cotton wool, so that when she tried to think – really, properly think – the thoughts all went skittering away from her. Her sight did not seem to be working in step with her mind, either; it was as if she was seeing things a second after they happened. That had been when she had known that there was a conspiracy to keep her locked away, and that she would have to be very clever and very cunning, and never trust anybody.

Once or twice she had tried screaming again, banging her fists against the harsh rough stone of the infirmary walls with frustration, because it was not to be borne that she should be shut away like this – 'At Her Majesty's pleasure', as if Her Majesty bloody gave a farthing fuck what happened to Mary! But as soon as she started screaming, they came running with the needles or the pills. You could spit out pills, but you could not spit out the hypodermic.

Leila had screamed in the dank wash-house all those years ago. She had screamed until her throat was bleeding and raw, and Mary had finally had to stop up her mouth to prevent people from finding her. Anyone would have agreed that this had been the action of a sensible, logical person.

Leila had taken several hours to come round from the large dose of sleeping stuff Mary had tipped into her tea – Mary could still remember how her wristwatch had ticked those hours away – and during those hours William's body had begun to grow stiff and doll-like. *Rigor mortis*. It had been rather strange to find out that the school biology lessons and the whodunnit novels had been right about *rigor mortis*. Mary had watched the process for herself, sitting on a blanket in the corner of the wash-house, a torch at her hand to switch on if she needed it, and a sharply-honed bread knife to hand as well, in case Leila did manage to break free.

As dawn started to lighten the skies, Mary saw that her father's face was taking on a mask-look, and setting down the knife she approached him and cautiously put out a hand to touch his skin. It felt exactly like a lump of dead meat. Revolting. But *rigor* was unmistakably happening. It was five hours after he had died, and the smaller muscles in his face and jaw were perceptibly stiffening.

The process was more advanced by the time Mary's mother started to wake from the drugged slumber: it was beginning to lock most of William's body into hard rigidity. But just as Mary had hoped, the first thing Leila saw when she opened her eyes was her husband's dead face, inches from her own. That had been when Mary had known that everything was all going to happen as she had planned it. She could still remember how she had felt at that moment, how she had sat forward eagerly, her hands tightly clasped, not wanting to miss a second of anything.

Leila had gasped in horror and had instinctively tried to pull back, only to come up against the thin strong rope that held her in place and the unyielding embrace of William's arms. Mary saw her blink and shake her head as if denying what she was seeing or trying to shake off an unpleasant dream, and then look blurrily about her, bewildered and confused. And then realisation slowly dawned in her face, and with it had come panic and revulsion, and that had been the best moment of all. Mary had laughed once again to see those emotions on her mother's face, although she had instantly put her hand over her mouth to push the laughter back down. But it had been a moment to store away and remember, and she could still recall it even now, even after so many years.

When Leila Maskelyne had realised that she was tightly bound to the body of her dead husband she had called out for help, managing to twist her head round until she saw Mary, seated quietly in the corner.

'Please – help me . . .'

'No,' said Mary, very quietly. 'There's no help to be had.'

'But – he's dead. William – your father— He's *dead*.'

'Yes, he is,' said Mary, and in case Leila should be in any doubt, she said, 'He's been dead for several hours. I killed him last night. There's a hole through the base of his skull into his brains.'

'But I don't understand— Mary what are you doing?'

'Killing both of you,' said Mary, and despite her control

another of the little laughs bubbled out. She waited for it to die away, and then said, 'I'm killing you for all the years you ignored me and didn't love me. And for all the years you fucked together to get my sister back.' She pushed her face closer to Leila's. 'I used to hear you,' she said. 'All those nights – I heard everything you did. You put Christabel above me all those years, and you tried to get her reborn. And all the time you had me, and I could have been just as good as she was.'

'This is mad,' said Leila helplessly, and this time the laugh that broke out from Mary's mouth had been not so much a laugh as a scream of anger.

'Don't say I'm mad! I'm not mad! You're the mad ones! You're the stupid mad things who have to die!' She had paused then, surprised to find that she was breathing hard, as if she had been running very fast.

'Mary, untie me. We'll go into the house and talk about this— My dear, of course your father and I loved you— Of course we didn't put Christabel above you—'

'Oh, yes you did,' said Mary. 'And you aren't going to be untied until you're dead as well. You're going to die, you selfish bitch, and you're going to die here, with *him*. Tied to him. It's good, isn't it? It'll be like the widows in India who threw themselves onto their husbands' funeral pyres. You'd know about that, wouldn't you? Because you never really left India, did you? I don't know how long it's going to take for you to die – it might be three or four days. But you will die, and I'm going to watch it happen.' The laughing came up by itself again, like vomiting, and Mary saw a look of the utmost horror in her mother's eyes.

That had been when Leila began to scream, throwing her head back, the muscles of her neck standing out like cords with the screaming. The sounds bounced off the stone walls and repeated themselves over and over, spinning around Mary's head, piercing and shrill. Dreadful. Not to be borne. Mary got up and stood over Leila, holding up the knife. 'If you don't shut up I'll have to make you,' she said. 'I'll cut your tongue out if you scream again. I'll really do it.'

'I won't scream,' said Leila at once, subsiding to a frightened whisper. Her face was smeary with tears and sweat and her eyes were huge with terror. 'I promise I won't scream again, Mary.'

But the bitch did scream again. She was cunning, that sly-faced Leila. She waited until Mary went into the house to get herself something to eat and use the bathroom, and until the outside world might be judged to be awake and about its lawful occasions. Postmen and newspaper boys, and people walking their dogs or taking their children to school. She screamed at the top of her lungs, and when Mary dropped the sandwich she had made herself and ran at top speed back to the wash-house she was still screaming, her head flung back, her lips flecked with blood and spittle. Her eyes were bolting from her head. She looked ridiculous and ugly, but someone might hear her, so she would have to be silenced, which was a nuisance.

Mary would quite have liked to carry out the tongue-cutting threat, but that might end in killing Leila before

Mary wanted her dead. Loss of blood. Shock. And Leila must die slowly, in her husband's rigid embrace. That was what the plan was, and that was what Mary wanted. There was also the strong likelihood that if Mary tried to mutilate her mother's mouth, Leila would seize the opportunity of fighting back and would bite. No, that idea would not work at all. What, then? Gag her? Stop up her mouth?

Stop up her mouth. With what?

By now it was a good twelve hours since William had died, and his entire body was rock-hard. Mary walked round the two grotesque captives, considering. From time to time the bubbling laugh came out, because this was all so very pleasing, it was appropriate, it was vindication and justification for all those years of listening to the whining about Christabel. She had thought that Christabel was with her earlier on, but she was no longer sure about that. Anyhow, it was better to be alone. There was no one you could trust as absolutely as you could trust yourself.

In the end, she sawed off two of her father's fingers to use. It took quite a long time, and she had to fetch two more knives because the knuckle-bones gave her a lot of trouble. But at last it was done, and after several experiments she managed to thrust the two fingers into her mother's mouth, like a plug. At the first attempt she pushed them too far back and Leila gagged and retched, but at the second attempt she managed to prop her mother's mouth open quite neatly.

Safe in the knowledge that Leila could not scream

again, she went back to finish her sandwich and to make a cup of coffee to drink with it.

The curious thing was that after they told her she was to go to Broadacre – after the screaming incident and the injections – Mary began to think about her dead sister more and more.

Every 8 June Mary remembered that this was Christabel's birthday: that today Christabel would have been twenty-eight, twenty-nine . . . Almost certainly Christabel would have been married by now, perhaps with children. Mary would have been an aunt to those children. She thought Christabel would have had a boy and a girl.

As the sun set on 12 September each year, she counted the years, and thought, 'Today Christabel has been dead for twenty-one years. For twenty-two, for twenty-three years.'

But most of all, Mary remembered how she had sensed Christabel's presence that morning in the squalid wash-house – *Set me free* . . . Christabel had whispered – and although Christabel had vanished immediately after-wards, Mary began to realise that she was returning. She did not come as a ghost like something out of a horror story – something that stood at the foot of your bed and stared at you with hollow eyes, or crept out of the shadows to lay icy fingers on your face – she came much more gently and much more subtly than that.

Inside Mary's mind. Ah yes, that was clever of Christabel, dead and enshrined and practically canonised by those two fools, her parents. It was what you would expect of

Christabel, who was for ever young, for ever beautiful and unspoiled.

Little by little, strand by cobweb strand, Christabel's thoughts slid deep into Mary's mind, until at times Mary could almost see her sister. To begin with it was all very puzzling, but then, quite suddenly, Mary understood. Christabel had been weighed down with all that sickly devotion and it had been a burden to her, just as Mary had found it a burden being unwanted and ignored, and having her own small achievements and aspirations belittled. Of course Christabel would be grateful to the little sister who had never met her but had lifted the burden of those clogging memories. Out of gratitude, Christabel would probably stay with Mary for most of her life now, and help her when she needed help.

It was rather comforting.

CHAPTER EIGHT

The Round Tower was beginning to get to Emily. She was starting to experience churning sensations in her stomach when she had to ride her motorbike past it, and quite often she dreamed about it and woke with her heart going at about ten times its normal rate.

People in Inchcape said it was a sad, neglected old place, and somebody ought to do something about it before it fell down where it stood. Turn it into a tourist centre, they said, or a museum. It could even become a kind of outpost of Stornforth Bird Sanctuary – enough of their charges came to it. Miss March told Emily that Great-uncle Matthew used to say much the same things. When she was a girl he had always been writing to people about getting something done, and about resurfacing the old road, but Selina did not think he had ever had any replies. Still, he had enjoyed writing the letters. He had been fond of writing to people in authority and pointing out their shortcomings, Great-uncle Matthew.

Emily did not think the tower was sad. She thought it was a sneery, sly place, and every time she growled the motorbike past it she had the eeriest feeling that somewhere within its depths there might be watchers. The trouble was that they would not be ordinary and unmenacing human watchers – tramps or winos or New Age travellers – they would be feathered and clawed, with hooded eyes and cruel talons and beaks— Here they were, back in the Hitchcock film again.

She mentioned the tower to Dr Irvine when he came to supper, not making a big deal of it, just dropping it into the conversation. Dad and Dr Irvine were cronies and they wanted to talk informally about some of Moy's people, so Emily had offered to cook supper for them. Mum used to do a mean chicken curry and Emily had found her recipe. She had not been able to look at any of mum's recipes for months, but when she did look it was surprisingly comforting. It made her feel near to mum to be measuring out the spices and seeing the little splosh of yellow on the corner of the page where mum spilt the turmeric that time.

Dr Irvine seemed interested in the Round Tower and in Emily's reactions to it. She said, deliberately vaguely, that it reminded her of a nightmare, and Dr Irvine looked at her thoughtfully for quite a long time so that Emily began to feel as if she had said something utterly stupid. He had nice eyes, Dr Irvine; very dark blue, with black lashes. You felt as if he could see straight into your thoughts, but as if he might like what he was seeing. And he had dark hair with just a few tiny flecks of grey in it, like the cloth of an expensive overcoat. Emily reminded herself that he was nearly twenty years older, and therefore obviously out of bounds as far as sexiness went, never mind what the girls in Moy's offices said about older men often turning out to be absolute dynamite in bed. Actually Dr Irvine probably was dynamite in bed if you considered it. Emily did consider it, and then was abruptly so embarrassed that she bent over the pot of curry, spooning out helpings.

Dr Irvine took his plate, and added rice and mango chutney. He said, 'A nightmare place, is it? D'you know the best thing to do with nightmares, Emily?'

'What?'

'Spike their guns. Confront them head on.'

Emily looked at him. 'You mean go right up to the tower?'

'Go right up to it,' said Patrick Irvine. 'Squash the nightmare, Emily. Lay the ghost.'

Lay the ghost. It sounded like a joke, the kind of thing a gang of lads might say down at the pub. Hey fellas, I'm laying a ghost tonight.

But Dr Irvine dealt with all those wild murderers and rapists – Mary Maskelyne had just come to Moy for heaven's sake! – and he had those eyes that walked in and out of your mind, and what he did not know about nightmares and phobias was probably not worth knowing.

Emily waited until Miss March went into Stornforth. It was a blustery afternoon, and Selina wore a mackintosh that buttoned up to the neck, with a headsquare tied over her hair in case it rained. Lorna Laughlin was driving her in: it was half-term and they were going to do some shopping together.

Once she had gone Teind House sank gratefully into its afternoon silence. Joanna Savile was in her room working. She played classical music while she worked – just very softly, but Emily had sometimes heard it, and she could hear it now. She had told Emily she was preparing a talk to give to a group of the inmates at Moy. Emily hoped the group would not include Flasher Logan.

Great-uncle Matthew's clock was on guard duty in the hall, but she stuck her tongue out at the horrid ticking thing as she went past it, jammed dad's mobile phone into the pocket of her leather biking jacket because you never knew, and zipped the jacket up to the neck.

She went out through the side door, which Miss March called the garden door, locking it carefully so that nothing spooky could sneak in and hide inside Great-uncle Matthew's clock, and set off through the orchard.

It was a sharp cold afternoon – the kind of late-October afternoon that Emily liked. The cold pricked tears in your eyes so that you kept seeing things through a little blurry mist until you blinked the tears away, and there was a scent on the air that was a mixture of bonfires and wet leaves and woollen scarves that got into your mouth.

The little orchard smelt of apples and the leaves felt dry and crackly as you walked across them. Nice. The disused road was nice as well. You had the feeling that you were walking backwards in time, or even into a different world altogether. Cowardly lions and white rabbits, thought Emily. Still, it's easier than Alice's rabbit-hole.

She thought, at first, that she would not be able to go up to the tower, even like this, even in the middle of the afternoon for God's sake, with people around, and a mobile phone in her pocket. But Dr Irvine's off-hand remark – which Emily knew had not really been off-hand at all – had lodged in her memory, and Emily touched it in her mind for reassurance. Spike the nightmare's guns. Confront the ghosts.

Seen from right down on the ground, the old tower was as horrid as she had thought. It was dark and menacing and it was *old*, so old that you could almost smell the oldness breathing out from it, and you had the feeling that if you stretched out your hands you would be able to plunge them, wrist-deep, into the swirling miasma of the long-ago. As well as that, it seemed to lean over, as if it might be threatening to topple down onto her – Emily could just imagine that sudden tumble of blackened crumbling bricks cascading around her head, and the centuries of dust, and the dozens of bird skeletons, light and fragile and unbearably pitiful, in the way that bird skeletons were if you found them in a chimney. The absolute last thing she wanted to do was push open the deep-set little door and go inside. The door would probably be locked, anyhow.

But it was not locked, wouldn't you just know it? It swung gently inwards at her touch, and the hinges did not even creak. So it wasn't a Hitchcock film after all, because a Hitchcock film would definitely have a creaking-hinge door. Emily hesitated, and then remembered that once she had looked properly inside, and *seen* that there was nothing to be afraid of, she would feel better. It would be nice to be able to ride past the tower without her heart hammering in panic every time.

She had been prepared for a really bad smell the minute the door moved inwards – she had, in fact, been half holding her breath so that she would not get a faceful of wet-leaves, bird-droppings smell – but there was only a faint mustiness, and overlaying it the atmosphere of extreme age. But Emily received a strong impression of immense unhappiness, almost as if, once upon a time, someone had come here to deal with a huge sadness that could not be admitted to the world. It was as if that someone had spent hours and hours here, and as if all the sadness and all the brooding and the despair had eventually leaked into the crumbling black stones . . .

That was completely absurd, of course. This was just a beaten-up old ruin, vaguely eerie, in the way beaten-up old ruins were eerie, and the sooner Emily came to grips with it, the better.

Her eyes were adjusting to the dimness now, and she could see a flight of stone steps twisting their way up. They looked pretty steep, as steps went; those monks or whoever had lived here must have been very fit, although you would expect that of monks, what with all that fasting and stuff.

Emily considered the steps, chewing her lower lip. She could hear, very faintly, the occasional beating of wings from the birds who flew across from the Stornforth sanctuary and perched on the tower, or sometimes came in through the narrow windows. But she did not think she was going up into all that twisting darkness, never mind if the view from the windows was the most extravagantly marvellous thing in the entire western hemisphere, and never mind if the birds were the long lost representatives of the great auk or the dodo. The steps were probably unsafe, anyhow, so that if you did manage to bring yourself to start climbing, you would probably end up beneath a pile of collapsed rubble. Scared? jeered an inner voice. You're meant to be laying a ghost, remember? You might have known you'd duck out when it came to going all the way to the top. You're a stooge and a coward, Emily Frost. But if it was being a stooge to stay safely on the ground floor, Emily would rather be a stooge than break her neck falling through crumbling stones.

It was very quiet in here. There was nothing to be seen, but Emily was beginning to feel a bit spooked. She went outside, closing the door carefully, and walked back along the little rutted road that did not really lead anywhere except to Teind House.

She was just in sight of the gap leading through to the orchard when a car drew up alongside, and Dr Irvine's voice said, 'Exorcising the ghosts, Emily?'

*   *   *

He was just about the last person Emily had been expecting to see, and he looked so wildly attractive seated at the wheel of his car, so fiercely masculine without Moy's background of filing cabinets and locked doors, that for a moment she simply stared at him and could not think of anything to say.

But he made it all right; he said, 'I hoped I might meet you – I called at the cottage, but Don said you were at Teind House this morning.' His eyes went to the grim outline of the Round Tower. 'You really were exorcising the ghosts, weren't you?'

'Sort of.'

'Are you going back to Teind? Well, get in just for a minute, would you?' He leaned over to open the passenger door. 'I've got a proposition for you.' When she was in the car, he said, 'Don was telling me that you were looking round for things to occupy your time.'

'Well, yes, although I've got two days at the school, and now Teind House—'

'Could you fit something else in? Because I wondered if you might like to help me by visiting one or two of the inmates at Moy.'

Emily regarded him. 'Is this for real, or is it a made-up thing just to give me something to do?'

'No, it's real, I promise. And it'd be very low-key. I had the idea that you might try visiting one or two of the women – just to talk to them for half an hour or so. Quite ordinary conversation: current events or last night's TV, or hairstyles or clothes.'

'Would I visit them in their rooms?'

108

'No, we'd probably set it up for you to be in one of the common rooms,' said Patrick. 'Easier from the security angle.'

'You mean so that there'd be staff within reach?'

He smiled. His eyes creased at the corners when he smiled like that. 'Yes, you'd have to be within reach of the alarm bells,' he said. 'And there would be a few subjects to avoid, but I'd prime you on those beforehand. You'd be perfectly safe.'

'I think I'd quite like to do it,' said Emily after a moment, hoping he had not sensed that the comment about having to be within reach of alarm bells had sent a slight chill across the back of her neck. 'I mean – if you think I could be of some help. It might be a bit awkward at first – a bit false and forced, until I get used to it. But it'd be quite a worthwhile thing to do, wouldn't it?'

He did not seem to have picked up the momentary chill. He smiled again, and said, 'Good girl. I'll set it up and phone you, shall I?'

So that meant that now Emily would find her heart jumping with anticipation every time the phone rang. This would not do, it simply would *not*.

'And listen, Emily, you'll find it easier if you can think of these people as just unwell, or crippled.'

'Cracked minds and damaged emotion-circuits. Battered souls who once stained the world with blood.'

'Yes. *Yes*.' He glanced at her, but this time he did not smile, he looked at her more thoughtfully. 'That's rather a good way of putting it,' he said. 'People flinch from mental illness – especially this kind of violent mental illness – but they wouldn't dream of flinching from someone with a broken leg or a furred-up set of arteries, or from a man in a wheelchair. And most of the people inside Moy have – patches of immense despair. Times when they know that what they've done and what they are makes them outcasts. That's a terrible thing for any human being. It's why I want you to visit some of them.'

'Just as if I'm a friend.'

'Yes.' He had not restarted the car; he was turned towards her, his eyes alight with enthusiasm. 'It's quite tiring to talk to them, in fact it's bloody exhausting,' he said. 'They draw on you – you can feel it happening sometimes. As if they're trying to suck out your own sanity and absorb it. And at times you get glimpses of the – the aching loneliness, and the *darkness* in their minds—' He stopped. 'Sorry. I get carried away sometimes.'

'I like hearing about it. In fact,' said Emily, hoping this did not sound arrogant, 'the more I know, the more I'll understand and be able to help.'

'Good girl,' said Patrick again, and started the car.

Emily, hearing the note of discussion-closure in his voice, felt unreasonably depressed.

CHAPTER NINE

Robbie Glennon was practically speechless with gratification when Dr Irvine asked him if he could be available for Thursday afternoon's talk by a writer of mystery novels.

'I want the right warders in attendance,' Dr Irvine said. 'I don't think there's going to be any trouble, but there'll be twelve of our people in one room – four of them men – and there'll be a good-looking female talking to them, so we need to be watchful but not intrusively so.'

Robbie said at once that he understood. This was a bit of a departure for Moy, and it was important and serious. They did not want the likes of Flasher Logan upsetting people, not that the Flasher would be present, of course, but there might be others who would think it was funny to disconcert this Joanna Savile. He studied the list that Dr Irvine gave him, and said that it looked like a good mix of people, hoping this did not sound like crawling to the boss.

'I think it'll work all right,' said Dr Irvine. 'I'd like to have included Pippa from Don Frost's wing, but when I suggested it to her she scuttled into a corner and crouched there for hours, her hands over her head. It's a pity; I think she might have got something out of it.'

Robbie thought so, as well. The odd, mostly silent Pippa was so clearly intelligent and interested in books, and if nothing else she might have enjoyed listening to the talk. But everybody knew that she never spoke, and she usually had to be coaxed even to come out of her own room. It was a sad case, said Dr Irvine, but they would keep trying to break through to her. He had it in mind to get Emily Frost to come in to talk to Pippa, he said; Don Frost had been asking around to see if there were any odd bits of voluntary work that Emily could do, and he thought they might kick off with this. If nothing else, Pippa would enjoy having someone as bright and young as Emily around, said Dr Irvine, and Robbie did not say that he would rather enjoy having Emily around himself, because Dr Irvine would hardly be thinking of Emily in quite the way that Robbie was thinking of her.

So he just said that yes, he would certainly be on duty for the talk, it would be an interesting exercise and he would like to be part of it, and no, it did not clash with an off-duty period at all.

Dr Irvine never knew who was supposed to be on duty at any given time, and so Robbie forbore to add that he was supposed to finish at midday on Thursday.

He had, in fact, been revving up to ask Emily out to the cinema in Stornforth that evening – he had just acquired a third-hand Volkswagen, which Em would probably like, although he would not mind if she wore her black leather motorbike gear for the date, because she looked an absolute knock-out in black leather, that Em.

Still, you had to get your priorities right, and in the light of Dr Irvine's request Emily would have to be put on hold for a couple more days.

The talk was very interesting indeed. Robbie had half expected it to be a bit boring, but it was not boring at all. He made a mental note to get hold of one of Joanna Savile's books.

There was a little quiz at the start – bits of music taped from TV commercials, and the group had to identify the product being advertised, and say why the music was appropriate. Robbie noticed almost at the outset that Ms Savile was keeping away from anything involving alcohol or sex. Probably Dr Irvine had warned her off.

The quiz was so interesting that Robbie wished he could have joined in. He recognised several of the pieces: there was the dreamy, string-plucking music for Hamlet cigars, of course – Robbie had always thought it was called *Air on a G String*, but it turned out to be just *Air in G*. Bach. Then there was one for cars, and then a spicy Italian-sounding piece, which even had Dr Irvine joining in and trying to guess. Spaghetti? Pasta sauce? It turned out to be pasta sauce.

And there was the famous 1990 World Cup *Nessun*

Dorma, with Pavarotti or someone sobbingly singing his heart out. When Joanna Savile said, 'Now think about this one. Why do you suppose that was picked for a football event?' several of them said, 'Triumph.' And a couple more said, 'Celebration,' and she nodded, pleased, and said, 'Victory over the opponents, maybe? Or even, "We're going to score twenty goals and win this match"?' and three of the four men present and two of the women instantly said, 'Yes!' with enthusiasm, and punched the air in the classic gesture of triumph.

The next part was writing down images that music brought into your mind, which followed on very neatly from the fun of the competition. Robbie was not very knowledgeable about the kind of music that was played for this, but he recognised part of Vivaldi's *Four Seasons* because it was the one Nigel Kennedy had put in the Top Ten, and he knew *The Hall of the Mountain King*, as well. It was a good choice, that one, because it made you think of hobbits and things: goblins and dwarfs marching through huge underground caverns and stuff like that.

It was clever, this getting them all to join in. If Ms Savile had simply talked to them for an hour or so, she would probably have lost them in the first five minutes; Robbie had seen that happen before with outside speakers. But it was going well, and Robbie was glad because Joanna Savile had clearly spent a lot of time preparing everything. He was glad for Dr Irvine, as well, because the afternoon had been a bit of an experiment, and it might easily have gone wrong. He wondered if Dr Irvine fancied Joanna Savile. She would not be Robbie's cup of tea, in fact she might be a bit of a ball-shriveller if you were not careful, but she might be very much Dr Irvine's cup of tea. They said he liked them sharp and bright and successful. She had a nice voice to listen to as well.

Patrick was relieved that things were going so well.

'There's absolutely no guarantee of anything,' he had said to Joanna beforehand. 'As far as I can be sure they're all pretty much genuine, although some of them might have their own agenda. But you should be prepared for anything from them. Oh, and don't be fazed by questions about porn, will you?'

'Not in the least.' She had sounded amused and Patrick had been slightly annoyed, and then had wondered if he had been hoping the question might discomfit her. That was the trouble with working with people's minds all day: you got into the habit of planting loaded questions in perfectly ordinary conversations, just to see what response you got.

He said, 'We'll see how they behave and respond, and then we'll make the decision about a second session. Is that all right with you?'

'I'm in your hands,' said Joanna, and Patrick had smiled courteously at her. She was wearing a rather severe outfit today: a dark grey trouser suit with a white shirt, pinstriped in grey. She had probably picked it to look anonymous and sexless, but she did not look either of these things, because she probably never would look anonymous or sexless, even if she put on a sack. Patrick, seating himself at the back of Moy's small lecture room to listen and to intervene if things took a potentially difficult turn, wondered about her husband. Ideally, he should be either a complete wimp so that they would never clash, or a very strong character indeed so that he could master her. He could not in fact see Joanna married to either of those types.

He looked covertly around the room. The young, eager-faced Robbie Glennon was conscientiously on duty. He was a useful recruit to Moy, that one; Patrick had already had a word with Don Frost about the boy, because he would quite like to have Glennon permanently attached to the psychiatry wing – maybe even set up some extra training for him. Don had thought it a good idea; he had said that Robbie was keen and intelligent and more ambitious than most of the recruits you got these days. He believed Emily was going out with him somewhere or other at the weekend, said Don – a disco or a wine bar in Stornforth or something. It had made Patrick feel unexpectedly old to think of the nice Robbie Glennon and Don Frost's pixie-faced daughter at a disco together. He wondered what colour Emily Frost's hair would be for the occasion.

Most of the group were listening fairly seriously to Joanna and the music, and most of them were scribbling down ideas. The chairs were arranged in a semicircle because seating people in rows made it too easy for drugs or smuggled porn magazines to exchange hands. A couple of females at the far end were being a bit giggly, and appeared to be compiling their notes as a joint project, but that did not matter. Patrick wondered if Joanna was getting the background she needed. Once or twice she interposed a question to one or another of the group, and listened intently to the answers.

Mary Maskelyne was seated quite near to Joanna. At first she had said no, she did not want to join in, she had had enough of being talked to and talked *at* in Broadacre. But then she had changed her mind, and laconically said OK, if they liked, she would come along to make up the numbers, making it sound as if she was conferring a favour. Patrick had instantly thought, Arrogant bitch! and then had been horrified at this swift, instinctive reaction, because although you could not actually like all the people you treated, you should manage a degree of tolerance.

And normally he did not care if these odd, drift-wood creatures were arrogant, just as he did not care if they were aggressive or whining or even downright dangerous. Like the child-beaters and the paedophiles, most of whom were victims of beating or sexual abuse themselves.

But Maskelyne – no, call her Mary for God's sake Patrick, let's at least try to humanise her a bit! – had a curious effect on him. He sought for an analogy. Like pine needles sliding pricklingly under your bare skin on a hot afternoon in a forest. No, stronger than that. Into his mind slid an old proverb – Chaucer, was it? Or maybe it was one of the old Scottish legends his father had taught him. Beware of three things, ran the ancient saying: the tongue of the snake, the fletch of the archer, and the smile of the Saxon.

The smile of the Saxon . . .

Maskelyne had taken a seat at the end, nearest to the table, and Patrick watched her covertly, struck, as he had been from the outset, by the difference between the defiant fourteen-year-old of the file photographs from over thirty years ago, all blazing eyes and mutinous lips, and the quiet woman of today. She was dressed plainly and unobtrusively in a dark skirt and sweater, and her hair was cut quite short, and streaked with grey. Most of the time her eyes were downcast as if she was shy of meeting anyone's direct regard, and when she spoke she did so softly and unemphatically, with not much trace of any accent, so that you would be hard put to know what part of the country she came from, and from what stratum of society. Put amongst the odd, sometimes-sinister, sometimes-pitiful inhabitants of Moy, she ought to have been unremarkable.

Except that no woman who had killed twice before her fifteenth birthday, and twice more in the next five years – both times while held in a high-security unit – could possibly be unremarkable.

The pine-needles-beneath-the-skin feeling increased.

But it was not until the talk was nearly over that Patrick realised what was disturbing him so much about Mary Maskelyne. It was quite simply that her absorption was not with what Joanna was saying: it was with Joanna herself.

Mary had not expected this writer woman, this Joanna Savile, to affect her so strongly. She had meant to listen to the talk, and store away any snippets of information that might help her to set about writing the book that would take her back into the headlines.

(*Extraordinary account of Mary Maskelyne's life* . . . the reviews would say. *Scalding glimpses of a monumental miscarriage of justice* . . .)

What she had not been prepared for was her own reaction to Joanna. The instant Joanna came into the room, Mary felt a shutter-flash of memory flicking upwards for a moment. Like lightning flaring and briefly illuminating a darkened landscape before blackness closed down once more. She had stared at Joanna and felt a sudden lurch of half panic, half excitement. Something to do with the way she looked? No, something to do with the queer sense of familiarity. *I've never seen you in my life, but I think I know you . . . From a dream, from a nightmare, from another life, or a different time . . . ?*

And then her mind said *Ingrid!* and the vagrant memory clicked into place. Ingrid. Joanna did not resemble Ingrid in looks – Ingrid had been much fairer and more squarely built, but there was something about the way Joanna entered the rather drab room – something about the way she looked round at everyone as if she was interested and eager to find out about them all – that brought Ingrid back, sharply and painfully.

Because Ingrid used to look at people with exactly that air of pleased expectancy. She used to tilt her head in the same way, as if she might be listening to them on a deeper level than ordinary hearing. It was the way she had looked at and listened to Mary in Broadacre, not so much interested in what Mary had done in the past as in what she had become in the present.

Mary sat quietly in her chair in the half-circle, watching and listening to Joanna Savile. She had thought they were all safely buried, those old memories, those Ingrid-memories, but here they were pushing their way up to the surface, nearly thirty years on.

Broadacre was where Mary had been taken after the Young Offenders' Hostel, and Broadacre had been the absolute pits. Christabel had whispered that they would have to find a way to get out of this place, or, if that was not possible, they would have to find a way to make it bearable. Mary had clung to this thought, just as she had clung to Christabel's strength. There would be a way to make Broadacre, this place of clanging doors that shut inexorably at eight o'clock every night, bearable.

In the YOH you had to know whom not to offend, otherwise you might get beaten up in the lavatories, and you had to know the people who dealt in drugs so that you could avoid them and their sly offers of coke or heroin. Drugs were smuggled in from outside and people bought and sold them with furtive desperation, and there was a subtle hierarchy that you had to respect.

But if Broadacre had a drug culture, Mary never found out about it. Far worse than the complex drug syndicates were the barred windows and the bleak soulless rooms and the dormitories with rows of iron-framed beds. There were no individual rooms at Broadacre except the isolation rooms, and the only concessions to privacy you got in the dormitories were skimpy curtains that were supposed to close round your bed, but did not quite meet so that you were always on display.

It was a place where people screamed as Mary had screamed in the YOH, and where people beat their hands on locked doors for hours upon hours, and it was a place where injections were given not just to stop inmates from screaming, but to prevent them from attacking the attendants and the doctors.

On Mary's first night everybody had seemed to be busy on some ploy or other, watching television or playing table tennis in the recreation room where vacant-eyed people sat blankly in corners.

Mary had not known what she was supposed to do or where she was supposed to be, and she was certainly not going to ask one of the cold-eyed attendants, snooty bitches. In the end she had gone to the dormitory, and a young man had followed her. He sat on the edge of her bed, asking her about herself; he had been pleasant and nicely spoken, and she had thought he was one of the orderlies. But after about ten minutes he had suddenly pushed her down on the bed, and leapt onto her and tried to tear all her clothes off. His hands had been clumsy, the nails jagged so that they had scratched her skin, and his breath had been hot and smelly. He had unzipped his trousers and Mary had felt the hard bulge of his erection pushing against her – like a hot thick stick! Horrid! – and it had seemed a very long time before the attendants came running in and dragged him off.

Ingrid had been one of the attendants. That had been

the first time Mary had seen her. She had come back to the dormitory after it was all over, bringing a mug of hot milk and two aspirin tablets for Mary. She seemed genuinely sorry about what had happened; she said Mary must have found the experience horrid and terrifying, and imagine it happening on her first night at Broadacre, as well. But there would not be a repeat performance, Mary could be sure of that, said Ingrid. She put her arms round Mary and hugged her.

'I shouldn't have done that,' she said, stepping back. 'You're so very young— How old are you, Mary?'

'Eighteen.'

'Eighteen.' An odd look had come into Ingrid's eyes, as if she were calculating something. But she only said, 'God, you're not much more than a child. Don't tell anyone I hugged you just now, will you? But you're so pretty I couldn't help it.'

You're so pretty . . . Mary had stored these words away, to be taken out and looked at later, when it was dark and everyone was asleep. Her parents had never said that she was pretty, although perhaps if she was in a school concert or a gym display, or going to a schoolfriend's birthday party, Leila might say, 'You look very pretty, Mary,' always adding *in that dress*, or *in your gym outfit*. Implying that Mary needed a party dress or a smart gym outfit to look halfway decent.

And 'I enjoyed the singing,' William might say, after the concert was over. But he never said, *You sang well, Mary*.

And then would come the hurtful comparisons. 'Your

sister had a dress just that colour,' Leila would say. 'Do you remember it, William? Only it was a softer green than Mary's. Oh, and she had little velvet bows on it – emerald shade – and there was a velvet bow for her hair. She wore the dress on her sixth birthday – we gave her a tea party in the gardens at Alwar. She looked like a little princess.'

Mary had not been given parties in gardens, or had velvet bows added to her dress, and she had never been anybody's princess.

In the early years in the Young Offenders' Hostel she had certainly never been called pretty. Sulky, said the warders and the slab-faced matron. Mutinous. 'Miss Sullen', matron called her. Matron was an old bag, everyone agreed on that, and she had a way of calling people out in front of everyone – usually at dinner-time in the long, wooden-floored refectory – and saying insulting and humiliating things. She had names for most people: Mary was 'Miss Sullen', or 'Madam Sulky Drawers'. She had an ugly grating voice and an even uglier Midlands accent, which she tried to cover up in front of the doctors, or if health workers or NHS inspectors came round.

But she ran the hostel firmly and efficiently, and people who were not patients admired her. Doctors and the lay workers and the office staff often said, Oh, isn't she selfless! And she never spares herself, you know. There was talk of her being given an MBE in the New Year's Honours, and after that the old bat went around simpering and hunching one shoulder when anyone asked her about it, and saying, Oh my goodness me, ai don't know *how* these rumours get around, ai don't reely. Ai don't expect to be rewarded for just doing mai job.

When matron fell down a flight of stone steps, splitting her head open like an egg on the concrete floor below, everyone was shocked. There was an inquest, and the coroner recorded a verdict of accidental death, and said it was sad that matron had not lived long enough to receive her MBE from the Queen.

After it was all over, the new matron told Mary and two of the other girls to scrub the hall floor thoroughly, because there was an unpleasant stain where matron's brains had spilled out, and people did not want to be reminded of the accident.

But everybody agreed that it was a great tragedy.

CHAPTER TEN

When Great-aunt Rosa died, falling down the stairs at Teind House, everybody agreed that it was a great tragedy.

Selina was told she would have to be a very, very brave girl, and not cry for Great-aunt Rosa. People all died in the end, said Great-aunt Flora, and some of them died when you did not expect it. But you had to accept it, and remember that what it really meant was that they were with Jesus in heaven.

What it actually meant in this case was that there was a great deal of crying (by Aunt Flora), and tetchy grumbling (by Great-uncle Matthew), and a lot of scurrying about and taking photographs by policemen, who had to make sure that the fall had been accidental.

'Not,' said Great-uncle Matthew crossly, 'that anyone really thinks otherwise, but there it is: one knows these people have to do their jobs. Flora, I'll take luncheon in my study quietly, I believe. I don't mind a tray, just this once.'

Between sorting out Great-uncle Matthew's trays (he had supper as well as lunch in his study in the end), and making cups of tea for the police officers, and telephoning people to tell them what had happened, Aunt Flora cried. She cried on and off for most of the day. Selina helped with the tea-making and Great-uncle Matthew's trays, but she did not cry because secretly she was glad that Aunt Rosa was dead. When the flurry died down a bit she went up to her room, and sat on the window seat and stared out over the orchard. The window was a big one, but it was made up of lots of tiny panes of glass. The glass felt cold and a bit damp when she leaned her face against it, and the room felt cold as well because Great-uncle Matthew did not believe in heating in people's bedrooms. Selina had hated the cold, stuffy bedroom at first, but she had discovered that you could keep pretty warm by putting your dressing gown on over your day clothes, and wrapping the bolster round your feet. That way you could curl up on the window seat and read or draw, and nobody knew where you were.

She could see the Round Tower just beyond the tops of the trees. If Aunt Rosa had not poked and pried inside the tower, she might still be alive. But she had been a quizzy old witch, that Rosa; she had followed Selina out to the tower one afternoon, and she had seen the beautiful shrine that Selina had made before Selina could hide it. She had not even heard Aunt Rosa come creeeping and snooping up on her, and the first she had known was when she turned round to see the horrid old creature standing in the doorway, her arms folded, staring round the room, her thin lips clamped tightly together.

Aunt Rosa had been angry and shocked, and she would not listen when Selina had tried to explain that the shrine was secret and sacred, and also hugely important.

Wicked heathenism, Aunt Rosa had said, and her thin nose had quivered so that Selina had suddenly realised that Aunt Rosa looked exactly like the picture of the witch in the story about Hansel and Gretel. She had tried to explain that a memorial in Inchcape church was not enough for her parents, and she told Aunt Rosa about the *patet*, and the worrying possibility of her mother and father's still being sinful and not, as a result, being allowed to go over the old and holy Bridge into paradise. Aunt Rosa had not understood, and (Selina did not realise this until much later) she had not wanted to understand. She had said it was pagan rubbish, and Selina ought to think shame on herself for talking like that, a great girl of eight and three months. There must be no more of it, was that understood?

'Yes, Aunt Rosa.'

As for heaven, said Aunt Rosa briskly, most certainly Poor Elspeth and very likely That Man as well would have gone straight to heaven. Why on earth should they not? And when it came to honouring their memories – well, Selina would do better to say her prayers every night, and put her mind to her schoolwork and her household tasks. That was the way to honour the dead, and there was to

127

be no more of this nonsense about ghosts hiding in the bedroom and pleading for help, said Aunt Rosa briskly, her witchy mouth prim and tight so that you could see the rows of little wrinkles round it, like a drawstring purse. This pagan shrine or whatever Selina called it, was to be removed and everything tidied neatly away, was that quite clear?

'Oh yes, Aunt Rosa,' said Selina.

Dismantling the shrine was heart-breakingly easy. Taking to pieces the carefully arranged photographs and books and cuttings felt like breaking up the final bits of father and mother. Mother's evening stole was already cobweb-thin with age, and the page with father's newspaper article about Mr Nehru was dry and brittle. But it all had to be done; Aunt Rosa would certainly check that Selina had done it.

She put all the things in the bottom of her wardrobe, and tried to think that mother and father would have long since taken the three steps of Humata, Hukhta, and Hvarshta that would get them across the old and holy Bridge into paradise, and that it would not matter about the shrine's being destroyed.

But she knew that it did matter. She thought that something had been broken: a promise, a link, something invisible but vital. And it was Aunt Rosa's fault. Yes, that was something to think about very carefully.

It was necessary to stay awake for quite a long time that night, to see if anything happened. Selina heard Aunt Rosa come to bed, and then Aunt Flora, a bit anxious and twittery because there was so much to remember when you retired for the night. There was her library book and her reading glasses, and her pills that had to be taken last thing, and the woolly scarf she liked to use as a bedjacket. She was a bit like the white rabbit in *Alice*, Aunt Flora, only she was plumper and wore spectacles which Selina did not think the white rabbit had done, and also she was woollier on account of the mufflers round her neck. She wore little soft slippers that went pitter-pat on the bare old floorboards.

Great-uncle Matthew came up to bed half an hour later. Selina heard him go round the house, making sure everywhere was locked up, tapping the barometer to see what kind of weather they would have tomorrow, winding up the clocks as he went. He always did it in exactly the same order every night.

And then the house was quiet, with the familiar, slightly creaky quiet that it sank into every night. Selina knew the house's noises by this time: she knew that the floorboards always creaked ten minutes after Great-uncle Matthew had come up them, so that you might think that a burglar was creeping up the stairs. She knew the sound the roof timbers made after dark and how the range in the scullery clunked a bit as it cooled down. Normally these were all unremarkable, rather friendly noises, but tonight they did not feel friendly at all. Selina lay on her left side so that she could watch the door and the deep old wardrobe in the little alcove just inside it. If the ghosts came they would come out of the dark puddles of shadow made by the wardrobe's bulk.

Great-uncle Matthew had not pulled the chain in the bathroom firmly enough tonight; Selina could hear the tank filling up in the growly clanking way it had if you did not give the chain a good sharp tug. When she first came to Teind House she had thought that there was something hiding inside the thick old lead pipes that connected into the cistern and were wrapped in bits of Great-aunt Flora's wintergreen to stop them from freezing in cold weather. For weeks she had been terrified to go into the cold bathroom after dark in case the lid of the cistern was suddenly lifted from inside, and mad eyes, half hidden by wet matted hair, glared out.

The rusty coughing sound was only the water going reluctantly into the cistern, of course. Selina knew that now. Or – did she? What if, just for tonight, it was something else? What if it was really something huddled in the corner of her bedroom, slowly and thickly choking on its own blood, coughing its life away and unable to call for help because its throat had been torn away . . . ?

She sat up in bed, cautiously because it was important not to make a noise until she saw what might be happening. You had to be quite cunning with ghosts, even when they were the ghosts of your own parents; you had to remember that they would probably be filled up with the panic and the desperation they had felt as they died, and that they would most likely look as they had looked at that moment—

Father, his chest burst open where the bullet had gone in. Mother, her whole body shredded and tattered. It was not too bad seeing father, but mother, oh, poor mother . . .

Don't come, whispered Selina into the unquiet darkness. Oh, please don't come. Please be all right, please be already on the other side of that Bridge.

It was no use. The shadows were moving, they were like curdled ink or clotted blood; there was a horrid dull red tinge to them that might have been the light from the harvest moon beyond the bedroom window, but Selina knew was really the blood from her parents' wounds, oozing out into the darkness . . .

Father appeared first. That was all right, that was not so bad at all, because his jacket was hiding the ragged-edged hole where the bullet had torn into his heart. His face was spattered with blood where his chest had burst open, but he could still smile in the way he had always smiled, and his hair was still crinkly and dark and nice. Selina loved him very much indeed.

But mother was with him. She was just behind him and she was holding out her hands exactly as she had held them out in Alwar that night, imploringly, pitifully. Mother had once had such pretty hands, but now there were only bloodied stumps. Blood poured down her face and dripped from her chin.

I'm sorry, whispered Selina to the terrible thing that had been mother. I'm so sorry. But it wasn't my fault, it truly wasn't.

Mother's hands were still groping blindly in front of her. Selina could see the wedding ring glinting in the mess of squelched-up bones and raw flesh. It was suddenly unbearable and pitiable that mother should still have this symbol of her marriage to father when her flesh was so torn.

Selina wanted to look away, but it was impossible. She clutched a fold of the sheet tightly and after a moment she said, very softly, but very earnestly, 'I'll find a way to make the shrine for you again – I *swear* I will! – and then you can go back to crossing the Bridge and the three steps you have to take, and then you'll get to where you should be. And I'll pray much harder for you, I'll do it every day – I'll be so good, I promise I'll be so good—'

Had they nodded then, just very slightly? Had father made to touch mother's shoulder, as if to pull her back? Selina waited, not daring to breathe, her hands trembling.

And then it was over. There was only the moonlight lying in bars across the floor, and the feel of the crumpled sheet in her hands, and the stickiness of fright-sweat prickling her scalp.

The children had not tried to fight as the sun went down behind the terrible tower on the edge of Alwar. They had been much too frightened to even think about fighting by that time. Christy had whispered to Selina and Douglas that they must watch their chance and make a run for it if they could, and Douglas said something about grabbing the reins of the pony and driving back down the bare dusty road, leaving the men behind. 'But what about the guns?' said Selina. 'What if they shoot us?'

'They won't, not when it comes to it,' said Christy

valiantly. 'They wouldn't shoot children. And my father will be here by then, anyhow.'

'And mine,' said another of the children. But they all knew that nobody really believed this any longer.

In the event, there was no opportunity of taking over the cart, because once it stopped the men pointed the guns at the children and ordered them out. 'Out of cart now,' they said. 'You get out of cart, and line up against tower.'

'Why are we here?' demanded Douglas. 'This is a funeral place. This is where people bring their dead. I thought you had respect and honour for dead people in this country.'

The man who had ordered them out of the cart, who seemed to be the only one who could speak English, said, 'This place where no one come. No one think to look here. That why we use it.' He grinned suddenly, displaying his rotting teeth. 'You die in Tower of Silence. Place of dead,' he said. 'That how it should be. A good message to send to your British government who refuse to let our people go.'

Christy said, 'But it isn't our fault that your friends are in prison,' and Selina wanted to say, 'And people who do wrong deserve to be in prison,' but she did not quite dare.

The man gestured to the tower again, this time using the gun to indicate what he wanted. 'All line up before wall. Do it now, or we not wait for sunset to shoot.'

As they shuffled into line there was a moment when Selina thought Christy was going to defy their captors.

Her lower lip jutted out mutinously, and her eyes shone angrily in the glow of the dying sun. Her fists were clenched as if she might be going to hit the man, and Selina's heart gave a huge bump of panic and excitement, because one half of her was terrified that Christy would do something that would get them all shot there and then, but the other half – and it was a bit more than half, really – wanted somebody to get them out of this. And Christy or Douglas were the only two who were brave enough.

Seen like this, the tower was much, much worse than it had looked from the road. It was built from harsh stone that would graze your hands if you touched it, and its sides sloped steeply, so that it was narrower at the top than it was at the base. Most of the time it would be black, but with the setting sun directly behind it the dark walls were streaked with crimson. Selina stared at it and remembered all over again about the ogre's tower. You could very nearly imagine that the walls were that colour because all the squelched-up bodies inside had reached the top and all the blood was slopping over the rim and oozing down the outside.

When she looked right up at the very top, she saw a dark outline against the fiery sky. Something round-shouldered and dark-cloaked seemed to bend its head to look down at her, and she shuddered and felt an icy fear clutch the pit of her stomach because she knew what it was. It was not the ogre who caught men to grind their bones for bread, but it was something very near to it. After a moment, a second shape came to sit beside the first, and then a third.

Vultures. Huge, clawed birds who ate the dead bodies brought out here, and left only the bones. At Selina's side, Douglas said, 'Don't look at them. They won't come down here; they don't attack people who are alive.'

But his face had the white, scared look again, and with the idea of trying to take it away, Selina said, 'Why do they bring dead people here? Why don't they just – well, bury them, like we do?'

'My father says it's because their religion won't let them – um, what's the word? – when you foul up something?'

'Defile? Corrupt?' Christy liked words and was good at them.

'Yes. If they bury people it defiles the ground, and if they burn them, like we cremate people, the smoke defiles the air. So they let the birds take them.'

'You mean *eat* them?'

'It's quite a – a *pure* thing to happen when you're dead,' said Douglas, trying to sound as if he believed this.

The armed men were glancing along the road, consulting the large wristwatch belonging to their leader every few minutes. Several times they shaded their eyes to look into the sinking sun, pointing and nodding to one another. There was still a thin crescent of the bright orange sun showing over the far horizon, but Selina understood that the men were waiting for the exact hour of sunset. They were giving the children's parents until the very last minute to release their friends from prison. Once that brilliant rim of sun went down below the dark horizon they would shoot all the children, exactly as they had said.

Selina's heart was pounding so hard she thought it would burst out of her chest. She felt for Christy's hand. It was cold and it felt small, but it held on to Selina's hand firmly. Selina stood there and thought: I will never forget this. If we escape from this, I will never, ever forget how it felt to stand in front of this giant's tower, holding Christy's hand, watching the sun go down and down into darkness.

With the hunched-over shapes of the ogre-birds watching from the tower's topmost rim, waiting until they could swoop on the bodies . . .

But the men won't shoot us, she thought. I don't believe that they'll do it, I really, absolutely don't—

And then one of the men gave a shout, and pointed down the road, along the way they had just come, and Selina's stomach did a flip-flop of hope, and she turned round – everyone else turned round as well – and saw a jeep being driven along the road at a furious rate.

Douglas said in sudden anguish, 'But I can't see who's in it—'

'It might not be anyone,' said Christy. 'It might be some more of the plotters.' In a whisper, almost to herself, she said, 'Oh don't let it be that, please don't let it be that—'

'It'll be our parents,' said the smallest of the girls. 'I've been asking God to send them, and my daddy says God never lets you down.'

The jeep was coming towards them, and whoever was driving it was doing so very fast indeed. It bounced and bucketed over the road's dry surface, and even at this distance Selina could smell the hot red dust that its wheels were churning up; she could feel it stinging the back of her throat and scratching her eyes, but none of that mattered because it had to be some of their parents in the jeep – she did not care whose parents they were, as long as they got here in time.

The jeep slewed to an abrupt halt on the side of the road, and two people got out and came running towards them. The man had dark crinkly hair and he carried a gun. The woman was sobbing as she came, holding out her arms.

Selina said, in a queer tight little voice, 'It's my mother and father. They've found us.' She made to run forward but one of the men snatched her arm and jerked her back. A second man grabbed Christy and put the muzzle of the gun to her head. 'Englishman, you throw gun down,' he shouted over his shoulder. 'You throw gun down, or I shoot this one and then all the others.'

Selina's father stopped dead, his eyes going from the gun-men to the children. Selina wanted to call out to him to please do what the man asked, because they were evil and bad, these plotters, and they meant it about shooting everyone. And now there was only a small piece of sun left, like the top of a blood-orange . . .

'We not talk to you if you have gun,' said the leader. 'We shoot. Put gun down.'

John March looked at the children again, and Selina thought that a kind of angry helplessness showed in his face. She said, 'Do what he says – you must—' and her father made an angry gesture as if he would like to punch the man and kill everybody. Then he nodded and the small gun he had been holding fell to the ground. Selina's mother gave a sob, and clutched his arm.

'Better,' said the leader. 'You are sensible man. Now you tell me if you bring what we want. You bring freedom for our people that British government imprison?'

This time Selina did not just see her father's hesitation, she felt it. She felt his thoughts in the way she occasionally did when he read a story to her and put his own bits in, and she knew before he spoke that there was no pardon for the imprisoned men. She was not sure if her father was here because he had been told to bring the message about not freeing the gaoled men, or if he was here simply because he had somehow managed to find out where the children had been taken and had driven out here to get to them. It did not matter. She loved him for coming here – and her mother, of course – with a huge hurting love. But if he told these men a lie they would know it, and they would shoot everybody.

John March did not lie, but Selina did not think he told the complete truth. He said, 'They're still talking. Trying to arrange things. You haven't given us enough time. That's why I'm here – to ask for another twenty-four hours.'

'Let us take the children back,' said Selina's mother. Selina could see now that her mother was crying and that she had probably been crying for hours. She was usually so neat and pretty, her hair always combed nicely into a shiny shape, but now she looked as if she had dragged on the nearest clothes she had, and her hair was streaming over her shoulders. Her face was swollen and streaked with tears and dust, and she was holding out her hands imploringly as if she could reach Selina and snatch her up and keep her safe.

'You not have children back,' said the man sharply. 'If you not do what we ask, we carry out our promise. Then you see – your country and your government see – that we are people of our word.'

'But you can't murder children,' began Selina's father, and at his side Selina's mother gave a cry of pain, and half sank to the ground.

'We do what we have to do,' said the leader, and as if these words were a signal, the last thin orange-paring piece of the sun went below the horizon.

The darkness surrounding the dreadful tower was not a complete darkness; Selina could still see the faces of the other children, and she could see her parents' faces as well. She could see that the plotters were lighting chunks of wood and sticking them in the ground to give some light, and this was almost worse than the darkness would have been, because the twisty flames cast moving shadows everywhere. When the gun-men moved, their shadows moved with them, but they were huge shadows, ugly and misshapen, and they did not quite match the men. You could easily think the shadows might suddenly take on a life of their own, and come prowling towards the children. You could even more easily imagine the ogre-birds unfolding their cloak-wings and swooping down to snatch them up.

Selina had been trying very hard not to cry because when all this was over she wanted her parents to say she had been brave: to say they had been so proud of her for being brave. But the shadows were frightening her very much and the watchful birds were frightening her even more. She thought she might start crying quite hard at any minute, and she swallowed hard to force the crying down.

Four of the men had surrounded Selina's parents, and pushed them forward so that they were standing with their backs to the tower, only a little way along from the children, but not close enough to reach them. Selina's mother had thrust her clenched fist into her mouth to try to force the tears back, and her father had his arm round her shoulders.

'They won't do it, Selina,' shouted John March. 'I promise you it'll be all right.'

'Hold on, darling,' cried her mother. 'All of you must hold on – Christabel, Douglas – everyone.' She sank to her knees, as if her legs would not hold her upright any longer. 'We'll get you out of this.'

'Keep on being brave,' said Selina's father.

'No more time left,' said the leader suddenly, and he swung round and levelled the gun at her parents. 'And because you two have lied to us, you die as well.' There was a click of something within the mechanism – the gun being set to fire! thought Selina in terror, and the fire-streaked darkness began to spin around her, making her feel sick.

'We love you, Selina,' cried her father, and her mother

shouted with him, 'We love you more than anything in the world, Selina,' and through the sick dizziness Selina felt the hurting tears coming up from her throat, because she loved them so much and they were going to die, and she would not be able to bear it. She thought she said, 'I love you,' but her throat had closed up with the crying and the being afraid, and she did not think they heard her.

Two shots rang out, one after the other, splitting the quiet night, and John and Elspeth March fell to the ground.

CHAPTER ELEVEN

For a moment there was absolute silence around the tower. The children pressed close together, their eyes huge and scared, all of them staring in horror and disbelief at the two prone bodies.

Christy threw her arms round Selina and hugged her so tightly that Selina could hardly breathe. 'I hate them!' she said into Selina's ear. 'I hate them, those men, and I'll kill them if I can!'

The smaller children were crying with fright, their wails echoing around Selina's head. She felt peculiar and unreal, as if none of this was really happening. Perhaps it was not. Perhaps it was a horrid dream, and she would wake up in a minute and find that everything was all right. But there on the ground were the crumpled bodies of her parents, looking somehow much smaller than they used to. Selina's father had an expression of frozen surprise on his face, and it was nearly possible to believe he was still alive. But his eyes are open, thought Selina, cramming her clenched fist into her mouth in case she began to scream. I didn't know that people had their eyes open after they died. She could not see her mother's face, because her hair had tumbled over it. She's untidy, thought Selina. She'd hate that, looking untidy. Perhaps they'd let me go and smooth down her frock and put her legs straight. But when she looked back at the gun-men she knew they would not let her do anything of the kind.

The six children were pushed into line again. Douglas was at the far end, and Christy was standing next to Selina. This is it, thought Selina. We're going to die. We really are. She heard Douglas say, valiantly, 'Don't worry, any of you. Remember Peter Pan? "To die will be an awfully big adventure",' and she saw the little ones' faces turn to him.

'It's true,' said Christy. 'It'll be the biggest adventure of all, and listen, Selina's mummy and daddy are waiting for us. They'll meet us, and they'll help us, won't they, Selina?'

'Yes,' whispered Selina. 'Yes, they'll be there. They're probably waiting now. And they're wonderful – my daddy tells the best stories in the world. You'll all like him so much. And we'll all be together, that's good, isn't it?'

'We'll always be together,' said Douglas defiantly, and Selina stared at him, and thought: yes. That's what I've got to hold on to. Always being together. Whatever happens, wherever we all go, we'll be together. That's what matters.

She thought Douglas started to say something else, but before he could do so a gunshot rang out again, and he gave a half-cry and fell forward, and Selina heard Christy scream. The second shot came then – the little girl who had thought God would send their parents to save them. She did not fall forward, she fell back, her body tumbling onto Douglas's. I'm going to be last, thought Selina wildly. They're going down the line. I'll be last – I'll have to watch everyone else be shot—

Third shot. Fourth – that was the other boy: he and Douglas had been good friends, they had played football together. Christy would be next— And then it will be me. I can't bear it, thought Selina. She tightened her hold on Christy's hand.

It was at that instant that the torches that had been sending the fantastical shadows dancing halfway up the tower's sides flickered wildly, and went out.

Darkness, velvety and thick, closed down, and the fifth shot – Christy's shot – rang out.

If there had been time for Selina to think she would not have done what she did. She would have seen the stupidity of trying to run away, and she would have stayed where she was, fixing her mind on the image of her parents waiting for her on the other side of death.

But the heavy darkness closed around her like a stifling curtain: it smelt of fear and the mad excitement of the gun-men, and Selina dodged back instinctively. The gun-men were stamping around and you could tell they were cursing each other even though they did not speak

144

in English, and at any second they would relight the torches and finish off the shooting. Christy, if that last shot had not hit her, was next, and then it would be Selina's turn.

Christy's hand was no longer holding Selina's, but that did not mean anything. The shot might have missed Christy by yards, and Christy could now be trying to escape, just as Selina was.

Escape ... Could she do that? How? I can't run, thought Selina, because there's nowhere to run *to*, and once they've relit the pieces of wood they'll see me. But I might be able to hide. Yes, but where?

She had been moving cautiously back from the group, feeling her way round the base of the tower. It was horrid to have to keep one hand on the harsh stones, but at least it stopped her from getting lost. It was what her father had called a point of reference. Would he have a point of reference to help him get to heaven with mother? Would they have waited for Douglas and the others, and Christy? They'll all be together by this time, thought Selina. But Christy might still be alive – yes, I'll keep thinking that she's alive and that I'll find her.

She thought she was about halfway round the tower – if you regarded the plotters as being at the front, she was about at the back – when the smeary lights of the burning torches flared up again. Selina crouched fearfully against the tower's sides but there was no sound of running feet, or shouts of men looking for her. Don't let Christy be dead, she prayed. Oh, please, *please* let her not be shot, and let her have got away.

It was just as she reached the end of this scrappy prayer that she saw the dark outline cut into the side of the tower, and realised with a mixture of horror and hope that it was not the doorless tower of the nightmare after all. The dark patch was where a bit of the wall went inwards – Selina thought it was what you called an alcove – and set into it was an iron gate, a bit like the gates in stories that opened onto secret gardens. Beyond the gate she could make out a small door. It'll be locked, said Selina to herself. The gate will be locked and the door will be locked as well. *Of course* they will. People won't be allowed to just walk into this place. But if they aren't locked—

She glanced behind her but there was no one to be seen anywhere, and then stepped into the alcove. It was cold and dank, and there was a faint smell that made you think of meat when it had been left out of the cool marble-slabbed larder by mistake, and had gone bad. Selina was not conscious of reaching for the gate's latch, but although it was very dark she could just make out her own hands reaching up to it. She saw the latch lift and the gate swing open. There was no creaking sound, only the whisper of the hinges.

The door had a huge iron ring for a handle, and at first Selina thought it was not going to turn. She tried twisting it to the left and then to the right, and she was about to give up when she heard the men shouting, and the sound of running feet. Her heart began to pound with terror. They've found out that someone's missing! thought Selina. They've counted the bodies and they've only found five – or maybe even four – and they know that one's missing! And they're coming to find me! And whether it was sheer panic that lent strength to her hands, or whether she had suddenly fathomed the trick of the handle, she did not know, but whichever it was she jerked the handle one last time, and this time it yielded, and there was the faint *click* of a lock's being released. The door moved back.

Selina took a deep breath and stepped inside the tower, and the door swung gently into place after her.

The stench inside the tower was dreadful. It rose up to meet her like a solid wall and it was the absolute worst thing she had ever known. It was like rotting meat and decaying vegetables, and pulpy fruit with wriggling maggots. Selina gasped, and put a hand over her mouth, but the stench had already reached her stomach. She retched and was violently sick on the ground. Terrible! She shuddered and gulped, and after a moment managed to find her handkerchief to wipe her lips. Better now. And if hiding in here meant she would escape being shot, she would manage to do it.

It was very quiet in the tower, a thick smothering quiet. She could hear the men's voices outside but they were very faint, as if they were coming from a long way away. It's as if I've crossed some kind of line into a different world, thought Selina, trying not to breathe in too deeply, trying not to notice the smell. Like in a story where you stumble across a magic doorway without realising it. Only I don't think this is a doorway that's taken me into a good place; I think this is a very bad place indeed.

She could not decide if the darkness was a good thing or not. On the one hand she would have liked to see what was in here with her, but on the other she would prefer not to see all the half-eaten dead bodies. But the trouble with the dark was that you did not know what might be creeping towards you . . .

I can't stay here, thought Selina. I really can't. But then she remembered that the men outside had guns, and that they had shot the other children and her own parents, and that if she went back outside they would shoot her as well. And it was worth hiding here for as long as possible, because if her parents had come out here to find her, it meant that people knew where the children had been brought. It meant that other people would come to find them.

She had absolutely no idea whether the gun-men would come into the tower or not. Douglas had said this was a holy place, and so it might be that the men would not dare to enter. She stayed where she was, just inside the door, afraid that if she moved away from it she would get lost.

Little by little her eyes were adjusting. The tower might not have been the doorless tower after all, but as far as Selina could tell it was certainly a windowless one. But far above her head, higher than the highest house, the tower was open, and a faint grey light trickled down. It showed up a black iron stair at the centre: it was very wide, and it twisted all the way up to the top. Selina could see its outline quite plainly at the top, although nearer the ground, where the faint light did not reach, it was smothered in darkness.

The tower had to have that staircase, of course, and if you thought about it it had to be open at the top as well. The dead bodies had to be carried up those stairs so that they could be arranged on the ledge at the top. The ledge was where the vultures came: it was where they ate the dead bodies, dropping pieces of them down the insides of the stone walls—

A hand came out of the darkness and touched her face.

Selina did not quite scream, but she nearly did. The only thing that stopped her was the knowledge that the gun-men were outside the tower, and that if she screamed they would probably hear and come running.

She pressed back against the door, fumbling behind her for the handle, so absolutely panic-stricken that for several endless seconds her hands would not obey her brain. Find the door handle, said Selina's mind in panic to her hands. *Find it!* Find it and get out—

It was about ten nightmare seconds before she realised that there was no handle on this side of the door, and it was another ten before she understood that there was no need for a handle on the inside, because once alone in here you would never need to get out again, because you would be dead . . .

And the door itself fitted so snugly that Selina could barely even feel the edges. She would certainly not be able to open it again. I'm trapped! she thought in rising horror. I'm shut inside this place with all the eaten-up bodies – bones and nails and arms and eyes— There're probably huge mounds of them, all piled up on the ground. Only something isn't quite dead, because it's crawled through the darkness, and it's found me: it's patting my face and if only I could *see* what it is . . .

She had just clenched her fists, preparing to hit out at whatever it was, when the hand came again, and this time it touched her hair and a whispery voice said, 'Selina?'

Selina felt a huge rush of relief. She said, 'Christy? You're *safe*!' and Christy said, between a sob and a laugh, 'The torches went out, didn't they? Just as they were going to shoot me.'

'I thought you got shot. I really did.' Selina could not believe how wonderful it was to find Christy here.

'I thought I did, as well. I heard the shot, but I ran round the side of the tower and came in here.' Her voice, which had sounded thin and weak to start with, sounded a bit stronger now. 'I think they must have missed me in the dark,' she said.

'I ran away as well.' Selina felt dizzy with relief at not being on her own any more. She loved Christy hugely for being alive, but she also felt as if she had been running for ten miles without stopping, or as if somebody had been beating her arms and legs until they quivered like jelly. She put her hands out and after a moment she felt Christy's arms come round her and hug her. Christy felt cold, and she felt somehow thinner than Selina had expected. She drew back a bit. 'Are you all right?'

'Yes, but it's horrid in here. I don't like it.'

'I was sick when I came in,' said Selina. 'On account of the smell.'

'I know, I heard you. But I wasn't sure who it was, so I didn't say anything until now. It doesn't matter about being sick. You got away from the plotters. Will we have to stay here until they stop looking for us?'

It was not like Christy to sound so unsure. Selina said firmly, 'Yes, we'll have to. But it's better with two of us.'

'Yes, but, um, wouldn't you have thought they'd have come in here by this time? I mean – they'll know by now that we got away, and they'll know there's only one place we could be. Why don't they come inside and get us?'

'I thought of that.' Selina was pleased that she could offer a solution. 'Douglas said this was where the dead have to be brought.' She felt Christy's sudden shiver at Douglas's name, and hurried on. 'So I expect it's forbidden for people to come in here. Like church at home, only even more important.'

Christy said, slowly, 'But would those men care about that? They're *evil*. They shot Douglas and the others. They shot your mum and dad as well.'

'I know. I can't think about that yet.' If Selina had started to really think about her parents' being dead, she would have cried until she was ill. So she said, 'The plotters haven't come in here at all. And if my parents knew we were here, other people must know it as well. So what we could do is wait until we hear another car come, and then go outside.' She stopped, suddenly remembering that Christy might not know about not being able to open the tower door from this side, or about the walls being so thick that it might blot out the sound of a car.

But when Christy said, 'I expect my parents will come pretty soon. I don't expect we'll have to wait very long, do you?' Selina at once said, 'No, I don't expect so.'

But they had to wait for a very long time. Selina thought that hours and hours went by, although Christy said it could not be hours and hours because the sky through the open top of the tower showed it was still night.

They did not want to move away from the door and so they sat on the floor, leaning back against it. 'Mind the sick,' said Christy. 'It'd be horrid to sit in it.'

Selina was actually past caring, but she said, 'Yes, it'd be horrid.'

They sat close together because it was less frightening that way, but it was still very frightening indeed. As the night wore on, the tower seemed less silent. It seemed to fill up with tiny stirrings – Selina had to try very hard indeed not to think about all the poor half-eaten bodies in here.

After a while a horrid little night wind got up and hissed around them, and small dry rustlings sounded within the darkest part of the tower. Bones being rubbed together, thought Selina, shuddering. They had stopped noticing the stench by this time, but the wind seemed to stir it up and she was sick again. Christy lent her a handkerchief, and when Selina had mopped her face she sat down again and said, 'Christy, dead people don't really come back, do they?'

It seemed a long time before Christy answered this, but at last she said, 'No.'

152

'But even if they did come back, they wouldn't hurt anyone, would they?'

'No,' said Christy again. 'If they loved you when they were alive, they love you even more when they're dead. They want to help you.'

'My father—' Selina stopped and had to gulp down a sob. 'My father would want to help me. And my mother.'

'And Douglas and the others.'

'Oh yes. We'll keep thinking about that, shall we, because—' Selina stopped speaking. Something was moving on the other side of the door.

Selina had not realised that she had stumbled to her feet until she felt Christy's hand pulling her back from the door.

'Someone's coming in,' whispered Christy, and Selina nodded, her eyes on the faint rim of light that indicated where the door was. 'We'd better keep back until we see who it is. I didn't hear a car, did you?'

'No, but I was being sick. You can't be sick and listen for cars at the same time.'

The light around the door became stronger. It was the same red, smeary light that the burning torches had made earlier, and Selina hated it. But as the door slowly opened she saw with despair that it was not Christy's parents; it was not anybody's parents. It was the plotters.

There were six of them – one was the man the children had all thought of as the leader – and between them they were carrying two objects that Selina could not instantly identify. Two sacks, was it? Whatever they were, they were wrapped in pale cloths, like sheets. The door was pushed wider, and the sulky torchlight trickled in, showing up the iron staircase, and something else – something that Selina had not seen until now.

A wide yawning blackness in the centre of the floor. A deep, deep well, going down and down into the earth. Its sides were lined with black brick, and Selina realised that it was from there that the bad-meat smell came. It looked about a thousand years old, that black, evil well, and it was where the poor bodies went when the ogre-birds had finished with them. All the spat-out bones and bits of flesh and eyes that they couldn't chomp up or didn't want, she thought. For hundreds and hundreds of years. She could see bits of bone and dried-out skin around the edges of the pit, and it was absolutely the horridest thing she had ever seen in her life.

As the men came right inside, propping the door open, she pressed back into the deep shadows, terrified of being seen and dragged out. But they did not seem to be here to search the tower, or to be concerned that two of their prisoners had escaped. They were intent on the sack-like things they carried.

As they began to cautiously mount the iron stair, one of the pale wrappings fell back a little, and Selina, crouching in the darkness, had to bite back a sob. The things were not sacks after all. Under the wrapping had been her father's face.

The sack-like things were the bodies of her parents, wrapped in clean white linen, and they were being carried to the top of the tower for the ogre-birds.

CHAPTER TWELVE

If Selina could have run out of the tower, she would have
done so then. The door was still propped wide open, and
it would have been easy. And having Christy with her had
made her feel much braver and much stronger, and she
thought that together they could have dodged out when
the men were near the staircase's top.

But through the door she could see the other plotters:
they were moving to and fro and the pieces of wood were
burning up strongly again, so that red shadows danced
everywhere, making it look as if there were at least a
dozen men. Selina thought it was only the flickering
shadows that made it seem like that; she thought there
were only about three or four of them. But they still had
their guns, she could see that clearly.

She did not dare whisper to Christy in case the men
heard, but Christy would have seen the men; she would

know that it was important to stay in hiding. That was one of the really good things about Christy: she understood things without them having to be explained.

The men were almost at the top of the stair. It was a long climb – probably as many as a hundred steps – and they had had to go carefully and slowly because of carrying the two bodies. The leader had gone up first, carrying the flaring torch, and four of the men carried the bodies after him, two to each one. The other man followed, with another burning torch. There was a little platform at the top, and when the men reached it they stood for a moment, propping the bodies against the tower's sides, straightening up as if to catch their breath.

Selina had tilted her head right back, into the position people called craning your neck, in order to see what the men were doing. As they began to lift the bodies onto the wide ledge there was a movement deep inside the night sky that made her shiver all over. It was exactly as if something that had been crouching in the dark had stirred and was creeping forward. The ogre-birds, stretching their claws, spreading out their wing-cloaks, getting ready to pounce on their prey? Selina had not known that word 'prey' until Douglas had used it. It was a bit worrying that the word sounded the same as when you talked to God in church every Sunday. Selina had been asking God to let them escape ever since the men had snatched them all up in the garden, and she had thought that was praying. But then Douglas had said about the tower and the vultures and the prey, and Selina had had a sudden doubt. Supposing she had been talking not to

God, but to the ogre-birds all along? It was difficult when one sound had two quite different meanings; it meant you could not tell if things got mixed up. Selina could not be sure, now, if she had been praying to God, or if she had been telling the ogre-birds that there was prey waiting for them in the tower.

Whichever it was, the birds were up there. Two of them were already on the ledge, their round-shouldered outlines grimly black against the night sky. Three more were hovering: in the crimson torchlight their wings looked wet and ragged at the edges. It looked as if they had been dabbled in blood.

Even down here, Selina could hear the sound of the beating wings on the air. There was a rhythm about it. Dreadful. Like somebody tapping on a drum. Like a rude man banging impatiently on a table for food . . .

She was shivering violently, and she was so cold she thought she might die from it. She was huddled into a tiny dark space as far from the iron stair as possible, her knees drawn up to her chest, both arms wrapped around them.

She thought Christy was a little way along the wall – she could not see her, but she could feel that she was quite near. I'd probably be able to reach her hand if I dared move, thought Selina. But she dared not move.

The plotters were lifting the two wrapped shapes onto the ledge: the birds moved again then, swooping up into the air and hovering over the tower, almost as if they might be saying, We must give these humans room to arrange our food. It did not take very long; the plotters did it quickly, looking up at the birds as they laid the two bodies out. Selina supposed she ought to be thinking that that was her father and mother up there, but she could not. The pale bundles were simply sacks; they were nothing. There was a word – anonymous. It meant no name and no face. Even when the men twitched aside the wrappings, they were only arms and legs and hair, vaguely embarrassing because they had no clothes on.

The iron staircase shuddered as the men came back down: they descended very fast indeed, glancing uneasily upwards all the while, and for the first time Selina wondered if the ogre-birds could actually come inside the tower. But no, they were perched on the ledge – there were at least eight of them by now, and they were hunching over the two bodies. The plotters had reached the ground and they were about to go out of the tower. They'll slam the door, thought Selina, in panic. And then we'll be trapped all over again, with those things eating my father and mother up there, and I don't think I can bear it—

It was then that two things happened, not absolutely together, but so close that Selina was afterwards to almost believe that one had set off the other.

The first thing was the sound of several vehicles, being driven very fast, coming towards the tower. The glare of headlights swept across the dark interior, and there was the sound of car doors being opened and slammed, and of people shouting. The gun-men began to scatter, dropping their weapons as they did so. It's the rescue! thought Selina. They've found us! I can see Christy's father, and

Douglas's! And lots of other people in uniforms! But she stayed where she was, until she was sure that there were enough people out there to grab the plotters and their guns, and then she stood up, brushed down her frock which was filthy, and walked a bit unsteadily out into the glaring headlights and the people.

It was then that the second thing happened. As Douglas's father lifted her in his arms, and said, 'My poor child, you're safe now,' Selina heard – they all heard – the most terrible scream coming from the very top of the tower.

For a while everything was blurred. The night seemed to suddenly fill up with terror, and people began to run into the tower. The iron stairs clanged as they raced up them, shouting as they went.

Selina was carried to one of the jeeps, and wrapped in a blanket and given something hot to drink. Everyone was saying, 'You're quite safe, Selina; it's all over,' but there was horror in their voices when they said it, and Selina knew it was not over: there was something in the darkness that was screaming, over and over, dreadful terrified screams, so that you wanted to clap both hands over your ears and shut out the screaming and the panic and the red-streaked night.

Two shots rang out, and something screeched in anger. One of the ogre-birds? And then somebody said, 'Sod it, I missed the bloody thing! It's too dark and it's too far up – I can't even see the damned creatures!' and somebody else – Selina thought it was Douglas's father – said, 'For Christ's sake, try for it again – she's still alive up there—'

'Up there' meant the tower, of course. Selina tried to sit up to see what was happening, and she tried to see where Christy was as well, but people kept coming in between her and her view of the tower, and voices were saying something about 'Keep the child away' and, 'Get her back to Alwar – there's a British hospital there'. Somebody else told her to stay where she was; everything was all right.

One of the men had managed to tilt the other jeep so that its headlights shone onto the terrible ledge, and Selina could see the tower's top pretty well. She could see that something was moving up there, on the ledge. It was something that had pale arms and legs and body, and hair that streamed untidily in the wind. It was crouching over, its arms coming up to cover its head, but the ogre-birds were all round it – they were flying at it over and over again, their great wings beating on the air, their hunched-over bodies leaning down.

The screaming went on and on, but by the time the men reached the top of the iron staircase it had stopped.

Great-uncle Matthew did not approve of fires in children's bedrooms. He said it was a ridiculous waste of money: children were notoriously hardy creatures and they were better for not being pampered and cosseted. He demanded to know whether Flora thought money for coal and coke grew in the garden, because he was not a millionaire, said Great-uncle Matthew testily, dear goodness he was not, and there was already enough wanton extravagance to contend with as it was, what with Rosa's funeral to arrange, and very likely half of Inchcape coming to Teind after the service, expecting to be fed.

But Aunt Flora, who was puffy-faced from crying, had insisted that Selina had a fire in her bedroom on the night Rosa's body was found. She said fires were comforting, and they must remember that it had been Selina who had found poor Rosa's body, and the poor child was bound to be suffering from shock. They were all of them suffering from shock, said Aunt Flora, and oh dear, *what* were they going to do without Rosa? She sat down on one of the over-stuffed chairs in the dining room and gave way to another noisy bout of weeping, and had to be given a teaspoonful of brandy in a small glass as a restorative by Great-uncle Matthew, who did not approve of females drinking spirits but did not like it when Aunt Flora cried, because it upset his digestion.

Selina went to the funeral, of course. In church she sat in between Aunt Flora who smelt of the mothballs she used to preserve her good black coat, and Great-uncle Matthew, who smelt of pipe tobacco and unwashed feet because in all the upset nobody had remembered to light the boiler for hot water. Aunt Flora had said that she would heat up some water for washing, but Great-uncle Matthew said he would not dream of allowing Flora to struggle up two flights of stairs with heavy kettles of boiling water.

Selina had washed in cold water, and she wore her school uniform which Aunt Flora thought would be the most suitable thing. Everybody was very solemn and a few people shed tears at the graveside, but Selina did not, partly because Great-uncle Matthew had said she must not make a scene.

It was nothing like a funeral in India would have been. Selina had not been allowed to go to the funeral they had held for Douglas and Christy and the others, because it had been thought too upsetting for her. But she knew about funerals in India, because her ayah had told her about them.

In India, the dying person had to chant the *patet* along with all the family, or, if that could not be managed, the *ashem vohu*. 'Very good, the prayer for *ashem vohu*,' Selina's ayah had said. 'It make for a happier time beyond death.'

And then, after the death, wherever possible there was the visit of the *sagdid* to the body – the four-eyed dog. 'Not truly four eyes,' the ayah had said. 'But a dog with two spots over its eyes.' The *sagdid* had to be brought into the house to see the dead person, 'For the forces of evil retreat at the sight of a dog,' said the ayah. 'And there must also be fire, because the burning of fragrant sandalwood and frankincense destroys all ills. And after all is over, the family must eat only vegetable and fish for three days as a sign of mourning.'

Selina thought this all sounded very reasonable. You would want to drive away all the bad things when somebody died – the forces of evil, the ayah had called them – whether you did it by introducing a spot-eyed dog or burning nice-smelling things. Sandalwood was very nice indeed: mother had had a bottle of perfume called *Sandalwood*. And if you were upset at the death of somebody you loved, you would not feel like eating anyway.

The children in Alwar had not been able to chant the repentance-prayer, but Selina thought it might not matter so much for children. They had not had the *sagdid* either, but Selina thought that they would have crossed the old and holy Bridge all right, because they would have been together. Sometimes she could see them all, holding hands together, walking across the Bridge, Douglas and Christy helping the younger ones, all of them fearful but a bit excited, because to die was an awfully big adventure. Douglas had said that, right at the end. At times Selina wished very hard that she had gone with them to share the adventure.

There was no spotty-eyed *sagdid* dog at Great-aunt Rosa's funeral, of course – Great-uncle Matthew could not abide dogs or cats and would not have one in the house – and there was no frankincense or sandalwood, either. Selina had rather timidly asked about this, and both Great-uncle Matthew and Aunt Flora had been shocked. 'Popish practices,' said Great-uncle Matthew, and then, to Aunt Flora, 'If you ask me, it's as well that child was got out of India when she was. Frankincense, of all things! I could hardly believe my ears.'

There was no vegetables-and-fish mourning, either; in fact it almost seemed to Selina as if Aunt Flora was preparing for a party after the service. A ham had to be ordered from Stornforth's best butcher, because Mr McGibb in Inchcape could certainly not provide what was wanted, and two large pork pies were delivered as well. Jeannie from the village who came in to do the laundry and what was called 'the rough' was summoned, and the morning of the funeral was spent in cutting ham sandwiches and arranging wedges of pork pie on large plates.

'Cake?' Selina asked, hopefully. Aunt Flora baked the most delicious cakes, especially when the vicar was coming. But it seemed that refreshments after a funeral must be decent and restrained, and that to be seen eating cake would be disrespectful. Great Uncle Matthew said afterwards that he did not know about restraint; four bottles of his best sherry had been drunk, and a good three-quarters of the whisky. He shut himself in his study to calculate how much everything had cost, and told Aunt Flora to be sure to have the ham bone boiled up for soup. A good ham soup made a filling and nourishing dish.

Once Aunt Rosa was safely dead the shrine could be put back in place because nobody else was likely to go out to the Round Tower. Selina waited until after the funeral, and then scurried out to the stone room. The photographs, the books that father used to read to her – including her very favourite *Heidi* – and the silk stole mother had liked to wear in the evenings. It still smelt faintly of *Sandalwood*.

Nobody saw her do any of this, and she whispered to father and mother that she was sorry about what had happened – she thought they would know it was not her fault that the shrine had been taken away. It was to be hoped that it had not disturbed their journey across the old and holy Bridge, because Selina was not sure if she could bear the sight of those poor tattered ghosts in her bedroom all over again.

She wondered about Aunt Rosa's ghost. It would be just like the horrid witchy old thing to come into her room when it was dark, but Selina thought she would not mind it very much, because of not liking Aunt Rosa, and certainly not loving Aunt Rosa in the way she had loved her parents.

When she thought about it again, Selina was very glad she had stretched the black string across the top of the stairs that night. She had tied one end onto a nail in the skirting board and then wound the other end round the banisters, doing it carefully and quietly after everyone was in bed, creeping out in her dressing gown and slippers. Nobody had heard her and nobody had seen, although she had had the spookiest feeling that Christy had been with her. This was such a strong feeling that she had to keep looking over her shoulder, in case Christy might be crouching in the shadows watching her. But she was not, of course, because she was dead; she had died on the night the men took them to the Tower of Silence, and if anything had held Selina's hand and talked to her in the darkness, it had been Christy's ghost. Selina thought it would be like Christy to come back, just for that short time, so that her friend would not be alone in the scary Tower of Silence. And Christy would approve of what Selina was doing tonight, because she would understand about the shrine; she would understand that Aunt Rosa could not be allowed to destroy the shrine.

The string across the stairs was about six inches from the ground – just the height of a person's ankles – but because it was black it would not be seen. Aunt Rosa had not seen it when she got up next morning, which was why it had tripped her up and sent her tumbling headlong down the stairs. The police doctor had said that the fall had broken her neck. Her legs had been broken as well, and one wrist, but it had been breaking her neck that had killed her.

After the funeral Aunt Flora had been worried that Selina, poor motherless scrap, might find it difficult to go to sleep, what with it being hardly a year since her parents had died, but the fire in the little hearth had burned up bright and warm and the bedroom was cosy and snug. Selina went to sleep without any trouble at all.

CHAPTER THIRTEEN

———⊷◆⊷———

Mary had slept very deeply on the night after Ingrid died. The doctors at Broadacre had forced some kind of tranquilliser into her, but she thought she would have slept deeply anyway, on account of having been revenged on that bitch Ingrid. It was strange that after all these years it still hurt to remember how much she had trusted Ingrid and how Ingrid had betrayed her trust. It taught you a lesson, that kind of thing; it taught you never to trust anyone, except for that secret strong voice inside your own mind. It taught you to not even trust people who seemed genuine and kind, and said that their sole purpose in life was to help you.

Ingrid had said that at the start. 'I want to help you, Mary,' she had said on that first night, the night of the rape attempt. She had sat on the edge of the bath while Mary got undressed, and she had talked soothingly, her hand on Mary's thigh. Mary did not really want anyone in the bathroom with her – she wanted to be on her own to scrub away the smell of the man's body from her skin – but they would not let her, because she had to be examined to see exactly what the man had done and how far he had got. Ingrid had probably been told that Mary must not be left alone in case she washed away the evidence.

But at least she had been able to wash her face and hands, and shampoo her hair, which helped a bit. Ingrid helped her to dry her hair. 'Pretty,' she said. 'You ought to let it grow a bit.' *Pretty* . . . That word again.

When Ingrid hugged her Mary could feel Ingrid's body through the thin pyjamas she had put on; she could feel Ingrid's breasts pressing against her own breasts. It felt peculiar. When she said, 'I shouldn't have done that,' a little pulse of excitement started up at the pit of Mary's stomach. She felt her nipples harden, and she stared at Ingrid, feeling her face grow hot with embarrassment and apprehension. Ingrid was breathing a bit faster and there was a faint line of sweat on her upper lip. Will she do anything else? thought Mary. I'll hate it if she does; I'll hit her, hard, and then I'll run back to the dormitory – there'll be people around by now.

But when Ingrid bent over and kissed Mary, full on the lips, her mouth open so that Mary tasted her breath, she did not run away and she did not try to hit Ingrid. She kissed her back, at first fumbling because she was so inexperienced, but then with more confidence. She gasped when she felt Ingrid's tongue, and when Ingrid stepped back, and said with unmistakable regret, 'I mustn't and I

daren't. Go along to the dormitory, Mary. Goodnight,'
Mary felt a sharp pang of disappointment. She had
expected Ingrid to do more than just kiss her. She had
not expected this incomplete love-making.

'Incomplete,' Broadacre's duty doctor had said, making
his brief humiliating examination. 'No penetration.'

'We didn't think there had been,' said the slab-faced
nurse smugly.

'No, nor did I. Oh, and for the record, she's *virgo
intacta*.' The doctor had straightened up and peeled off
the thin surgical gloves and dropped them into a bin, and
then said, apparently as an afterthought, that Mary could
have a bath now if she wanted.

Broadacre had been so vast and so bewilderingly complex that at this distance Mary could not sort out any
particular strand from those early, tangled memories.
There had been so many new impressions and new
faces: new routines to learn, new mealtimes to adjust
to, different arrangements for recreation and work, and
sessions with unfamiliar doctors and psychiatrists.

Christabel had stayed with her throughout it all, of
course, her strength forcing Mary to cope, helping her
to look for ways to make this unbearable place endur-
able, her thoughts tangling with Mary's to make up
the pattern of those years. At times it was difficult to
know which were Christabel's thoughts and which were
Mary's own.

But the one memory-strand that had never become
tangled or indecipherable was the memory of that doctor

who had examined her after the rape attack, and of his look and his tone.

Virgo intacta, he had said, and he had given Mary that look half of pity, half of contempt. As if he was faintly bored. As if he was relegating her to some lower-class, inferior pigeon-hole. And as if he might be thinking: this one's never even been laid, and she's never likely to be either, stuck in here. So put it on the file that she's a virgin and close the filing cabinet, and draw a line under the whole thing. Mary had hated him with a deep and passionate hate. Fine sodding chance I've had to be anything *but virgo* bloody *intacta* when I've been locked up inside madhouses since I was fourteen.

That had been the moment when she had looked down the years that stretched out in front of her and seen their unutterable dreariness. Unless she was very clever or very lucky she would live her life inside Broadacre, or a place very like it. She would spend her days doing stupid unimportant work that they said, patronisingly, was 'rehabilitating' and 'worthwhile'. Mary knew the work was neither of these things, because anyone with half a brain could see it was invented work, trivial work. Trivial. The word rasped against her mind, hurting, humiliating.

Mary Maskelyne, trivial! The Sixties icon, trivial! The teenager hailed as an anti-heroine almost before the word was common currency – the girl to whom all those other teenagers had written, asking for advice, asking how to find the courage to do to their wicked, abusive parents what Mary had done to hers! Dubbed as trivial and of no interest! How *dared* the doctor imply that! And written in the records as a virgin! Did that mean that in the years to come – perhaps after she was dead – when people wrote biographies of famous murder cases, they would say things like, *In the 1960s there was the famous multiple-murderess, Mary Maskelyne, who lived and died a virgin* ...? And all those people in the future would think, Imagine that, Mary Maskelyne was never screwed. She killed people but she never got fucked, poor old cow. There was something faintly pathetic and slightly comic about elderly virgins. They were a sub-breed by themselves – twittery old spinsters, eccentric great-aunts, all a bit peculiar because they had never been laid.

A little pulse of anger had started to beat inside Mary's mind then – or was it anger? Mightn't it be the secret, hunched-over thing in her mind again, four years older, but uncurling just as strongly as it had done that other time? With the thought the anger-pulse seemed to change pace very slightly, so that it was no longer anger, but excitement. I'm planning again, thought Mary. I'm weighing up ways and means, and I'm calculating what to do to be revenged – yes, and to make life more interesting, and it feels *good!*

She lay on her bed in the ugly dormitory that smelled of stale sleep-breath and sweat, and stared up at the ceiling. It was covered with myriad cracks and it looked a bit like the map of Europe, although if you turned your head it looked more like an elephant, with Italy where the trunk was.

If the rape had been complete that doctor would not

have spoken so dismissively. If she had conceived a child as a result of it he would have looked at her with very different eyes indeed. A child. They would all sit up and take notice of that, because they would have to! The whole country would sit up and take notice, as well. Press releases would be issued, and the papers and the television and radio stations would all take it up. The newspaper headlines would be banners, exactly as they had been four years earlier. *Maskelyne raped inside Broadacre* . . . they would scream. *Killer to give birth to rapist's child* . . .

There would be public inquiries and news items. They would resurrect the film footage of Mary arriving at court for the trial, and there would be interviews with psychiatrists and social workers. The letters would all come pouring in once again, and once again Mary would be important. And that doctor would be made to feel a fool, because he had got the whole thing wrong.

The cracks in the ceiling stopped being Europe, and rearranged themselves into a different pattern. Christabel's face. Not quite as it was in the old photographs from home, because Christabel was older now. But unmistakably Christabel, looking down at Mary, the sister she had never known, smiling at her, whispering into her mind that it would serve them all right if Mary could lose her virginity in here, if she could become pregnant. Telling her to go for it, Mary, make the bastards look stupid, get yourself screwed and enjoy what follows.

Get yourself screwed . . .

How? And who? And when? The curled-up blackness

deep within her mind went on planning and calculating, and the golden strength and the glowing energy of her dead sister trickled in and out of Mary's thoughts.

Ingrid had not minded about the virginity thing, in fact she had seemed rather pleased about it.

The night after the rape she had come into the bathroom again while Mary was there, and she had perched on the edge of the bath exactly as she had done last time, except this time Mary was actually in the bath, covered in soapy water.

Ingrid had wanted to know about the doctor and his examination, and she listened carefully, her head tilted to one side as if she were trying to hear not just what Mary was saying, but what she was thinking and feeling as well. She said there was nothing wrong with being a virgin, in fact it made Mary special. It meant there were things they could explore together, said Ingrid: feelings that Mary could experience for the first time. This time she did much more than stroke Mary's thighs and give her that single wistful kiss: this time she explored Mary's whole body, reaching down into the warm water to caress her breasts. To start with Mary had the curious feeling of being pulled out of her skin, and forced into another that did not quite fit her, but after a while she quite liked it.

What Ingrid did in the damp, soap-smelling bathroom, the door locked against intrusion, was worlds and light years away from the gruntings and heavings of the semi-rape of twenty-four hours earlier, just as the soft fragile fluttering of a butterfly's wings or a bat's was worlds and light years away from the heavy, leathery pounding of an eagle's wings or a gryphon's.

But both sprang from the same root. Both rendered the creature airborne.

Ingrid's fingertips and Ingrid's flicking tongue rendered Mary airborne that night; they took her up and up into a breathless, coiled-spring excitement, and she had thought that if only it would go on she would be for ever grateful to Ingrid—

And so she had been. She had been breathlessly, enchantedly grateful to Ingrid, until the day that the enchantment had dissolved, and she had seen what lay beneath the magic. Betrayal. Ingrid had not cared about Mary at all. She had probably been laughing at her all along – telling the other staff at Broadacre about the things Mary had let her do, bragging to them about Mary's wide-eyed gratitude.

And in the end, Ingrid had betrayed her.

Get yourself screwed, Mary . . .

It was easy to slip out of the dormitory during the recreation time one week later – Mary had rehearsed it three times, and each time she had been able to go unchallenged more or less anywhere she wanted.

Recreation time was seven until eight: the hour after supper and before the bedtime bell. Most people watched television, although as Mary went cautiously out of the block she could hear that some of them were playing stupid Monopoly or Ludo – she could hear them screeching with silly glee, and she could hear the pit-pat of the table tennis game as well. It was a good time to pick, though, because it was a time when the warders thought they knew where everybody was. But Broadacre was so big it was easy to get lost for an hour or so, and there were so many staff that they had not all got to know Mary yet. They knew the fourteen-year-old whose features had been blazoned across all the newspapers, of course; they knew the back-combed hair and skinny-rib sweater and the heavily made-up eyes, because everybody knew that. But they did not know what Mary looked like now, four crucial years on, with her hair cut into short, feathery fronds, and her face almost free of make-up. It was laughably easy to give the warders the slip, and go along to the men's dormitory. If anyone recognised her or stopped her, she would say she was looking for the library because she wanted a book to read.

The man who had attacked her on that first night was called Darren Clark, and he was in Broadacre because he had raped several little girls. Ingrid had said that the attack on Mary would have been a kind of initiation ceremony to him: he had done it before with new patients and the attendants were supposed to keep him under supervision when new people came in, but he liked giving them the slip.

Darren Clark's family were quite well-off, and they had been able to employ a very good barrister to defend him against the rape charges. They had paid doctors to provide reports saying he was not responsible for what he had done, because they had not wanted the shame of having a son who was a criminal. They thought it was far less shameful to have a son who was mad, said Ingrid.

Mary did not care whether Darren Clark was mad or not, providing he could do it to her properly, providing no one interrupted them – and providing she got pregnant as a result.

It was an awful lot of 'providings'. But she had sent the note to him – 'Please meet me in your dormitory at seven o'clock tomorrow night' – and if he did not turn up it would not matter all that much. If he showed the note to anyone, that would not matter either, because Mary had not signed it. The end would simply be that she would have to look for someone more suitable. But she thought Darren Clark would come. She thought he would be intrigued and flattered; Ingrid said all men were screamingly vain. She had said, as well, that Darren Clark was quite intelligent most of the time. Mary supposed this meant when he was not raping children or initiating new inmates.

Mary had told Ingrid that the rape attempt had been loathsome. She said she had hated the feel of Darren Clark's body writhing against her, and the hard stick of his erection pushing between her legs had made her feel so sick she had nearly thrown up in his face. Ingrid had laughed softly, and said, 'Poor baby. He wanted to piston-pump you, Mary, that's what he wanted. I'm glad he didn't get that far; you'd have hated that a whole lot worse.' Mary had said whatever you called it and however far it had got or not got, she had hated it anyway. She had wanted to scrub her skin for about a month to get rid of the memory of him touching her and slobbering over her.

But she was no longer sure if the encounter had really been all that hateful. Writing that careful note, going stealthily through Broadacre tonight, was beginning to feel fiercely exciting. It was much more exciting than waiting for Ingrid to come on duty and signal to Mary that they should meet in the small bathroom at the end of the corridor, or somewhere equally secret. And after the first time Mary had been aware of a faint impatience with Ingrid. 'No penetration,' the doctor had said that night, but there was no penetration with what Ingrid did, either. What Ingrid did was ineffectual. Incomplete. It was all very well to stroke and kiss and lick, but after a while it had made Mary remember how her attacker's body had felt – hard, insistent, masculine. How would it have been if the attendants had not come running to separate them . . . ?

The male dormitories were in a different wing from the female ones. You had to go along a dingy corridor that crossed a stretch of scrubby garden where the inmates were supposed to plant spring bulbs and make herb borders. There were not many people about at this time of early evening but there were some, and so Mary walked swiftly and purposefully, nodding absent-mindedly at anyone she met so that it looked as if she was expected somewhere.

The corridor was draughty because of having windows on both sides all the way along, like a railway carriage, and it smelt of damp. But underneath the damp was another smell that Mary could not at first identify. And then she knew what it was. Human despair. The agony of minds that were locked away – not just locked inside Broadacre, but locked inside their own bitter, lonely incomprehension. For the first time since coming here Mary saw that Broadacre was different from the Young Offenders' Hostel; the YOH had been where the yobs and the joyriders and the teenage drug-dealers were put because they were not old enough for grown-up prisons. But Broadacre was where the helplessly mad people went. And if I am not very careful, I shall become part of the madness.

There were cold electric light-bulbs overhead, and at this time of day they were switched full on, making the windows into oblongs of blackness. Mary could see her reflection in them, a bit blurry because the windows were misty with condensation, but recognisable. She glanced across to the other side. Yes, the reflection was there as well. And then her heart leapt suddenly, because wasn't there another reflection there? – a second person, no more than a hazy shape, like a ghost twin or a phantom image, walking alongside her?

Christabel?

Mary's heart began to thud against her ribs. She had surely imagined it. No, there it was again, an indistinct outline against the dark garden. Small and thin and pale. Like something struggling to materialise. Christabel, walking alongside the sister she had never met, her mind locking into Mary's and filling her up with that dark strength, just as she had done four years earlier . . .

Do it, Mary . . .

Yes, whispered Mary to the night-garden. Yes, I'll do it.

The men's dormitory was almost identical to the women's – there were the same rows of iron-framed beds, and the same curtain tracks overhead so that you could curtain off your few feet of space and feel private. In the women's dormitory there were odds and ends of make-up on the lockers, and magazines with articles about pop stars and royalty strewn about. Here, there were shaving brushes or electric razors. There were magazines as well, but Mary thought they were different ones. At the youth place there had been a lively trade in porn mags; there would be sure to be something similar here.

If you were romantically minded you would not think this a very nice place to lose your virginity – properly lose it, not fiddle and finger around with it as Ingrid did. But it did not matter that there was no scented garden or flowery bower, and in any case that stuff was for those wimpish creatures you read about in books. This was not about romance, it was about getting screwed as thoroughly as possible, and getting pregnant. It was about showing that doctor that she was neither trivial nor boring, and it was about reminding the outside world that she still existed.

Yes. Good. And stay with me, Christabel.

She moved along the row of narrow iron-framed beds, searching. Here was his bed – there was a plastic name-tag at the foot, with 'Darren Clark' written on it in a round, careful hand.

The large plain-faced clock over the door pointed to three minutes to seven. Exactly right. Mary lay down on the bed, listening intently for sounds beyond the door, watching for signs of movement beyond the square of frosted glass in the door's top half. The minute hand ticked its way up to seven o'clock, and there was a stab of disappointment – he's not going to come! – and then hard on the heels of this a lurch of hope, because soft footsteps were coming along the corridor. Was it? Yes, it must be.

There was the dark outline of a man beyond the frosty glass, and then the door was pushed open, and Mary smiled the secret smile and felt the excitement spiral upwards. He had come, just as she had known he would.

What surprised her was not the physical side – she had known what to expect, more or less. It was the way she felt after it was over.

For what seemed a very long time he stood uncertainly at the foot of the bed, not moving, not even seeming to want to touch her. Well, what did you expect? jeered the inner voice. That he'd sit on the bed and read poetry to you? That you'd discuss love and life and undying devotion before he tore your clothes off and – what did Ingrid call it? – piston-pumped you? And then Mary realised that he was not going to be turned on purely because she was here; he needed more than that. He needed violence, and he needed his victim to be frightened. Of course! So rewrite the script, Mary, and do it quickly!

Speaking slowly, testing each word before she let it go, she said, 'I came to ask why you attacked me that night,' and saw his eyes widen with interest. Yes! Good!

He said, 'Were you frightened?'

'Yes. Yes, I was.' Had he taken a step nearer? 'I didn't want you to do that to me,' said Mary. 'I mean, I didn't want you to screw me.' Was that right? Should she have said 'fuck'?

'They all say they don't want it.' Yes, he was moving nearer; he was on the edge of the bed now. 'But really they do want it. I know they do. You want it now – that's why you're here.'

'No—' Had that sounded convincing? She shrank back against the bedhead. 'I came to tell you I hated you—' Remember Ingrid's remark about initiation ceremonies, said the inner voice. 'It was my first night here,' said Mary.

'I know it was. I like to check out the new females.' He reached out a hand, and his fingers suddenly grabbed Mary's wrist. Mary gasped, quite genuinely. 'You won't scream this time, will you?'

'You've got it all wrong. I didn't come here for this—' Oh, get on with it, you prat, before somebody comes in . . .

But it was going to be all right. He was bounding onto the bed, dragging her skirt up to her waist, still holding her wrist with his left hand, but thrusting his right hand up between her thighs. Mary felt his fingers brush her – *there*, in the place nobody had ever touched, except for Ingrid, except for that disdainful doctor – and she struggled and tried to push him away. At once his hand came up to encircle both her wrists, forcing them over her head, and he half knelt on her, one knee pushing her legs apart. His breath gusted into her face, and Mary struggled again, panic rising despite her resolve.

He fumbled at the zip of his jeans, and pushed them down, half over his thighs. There was the feeling of hard warm flesh against her legs – masculine, intrusive . . . OK, this is it. He's about to do it—

But when he rammed into her body, she gasped, half with the sudden pain, half because she had truly not expected it to feel like that – she had not expected him to feel so huge and so hard . . . She had not expected the urgent pushing, either, and she cried out, wanting to stop him or at least slow him down, because this was hurting, it was a deep bruising feeling far inside her and nobody had told her about the frantic thrusting, like a sledgehammer, over and over—

And then, with a rush of movement and a sudden burst of wetness, it seemed to be over. He sagged onto her, heavy and awkward, and Mary lay absolutely still. That was it, then. He did it. He did *me*. With any luck I'll be bleeding, and with just a bit more luck I'll be scratched and bruised where he grabbed my wrists and grazed my neck with his teeth. Evidence of rape.

She managed to push him off her and he half fell off the bed, landing on the bare floor. Mary propped herself up on one elbow and looked down at him. He looked absolutely ridiculous, sprawling on the floor, not exactly shame-faced but not meeting her eyes. He was ugly and gross, squirming round to try to pull up his jeans. His face was red and sweaty and his neck swollen with exertion and pride like a bullfrog, and he was stupid and hideous.

And now that he had done what Mary had wanted, he was expendable.

The thought slid into her mind, soft and serpentlike. Expendable. In fact, it might be better to be rid of him in case he told anyone about the note – in case, after all, they could see who wrote it. Handwriting experts – yes, she had forgotten about that. They might piece together what had really happened, which would spoil the whole plan. It would be better on all counts to cover her tracks, really. Kill the bullfrog? Well, why not? Wasn't there a creature in the insect world – a spider, was it? – who killed her mate after he had impregnated her? Mary remembered learning about it in some pointless biology lesson. She remembered, as well, that this was someone who was in Broadacre for raping children, and who was known for his bizarre initiation ceremony with new female patients. Nobody would be surprised if he got his come-uppance, in fact a good many people would probably secretly be pleased. People hated child-rapists worse than anything – Mary knew that. Prison's too good for them, they said. And they said, String the bastards up. Cut their balls off. Yes, this could be as foolproof as they came.

She got slowly off the bed, and looked about her for something to use as a weapon. Something to squash the ugly bullfrog or to slit him open. How about that shaving stuff on the locker? Was there a razor there? No, they would not let these people have dangerous razor blades lying around. Then what about that empty Coke bottle on the table? She pattered across the room to get it, feeling strong and indestructible, feeling as if she could do anything in the world and get away with it. Was that Christabel's strength and Christabel's confidence again? She paused to listen, her head on one side, but wherever Christabel was she was staying very quiet and very still.

It was surprisingly easy and incredibly satisfying to smash the bottle over the bullfrog's head. He had been half standing up, fastening his jeans, trying to stuff his disgusting sex-thing into them, but when Mary hit him he went down with a grunt, exactly as her father had done all those years ago. A rim of white showed under his eyelids and there was a trickle of blood from where the bottle had cut his scalp a little. Mary considered him again. His jeans were still open and he looked grotesque. He had raped little girls and he had tried to rape Mary that first night, and he deserved to die.

Cut their balls off, people said about child-rapists.

Mary nodded to herself very slowly two or three times, and then, wrapping her skirt around the neck of the Coke bottle to protect her hand, she smashed it hard against the iron frame of the bed. The top section splintered at once, leaving several glinting jagged spears of glass sticking up from the neck. *Good*. Mary walked across to where the bullfrog lay on the ground, and then turned him onto his back.

As she crouched over him, lifting the broken bottle

high in the air preparatory to bringing it hard down on his groin, Christabel came back to her. Christabel watched from the shadows as Mary did what had to be done.

CHAPTER FOURTEEN

'It's important,' said Patrick Irvine, 'to always be just a little bit frightened in here, Emily. That way you stay on guard.'

'OK,' said Emily. 'I understand that.'

'Don't let it take you over, though,' he said. 'Just keep your wits about you, and make sure that there's always – *always* – somebody within yelling distance, and that you know where the nearest alarm bell is. I'll point those out to you as we go, and there'll be at least two or three in the day-room as well.'

'All right. Dr Irvine, this Pippa I'm going to be see-ing— How much should I know about her? How much are you allowed to tell me?'

'She's potentially very, very dangerous indeed,' said Patrick at once. 'But also, she's a very sad case, poor Pippa. There's never anyone for her on visiting day –

at least, not to my knowledge – and I don't think there ever has been. She's been inside one asylum or another for most of her life, and she's as institutionalised as they come. It was probably inevitable that she would end up in Moy.' He paused and Emily waited, and then he said, 'She doesn't speak – not ever. There's no physical reason why she shouldn't, and we think she's quite intelligent. But she's locked the doors of her mind against the world, and no one's ever found a way to unlock them. I certainly haven't. Oh, and I should tell you that she lost an eye some years ago – you won't find that distressing, will you?'

Emily said of course she would not.

'There's a bit of a scar, but it isn't very noticeable, and she normally wears darkish glasses, which hide it fairly effectively. She's been an inmate here for about three years, and I've been trying to reach her for all of that time. I've no idea what goes on inside her mind, but I'll keep trying to find out. If we knew why she never speaks we might make sense of some of the things she's done.'

'Ought I to know what kind of treatment she has or anything like that?'

'Oh God, she's had every kind of treatment we know,' said Patrick, thrusting the fingers of one hand impatiently through his hair. Emily wanted to touch his hair so badly that she nearly had to sit on her hands to prevent herself from reaching out to him. 'But nothing's worked, and although we'll never dare let her go out into the world we'll keep trying to get through to her,' he said. 'She reads a lot and she likes music so we've tried all of those

therapies and I've tried hypnosis as well, of course—'
He broke off. 'That surprises you,' he said. 'That I use
hypnosis.'

'Yes. I don't know why, though.'

Patrick said softly, 'But didn't you realise I sometimes
play Svengali?'

He looked at her and Emily stared back at him, and
eventually managed to mumble something about his
having to be Russian or Romanian or something to
really be Svengali. But she must still have looked a bit
disconcerted, because after a moment he leaned forward
over the desk, clasping his hands.

'It *is* Svengali I play, and not Baron Frankenstein,
Emily,' he said, very gently. 'And hypnosis is sometimes
a way into their minds – it's a way for me to find out
what's happened to flaw them – what's made them rape
and mutilate and kill, apparently without any compassion.
I don't know if evil is a disease, or if it's something
created by childhood abuse or adult tragedies – I don't
think anyone knows for sure. We've progressed since the
Middle Ages and the superstitions about possession and
demons: we know that there are malformations of the
brain that account for some of the conditions we have
to deal with. But no matter what name they're given,
the devils and the demons are still there. And it's those
devils that I'm trying to help exorcise.'

Emily considered this, and then, because it seemed
an appropriate moment, she dug into her pocket and
produced a sheet of paper.

'I wrote this out – I thought you might like to read it.'

Her voice sounded infuriatingly defensive. 'It was after you talked about the darkness and the loneliness when we were outside the Round Tower,' she said. 'It sort of struck a chord in my mind.' In her own bedroom it had seemed rather a good idea to copy out the few lines and bring them with her, but now she was not so sure.

But he seemed instantly interested, and he read the lines over, once to himself, his face absorbed, and then aloud. Emily could have died just listening to his voice.

> *I reached a place where every light is muted,*
> *which bellows like the sea beneath a tempest,*
> *when it is battered by opposing winds.*
> *The hellish hurricane, which never rests,*
> *drives on the spirits with its violence:*
> *wheeling and pounding, it harasses them.*

'Emily, that's inspirational,' he said looking up at her, his eyes shining. 'The hellish hurricane that never rests, but drives the spirits on with its violence . . .'

'It doesn't forgive the violence,' said Emily. 'And it doesn't condone it. But it doesn't exactly punish it, either, does it? It tries to give a reason for it.'

'It's eerily descriptive. Where did you find it?'

At least he did not think she had written it, like some over-eager schoolgirl. Emily said, 'It's a bit of Dante's *Inferno*.' And then, in case he might think she sat in her room poring over poetry to give to him, like a romantic adolescent, for God's sake, she said, 'Odd bits stick in your mind sometimes, don't they? I mean – you're made

189

to learn them as a kid, and they stay with you. That stayed with me, so after you said that about darknesses and lonelinesses, I looked it up.'

He eyed her for a moment, but he only said, 'If you were made to learn Dante as a child you must have had a pretty unusual schooling.'

Tell him, you stooge! Tell him about Durham, and about having to come back home before Finals because of dad going to pieces when mum died! No, I can't. It'll sound like boasting. Emily said, vaguely, that she liked squirrelling away unusual scraps of things, that was all.

'Can I keep it? I'd like to get it properly printed, and frame it to have on my desk. As a reminder of what some of the inmates suffer. Would you mind?'

'Of course not. And it'd be out of copyright by this time, wouldn't it?' said Emily gravely, and he grinned at her, and her heart lurched with pleasure. And then, since she was here to do some useful work, and not to talk about fourteenth-century poetry, she said, 'We've got off the subject, haven't we? Tell me a bit more about Pippa.'

Patrick had regretted making the Svengali crack to Emily Frost almost as soon as the words were out of his mouth – you can't resist the temptation to exert a little charm, can you? demanded his inner voice crossly. Even on this one who's certainly young enough to be your daughter. As well as that, he had had to beat down the impulse to tell Emily that at times – such as the times he tried to reach Pippa and the others who were like her – he was uneasily aware that it would not take much for Svengali to cross over into Baron Frankenstein.

He had not thought Emily would pick up the Svengali allusion – he kept forgetting how extremely young she was. But she had; she had given him the urchin-sprite smile, and made that answer about his not being Russian enough for Svengali, and had walked at his side through the fearsome system of locked gates and doors to the day-room inside A wing. The top of her head was level with his shoulder, and her hair was two-tone today: the underneath part was vivid magenta and the top was silver-gilt. It looked like a slightly ragged cap, donned in a moment of absent-mindedness.

(A cap of silver-gilt, spun from moonlight and bog-flowers and mushroom caps . . . ? Oh, for goodness' sake!)

He noticed that there were dark shadows around her eyes, as if she might have been out somewhere until the small hours the previous night, and he wondered where and with whom.

And *now* you're imagining midnight revels in the depths of the greenwood shade, said his mind jeeringly. Oh sure, orgiastic cavortings with priapic elves on a bank over-canopied with luscious woodbine, all of them high as kites, banging away until dawn, was that what you were thinking, Patrick? More likely a pubful of lager louts discussing football and getting smash-drunk or out of their minds on Ecstasy—

Yes, but she knew that Dante stanza – or at least, she

knew enough to look it up and she cared enough to write
it out and let you see it— God, I've got to stop thinking
like this!

But Oberon's sweet woodbine-couch aside, one might
reasonably suppose that Emily had a fairly colourful
social life. Patrick did suppose it, and it made him feel
profoundly and irrationally depressed.

All the way through the maze of corridors and locked
doors Emily was planning how she would talk to this
woman, this Pippa, about ordinary trivial things. Things
like helping with the children at Lorna Laughlin's school
and how they were having a painting competition. She
had thought she could talk about Herbert, her cat, as
well, and how he had caught a mouse and left it on the
doorstep and given everyone hysterics, but Dr Irvine had
said, 'No reference to animals when you talk to Pippa,
Emily. Not in any form at all,' and Emily had not liked
to ask why, but had just nodded.

The slightly battered day-room managed to be both
cold and stuffy at the same time, and smelt faintly of
stewed tea. Pippa was sitting in a straight-backed chair,
one of the attendants with her. Emily noticed that Pippa
had chosen a chair with its back to the window and
remembered about the damaged eye and felt sympathetic.
She saw that Pippa was waiting patiently and tidily, her
hair carefully combed and the buttons of her cardigan
done up to the neck. She looked like a schoolchild who
has been told to sit quietly until its mother arrives, and
Emily suddenly found this so unbearably poignant that

a stupid lump came at the back of her throat and tears stung her eyes.

And then Dr Irvine said, very softly, 'You have to be a bit detached about these people, Emily.' And, as Emily looked involuntarily up at him, he smiled the real smile, and said, 'But I wouldn't want you not to have feelings, my dear.'

My dear. It was the wildest maddest thing in the world to feel so absolutely thrilled because he had called her 'my dear'. All it meant was that he had seen she was affected by Pippa, and was giving her a bit of confidence. He probably did it to everyone.

But it worked. Emily went forward, and said, 'Hi, Pippa. I'm Emily. They said I could come to talk to you – they said you'd like a visitor for half an hour or so.' She had rehearsed this beforehand, and it came out about right. 'I'm not very used to doing this,' she said, which was the next bit of the script. 'But my dad works here, and I thought I'd like to talk to some of the people he knows. I expect you've met my dad – his name's Donald Frost. He and Dr Irvine said that you'd be a good person for me to start with. So this is a rehearsal, really. I hope you don't mind being a rehearsal.'

There was no reply which was a bit off-putting, but Dr Irvine had already explained about this. 'Just assume she's understanding you,' he had said. 'Just talk to her.'

Emily cast a glance at the attendant who was sitting in one of the chairs, leafing through a dog-eared magazine, looking bored. She said, 'I don't know what you like to talk about, Pippa, but what I'll do, I'll tell you about the things I do and we'll go from there. One of the things I do is help in the school for two afternoons, and that's good, because the kids are great.' Patrick had said not to talk about animals, but he had not said anything about children. So Emily ploughed on. 'The kids are having a cookery day at school on Monday – I'm helping with it, and I'll bring you some of their cakes if you'd like.' Nothing. Emily said, 'I don't know what they'll taste like, but I'll bring them anyhow. I'll come on Monday afternoon – would that be all right? We'll have a cup of tea and try the cakes.'

Pippa turned to look at Emily as if trying to understand what was wanted of her. Then she nodded slightly, submissively. As if she was saying, Yes, if that is what you want of me.

This was encouraging, so Emily pressed on, and all the while there was the memory of Dr Irvine – Patrick – calling her 'my dear', and smiling the special smile. Every time Emily thought about that, she felt as if she could run all the way up the nearest mountain and back down the other side.

After he had delivered Emily safely to the day-room, Patrick went back to his office, and reached for the overflowing in-tray. It was annoying that Emily's face kept getting between him and the case notes awaiting his attention. Don Frost had said something about her going out with Robbie Glennon: Patrick wondered if the heavy-eyed look was because of him. If she did get together with that young Glennon, it was to be hoped the boy would appreciate her.

When he left her in the day-room, she had thanked him, and said, See you soon, Dr Irvine, and Patrick had had to beat down a sudden impulse to say, For God's sake, ditch this bloody formality, and call me Patrick!

He was working steadily through a batch of case notes when the phone on his desk rang.

It was Miss March from Teind House. After a moment, Patrick recalled meeting her at some charity supper or other he had attended earlier in the year. He did not much like the slightly constrained, slightly false gaiety of these events, but it would have been churlish not to take some role in Inchcape's little community.

Selina March had been on his table that night; she was, it appeared, one of the stalwarts of Inchcape's little church, and an indefatigable worker for various worthy causes. Patrick had judged her to be in her early fifties, and remembered that she had worn an unbecoming camel and brown print two-piece, that her hair was arranged in no particular style at all, and that her face was innocent of make-up except for a light dusting of powder and a trace of pink lipstick. He had tried to talk to her, but she had been painfully shy, and had blushed furiously and looked down at her feet when the after-dinner speaker told a faintly *risqué* joke.

He had thanked her for her company at the dinner, and had not given her another thought until he heard her voice on the other end of his phone.

She was apologetic, breathless, and not very coherent. She was so very sorry for troubling him, she said, and of course he must be extremely busy— Doctors were always so very busy, of course, one knew that—

Patrick said patiently, 'Is there something I can do to help you, Miss March?'

'I am so sorry, I must be more concise. It's just that I am so worried by what has happened, Dr Irvine—'

'Worried?'

'Mrs Kent,' said Selina. 'Joanna Savile, you know. She is staying with me – I have a little paying guest arrangement here— She came to Moy to talk to some of your people yesterday—'

'Yes, she gave us a very good talk,' said Patrick, and waited. What on earth was the old dear trying to say?

'You see, she didn't come back last night,' said Selina. 'And really, I don't quite know what to do.'

Patrick said, 'You mean – she's missing?'

'I can't be sure about it, Dr Irvine. But I telephoned her flat in London – she had given me her number – and there was no reply. Her husband is abroad, of course, but I thought perhaps he had returned early— But there's no message, and I'm beginning to feel quite worried, although I don't want to start any panic if there's a simple explanation.'

Patrick said, 'But Joanna wouldn't just have gone back to London without telling you, surely?'

'Oh *no*, I'm quite sure she wouldn't. She was a very thoughtful girl. And her car is still here – a very nice car, which she hired for the journey. That's what I find so worrying. Wherever she's gone, she hasn't gone in the car. I do find that odd.'

'Have you phoned the police?'

'Well, not yet. You see, I thought perhaps there had been something at Moy that might have necessitated her staying out . . .'

Like running off with a lover? thought Patrick. Or is she wondering if I seduced Joanna after the talk and she's still languishing in my bed? He said, 'Miss March, Joanna left here at around five o'clock yesterday. I'm sure she did, although I'll ring down to the gatehouse now, to make sure. Could I phone you back to confirm that for you?'

'Oh, well, if you wouldn't mind – I don't want to be a trouble—'

'Give me your number, and then give me ten minutes,' said Patrick. 'But if Joanna really hasn't been seen since yesterday, I'm afraid you'd better call in the police.'

CHAPTER FIFTEEN

If Selina had known that Joanna Savile – Joanna Kent – would cause so much trouble she would have made some excuse to stop her coming to Teind.

Now that Selina had admitted that Joanna was missing – now that she had burnt her boats by telephoning Dr Irvine – it was difficult to know what ought to be done next. Selina had never really had anything to do with police investigations – at least not since the aunts had died, and even then she had not really been old enough to be much involved.

Dr Irvine had kept his promise about telephoning back: he had rung Selina well within the promised ten minutes to say that Joanna had definitely left Moy around five o'clock – the man on duty at Moy's main gate had signed her out and had unlocked the doors himself, and seen her get into her car and drive away.

'But you said her car's still at your house?'

'Yes.'

'Ah. Yes, that's worrying, isn't it?' He had sounded genuinely concerned. Selina wondered if he had found Joanna attractive. He said, 'Would you let me know what happens? Could I phone you tomorrow, to see if there's any news?'

Selina had said, Yes, certainly, and Dr Irvine had said that if he could help with any of the practicalities of the situation Selina was to be sure to let him know.

It was the practicalities of the situation that were concerning Selina now. What to do, and in what order to do it. Whom to telephone. Joanna's husband? But he was travelling in Spain somewhere. The police? But would the police be interested in an adult who had only been missing for twenty-four hours? Selina thought it was more likely that they would assume Joanna had gone off with a lover – her car was still here, and there were no signs of a struggle anywhere, surely mute proof that wherever she was, she had gone there voluntarily? Was it possible – was it credible? – that Joanna had stolen out at dead of night while Selina slept, to meet someone and run away with him? Selina was not very familiar with the ethics of running away with a lover, but she thought this sounded possible.

But one of the first practicalities was clearly to make a check on the things in Joanna's bedroom to see what might be missing. Selina did this conscientiously, asking Emily Frost to help her so that no one could later accuse her of stealing anything or reading any private letters.

Today Emily was wearing her hair slicked flat to her head, held there by some kind of unguent. It made her look as if she had been half drowned in a rainstorm.

'I would not, of course, *dream* of reading letters not intended for me, or invading a guest's privacy in any way whatsoever,' she said to Emily, who had drifted across to the window and was staring out over the old orchard. 'But people are so suspicious nowadays. My great-aunts, Rosa and Flora, who brought me up, were very strict about respecting other people's privacy, although we did not often have people to stay.'

'No visitors?' asked Emily, coming back into the room, and Selina said, Well, the vicar sometimes came to Saturday afternoon tea, and the doctor and his daughter used occasionally to come in for sherry before Sunday lunch. Or one of Aunt Flora's church groups might meet in the sitting room if the church hall was booked.

'What about your friends?' Emily was peering into the deep old-fashioned wardrobe. 'Didn't you have schoolfriends at weekends or anything like that?'

But Great-uncle Matthew had not cared for shrieking schoolgirls stravaiging about the place. Selina had occasionally been invited to birthday parties or picnics, but Great-aunt Rosa had said you could not really accept invitations without returning them, and to do so was difficult on account of disturbing Matthew's work, so most of the invitations had to be declined.

But Selina was not going to say any of this, and certainly not to someone employed to help with the cooking. She said, briskly, that they must get on; they must see if there was anything that might give them a clue as to Mrs Kent's whereabouts.

Emily was surprisingly helpful when it came to sorting through Joanna's clothes. She said there were quite a lot of things still here – the bronze chenille jacket, for instance, and that smashing red silk skirt as well. 'I don't think she'd have left those behind if she was running away with a lover, do you?' she said. 'They're much too nice to leave. Expensive as well. But I think there was a darkish suit, and I can't see that in here, can you?'

Selina was not very sure what Joanna might have worn to give her talk to the Moy prisoners, but a darkish suit sounded appropriate. She volunteered, rather hesitantly, the suggestion that there seemed to be a couple of other things missing – a jacket and some trousers, she thought, and one or two blouses. Emily had not heard anyone use the word *blouse* for years. She asked about underthings. Would Joanna have put them in the chest of drawers?

But Selina did not think they could look through undergarments which would not tell them anything anyway, for how could either of them know what Joanna had brought with her?

Emily considered saying that if Joanna had really gone off with somebody, she might well have invested in dazzling new underwear anyway and ditched the existing lot, but decided against it. She opened the drawers and glanced over the contents without disturbing them in case there was anything that might help, but there seemed only to be underwear and tights and a couple of cotton nightshirts. She asked about shoes and bags.

'Now shoes and handbags I *do* know about,' said Selina. 'I always notice good shoes and handbags.' She told Emily what Great-aunt Rosa used to say about being able to tell a lady by her accessories, and Emily said, rather blankly, 'Oh, right.'

'Her *black* shoes are missing, and also a black handbag. But the large *brown* bag – the one she had when she arrived – is here.'

'Two handbags?' Emily usually stuffed anything she needed into a jazzily coloured tote bag. 'Would she have brought two handbags with her?'

'Oh, yes. She would *never* have carried a brown bag with that dark grey suit,' said Selina at once. 'And both her suitcases are here, as well.'

'And,' said Emily suddenly, 'the computer.' She crossed to the small table that Joanna had used for working, and flipped the laptop open. 'I didn't see it before. Uh – Miss March, I don't think Joanna would have left this behind. Not voluntarily.'

'But she'd have taken any papers with her.' Selina had seen the laptop, but she had not realised that it was a computer. She had thought it was a briefcase. 'She'd have put typed notes or anything of that kind into her bag.'

'Not really. She'd more likely have everything stored on hard disk,' said Emily. 'For printing out when she got home. There's no printer here, and I don't remember seeing one.'

This was all incomprehensible to Selina. She regarded the flat leather-topped oblong, wondering if this was one of the practicalities she had been worried about.

'I think,' said Emily after a moment, 'that you'd better phone the police after all, don't you? Or maybe it would be better to try reaching her husband first. Is there any way you could do that?'

Gillian, phoned for help, thought the Rosendale Institute would certainly know where Joanna's husband might be reached: they were a very reputable organisation and they should be contacted. Selina did not like to say she did not want to get involved in discussions with unknown people about Mr Kent's possible whereabouts and Joanna's disappearance. She said, non-committally, that she would think about it.

'If you've got Joanna Savile's address I could drive round there and see if there're any signs of recent habitation,' said Gillian, but Selina did not think this was necessary, or at least not yet.

'But you ought to phone the police,' said Gillian. 'They'd be able to get a message to her husband. If she's really vanished, he'll have to know.'

'But, Gill dear,' said Selina a bit awkwardly, 'supposing Joanna has – well, run away with somebody?'

Gillian paused, and then, obviously choosing her words carefully, said, 'I don't think that if you were planning on going hand-in-hand into the sunset with a lover, you'd do the vanishing from Inchcape.'

Selina said, oh yes, she quite saw that.

'There's probably some very ordinary explanation,' said Gillian. 'I should just go on with life as if nothing's happened. Would you like me to come up? For moral support? I expect it's a bit daunting for you on your own—'

'Oh, there's no need for you to come all this way,' said Selina at once. 'I believe I'll just report it to the police, and let them do whatever is necessary. And I can always telephone the vicar or Lorna Laughlin in a crisis. You remember Lorna?'

Gillian did remember Lorna, who had recommended Emily, and was the nearest thing Selina had to a friend. She was glad to think that at least Selina, funny old darling, had someone to call on. She asked how Lorna was.

'She's very well,' said Selina. And then, 'D'you know, I believe you're right about going on with life as if nothing had happened, Gill. That's exactly what I shall do.'

It was almost dark when Krzystof Kent eventually reached Inchcape, and huge bunches of purple storm-clouds were massing overhead. It was probably symptomatic of his state of mind, but as he swung the car off the main road and followed the signs for Inchcape, there was a moment when it felt as if the storm was stalking him. It seemed to be staying about half a mile behind him, never quite catching him up, but persistently there.

It was the kind of thing that Joanna would have turned into a joke: she would have made some comment about warnings from the old forest gods and probably sketched a vivid word-picture of Thor, petulant and shoulder-hunching with Donner and Blitzen – 'You said *I* could have the next storm, you *promised*,' and Thor dropping his hammer on somebody's toe – 'I *told* you to mind where you left that thing.'

Joanna would have conjured up the absurd cartoon images vividly and swiftly because she always did, and if she turned out to be dead that was one of the many many things about her that would haunt Krzystof.

'There's probably some perfectly ordinary explanation,' his boss had said, when he finally managed to reach Krzystof at the villa near Pamplona that the small team had adopted as a temporary headquarters. 'I only got the call about it yesterday, so it really is still only a matter of forty-eight hours . . . well, seventy-two to be absolutely accurate. Can you get a flight back to the UK right away? You'd be better to fly up to Aberdeen and hire a car to drive across, from the sound of things.'

Krzystof said this was what Joanna had done. It was a fearsomely long drive from London to Inchcape.

'We'll set that up for you,' Krzystof's boss had said. 'It'll be easier to do it from here than from your end. We'll get you on a flight, and arrange for a car at the other end. Take as long a leave as you need, of course, and don't hesitate to call on me for anything.' He had repeated, in his kindly way, that when Krzystof reached Scotland he would probably find that there was a quite straightforward explanation.

Krzystof devoutly hoped that his boss was right, but the trouble was that the explanation might be simply that Joanna had run off with somebody else.

She had certainly not sounded as if she was going off with a lover when they parted. 'If you're swanning off to

205

northern Spain I might as well soak up a bit of Scottish atmosphere for the new plot,' she had said. 'I've got to deliver the new manuscript in six months – I must have been mad to agree to that deadline, because it's going to be a bit of a scramble. But I expect I can get a cottage or maybe a peaceful b and b for a week or two, and when you get back you can join me. I'll work during the day while you scour the glens for some new relics for the Rosendale – the dagger that Rob Roy used or Charles Stewart's drinking mug or something. It'll make a nice change for you after looking for Inquisition torture instruments. And we'll meet up every evening and I'll tell you what Jack Tallent's been up to and whether he's solved the murder, the old goat, and we'll eat Scotch salmon and fresh trout, and drink Glenfiddich in front of a log fire.'

Would anyone contemplating running away with a lover really have talked like that? But then maybe Joanna had not met the lover until she got here.

She had not found any holiday cottages for rent, but the Tourist Information Centre near to Stornforth had put her onto a bed-and-breakfast place. 'It's a tiny place called Inchcape,' Joanna had said. 'It's about midway between the Cairngorm and Grampian mountains, and it's so remote it's barely a dot on the map. In fact it's very nearly as far north as you can get without actually falling off the edge and having to swim for Norway. But I think I'll like it there.'

She had liked it very much. When Krzystof checked in at their flat before flying to Aberdeen, he found a long, diary-type letter from Joanna on the mat. 'This is so you'll know where I've ended up,' she had written. 'And also how to reach Inchcape. I know from bitter experience that anything sent into the field won't reach you, so I'm adding a bit to this letter as I go along, which is a bad substitute for actually being able to talk to you, but all I've got at the moment. I'll send it to the flat for when you get back there.'

She had fallen in love with Teind House right away. 'It's a marvellous old place,' she had written. 'I don't think it's been modernised since about 1930, and the lady who owns it – Miss Selina March – doesn't look as if she's been modernised much, either; in fact she looks as if she fell into a fragment of some pre-World War II era and never managed to climb out again. Remember when we went to see my grandmother before we were married? Domed glass covers with wax flowers underneath, and sun-faded rooms and dark heavy furniture glowering in corners? That's Teind House. But just for contrast, flitting in and out of it all is a delightful child called Emily Frost who's somehow connected with Moy but comes up to Teind to help with bits of housework. She's rather attractive: she's got one of those three-cornered faces, and she has the most amazing wardrobe of hairstyles.'

On what seemed to be her second day at Inchcape, she had written, 'I've agreed to give a talk to some of the inmates of Moy – the asylum for the criminally insane, which is probably Inchcape's main, if macabre, claim to posterity. It won't be in the least dangerous – there's a rather good-looking Dr Irvine who's going to hold my hand while I'm there. I suspect he might like to hold a bit more than my hand if I gave him the signal, because he looks as if he might be a bit of a wolf on the quiet. Did you look Hungarianly brooding and revengeful when you read that, Krzystof darling? You needn't. I'll let you know how the talk goes, and we'll take Patrick Irvine out for a swish dinner when you get here, as a thank you. As a matter of fact, I suspect Emily has a bit of a yen for him, although I'm not sure if either of them realises it – he's years older than she is. I hope it doesn't end with him breaking the child's heart, because like most wolves he's probably a heart-breaker. Maybe it's a reaction to being shut up with those poor mad killers for most of the week.

'But mad or sane, Moy's a dour, bleak old place, Krzystof . . .'

Moy, when he saw it from the road, surprised Krzystof. It was stark and bleak, just as Joanna had said, and it stood on a ridge of high ground, a little apart from the village, so that it gave the impression of frowning down over the little cluster of houses and the village shop and the church.

It was more modern than Krzystof had been visualising – concrete block walls and efficient, intercom-wired gates – and he supposed his image had been coloured by all the fearsome legends that trickled down from the nineteenth century. Without realising it, he had been expecting to see a dark brooding madhouse – a nightmarish blend of every bleak house ever created. Dotheboys Hall and Mr Bumble's workhouse. That stark and pitiless institution in William Horwood's remarkable book *Skallagrig*. All fiction, though.

It was dusk when he eventually reached Teind House, bouncing the hire car over the rutted track, and peering through the strong, savage thunder-rain that had just started to lash against the windscreen.

But there was more than enough daylight left to see the irregular-shaped old house that seemed to have grown up out of the hillside of its own accord. A dull, heavy half-light trickled down over it, and as Krzystof drew up he caught sight, through the surrounding trees, of what looked like an old Celtic round tower. In the dying light the house looked grim and faintly uncanny, but there were squares of yellow at the downstairs windows, which looked warm and welcoming, and Krzystof, exhausted from the journey, was insensibly cheered by them. There was an old-fashioned wrought-iron carriage lamp over the door, as well; it sent out a friendly amber glow. Journey's end.

He climbed out of the car, and plied the door knocker. As he heard footsteps approach from the other side there was a crash of thunder overhead. Lightning split the skies and, as if some celestial lighting man were obeying a cue, Teind House's lights flickered uncertainly several times, and then went out.

CHAPTER SIXTEEN

———❖———

As Joanna had said in her letter, Teind House seemed to belong to an age that had vanished fifty years ago, and Selina March seemed to belong to it as well.

She was a rather colourless lady with indeterminate features and soft brown hair, and she was apologetic about the power failure, which was apparently a regular occurrence during a storm. After she had explained this, she was timidly welcoming, hanging up Krzystof's raincoat, and then anxiously deploying oil lamps at predetermined points around the hall. Two, it seemed, had to go on each side of a huge and hideous grandfather clock that was ticking sonorously to itself like a beating heart encased in mahogany, and not until all this had been satisfactorily dealt with did Miss March lead the way to the second floor, where Krzystof's room was situated.

'Strictly speaking, Mr Kent, it's really an attic,' explained

Miss March, a touch defensively. 'And normally I would not *dream* of housing a guest up here. But it has been repainted and everything is quite clean, and there is a bathroom on the half-landing. My goddaughter said it would be ideal for your wife to work in.'

'Yes, she was right.' Joanna would have liked this room with its innocent old-fashioned charm; she would have found it congenial and peaceful.

'It's rather a – a *feminine* room, I'm afraid, but I thought you would like to have it,' said Selina. 'I thought it might make your wife seem nearer.'

'That's very thoughtful of you.'

'Mrs Kent's things are still here, but of course I asked my helper, Emily Frost, to give it a really *thorough* turn-out before you arrived.'

The room was quite large, and even by the light of an oil lamp Krzystof could see that it was spotlessly clean. The high, old-fashioned bed with its beautiful patchwork quilt was neatly made up and there was a faint scent of lavender furniture polish and of old, old timbers and generations of wood fires.

And despite Emily Frost's really thorough turn-out the room was so piercingly redolent of Joanna that for a moment Krzystof thought he was not going to be able to stay here after all. He stood in the doorway, holding up the oil lamp so that golden pools of light lay across the old polished floorboards, and the sense of her presence, the feeling of the essential Joanna-ness, was suddenly so strong that the sick fear and loneliness almost overpowered him anew.

To dispel this, he set his case down and crossed the room to the window. 'It's a remote place, isn't it? Is that an old Celtic round tower beyond the trees?'

'Yes, it is.'

'I saw it from the road. I thought that was what it was.'

'How interesting that you recognise it,' said Selina March. 'Very few people have ever seen one.'

'I've seen them in Ireland,' said Krzystof. 'While I was working. There's quite a famous one in Cashel.'

'My Great-uncle Matthew used to tell me that round towers were built by monks around the ninth and tenth century as watchtowers, or for storing valuables.'

'That's the commonly held theory,' said Krzystof, still peering through the darkness. The storm seemed to be grumbling itself away somewhere across the North Sea, and a watery moon was starting to come out. He could see the tower quite clearly across the tops of trees. He said, 'But I have heard one bizarre hypothesis that claims the towers were built as antennae – huge resonant systems that could collect and store energy from the earth and from the skies.'

'Goodness me.'

'It's not a very widely accepted explanation,' said Krzystof, turning back from the window, 'although like most quirky ideas there's a bit of a basis for belief. And quite a lot of the round towers in Cashel are constructed of materials that do possess magnetic properties. Limestone and red sandstone and granite. The theory is that the towers were once used to draw down power from the sun, or tap into the cosmos.'

'How remarkable.' Krzystof glanced at her and saw that she meant this, and was not just offering a polite platitude. She was staring through the window towards the tower, as if seeing it with a new perspective. But then she seemed to recollect her guest, and asked, a touch anxiously, whether Krzystof had eaten supper. 'The Black Boar would usually provide a meal, but with the power being off there might be problems—'

'I ate on the plane,' said Krzystof. 'I truly don't need anything.'

'Oh. Oh, then perhaps I could offer you a – a cup of tea? The range will still be burning, and a kettle can easily be boiled. Or, no, wait now, after your drive you will be chilled. My great-uncle Matthew kept a very good stock of liquor, and I believe there are one or two of his bottles left . . . A glass of whisky, perhaps?'

'Miss March, you're a delight,' said Krzystof. 'A glass of whisky is exactly what I need.'

He saw he had pleased her and once downstairs she produced a dusty bottle of something dark and faintly oily looking. Krzystof saw that it was usquebaugh and that the label was handwritten. Illicitly brewed on some local still in the days of Great-uncle Matthew, perhaps? His hostess poured it into a small glass with the nervous air of one expecting an explosion. 'Occasionally I take a glass of sherry, or a small glass of rum if I have a cold. But my Great-uncle Matthew always spoke very highly of this.'

'I'm sure it'll be very good,' said Krzystof, eyeing it with misgiving.

'I expect you're used to something more exotic.'

'You're getting hung up on the name, Miss March,' said Krzystof. 'I'm only half Hungarian, and I was born in England and brought up here. I'm very English indeed, really. I even watch cricket and drink English beer.'

'Oh, well, in that case . . .'

Krzystof took the glass, and said, '*Ege'sze'ge're!*' which was 'Cheers' in Hungarian and which pleased Miss March, as he had thought it might. It was interesting to hear other languages, wasn't it? She did not, herself, speak any language other than English; the aunts and the great-uncle who brought her up had not thought it necessary.

'The Tower of Babel has a lot of answer for,' said Krzystof, and drank the contents of the glass.

The usquebaugh was terrible. It went down like scalding turpentine and threatened to come up again like broken glass. Whoever Great-uncle Matthew had been, and whenever he had lived, either he had had no palate and a cast-iron digestive system, or the stuff had simply not been properly distilled in the first place.

But under Miss March's anxious eye Krzystof managed to down it with a modicum of equanimity, although in case she should offer a refill he set the glass firmly down and asked if she could tell him anything more about Joanna's disappearance. 'I only had the sketchiest of details from my boss, and I flew back from Spain and then up here almost immediately.'

Selina March plunged at once into voluble explanations, starting with phone calls made to the Black Boar

214

where Joanna had apparently eaten lunch and supper most days – 'since I cannot undertake to provide anything other than breakfast' – progressing to the conversation with Dr Irvine at Moy where Joanna had given a talk, and ending up with the appeal made to the police station at Stornforth, requesting assistance and advice.

'And they were very courteous and came out to the house the same day, but they explained that in the case of an adult, and where there is no evidence of *violence*, they have no mandate to set up a search for forty-eight hours.'

'But her things are all still here? Her clothes?' Krzystof had not looked in the wardrobe in his room yet, but it was a safe bet that either Miss March or the Stornforth police had done so. 'Suppose she just went walking somewhere, and broke her ankle or something—'

'The police did search the immediate area, of course, with that in mind. But although most of your wife's clothes are still here I am reasonably certain that a couple of outfits I had seen her wearing have gone. A darkish suit that Emily Frost thinks she wore to give a talk at Moy, and also a brown jacket and trousers. And a brown skirt and two blouses, I think – a cream one and a coppery-gold one. Oh, and shoes and a black handbag – she brought two bags with her, I do know that, because I admired them.' She glanced at him and said, rather diffidently, 'You would be better able to tell if anything was missing, of course—'

'I don't know that I would,' said Krzystof. 'I've been abroad for two months, remember. Joanna might have bought any number of new things while I was away.'

But by this time it was fairly clear to Krzystof that Selina March, the Stornforth police, and probably anyone in Inchcape who had met Joanna, all believed she had gone off with a man. Krzystof would probably have thought so himself, given the circumstances, given Joanna's looks and personality, and given his own apparent lack of attraction, as well. He remembered that he had meant to have his hair cut before coming back to England.

He thanked Selina March for the drink, and stood up. It had been a long and difficult day, he said, and Miss March said, dear me, yes, all that *travelling*, and gave him one of the smaller oil lamps so that he could see the way back up to his room.

Joanna's clothes were hanging in the deep old wardrobe, just as Selina had said. Krzystof opened the door and surveyed them. He recognised Miss March's description of a dark suit – it was one that Joanna usually wore if she had to look businesslike, and it was certainly not here. Exactly what *was* here?

It felt like the worst kind of invasion to search through his wife's clothes – to look in all the pockets and then to open the dressing-table drawers – but it was the only link Krzystof had with her and it had to be done. Everything was faintly imprinted with the scent Joanna always used; Krzystof could have done without that additional agony.

But there was nothing to be found, except for the occasional crumpled tissue or handful of loose change in a jacket pocket. There were no receipts from bars or petrol stations or shops, and there were no mysterious telephone numbers or names scribbled on scraps of paper.

Of course there were not. He frowned and closed the door firmly.

How about the suitcases and bags? In common with most men, Krzystof did not pay a great deal of attention to handbags, but Selina March had been definite that as well as the two cases Joanna had brought two handbags with her and that the black one was missing. A brown bag was lying in a corner of the wardrobe, but when Krzystof opened it there was only a comb and a scribbled note of directions in Joanna's writing for finding Inchcape and Teind House. He had a sudden image of his wife driving out here, the directions propped up on the dashboard. The car had been collected by the hire firm, but presumably it had been checked by the police for any clues. Still, it would not hurt to make sure. He would ask about that while he was in Stornforth.

After ten more minutes he sat down on the bed, a mounting puzzlement shouldering aside the other emotions. He had no idea what clothes Joanna had brought with her – obviously she had not brought her entire wardrobe to Inchcape – but it was difficult to believe she would voluntarily have left so much stuff behind. Clothes could be bought new, of course, always supposing there was enough money, and Krzystof admitted, a trifle grimly, that if you were running away with somebody you might very well want to buy enticing new underthings. There was no toothbrush or sponge to be found, but the small travel hair-dryer was still in its case, and the zipped-up cosmetic bag of cleansing cream and hand lotion and deodorant was tucked into the side

217

of the suitcase. Would any female really run away with a lover and leave her hair-dryer and deodorant behind?

It was almost midnight. Krzystof remembered that he had been travelling for a good part of today and for most of yesterday as well, and that he was unbearably tired. He went along to the bathroom for a quick wash, and once back in the attic room rummaged in his suitcase for his favourite photograph of Joanna, setting it on the window sill where it would be the first thing he saw when he awoke tomorrow morning. It was a good likeness; it showed very clearly the dark eyes and brown hair. Krzystof had taken the photograph himself shortly after they were married, which was probably why it was one of the few shots that showed Joanna's extraordinary look of mischievous seduction: eyes slanted, mouth curved. Until this week he would have wagered everything he possessed that nobody save himself had seen that look since their wedding, but now he was not sure. Had there been a lover? Had he been waiting for her, here in this odd, ghost-ridden house that had somehow got itself stuck in another era, and had they gone off together?

Or was the explanation more macabre: had Joanna fallen to her death somewhere out here, and was her body lying undiscovered in some lonely glen? Selina March had said Joanna's car had been neatly parked outside the house, which seemed to rule out the possibility of a road smash. But it did not rule out the possibility of other accidents. Krzystof remembered with unease the closeness of Moy. But surely if there had been any trouble there – any escapes – it would be known.

He was dizzy with tiredness by this time, but he sat on the window seat for a while longer, staring through the uncurtained glass. Teind House was still in darkness, but one or two lights were showing in the distance now, which presumably meant that electricity was being patchily restored.

The Round Tower reared up over the tops of the trees: Krzystof could see the top of it, and he could make out a couple of narrow slit-like windows. Miss March had said the place was fenced off these days because it had been pronounced unsafe; most people were a little afraid of it, she had said. She had especially mentioned to Mrs Kent not to go too near it.

Krzystof had not said that Joanna would have been attracted by the tower and would certainly have been intrigued by the faint whiff of pre-Christian rites that clung to it, because it had not seemed relevant. But he found himself wondering whether Joanna might have gone to look at the tower, and he thought he would walk across to it himself tomorrow morning. By daylight it would probably simply be an ugly ruin, but tonight, its dark walls silvered with the cold northern moonlight, and with the scudding stormclouds behind it, it was more than enough to dredge up reminders of all of those ancient pagan customs that clung to round towers.

He came back into the room and got into bed. As he tried to sleep, he felt his mind reaching out to Joanna who had slept in this bed and used this room. He had never been able to decide about telepathy, but he and Joanna had been so well attuned that they had often picked up one another's thoughts or started to say exactly the same thing at exactly the same moment. If Joanna was still alive surely she would be picking up his frantic anxiety about her now? But I can't feel anything at all, thought Krzystof, and was aware of a cold clutch of despair. Don't be dead, Joanna. I couldn't bear you to be dead.

But although he could not sense anything of Joanna, he could sense other, slightly uncomfortable, things inside this dim, old-fashioned house. 'That's the Hungarian half coming out, Krzystof darling,' Joanna would have said, grinning the urchin-grin. 'The half that thinks it ought to be fey, and know about old romances and ancient ghosts and weird forest-spirits. *Rusalka* and *vila* and what not. You do trade on your Hungarian mama at times, don't you?'

Nobody but Joanna had ever spotted that Krzystof, born and brought up in England, did trade on the Hungarian half, usually at times when he was feeling particularly unsure of himself. It was a mask to hide behind and it was a good mask. But Joanna had seen the mask from the first, of course; she had seen behind it to the real person, and that was one of the reasons why Krzystof had fallen in love with her.

He thought he was not being Hungarian or fey about Teind House, though. At first encounter it felt like an ordinary, rather quiet, house, its atmosphere the atmosphere you got in places where people had lived uneventful lives, and there had mostly been old people and no children. As if the walls soaked up the long periods of silence and stillness.

220

But Krzystof had the feeling that Teind House might have other, less tranquil, things beneath its façade: he thought it might have dark memories and old unhappinesses, into which, if you were not careful, you might stumble by accident, in the way you could stumble into a pool of sour icy water in the dark . . .

He sat up in bed, punched the pillows crossly to make them more comfortable, dragged the covers around him, lay down again, and finally fell down into an uneasy sleep where he dreamed that Joanna was drowning in a bottomless pit of black and freezing water, and he was unable to reach her.

CHAPTER SEVENTEEN

A watery sunlight trickled into the small square room that Miss March had referred to as the breakfast room, and as Krzystof sat down at the neatly laid table a small, streak-haired creature wearing a purple T-shirt and rainbow-coloured combat trousers came in, bearing a platter of scrambled eggs and ham. Krzystof said good morning, and then realised that this must be Miss March's 'helper', Emily. He saw what Joanna had meant about the three-cornered face. It was a bit like being served breakfast by a Puck-character, who might disapprovingly have surveyed the mushroom table with its hazel-cups of mead and moon-parch'd grains of wheat and said, oh sod this, let's eat proper food this morning.

In addition to the eggs and ham, it seemed that the kettle was just boiling, so there would be tea any minute, although not orange juice because the fridge had defrosted itself during the power cut, and not coffee either on account of the percolator's having blown a fuse when the power came back on again.

'Tea's fine,' said Krzystof. 'Are you Emily? My wife – Joanna – mentioned you in a letter.'

The wood-sprite admitted gravely to being Emily, suddenly observed that the milk jug was missing and that Miss March would go ballistic if she spotted it, and darted into some nether region to remedy the omission.

When the errant milk jug had been brought, and with it a large pot of tea, she said, 'It must be agony having your wife suddenly vanish.'

'Yes, it is. The police think she's gone off with a lover.' He watched Emily covertly to see what reaction this got.

Emily said at once, 'She wouldn't have done that.'

'You're the first person I've met in Inchcape who doesn't think so.'

'She missed you,' said Emily. 'There wasn't anyone else.'

'Did she tell you that?' Krzystof poured himself a cup of tea.

'No, but she – when she talked about you – about missing you – her whole face changed. As if a light had come on inside. You don't look like that if you're having an affair.'

Krzystof stared at her. 'Thank you, Emily,' he said at last.

'Did you know her laptop's still upstairs?'

'Is it? Are you sure? I didn't see it.'

'Miss March put it inside the large suitcase. She thought it would be safer there.' Emily hesitated, and then said, 'Your wife came here to work, didn't she? To make notes for a new book, or research a plot or something like that. She was here for four days before she vanished, and I'm sure she did quite a lot of work in her room. She wouldn't have gone off and left all that behind, would she?'

'No,' said Krzystof slowly. 'No, she wouldn't have done that.' He took a sip of the hot tea, and as she turned to go he said, 'Hold on a minute, Emily. You've got some connection with Moy, haven't you? I'm hoping to go up there after I've talked to the police at Stornforth, to see if I can pick up any clues to Joanna's disappearance – she gave a talk there, I think. But I don't know who I should ask to see.'

It appeared that the Moy connection was via Emily's father who was one of the wing governors at Moy. 'He'd be very happy to talk to you, I should think – his name's Don Frost – but it's Dr Irvine you really ought to see,' said Emily, and Krzystof saw her cheeks turn pink when she said Irvine's name. 'That was who your wife saw,' said Emily firmly, and Krzystof remembered what Joanna had said about a bit of a yen, although he suspected that Emily was a bit old to be suffering from a bit of a yen. The look was deceptive; she was probably twenty or even twenty-one.

He said, 'Thank you. I'll phone him after breakfast and see if I can get out to see him later today.'

Krzystof had been in too many of the world's odd places

not to know that strong emotion could print itself on the air, could even bury itself in walls and stones and timbers as well, lingering on for years sometimes. But he had not been prepared for the bleak loneliness and the bitter despair that lingered within Moy.

There was a feeling of tension, as well: of anger and bitterness and bewilderment, all tangled messily up together, but all rigidly suppressed. As if a lid had been clamped firmly onto a seething cauldron whose contents were just that little bit too violent for it, so that tiny hissing spurts of emotion escaped at intervals.

'I don't think I can be of much help,' said Patrick, when Krzystof reached his office later in the morning. 'I wish to God I could – you must be absolutely frantic with worry. Let me see. Well, your wife was certainly here on Thursday afternoon. She got here just before two, talked to a dozen or so of the inmates, and left around five. I didn't see her actually leave, but I did check with the gatehouse when Miss March phoned. The man on duty was definite about her driving away.'

Patrick had seen, almost straight away, that he had been quite wrong about the kind of man Joanna Savile had married. Krzystof Kent was neither wimpish nor dominant. He was a thin, slightly untidy young man of around thirty-five, with gentle eyes and hands, and an intelligent mouth. He had very clear grey eyes, black-rimmed, and Patrick noticed the high, eastern European cheekbones. Had Joanna said Romanian or Hungarian or half Hungarian? Despite the gentleness, he thought there was a hidden core of toughness here, and he thought that this was a very good partner for Joanna. He hoped very strenuously that she would turn up unscathed, and then he hoped even more strenuously that she had not run away with a lover.

Krzystof Kent said, 'I've talked to the police in Stornforth. They've made a bit of a search, but because a few of her things are missing – extra clothes and shoes – it looks as if she went voluntarily. As if it was planned. So they aren't prepared to mount a full-blown search.' He leaned forward. 'But I don't believe she went off like that. I can't. Her letters— I'd have known if there was a lover in the picture. So I'm trying to scrape up a few clues – something that will help me find out where she is. Or something that will make the police think again about a proper search.'

Patrick felt an unexpected pang. How must it feel to be so extremely close to someone that you could speak with such absolute conviction? Krzystof Kent wasn't just hoping that Joanna hadn't gone off with another man, he *knew* she hadn't.

'I wondered,' said Krzystof, 'if Joanna had seemed to – to latch onto any of the people here? I'm groping in the dark, you understand. But the police have helped me to piece together a sketchy timetable, and it sounds as if she vanished just after leaving here. The car she hired was left outside Teind House, but Miss March didn't hear her actually come in.'

'The inference being that she parked the car and went off to – wherever she is now?'

'Yes. Either she went very quietly into the house and took some things from the wardrobe, or she had them in the car already and – well, transferred them to another car.' He paused, and then said, 'I know this sounds peculiar, but I wondered if anything was said while she was here that might have – well, unsettled her.' He made a quick impatient gesture with one hand. 'Or that might have dredged up some memory—'

'And triggered off a bout of amnesia, or a psychotic disturbance?' You're clutching at straws, my friend, thought Patrick. People with amnesia don't collect extra clothes before they vanish. But as if he had picked this up Krzystof Kent said, 'Agatha Christie vanished for a couple of weeks, and nobody ever really had a satisfactory explanation.'

'If I said that the disappearance was very good publicity for Miss Christie's books, would you punch me?'

'Yes, but I'd probably apologise afterwards,' said Krzystof, and smiled.

'Your wife struck me as being particularly well balanced,' said Patrick after a moment. 'But there was one very small thing—'

'Yes?'

'The talk she gave was by way of a *quid pro quo*. She was hoping to get some background for a book – I expect you know about that. She offered to give the talk so that she could pick up a few details about ordinary daily life inside Moy.' Patrick smiled. 'Always allowing for the fact that life inside Moy, or any other criminal asylum, is seldom ordinary.' He paused, and then said, 'I thought she seemed particularly interested in one of the inmates.'

'You did? Who was it?'

Patrick hesitated again. I could be wrong. I could be sending this nice, clever, worried young man onto a wildly wrong track. But there was that look in Joanna Savile's eyes—

'It was Mary Maskelyne,' he said, and Krzystof frowned, as if processing this information.

'The teenage murderess?' he said, at last.

'Yes. She was transferred here two or three weeks ago.'

'I don't remember reading about that. But I've been abroad for several weeks so I could easily have missed it. I can't think of any reason why Joanna would find her especially interesting,' said Krzystof. 'It was a *cause célèbre* in the Sixties, wasn't it?'

'Yes, Maskelyne killed both her parents. She was only fourteen at the time and it was just after the hanging law was repealed; if it had been three or four years earlier and she had been three or four years older she would probably have been hanged. She might have been released at eighteen but it was believed that she had killed the matron of the YOH – they never proved it and the verdict was accidental death, but I don't think anyone was in much doubt. So the Home Secretary was recommended not to release her. And then later, of course, Maskelyne killed twice more.'

'And Joanna seemed interested in her?'

'Yes.'

'She's presumably completely mad, this woman?'

'A lot of people would tell you that she has quite

228

prolonged intervals of complete sanity,' said Patrick dryly.

'You're hedging. Patient confidentiality?'

'Partly. I won't bore you with labels, but I can tell you that there's a strong personality disorder at base.'

'Multiple personality?' asked Krzystof, hesitantly. 'Schizophrenia?'

'The word covers a multitude of demons, but it's as good a one as any. She certainly has delusions.' Patrick had been watching the other man closely, but there had seemed to be no reaction at all to Maskelyne's name. He said, 'Joanna asked me about Maskelyne prior to the talk. She seemed particularly interested in her. It might just have been the publicity that had surrounded the transfer – the original murders were dragged out and re-examined by the wretched media, of course, and your wife might simply have been thinking it would be a good case study for her research. But—'

'But you think there was a bit more to it?'

'Yes, I do, actually.' Patrick hesitated. Do I tell him that the interest seemed to be two-way? That I saw Maskelyne's face take on that look – that *hungry* look – when she saw Joanna? Choosing his words carefully, he said, 'Is it at all likely that your wife had ever known Mary Maskelyne?'

'I don't think so,' said Krzystof. 'I should think she'd have mentioned it. And anyway there'd be a gap of about twenty years between their ages, wouldn't there?'

'Yes, but Joanna might have known the family. Or her mother or father might have known them. If that was so she'd probably have been a bit curious about Mary. Anyone would.'

'Joanna's parents died in a car crash when she was at university,' said Krzystof. 'And she was an only child. There are a couple of aunts and cousins, but they aren't very close. I don't really think there's any connection with Mary Maskelyne; in fact I think you were probably right about Joanna seeing the case as a good one to use for background.'

'I expect you're right.'

Patrick waited, and after a moment Krzystof said, 'Would you allow me to see her?'

'Maskelyne?'

'Yes.'

There was a longer pause this time. Then Patrick said, 'If you think it would do any good—'

'She might remember something that Joanna said. I'd be extremely careful,' said Krzystof. 'I'd observe any rules or security checks you wanted.'

'All right,' said Patrick, after a moment. 'We'll do it now, if you like. Her room's in D wing – that's at the centre of the building, on the first floor.'

'She has her own room?' Krzystof had been imagining wards, grim dormitories.

'They all do. It's the only way we can operate,' said Patrick. 'We simply can't risk putting them all together. And when they do meet we see to it that they're always accompanied by at least one attendant to every four.'

'They do get together at times, then?'

'Yes, certainly. Most of them eat together – there's

230

a quite cheerful dining room downstairs. Some of the patients are too severely disturbed to be allowed to mix, but quite a number can. We give them group therapy and occupational therapy – music sessions, educational classes.' He stood up and reached for a set of keys in the drawer of the desk.

'I'll have to come in with you, of course, but you can talk to her fairly freely. I won't interfere unless I think I can help. Or,' he said, 'unless I think she's edged you into a potentially dangerous thread of discussion.'

'Is that likely?'

'She might. How much do you know about her?'

'I know she butchered her parents, but I don't know very much more.'

'Looked at objectively she makes an interesting study,' said Patrick. 'She's extremely clever, by the way. That surprises you?' he said, for Krzystof had looked up sharply.

'Yes. I don't know why it should.'

'Maskelyne is clever and cunning and very devious,' said Patrick. 'However ordinary she might seem, she isn't ordinary in the least.' He thought for a moment, and then said, 'I don't think it's breaking confidentiality very much to say that in my opinion it's when she appears sane that she's at her most mad and her most dangerous.' He opened the door and stood back to let Krzystof go through. Krzystof noticed he locked the office door before leaving.

CHAPTER EIGHTEEN

The locking of her door every night was something Mary was still trying to get used to in Moy. After the outright no-privacy years in Broadacre, it was hard to adjust to Moy's covert watchfulness – to the sly spyholes in the door of every room, to the security cameras set high up in the corridors. It was difficult to sleep in a room where you knew the spyhole might slide back at any moment and someone might peer in.

It was difficult to sleep on the night after the writer woman, Joanna Savile, had given the talk. After lock-up Mary lay in bed, staring up at the ceiling, her mind seething with memories and images – Broadacre and the plan to become pregnant, and Ingrid.

Ingrid.

Beneath everything, like a dark and bitter undertow,

was the never-to-be-forgotten memory of how Ingrid, in the end, had betrayed her.

At the end of Joanna Savile's talk it had been quite easy and natural to go up to the little table and ask questions about writing. How did one begin? Ought you to choose your characters first and put them in your story, or was it better to think up the story first and then decide how to people it?

A couple of the others were there as well. They wanted to write short stories for magazines, or they wanted to write about their childhoods, or update *A Christmas Carol* for a play at Christmas. Mary thought all this was unbelievably dull, but she listened to everything that was said, nodding slowly at intervals as if she was finding it deeply absorbing, but all the time watching Joanna. Closer to, she was not as much like Ingrid as Mary had initially thought. She was thinner and her voice was different. More expensive. I hate you, thought Mary. You're successful and probably quite well off because you look fairly glossy. And you're wearing a wedding ring. I'll bet you've got a husband who's clever and successful as well, and I'll bet you had parents who doted on you.

Whether or not any of this was true, Joanna Savile was helpful and patient with everyone. She talked to the short-story aspirants about how you had to make every word count in that framework, and she talked to Mary about setting out a synopsis – a work-plan, she called it. Had Mary a novel actually in mind? Uh – was it OK to call her Mary, by the way?

'Yes, of course. And yes, I did think I'd like to try a

novel eventually,' Mary said. No need to admit to anyone yet that her book was going to be the story of her parents' cruel disinterest, and the story of Ingrid's betrayal.

Ingrid . . .

As she talked to Joanna, the curled-up darkness in her mind – the darkness that was becoming more and more enmeshed with Christabel's secret presence – was already starting to uncoil, and with it the familiar stir of excitement. I could do this. I could write my own story, and everyone would take notice of me again. Publicity. Interviews. The letters would come flooding in – perhaps a whole new generation would begin writing to her. And reviews – she remembered again about reviews in the newspapers. *Surprised to find such a degree of literacy from one who has been held at Her Majesty's pleasure for more than thirty years . . . Triumph for teenage murderess . . .*

There was something called the Koestler Prize as well; it was given for creative work done by people inside prisons or special institutions. One of the boys at Broadacre had been taking a City & Guilds course in photography and he had won a Koestler Prize. Mary had gone along to Moy's small library earlier today to find out a bit more about it, in case it might be useful. The write-up was mostly pretty boring, droning on about rewarding creativity and encouraging enterprise, and about how dedicated the judges were. Mary would just bet they got a fat fee for the judging, never mind that the article said they gave their services free.

But apparently there were several categories in the

award, and one of them was Poetry, Prose, and Play-writing. Hah! Exactly what she had hoped! She read on, and halfway down the page her attention was caught by one paragraph about the writing awards.

'In so far as the entrants have doubtless had enough judgement for one lifetime,' it said, 'we prefer to think we *assess* their contributions. So we look for imagination, verve and insight; writing which makes us stop and think. We cannot pretend it is always a joy to read; on the contrary, the outpourings of distress are frequently overwhelming. There are the tragedies of a thousand violent childhoods, loss and death; even the approach of release and freedom is sometimes recorded with a sense of fear.'

The outpourings of distress ... The tragedies of a thousand violent childhoods ... Yes.

Koestler Prize goes to Mary Maskelyne ... the headlines would read, or maybe it should be '*Prestigious*' *Koestler Prize* ... Yes, that was even better. And – *Astonishing confession of a child helplessly enduring the selfish cruelties of parents worshipping at the shrine of a dead daughter* ... *Betrayal and deceit from those she had trusted* ...

Mary could see the headlines as clearly as if they were already written. But it was necessary to appear modest and unassuming for the moment, and so when Joanna Savile asked if Mary was thinking of attempting a novel, Mary said, 'Well, I do know a novel's a big undertaking,' and smiled uncertainly. Was she sounding sufficiently diffident? She might as well embellish it a bit. She said, 'I expect a novel's what everyone wants to do eventually though, isn't it? But I thought I might start with some short stories. To get into training.'

'Short stories are very good discipline,' said Joanna March, smiling at Mary. She had a lovely smile, the bitch. Ingrid used to smile a bit like that, in the days when Mary still trusted her, in the days when Ingrid could still be trusted, in the days when Ingrid had still had a mouth that could smile and a tongue that could tell lies—

Ingrid . . .

Ingrid had not smiled on the night that Darren Clark died. She had not come to Mary's bedside until the next morning – until long after Mary had made her carefully hysterical accusation of rape, and long after the painful examination had been made. And *this time* there was no humiliating off-hand reference to no penetration, and *this time* there was no slighting instruction to mark her medical records as '*virgo intacta*'.

Ingrid had looked white and shocked that morning. She stood at the side of Mary's bed in the infirmary wing and looked down at her, her eyes unreadable. Funny how, when so much else had slithered from her memory, Mary could still remember Ingrid's eyes on that morning: bleak and hard. And Ingrid's mouth, the mouth that had done all those intimate things to Mary's body, had been thin and stern.

'You stupid, silly bitch,' she had said, speaking very softly so that the infirmary attendants in their little glass-walled office could not hear. 'What the fuck were you trying to do?'

'He raped me,' said Mary, staring at the unforgiving eyes. 'I wasn't trying to do anything. He made me go into the men's dormitory with him – he forced me there – and then he raped me. He hurt me a lot. I didn't know they could get as big as that; he was huge. I'm still bleeding from it.' Had there been a slight softening of Ingrid's expression at that?

'You killed him, though. Mary, you killed him.'

'I didn't mean to kill him. I was trying to defend myself. There was a Coke bottle— Listen, if you'd had that huge horrid thing rammed into you, making you bleed, you'd have grabbed anything handy and smashed it into him.'

'But you do know what you did to him afterwards, don't you, Mary?'

'Yes, I killed him. You've told me that.' Mary hunched a shoulder and turned her back on Ingrid. 'I can't remember it all,' she said, muffling her voice into the pillow. 'It's patchy, the things I remember. But I do remember that I was frightened. I'm still frightened if you want to know. I might be pregnant and that's very frightening indeed.'

'It's not that much of a possibility, surely—'

'Yes, it bloody is! He came inside me! I felt him!' It was unexpectedly embarrassing to say these things to Ingrid; Mary was glad that she was still burying her face in the pillow. 'What if I'm pregnant?' she said, mumbling the words.

'Oh, it wouldn't be a problem. They'll do a pregnancy test in a week or so, and if it's positive, they'll give you a D and C more or less automatically.'

'What?' Mary sat up in the bed and stared at Ingrid. 'You mean an abortion?'

'Mary, you wouldn't want—'

'They'll make me have an abortion,' said Mary, clenching her fists, feeling the hot fury start to rise. 'That's what you mean, isn't it?'

Ingrid said, very gently, 'Yes, Mary, that is what I mean.'

An abortion. And those hoped-for headlines, that new wave of interest in the infamous Mary Maskelyne who had been raped and who had given birth as a result, would never happen. All that would happen would be a squalid half-hour on some surgical table, and presumably a note on the medical record – another hateful belittling note! – and life would drag tediously and despairingly on.

It was at that moment that Mary began to hate Ingrid.

The pregnancy test was done one week later, and the result was positive. *Good*. Thank you, Darren Clark, poor bled-out body, stupid dickless corpse, lying in a cemetery somewhere. Thank you. A pity you never knew what you did for me, but there you are, life's a bitch and then you die.

Mary was allowed out of the infirmary after Broadacre's psychiatrists had finally stopped poking and prodding at her mind – '*Why* did you feel you had to mutilate him, Mary?' 'Because he fucked me, you wankers, why else d'you think?' – and after the other doctors had eventually stopped poking and prodding at her body.

'I'm going through with this,' she said to Ingrid. 'I'm

not having an abortion, not at any price.' Nor am I giving up those headlines, said her mind. *Teenage murderess gives birth to child after vicious rape . . .*

Ingrid said, 'But Mary, sweetheart, even if you could persuade the doctors to let you have the baby, once it was born they'd take it away and get it adopted. You couldn't possibly keep it. Not in here.' She took Mary's hand. 'They'll bring such a lot of pressure on you. Mostly because they'll all be afraid for their reputations. Rape in a government institution— If that got out, it would create such a row.'

'Oh, would it?' Innocent eyes, remember to give her the innocent-eyes look. (Yes, but hold on to those headlines, Mary, because that's what this is all for . . . *The notorious Mary Maskelyne yesterday gave birth to a son – a daughter . . . New episode in the tragic life of Sixties icon, Mary Maskelyne . . . 'I know I will never see my child again,' said Miss Maskelyne bravely, in an exclusive interview . . .*)

'I don't think they could actually *force* an abortion,' said Ingrid, after a moment. 'But they might make it very difficult for you to keep refusing.'

'I see,' said Mary slowly, not saying that what she really saw was that Ingrid was not prepared to put her head on the chopping block for Mary's sake. 'Yes, I see.'

To begin with, Broadacre's governor and Broadacre's doctors tried over and over to persuade Mary into what they called a termination.

'No,' she said, clinging to that one word. 'No.'

'Have you talked to your personal adviser?' they said. 'Really talked to her?'

'Personal advisers' were a new thing; an experiment of the Home Secretary's, who had gone on television to tell anyone who was interested that people in secure psychiatric units and asylums should be assigned personal advisers, each adviser taking on eight or ten inmates. This was a marvellous innovation, said the Home Secretary unctuously; it was the way forward for mental institutions and criminal asylums, and it was the humane way to treat hundreds of poor unfortunate souls. Most of the attendants and doctors at Broadacre who had listened had said, Jeez, what a lot of crap, the Home Secretary no more cared about being humane than Adolf Hitler: all he was doing was angling for a knighthood when he retired next year.

But the support Mary had wanted from Ingrid (and failed to get from the cold-hearted bitch!) came, in the end, from a totally unexpected quarter. It came from the prison chaplain.

To the chaplain, abortion, for whatever reason, was total anathema. He came to see Mary, talking to her for long hours, yacking on about the sanctity of human life, and about how only God, who bestowed life in the first place, had the right to take it back. He was ugly and tedious and it was a pity nobody had told him how distasteful it was to have hairs growing down from his nose, but he talked about sin and about restitution, and he gave Mary the argument she had needed to screw down the sanctimonious prigs who only cared about saving their careers and preserving their reputations.

Repentance. That was the reason she used to shut the clacking doctors and governors up when they came at her again with their representations and their persuasions. They wanted to hush everything up, of course; Mary knew that. But she donned the most innocent and the most hesitant of all her innocent and hesitant guises, and she said she understood, at last, how wicked she had been, and that she saw the birth of the child as a way to redress the balance. She had killed her parents, she said, and she knew now that it had been a truly evil thing to do. But with the chaplain's help she was presently groping her way towards some kind of forgiveness. Some kind of cleansing. Would they, then, have her kill again? she said.

It discomfited them, because these days a professing of religious beliefs did discomfit people. But it worked. She was allowed to continue with the pregnancy.

'But you do know that they'll take the child away for adoption?' said Ingrid. 'Mary, you do know that?'

Mary said slowly, 'The thing is that I've never had anything that was really and definitely my own. I never even had a dog or a cat. I'd like to know that I had a little boy or a little girl growing up somewhere in the world.' She took Ingrid's hand, moving her fingers intimately against the palm. 'We might even be together one day, you and I. They might let me out one day, and I might be able to have a share in the child.' She took a deep breath, and said, 'They might even let you adopt the child right from the start.'

'Mary, that wouldn't be possible—'

'Why not? People have children and careers these days. I read about it. There are day nurseries and things. You could do it if you really wanted to.'

'It simply wouldn't be allowed.'

'I thought you meant all those things you said to me,' said Mary, thrusting out her lower lip petulantly and snatching her hand back. 'About loving me. About wanting to be with me properly – a little house together somewhere, where we could grow old together.' Load of sentimental bollocks, said her mind; I wouldn't live with you if I was destitute and starving, you stupid ineffectual old dyke! Never had a man, and wouldn't know what to do with one anyway!

'Oh, Mary, sweetheart, of course I meant them! But—'

OK, time for a change of tactics. Mary said, very softly, 'Listen, Ingrid, if you don't do this for me – if you don't find a way to adopt this baby – I'll tell them all what we do together. I'll describe what you did to me that first time – up against the bathroom wall with the door locked. I'll say you forced me to do all those things.'

Ingrid's fear was instant and unmissable. She turned white, and the pupils of her eyes contracted to pinpoints. She's remembering Darren Clark, thought Mary. She's remembering what I did to him. In a tight, breathy voice, Ingrid said, 'Mary, don't threaten me— I'll do whatever you want. Of course I will.'

'I knew you meant what you said really,' said Mary. 'And I didn't mean to threaten you, it's only that I so long to be with you and to have the child— I'd do anything to have that, Ingrid.'

She saw with resignation the darkening of Ingrid's eyes that signalled a flood of emotionalism. Oh God, and *now* I'll have to go through one of those tedious sessions in a locked bathroom somewhere, or maybe the linen cupboard on the dormitory landing . . .

But there was a price to be paid for most things, and by this time she was good at faking things with Ingrid. And at least afterwards she felt surer of Ingrid, and she could whisper, 'You did mean it, didn't you? About taking the child?'

There was an almost imperceptible pause. But then Ingrid said, 'Yes, Mary. Yes, I'll take the child.'

The birth, when it finally came, was far worse than anything she had ever imagined. Agony. Hours and hours of unremitting pain. Grinding waves of torment so that she began to believe the child so easily conceived was biting and clawing its way out of her body.

They had put Mary in a little side ward off the main infirmary, because it would be more private. Really, she should have been taken to the nearby hospital, they said, but it happened that one of Broadacre's nurses had trained in midwifery not so long ago, and no complications were anticipated.

Only Christabel's presence enabled Mary to cling to her resolve. Freedom, whispered Christabel, as Mary writhed and moaned on the bed. The attention of the world once again. Maybe even escape from this tedious place. We wove the dreams and we laid the plans, Mary, but there's always a price, remember? There's always a price, Mary, every time, and this is the price we have to pay this time.

All very well for Christabel to say that. It was not Christabel who was gasping with agony in a bed, or whose hair was becoming stringy and sweat-soaked with the pain, and it was not Christabel who was humiliatingly sick during the birth, not once but several times, so that they had to prop her up in the bed and hold the basin under her mouth.

Dreadful. Disgusting. Yes, but hold on to the plan, Mary, remember the plan. *It was announced today that Sixties killer Mary Maskelyne gave birth to a son – a daughter – the result, it is thought, of a secret liaison with another inmate of Broadacre . . .*

Would that one work? Would people believe the story of a 'secret liaison'? Would they say, Oh, the poor creature, she found some love in her life at last, but even that was taken away from her?

Just as, after one final unbelievable cleaving of agony when she thought they were sawing her body in two, they took the child away from her . . .

'A daughter,' they said when at last the agony began to recede. 'A fine little girl. Dark hair and blue eyes. Six and a half pounds.'

Mary knew quite well that all new-born babies had blue eyes and she did not care how much the thing weighed. When they asked would she not like to hold the child, or suggest a name, she turned her face away, tears in her eyes, and the nurses murmured to one another that she was being so brave, poor thing. They gave her something to help her to sleep; it spun her down into a deep, velvety unconsciousness.

But just before she toppled over the end of oblivion, she heard quite clearly one of the nurses say, 'Shall I take the baby now, doctor? The foster parents have filled in all the forms. They're expecting us to phone them as soon as we can – I've got the home number and the husband's office number in London as well.'

And the doctor replied that yes, the phone call had better be made, but that the wife, rather than the husband, should be telephoned. Apparently as an afterthought he asked if they were aware of the child's parentage.

'Not the names, of course,' said the nurse. 'But they do know it's the child of a long-term prison inmate, and they don't mind in the least.' Her voice was muffled for a moment as she leaned over to wrap the baby more carefully. 'Poor souls, they can't have children themselves, and they've been so anxious to adopt.'

Parents. A husband with a London phone number. The words etched themselves into Mary's brain as if they were being traced in acid, and as she fell helplessly into the drug-induced slumber her last thought was that Ingrid had betrayed her.

The next night Mary asked for the sleeping pills again, and the night after that as well. The infirmary people thought she was grieving for the child, and gave them to her without question. Sleep was healing, they said.

You only had to be inside places like Broadacre and the youth place for a week to find out how to put pills under your tongue and pretend to take them. Mary had never done it before, but she managed it without any trouble, hiding the pills in a rolled-up tissue under her pillow.

The plan worked exactly as Mary had hoped. When Ingrid came to visit her in the little side ward two days later it was easy to offer the bitch a drink of orange juice from the plastic bottle on her bedside table.

'We have to drink to the child,' said Mary, pouring out two glasses. 'We could pretend it's champagne, couldn't we?' Please, said her eyes. Do this for me, Ingrid. I've had to give up my daughter.

Ingrid, the silly emotional cow, fell for it. 'We'll drink to her happiness,' she said, taking the glass from Mary's hands, not even looking at it, not seeing the faint cloudiness from the crushed sleeping pills.

Mary waited until Ingrid slumped back in the wooden visitor's chair, and then pounced.

CHAPTER NINETEEN

As Krzystof and Patrick walked through the bleak corridors, unlocking and relocking doors as they went, Krzystof asked how Mary Maskelyne came to be in Moy.

'An English inmate in a Scottish unit?' said Patrick. 'That's what you mean, is it? It's partly to do with a research project I'm heading. I managed to screw a grant out of one of the Edinburgh faculties last year, and then St Thomas's Hospital in London came up with some funding as well. That's made it possible for us to get quite a number of likely case-studies transferred here. The various government departments rather latched onto that.'

'Putting all the bad eggs into one basket?'

'Yes. It might sound a bit calculating to work like that – as if we take a begging bowl round – but it's the only way we can keep going with the research. That's a vital part of the job, for me. There's still so much we don't know about this kind of mania, or any kind of mania, and it's a sad fact of life that we need sordid dosh to study it.'

Krzystof said he understood only too well about grants and bequests. The Rosendale was reasonably self-supporting but they were always thankful when a large donation was made.

'I'd like to see your Rosendale Institute one day,' said Patrick.

'We're quite proud of it. Sometimes we give lecture tours or take exhibitions round to schools and history societies. I'm only one of the interpreters, so I'm mostly sent out with the buyers and the scouts, but I sometimes help with the tours – they bring us some of the sordid dosh. We were in Poland last year – they have some amazing things there.'

'Isn't there a Polish church filled with things made by people from the concentration camps?'

'Yes, several of them. We don't negotiate for anything like that, of course, but sometimes we're allowed to make videos. They can be quite an interesting part of an exhibition.'

D wing was at the top of a flight of stairs and along an upper corridor with doors opening off it. Each door had a spyhole at eye-level and a small name-board outside. Electric alarm bells were sunk into the wall at regular intervals, each one painted with scarlet enamel – an unpleasant reminder that this was a high-security unit.

Krzystof was finding Moy a dreadful place, even though he knew, logically, that the inmates had to be locked away, for their own safety and for the safety of everyone else. This is all they have, he thought, appalled, and this is all their life will ever be. Locked rooms, clanging iron bars, strict regimentation ... Yes, but most of these people have killed and mutilated other human creatures. They're mentally sick, and they're extremely dangerous.

At his side, Patrick said very gently, 'It's a cruel old world at times, Krzystof. We do what we can for the patients, and we're as humane as we can possibly be.'

'Do you make a practice of thought-reading?'

'Occasionally. I'm sorry you're finding this so distressing. Perhaps if you weren't here to try to trace your wife you'd be better armoured.'

Krzystof could not decide whether to be comforted by Irvine's swift comprehension or annoyed. But it was true that he was a skin short at the moment.

Patrick said, 'Being locked away in her room every night was one of the things Mary Maskelyne found difficult when she first came here. She had been at Broadacre, and Broadacre was never especially well run. Mary used that to her advantage, of course. In fact I suspect that if there had been more supervision there the wretched attendant she killed might still be alive.'

'Now that I do remember hearing about,' said Krzystof.

Patrick glanced at him. 'It was at least twenty-five years ago,' he said. 'Mary was barely twenty at the time. You couldn't have been very old when it happened.'

'I wasn't, but I remember seeing the TV news reports.

I remember hearing what was done to that attendant and it stuck in my mind. I used to have nightmares about it for weeks afterwards.'

'Yes, it was a nasty business,' said Patrick. 'Mary thought the woman had betrayed her in some way – she thought the woman had lied to her.'

'She knocked the attendant unconscious or something, didn't she? And then—'

'Say it,' said Patrick as Krzystof paused. 'Exorcise the childhood nightmare. Don't you know the old belief that in order to rout out and banish a demon you must first name it?'

Krzystof grinned. 'And I was thinking you were a man of science.'

'I am, but there's often a grain of good common sense in the ancient beliefs.'

Krzystof said, 'All right. The story was that Maskelyne drugged the woman or knocked her out, and then cut off her lips with a fruit knife.'

'That's pretty much what happened. The poor woman died from shock and loss of blood. Maskelyne said she had absolutely no memory of doing it, and it was only two or three days after she gave birth to a child. They said at the inquest that Maskelyne could have been suffering from some form of post-natal syndrome, depression, baby-blues, whatever label you like to give it. She could *just* have been suffering from something like that, of course, although I don't think anyone really believed it. And she's never referred to either the child or the dead woman since.'

'Curious, that,' said Krzystof. 'You'd expect any woman to have some feeling for her own child.'

'Mary isn't just "any woman",' said Patrick dryly, and stopped before a door. 'This is her room,' he said. 'You'll remember what I said about her being at her most dangerous when she seems most sane, won't you?'

'Yes, of course,' said Krzystof, but as Patrick unlocked the door his heart was beating fast with apprehension. He thought: I'm about to meet one of the dark ladies of the twentieth century. Mad or sane, this woman was a macabre legend by the time she was fifteen. Her name will certainly stick in the history books, along with all those other evil icons – Myra Hindley and Rosemary West and their sisterhood. Lizzie Borden with the axe. Ought I to be feeling more fear than I do? he thought. Ought I even to be feeling awed? I'd happily feel all the emotions available to mankind if it would give me a clue to where Joanna is.

The anger and the bitterness he had sensed earlier on was strongly present in Mary Maskelyne's cell-like room, but at first impression Mary Maskelyne did not look like a legend, and she did not even look particularly evil. She was a small slight figure with short dark brown hair. She had on a plain dark sweater with a grey skirt and if you saw her in the street or in a restaurant or a supermarket you would not give her a second look. You would barely give her a first look, in fact. It took a moment to superimpose onto this insignificant woman the famous photograph of the fourteen-year-old girl with the Sixties eye make-up and smooth Sixties hair. Krzystof was just thinking that after all there was nothing so very remarkable here when the small figure turned its head to look directly at him, and he felt as if something cold had trickled through his mind. This one was not unremarkable at all and she was not insignificant by any means. And if she had in any way latched onto Joanna . . .

But after that first look Mary Maskelyne seemed almost to retreat behind a veil of conventionality. She listened as Patrick Irvine introduced Krzystof and explained briefly what had happened, adding that as far as possible they were trying to piece together Joanna's movements before she disappeared. Mary had spent some time with her after the talk: could she remember anything that might give any clue to Joanna's state of mind? Any names mentioned, or places, perhaps?

'I'm sorry, but I don't think I can help you,' said Mary, and Krzystof heard with a further shock that her voice was rather gentle and soft. There might have been a slight accent – southern counties, was it? – but it was barely discernible. 'I don't think she said anything that you'd call significant.'

Krzystof said, 'I didn't think there would be anything. But I'm clutching at all possibilities. I'd be very grateful if you could tell me a bit about your discussion.'

'We talked mostly about writing,' said Mary, frowning slightly as if thinking back. 'She gave me a few very good tips, in fact.' A swift glance to Dr Irvine. 'I've been thinking of trying my hand at a short story.'

'Good idea,' said Patrick, non-committally.

'So I talked to your wife about it. She was very helpful.

Interested.' The curious eyes turned to Krzystof again and this time he pinned down the elusive flicker of recognition. Snake's eyes. Dark and calculating and watchful. 'She's very attractive, isn't she, your wife?' said Mary thoughtfully, and at once Krzystof felt a sharp stab of anger and panic slice through him. He remembered that it had been hinted that the murdered woman at Broadacre had been Mary's lover. Had this soulless, snake-eyed creature looked on Joanna with some kind of desire? But he said, as casually as he could, 'Yes, very.'

'She did tell me that she was staying in Inchcape for a couple of weeks,' said Mary, still apparently searching her memory. 'She didn't say exactly where, of course . . .' This time the glance she sent to Patrick was unmistakably malicious. 'That would be your instruction, wouldn't it, Dr Irvine? "Never tell the inmates where you live", isn't that what you always say?'

'It's a reasonable precaution,' said Patrick, unfazed.

'It's in case any of us manage to break out,' said Mary to Krzystof, and incredibly there was a glint of amusement. Before he could think what to say, she said, 'But she did say it was in Inchcape, because she said she thought it was a beautiful spot. Oh, and she mentioned the Round Tower – that's one of the famous landmarks, isn't it? She said it was intriguing. You've searched there, have you?'

'The police searched it,' said Krzystof. 'They didn't find anything.'

'Oh, and I thought I might be giving you a clue.' The unnerving eyes went on studying Krzystof. 'Have you seen the tower yourself?' she said. 'Do you know about its origins?'

'I've seen similar ones in Ireland,' said Krzystof, unsure whether this conversation was helping him but seeing no reason not to follow the direction it was taking. 'And round towers crop up in a number of cultures, although the basis for their existence varies with the country. As a matter of fact I'm staying with someone who encountered one in India as a child—'

He stopped at once. The reaction was unmistakable. As if a strong light had been switched on behind the blank eyes. But she only said, 'A tower? In India? How interesting,' and Krzystof glanced at Irvine for guidance.

Patrick said, smoothly, 'Mary's family had connections with India before she was born. She has always found it an intriguing country.'

This seemed safe enough. Krzystof said, 'Yes, I've always thought so. The ancient religions and the rituals. The – the friend I'm staying with was in a tiny northern province as a child. It was many years ago, but she remembers it quite well; she was telling me about it only this morning when I asked about Inchcape's tower.'

Mary Maskelyne was staring at him. Her hands were clutching the chair-arms so tightly that the knuckles had turned white, and although her face was so expressionless as to almost seem like a mask, that strong light blazed from her eyes. She said, 'Was the place where your friend stayed by any chance Alwar?'

'Yes,' said Krzystof, slowly. 'Yes, I believe it was.'

* * *

Alwar. *Alwar*. The word reverberated through Mary's mind, until her head throbbed and pounded with it.

After Dr Irvine and Joanna Savile's husband had gone, she sat for a long time, staring out of her tiny window, watching the sun setting in its crimson and bronze glory, trying to assemble her thoughts into some semblance of logic.

So. So, there was someone living in Inchcape who had spent a few childhood years in Alwar. So, let's not jump to conclusions, Mary. Yes, but Krzystof Kent said 'many years ago'. She was in Alwar many years ago, he had said. So she was not a very young person, this friend. But she could not be all that elderly or she wouldn't be having people to stay in her house.

But let's stay calm. Let's remember that even if she's the right age, this friend, this woman on Moy's doorstep, and that even if she was in India in the late nineteen forties, so were a lot of other people. Yes, but how many of them were in Alwar? Alwar was a small place in India's north-west. It had a palace and a museum and some industry, but its population then was only that of a small market town. Mary knew all these facts very well indeed; she had grown up knowing them.

But this woman had known about the tower at Alwar; she had told Krzystof Kent about it, because Inchcape's Round Tower reminded her of it. She *must* have meant the Tower of Silence at Alwar. She *must*.

Christabel would know if this not-so-young, not-so-old female had really been there, of course; she would know if this was the survivor from that blood-smeared

255

night when Christabel and those other children had died.

But Christabel was being infuriatingly silent. Mary knew she was close by, because she could feel her presence in the way that she almost always could nowadays. But there was no emotion coming from her, and no sense of her mind locking into Mary's. Because Christabel had heard what had been said, and was still stunned by it?

I hate that child who escaped . . . Leila Maskelyne had said, over and over until Mary had wanted to scream. *She has had the life our dear one should have had* . . . *Why couldn't she have died instead of our dear girl* . . .

Mary had always hated the unknown girl as well. She had spoiled their lives, that child. If she had been the one to die instead of Christabel, Mary's parents would have loved her. Mary would have known Christabel properly, as an older sister, instead of having this shadow-image who whispered into her mind.

It was stretching coincidence rather a long way to think that Krzystof Kent's hostess might be that unknown child who had escaped, but if you added everything up it was just about credible. If she could find out a name – yes, that was the crux of this whole thing. A *name*. She wondered who she could talk to on Moy's staff who might know the local people, and she began to frame apparently innocent questions. You could do that kind of thing without raising suspicions providing you were clever and cunning. And Mary could be very clever and very cunning indeed; none of the stupid sheep-creatures who guarded her really knew just how clever and cunning.

She went on thinking and thinking about this woman who lived in Inchcape.

Emily was trying to take more of an interest in current affairs at the moment, because of visiting Pippa. Pippa was intelligent – you could see that, even when she was just sitting limply in the chair in the day-room – and she might like to hear about what was happening in the world. So Emily was looking out for odd, amusing news stories that she could relay to Pippa: not upsetting things like war in the Middle East or famines in unpronounceable countries, but things that might make for an interesting discussion. It was admittedly difficult having a discussion with somebody who never spoke, but you just had to keep on talking.

'I think it's so brave of you to visit the poor soul,' Miss March said, when Emily told her about it. They were in the scullery at the time, with the lights all switched on because Great-uncle Matthew had always said that it was the constant switching on and off of electric lights that wore out the bulbs, so a light, once switched on in Teind House, stayed on all day. Emily had not been able to decide if Teind House was spookier with lights blazing than it was when the shadows crawled into it at dusk.

'My great-aunt Rosa used to do a little charitable work,' said Selina. 'Visiting the sick people in the cottage hospital was one of the things she did – my great-uncle Matthew was on the board of the hospital governors.' The once-a-month meetings of the hospital governors in

Stornforth had in fact been a fixed point in Great-uncle Matthew's life. Nothing had ever been permitted to interfere with those meetings. Selina said, 'And Great-aunt Flora made calves' foot jelly and egg custards for people in the village when there was illness. She was a very *domestic* person, Great-aunt Flora. She believed in good nourishing meals, especially for gentlemen.'

Emily, who had been making a pot of kedgeree for Krzystof Kent's breakfast the next morning because Miss March subscribed to Great-aunt Flora's maxim about good nourishing meals for gentlemen, furtively grabbed a handful of kitchen paper and guiltily mopped up spilt rice and haddock flakes.

'She was very housewifely, Great-aunt Flora,' said Selina.

As well as being housewifely, Aunt Flora had also been annoyingly inquisitive, especially after Aunt Rosa died. She had taken to asking questions – where was Selina going? Why had she not come home from school at the usual time? – and wanting to know about homework and lessons.

Great-uncle Matthew had never asked questions about Selina's activities, because Great-uncle Matthew never took any notice of anything that did not directly affect him or his comfort. After Aunt Rosa died he simply went on studying his bits of local folklore, and writing irritable letters to people whose opinions clashed with his own, and attending his beloved hospital meetings, and cataloguing his stamp collection. On the first Monday of every month he wondered rather querulously why they had to put up with Aunt Flora's Church Ladies' Guild in the sitting room because it meant a lot of clacking women in the house, and at frequent intervals he asked why Selina could not do her homework in her bedroom instead of on the dining-room table. In his day children had not been allowed to spread their messy schoolbooks everywhere, said Great-uncle Matthew, and, told that Selina's bedroom was apt to be chilly on account of being north-facing, said that in his day children had not been so pampered.

When Selina timidly asked if she might have a record-player for her fourteenth birthday so that she could listen to records like the other girls did, Great-uncle Matthew was shocked to his toes and did not know what the world was coming to. In his day there had not been such things as record-players and songs about kisses sweeter than wine – most unsuitable – or the yellow rose of Texas, whatever that might mean. Children had been the better for it, as well. Selina might, if she was so inclined, take piano lessons, said Great-uncle Matthew. He would make no objection to that, providing it did not cost too much, and providing she did not practise scales on Teind House's piano, because there was nothing less conducive to concentration than having to listen to somebody practising scales.

Selina did not much want to learn to play the piano, but it was something a bit different to do, so she had a lesson once a week and was allowed to practise on the schoolhouse's tinny piano on Friday afternoon after everyone had gone off full of excited weekend plans, leaving her on her own except for the janitor.

She and Aunt Flora sometimes listened to the Light Programme on the wireless in the kitchen: Aunt Flora liked Mantovani and the selections from Cole Porter musicals, but these were not as good as the things people at school listened to.

Selina had expected Great-aunt Rosa's ghost to come sneaking and prying into her bedroom after the witchy old thing had fallen down the stairs and broken her neck, but she had not done so, not once. This had been a bit surprising, because Selina had thought that even after Aunt Rosa was dead she would find a way to denounce the shrine, carefully rebuilt in the tower. She had waited, fighting sleep night after night, in case Aunt Rosa's ghost came but it never did, and the shrine stayed.

Selina went there regularly. She would have liked to follow the ritual called the *barashnom*, but it required you to wash several times and also to live apart from the rest of the house for nine days and nights before entering the shrine, and this was impossible in Teind House where the range had to be stoked up for four hours before you got any hot water. So she compromised by washing very thoroughly in a basin of cold water in her bedroom, and by making the visits to the shrine on Sundays, when Teind House had been quiet all day, or on Fridays, when she had stayed at school by herself for her hour's piano practice, and nobody saw if she had a strip-wash in one of the cloakrooms. Once inside the tower, she always chanted the *kusti* and the *patet*, which were repentance-prayers for the dead and in which you had to be careful to include the names of the people you were honouring. Sometimes, for good measure, Selina recited the creed, which was wholly Christian of course, but which might be well received on account of her parents' being English. You had to be polite about these things.

It was more than five years since her mother and father had died now, but there was no way to be sure that they had both crossed the old and holy Bridge. Several times Selina wondered if she had done enough honouring of their memories, and if she dared dismantle the shrine to see what happened, but she never quite had the courage.

And then, one bronze-and-gold autumn Sunday afternoon, Aunt Flora mentioned opening up the Round Tower.

CHAPTER TWENTY

———◆◆◆◆———

She and Selina were washing up the lunch things, doing so straight after the meal as they always did, because Aunt Flora's dear mother would have turned in her grave to see a sinkful of dirty dishes halfway through the afternoon, and it a Sunday.

'I said to the vicar this morning that I would walk across and take a look at the Round Tower,' Aunt Flora said, tipping washing soda briskly into the bowl. 'To see if it mightn't be suitable for a little exhibition, you know. The Ladies' Guild could display their needlework, or the school might set up an exhibition of pupils' work. Art, or pressed flowers. Hand me that plate, Selina, will you?'

'The Round Tower?' Selina stood stock still in the middle of the kitchen, clutching the newly dried plate and staring at her aunt in horror. 'Oh, but I don't think it would be very suitable for an exhibition, Aunt Flora.

It's horridly dirty, and . . .' A little improvisation could surely be allowed here? 'And Miss Mackenzie who takes us for history says it's dangerous. We're forbidden to go there,' said Selina, rather desperately.

'Yes, but we could just take a little walk towards it, couldn't we? We won't need to go very near to tell whether or not it's suitable.' Aunt Flora had finished putting away the plates, and had polished the glasses that had held her and Great-uncle Matthew's tonic wine which they drank with Sunday lunch. She spread the tea cloths on the range where they would dry out in the warmth, and untied her apron, folding it away in the drawer. 'We might even take a little walk out there now, Selina. A little exercise after a heavy lunch is a good idea, and it's a beautiful afternoon, and your uncle is working in his study . . .' They both knew that this was a polite way of saying that Great-uncle Matthew was taking his customary post-lunch nap. 'We'll be back in good time to cut the sandwiches for tea,' said Aunt Flora.

Sunday afternoon tea was a ritual in itself: there were usually meat paste or egg and cress sandwiches, a slice of Madeira cake or scones, and quite often tinned or bottled fruit. The fruit was usually apricots which Selina hated because they were like peaches with skin on, but Great-uncle Matthew liked apricots so that was what they mostly had. Supper was eaten at eight o'clock on Sundays, and was generally cold meat from the lunchtime joint with some of Aunt Flora's home-made chutney.

'We'll walk across to the tower now, just to take a look, and then,' said Aunt Flora happily, 'if the vicar *should* happen to look in for a cup of tea later – he might very well do so, you know – I could tell him what we think.'

It was possible to start hating Aunt Flora – nice plump dithery Aunt Flora – as abruptly and as thoroughly as once you had hated Aunt Rosa. It was possible to see, all at once, that although she had a stupid sheeplike face and a vapid, sheeplike mind, beneath it she was dangerous, threatening.

She would find the shrine and she would know what it was at once. The trouble was that she would not understand its necessity, just as Aunt Rosa had not understood.

But Selina gave Aunt Flora a chance. She waited until they were inside the Round Tower's little room, and she watched Aunt Flora look about her, and draw in her breath with a little puffy sound of surprise, and then say, 'My goodness me, Selina, have you done this?'

Selina knew then that Aunt Flora, for all her nice wuffly plumpness and her happy dithering about whether the vicar would come to tea and if she should bake her special cherry cake just in case, was as disapproving as her sister had been.

'Selina, it's – it's a *shrine*,' said Aunt Flora, staring about her. 'And those are Poor Elspeth's things – I recognise that black stole. And that's a photograph of That Man— A silver frame as well! My dear child,' said Aunt Flora, scarlet-faced with indignation and disapproval, 'my dear child, this won't do at all! Think what your great-uncle would say!' A pause. 'Think what the vicar would say!'

expostulated Great-aunt Flora, a picture of outraged Presbyterian horror.

'It's only to honour their memories,' said Selina hopefully, because if only Aunt Flora could try to understand that the shrine was absolutely and overwhelmingly necessary, it might still be all right. 'It's a way of remembering.'

'We don't honour memories like this,' said Aunt Flora firmly. 'We honour memories by flowers on graves—' Too late she recalled that neither Poor Elspeth nor That Man who had taken her to the outlandish Indian place had graves, so she said, in her briskest voice, 'Or by church services on birthdays and the anniversaries of deaths. By having photographs in your room.'

Selina could not see that having a photograph of her parents in her room and chanting a few prayers on mother's or father's birthday was very different from arranging things out here. She said, pacifically, 'It isn't hurting anyone to have this shrine, Aunt Flora.'

The use of the word *shrine* was unfortunate. Aunt Flora flushed all over again and her face seemed to swell like an outraged turkeycock's. She said, 'It's unChristian, Selina! And it's very very deceitful of you as well – sneaking out here to this – this pagan thing all these years. Well, one thing is for sure, this must stop and immediately, is that understood?'

'Yes,' said Selina in a colourless voice.

'You must take these things away at once, is *that* understood? Yes, you may well hang your head like that.'

'I'm sorry,' muttered Selina, staring at the floor, not

meaning, I'm sorry for what I've done; meaning, I'm sorry you had to forbid the shrine. She said, 'I'll do it at once, I promise I will. I didn't know about it being pagan and things. But, Aunt Flora, now that we're here, should we take a look round anyway? For the vicar's exhibition? It isn't really dangerous, you know, this tower. I made that up because I thought you might be angry if you saw the—' Better not to use the word again. 'If you saw all these things,' amended Selina.

Aunt Flora softened visibly. To be sure the tower was horridly dusty and desolate, she said, looking about her, but it could be spruced up quite easily. A few licks of paint and plaster, some rush matting on the floor— Some kind of temporary power supply for lighting— She could even visualise some nice cloth-covered tables with the Ladies' Guild needlework set out on them. And perhaps the History Society in Stornforth might be persuaded to write up a little background to the tower's origins: they could have leaflets on sale, and serve coffee and cakes to people visiting the exhibition. She wandered happily off into culinary realms, wondering whether they might boil water on a camping stove, or whether Thermos flasks would serve, and Selina hated her all over again, with an angry bitter hatred, because she had dismissed the shrine so casually and so completely.

She waited for a pause in the flow of Aunt Flora's discourse, and said, 'Shall we take a look at the upper sections while we're here? Those are the stairs leading up – I don't know how far they go, but they look pretty safe. I should think,' added Selina cunningly, 'that the vicar would want to know if the upstairs bits could be used as well as the ground floor, wouldn't he? He'd be awfully pleased if you could give him a report. If he comes to tea later on, I mean.'

The idea of the vicar's being pleased at anything Aunt Flora had done or attempted found instant approval. Aunt Flora began to look less angry; she said perhaps they might take a little look, although they would have to go carefully, and – Selina was to mind this! – they would have to come out *immediately* if they saw any signs of stones crumbling or ceilings being unsafe.

'Instantly, is that clear, Selina?'

'Oh yes, of course,' said Selina. 'We mustn't risk anything happening to either of us.'

The stairway was dark and narrow, and it wound round and round, exactly as the iron stairway inside the terrible Tower of Silence had done.

I must be careful, thought Selina, cautiously leading the way upwards. I must be calm and ordinary, and I mustn't let her suspect anything.

It was eerily difficult to remember that this was Inchcape, not Alwar. The higher Selina went up the stone stair, Aunt Flora puffing along behind her, the closer she felt to Alwar and the children – dear brave Christy, and Douglas who had tried so desperately to protect them all – and the more the gap of the years seemed to narrow.

This *was* Alwar, very nearly; the darkness was surely the same darkness that had clung to the evil blood-tainted tower outside the town, and the stone walls were almost the same walls that the plotters had scraped against as they carried the two wrapped-up bodies to the top— Selina could hear the beating of huge wings on the air as well, and she was suddenly afraid that if she looked up she might be able to see the round-shouldered shapes, peering down, waiting for the meals of human flesh that were being carried up to them . . .

No, this was absurd. This tower had long since been roofed over. Selina frowned and blinked several times to dislodge the images from behind her eyelids. But she *could* hear the soft beating of wings, and there might well be large birds up there, because they flew in from the sanctuary at Stornforth, she had often seen them. There were capercaillie and crossbills and larks and wood warblers and several exotically plumaged birds from other countries. Stornforth was rightly proud of its bird sanctuary. Lately there had been talk of eagles, which everyone thought would be exciting.

But besides all that, the sanctuary had hawks and falcons. Had it the cloak-winged ogre-birds, as well? If so, might they be up there now, waiting, just as they had waited for father and mother that night . . . ?

After the pale bloodied thing that was mother had stopped screaming, panic had taken over outside the tower. People had run back and forth, calling frantically to one another, shouting for more lights, shouting for someone to go up inside the tower and bloody *do* something! But two people had gone up there already, and no one seemed to quite know what else could be done.

Selina had stayed huddled into Douglas's father's jeep, and for a little space of time everybody seemed to forget about her. She saw Douglas's father go across to the horrid jumble of bodies at the tower's foot, and she saw him shine his torch and bend down. And then he recoiled, one hand going to his eyes, as if somebody had hit him hard across the face. Douglas, thought Selina miserably. He's seen Douglas's body. He didn't know until now that Douglas was dead. But her mind was still confused with what had happened and with trying to understand what would happen next. It was as if the pieces that were the facts were all in her mind, ready to be understood, but as if they had to be arranged into the proper pattern first and Selina could not manage to do it.

The men who had gone up the iron stair had reached the top of the tower; Selina could see them moving warily around – she could see that they had to keep dodging back as the angry birds flew at them. Somebody near to the jeep muttered that it was practically unknown for the birds to attack living humans, but Selina thought that it was fury at being cheated of their prey that had enraged the birds.

She watched the tower's top, her hands clenched tightly together in her lap, shivering violently even though the night air was so warm. The headlights from the cars were still tilted up to shine onto the Tower, and she could see everything very clearly. Her father lay where he had been put and the birds did not seem to have touched him, but mother was still in an awkward jumble on the stones. She would hate to be seen like that, her legs embarrassingly sprawled out, and her hair a tangled mess. She had liked to be always neat and shinily groomed, mother; she always made sure that her hemlines were well below her knees, and she smoothed her skirts down primly when she was offered a low chair, and sat with her knees tidily together. Father teased her about it, a bit.

But father would not tease her any more, and there was no longer anything tidy about mother, and there was nothing prim about her, either. As Selina watched, miserably frightened, still struggling to sort the pieces of information out so that they would make sense, one of the birds came angrily swooping down again, and the two men dodged back, covering their heads with their hands. The blood-streaked thing that had been Elspeth March moved slightly and Selina caught her breath and shoved her clenched fist into her mouth in case she cried out and everyone remembered about her being here and took her away.

With nightmarish slowness the helpless figure slid to the edge of the stone rim. It stayed there for an unmeasurable space of time, curled over, its hands covering its head. The hands had no fingers any longer, because the vultures had bitten them off when mother tried to protect her face.

As Selina watched, the thing that had been mother straightened up, and half turned to the men who were attempting to rescue her. She made a last despairing gesture for help, flinging her arms out, and taking a step towards them. But she could not see them, because the vultures had scooped out her eyes with their beaks, leaving dark bloodied holes, and before anyone could reach her she fell blindly over the edge of the tower, and came plummeting down to the ground.

It seemed to take a very long time for her to hit the ground, but when she eventually did so there was a dull wet squelching thud, and one of the men turned aside, covering his mouth. Somebody said, 'Christ almighty, she's fallen on the kids!'

The vultures came hurtling straight down onto the tangled heap of bodies.

Selina opened her eyes to firelight in a completely strange room. It was not the safe, warm kind of firelight that made friendly pictures on your bedroom wall when you were ill; this was a frightening firelight that cast images of ogres in raggedy cloaks who crouched on the top of black towers and waited for humans that they could eat up, and used their claws and their long curved beaks to rip into flesh and hair, and tear out eyes—

Selina sat bolt upright and gasped, and at once a completely strange lady in a nurse's uniform was there, patting the bed, telling her she was quite safe, everything was all right, and please drink this.

'It's something to help you sleep,' said the nurse, as Selina stared with scared eyes at the mug of *drink-this*. 'You're in hospital, you know.'

Selina frowned, because although her mind felt fuzzy it also felt as if there might be things she should be remembering. She said, 'My parents—' and then stopped.

There was something wrong, something bad. She would remember what it was in a minute.

'Doctor will come along to talk to you when you've had a nice sleep,' said the nurse brightly. Selina hated her. She wore a white apron that rustled, and she smelt of carbolic soap and cocoa. 'Drink this all up, first, and then off to the Land of Noddington for a while.'

Selina wondered how old the nurse thought she was. She started to say, in her most grown-up voice, 'I'm seven and a quarter, you know,' and then quite suddenly a piece of the blurry nightmare slid into her mind, and she said, 'Christy. She was in the tower with me— Where is she? What happened to her? Did they bring her out? I didn't see anyone bring her out—'

'We'll talk about that later.'

'No,' said Selina, glaring at the nurse, her fists beating angrily on the bedclothes. 'No, you must tell me now. If you don't, I'll—' Another sliver of memory skittered across her mind. Somebody who had screamed into the crimson-streaked night, on and on, until it hurt your mind to hear it. 'I'll scream,' she said mutinously. 'I won't stop screaming until you tell me about Christy.' She drew in a deep breath, and the nurse said hastily, 'Let me find doctor for you.'

The doctor came nearly at once. He was a nice jowly-faced man with shiny round spectacles and a fringe of hair round a bald head. He sat on Selina's bed and held her hand, and said, well now, what was all this about?

'It's Christy,' said Selina, clutching at his hands. 'Christabel Maskelyne. She was inside the tower with me

272

– I remember that part. We hid from – from something—
But then we couldn't get out because the door wouldn't
open from inside. They did bring Christy out, didn't
they? Because I didn't see her – not right at the end – not
when—' She stopped, clenching her fists in frustration.
'I can't remember. Not properly. I can remember some
but not much.'

'You'll remember a little bit at a time, Selina. Like
being out in the fog, and you think you can't see where
you're going, only then it clears in patches, and you can
see quite clearly. That's what your memory will do.'

Selina said, 'Yes, but I can't wait for it to do that.
Because of Christy. If they shut the door on her she
wouldn't be able to get out of the tower. And the walls
are so thick they wouldn't hear her if she called out.
They mightn't know about any of that.' She looked up
at the doctor. 'You must tell them to go back. Please,
you must.'

The doctor had warm strong hands that closed round
Selina's. He did not smell of soap and cocoa; he smelt of
clean shirts and the stuff Selina's father sometimes put
on his hair.

Father . . . Another tiny shard of memory flicked into
place. Something bad had happened to father . . . Part of
the nightmare. Part of the screaming and the iron stair
that clanged when you went up it . . .

'Selina, listen to me,' said the doctor. 'You and your
friends were taken prisoner by some very bad men—'

'Yes. They had guns. But Christy and I hid in the
tower.'

273

'That's right.' He paused, as if he was thinking what to say next. 'My dear,' he said, very gently, 'by the time you were rescued, all the other children were dead. It was very quick and they wouldn't have felt a thing, I promise you. But the tower was searched very thoroughly, Selina, and there was no one else in there.'

The firelight burned up, with a dry crackling noise. It sounded exactly like the greedy rustling of the ogre-birds' wings.

Christy was dead. All of them were dead.

Selina said, in a whisper, 'Then who was holding my hand in the tower?'

She had not been able to understand it for quite a long time. She had said, 'But she was there. Christy was there – she talked to me. She held my hand.'

They had h'rmphed a bit at that, in the way that grown-ups did when they were not sure what to say to you. Selina got fed up with them and burrowed back into the bed, because it felt safe being under the clothes. That night, she heard a nurse saying that it had been a long time before anyone could get near to the bodies at the foot of the tower, because the birds had been so fierce. When they had finally managed to shoot the birds, the children's bodies had been so badly mutilated that it had not been possible to identify anyone with any certainty.

'Some were almost completely eaten,' said the nurse to her colleague, shuddering, not realising that Selina was listening. 'The vultures swallow bones whole, you know. Even the large leg bones. And the skulls were broken in the scramble to beat the birds off, so that it was impossible to know if all the children were there or not. In the end they decided to bury what was there in one grave, and to put up a stone with all their names on it.'

'Oh, the poor mites,' said the other nurse, horrified.

So Christy must have been killed after all. But when Selina asked if it had been a ghost who was with her in the tower, the nurses said, oh well, it was easy to become muddled in all the panic and confusion, which was no answer at all.

It had not been until a long time afterwards – when Selina had managed to pick up most of the mind-pieces and sort them into a pattern – that she remembered what had happened to her mother.

She tried very hard not to wonder whether at the very end mother had realised where she was, and that she was falling to her death.

Great-aunt Flora had realised it. It was easy to persuade her to look through one of the slit-like windows near the Round Tower's top: to say, Goodness, what a marvellous view, you can see Teind House and as far as the rectory, and there the meddlesome sheep-faced creature was, breathlessly eager.

In the falling dusklight of the autumn afternoon the view from the Round Tower's highest window was not very different from that of Alwar's Tower of Silence. As Selina stared out over the countryside, she remembered how, when she first came to Teind House, she had looked out across the gardens and seen this tower, and how the garden and the tower had suddenly shivered and blurred, so that she had not been sure whether she was at Teind House at all, or whether she was being pulled back to Alwar.

And today the smoky dusk was beginning to dissolve, exactly as it had done that first night; it was melting, shred by shred, and the twilight that was usually so friendly was filling up with menace – it was crawling with evil-faced men who wanted to shoot children, and the sky was smeary with ogre-birds who liked to grind men's bones for their bread . . .

'You need to lean just a bit further out,' said Selina to Aunt Flora. Her voice seemed to come from a long way away, but that was because her mind was stretching to span the two worlds, and because she could smell the blood and fear again. She could feel Christy crouching next to her inside the tower, and she could feel Christy's hand in hers all over again, and Christy's voice whispering that it was all right, Selina, they were together, and they would find a way to escape.

Taking a deep breath, tensing her muscles, the faraway Selina said, 'It's perfectly safe, Aunt Flora. You won't fall – I've got hold of you. But do look – it'd be such a pity for you to miss this wonderful view.'

The stonework around the old narrow window held surprisingly firmly, which was a pity in one way. It meant that Selina had to shove very hard indeed before stupid, snooping Aunt Flora tumbled sufficiently far forward to be toppled out. She screeched as she fell, flailing her arms and legs wildly. Selina watched until she hit the ground with exactly the same squelching thud that mother had made five years earlier when she fell from the Tower of Silence.

It was easy to poke out some of the stones around the Round Tower's narrow window, so that people would think Aunt Flora had leaned on them too heavily and dislodged them. Several of the larger ones went smashing down on the silly old creature's head.

Selina stayed where she was for a while, looking down at Aunt Flora's body, and at the stones scattered on the ground. Most of them had broken up when they fell, but some of the larger ones were still intact. She thought the stones looked exactly as you would expect them to look if they really had given way under Aunt Flora's weight. She kicked out one or two more to be sure, and waited for them to go tumbling and smashing onto the ground. Only when she was satisfied with everything did she go back down the stairs. She carefully moved the shrine-things into a corner where they would not be seen if people came to take Aunt Flora's body, and after this she went home along the little old road and through the orchard to Teind House, deliberately running as hard and as fast as she could so that she would be breathless and dishevelled when she got there and everyone would think it was from the shock of seeing Aunt Flora tumble to her messy splattery death.

It all worked exactly as she had thought it would; everyone was appalled and Selina was made to go to bed with a hot-water bottle, and given aspirin crushed in hot milk with a half-tablespoon of brandy, and everyone said, Oh, what a terrible experience for the poor child.

There was a funeral service for Aunt Flora, of course, with the same mournful music there had been for Aunt Rosa, and everyone wearing black again. The vicar spoke for a long time about the work Aunt Flora had done for the church and for the parish of Inchcape and everybody looked solemn. Selina wore her school uniform for the service, and Great-uncle Matthew sulked because of having to pay for ham sandwiches and sherry a second time.

Afterwards, life went on and the only difference was that Jeannie came up from the village every day now, to prepare Great-uncle Matthew's lunch and to leave a meal that Selina could heat up for supper when she got home from school. Teind House became even quieter than it had been in the aunts' day.

Selina remade the shrine properly again a month after Aunt Flora's funeral. It was important not to risk its being found a second time. There were not many places to choose because the tower had been built as a watchtower and it was really only a flight of stairs enclosed in a brick and stone shell, but there were two or three little half-rooms opening off the stairway, which Selina thought might have been where the monks would have rested. You would certainly need a bit of a rest if you were stomping up and down those stairs all the time.

She chose the half-room nearest the top. It was not very likely that anyone would come all the way up here, but even if anyone did, there was nothing wrong in having set out photographs of her parents, and some of their belongings. It might look a bit peculiar, but it was not anything you could go to prison for.

Remaking the shrine took quite a long time because the little room had to be properly swept and dusted and then everything had to be carried up the stairs. But when she had finished it all, Selina was pleased. The place was better as well: it was more secret than when it had been just inside the door. So you could almost say Aunt Flora had done Selina a favour in showing her how vulnerable the shrine was down there on the ground.

Later on, she managed to smuggle more things out to add to the shrine. Great-uncle Matthew did not notice that the silver candlesticks were not in their usual place, or that the little Victorian silver matchbox which had belonged to his father had gone.

As the weeks went by Selina began to feel safe again. Both the snooping aunts were dead, and it was much easier to go out to the Round Tower and keep the shrine clean and fresh. It was easier, too, to take little posies of flowers or sprays of lavender, which would all help father and mother on their journey.

It was not very likely that Great-uncle Matthew would realise what Selina was doing, but even if he did he would not meddle. In any case, if she had to, Selina could deal with Great-uncle Matthew.

CHAPTER TWENTY-ONE

———❦———

Emily Frost woke to a grey, leaden sky and the insistent clamour of her alarm clock, and to the realisation that she had a dull headache and a vague feeling of apprehension. Something unpleasant in the day ahead? Or something regretted in the night gone before?

She stayed where she was. Dad had probably gone up to Moy ages ago – he was on an early shift this week – and her alarm had a snooze button which meant she could have an extra ten minutes before getting up.

The headache would be the result of too many drinks in the wine bar at Stornforth last night: Emily considered last night in case it was the cause of the vague apprehension. But she thought it was not. She thought she had behaved perfectly well, and she had managed to politely avoid the groping hands and gleeful suggestions of a leather-jacketed biker who had had too much to drink and who seemed to think Emily was anybody's.

Today was the day she was due to visit Pippa again at Moy, so that could not be the reason for the vague feeling of menace. Today was one of the days that if you were still at school you would have marked with a gold star, because Moy meant Patrick Irvine. Emily smiled and burrowed back into the pillow.

Patrick.

If she had been with Patrick last night they would not have spent the evening in a scrubby wine bar with people gusting cheese-and-onion-crisp breath into your face every time they spoke, and the prospect of going to bed with a lager-sodden biker after closing time. Emily tried to direct the lingering fragments of sleep into a dream about Patrick. You could sometimes do that with dreams, usually when you were drifting in the half-asleep, half-awake stage.

An evening with Patrick would have started with an elegant dinner in some lush, plush country-house hotel, after which they would have gone to bed together in a bed with silk sheets, and spent a mind-blowingly sensual night. They would have made love several times during the night, each time better than the last, and although Patrick might eventually have slept, Emily would not have slept at all, because she would have stayed wide awake so that she could watch him sleeping.

And when finally they did get out of bed, there would have been breakfast with fresh orange juice and smoked salmon with scrambled eggs on silver dishes, and hot croissants. They would have showered or bathed together, and there would be expensive soap and scented bath oils, and thick, thirsty towels. They would probably make love in the shower, as well—

Emily had just reached this luxuriantly soap-scented point in her daydream when the alarm clock went off for the second time, and Emily bashed it crossly with a fist to silence it and crawled irritably out of bed, because before she could join in with the school's cookery day she had to go down to Teind House to be on breakfast duty. Miss March only had Krzystof Kent staying at the moment and although she could perfectly well manage to prepare a single breakfast by herself and wash up afterwards, she was so clearly terrified of meeting a lone man at the breakfast table that Emily had said she would dash up for half an hour to help out.

Patrick had quite a full day ahead, because one of the larger drug charities was making a semi-ceremonial visit to Moy, which meant he would have to spend some time with them. Moy's governor always ducked away from actually admitting to the existence of drug-taking inside Moy, but everybody knew it went on. Patrick sometimes waxed eloquent about what ought to be done to drug traffickers, but despite all the care they took drugs still got passed around inside Moy, just as they got passed around inside other institutions like Moy. All you could do was try to deal with it when it surfaced, and hope to keep it out as much as you could.

The various drug charities were quite helpful and

practical though, which was why Patrick would spend as much time with them as possible, although it was a pity they had asked to come today, because Monday was one of the days on which he tried to see patients.

He tried to stick as closely as possible to the routine he would follow if Moy were a conventional psychiatric hospital, scheduling a half-hour for each inmate at least once a fortnight, leaving the day-to-day stuff to the junior psychiatrists. Moy was quite a good training ground for newly qualified doctors and therapists, and they had several very good people at the moment. It was important to keep strongly in touch with new techniques and new ideas; Patrick had instigated fortnightly forums, at which seniority went by the board and ideas and opinions were tossed back and forth, and discussion often crossed over into downright argument.

As he showered and dressed, he remembered that Emily Frost was coming in again today, to visit Pippa. It was nice of the child to give up her time; Patrick thought she had a good deal of unsuspected depth and considerable intelligence. The peculiar clothes and the hair were deceptive.

He whistled softly as he poured cereal and made toast, and glanced through the day's headlines as he usually did over a second cup of coffee. Everything in the world too frightful for words, as usual. He put the paper away.

There was a good hour before he was scheduled to start seeing patients, which meant he could work through some of his outstanding correspondence. Then, when he had seen the charity people, the afternoon would be reasonably free. He might look in on Emily's session with Pippa.

Emily wore her rainbow combat trousers for the visit to Pippa, along with a magenta waistcoat, because the vivid colours would be bright and cheerful in Moy's institutionalised bleakness. She could not find a clean T-shirt to go under the waistcoat so she plundered dad's shirt drawer, and unearthed an old dress shirt that had shrunk in the wash that he had not got round to throwing out. It looked pretty good under the magenta waistcoat. Emily added her black boots, gelled up her hair because it was her day for wearing it in spikes, and set off.

She had remembered the promise about bringing some cakes from the school's cooking day, and had told the children that she would like to take some of them to give to somebody who was not very well. The children had latched onto this; they had painstakingly traced out 'P' for Pippa in sugar or icing on several of the cakes, and then one of the little girls had offered her lunch-box for the transportation, only it must be brought back tomorrow or her mummy would wonder what she had done with it. Emily had gravely promised to bring it safely back, and they had packed the cakes carefully in the lunch-box, and covered them with greaseproof paper. The children's interest and the slightly uneven icing-letters would make a friendly little story to tell Pippa, even if the cakes turned out to taste as peculiar as Emily thought they very well might.

*   *   *

Alarm bells were dotted all over Moy. They were set into the wall behind little glass boxes like miniature fire alarms. Emily thought they were like single malevolent eyes, staring at you. It was to be hoped she never had to punch out one of those horrid red eyes, and she hoped even more that she never heard the sound of Moy's huge old-fashioned bell tolling inside its stone tower, to warn everyone within hearing that an inmate was on the loose.

Robbie Glennon had told her about the old bell. He had said it was one of the local legends; the bell-tower had been built at the same time as Moy, so that if any of the prisoners escaped the bell could be rung to warn people in the surrounding countryside. The last time it had been used had been in 1920, said Robbie, and added hopefully that, if Emily liked, he would smuggle her along to see it one of the days. It was a huge iron bell with a long dusty rope dangling all the way down to the ground and it hung in a little oblong stone tower by itself. You were not supposed to go into the bell-tower unless you had specific permission, but he would probably manage it, he said confidently.

Emily had no idea whether he was trying to impress her, or whether he really could get into the old tower. He was quite good company, though, that Robbie: Emily was going to take him into Stornforth this weekend. The wine bar had live music on Saturday nights, and he would probably enjoy it. Also, it would be nice to have a proper escort for once and not look as if you were on the catch and therefore prepared to go to bed with anyone who wore a cheap leather biking jacket and bought you a couple of drinks. Emily had not yet decided about the bed thing with Robbie Glennon, and she had not decided if she actually wanted to see Moy's bell, either, because it might be a bit spooky. Bells were like cats and mirrors; you always felt they had a secret life of their own.

Pippa did not look as if she had ever had any kind of life of her own, secret or otherwise.

She was brought into the glum day-room in A wing by the attendant Emily had met last time, and she was wearing the same shapeless clothes and ugly clumpy shoes. Her hair had been ruthlessly combed and pinned back and the impression of a too-obedient child, submissively dressed and tidied and brushed by its mother and brought to an outing, was impossible to miss. The bumpy twist of flesh over the damaged eye-socket was unnecessarily exposed, and Emily felt the pity of it clutch her throat. Patrick had mentioned glasses – surely they could have made sure she wore them to meet a visitor? Or at least combed her hair to fall forward in a fringe?

But she sat down opposite Pippa, and smiled, and said she hoped Pippa remembered her from last week, and more to the point, she hoped Pippa remembered about the cakes.

'The children baked some extra ones specially for you,' she said. 'I told them I was visiting a friend today and that her name was Pippa, so they wrote your initial on some of the cakes. We had a really good time with the baking, although some of the kids got covered in dough and flour.' It was a bit disconcerting to talk like this without getting any response. Emily wished the attendant would help out a bit, instead of sitting like a pudding in the corner, reading a magazine.

The mention of children seemed to have struck a bit of a spark at any rate. Pippa was watching Emily with sudden attention; Emily thought it was silly to suddenly feel a bit spooked. Was it the single eye that made it feel eerie? Probably. But surely it was all right to have mentioned the children? Dr Irvine had said not to talk about animals, that was all.

'We'll try the cakes, shall we?' she said, and she was just reaching for her haversack which contained the borrowed lunch-box when a shrillness ripped through the room. Emily looked round, startled, and then realised that one of the red alarm bells was sounding.

She had absolutely no idea what she was supposed to do or whether she was supposed to do anything, but the attendant was already talking into the small intercom clipped to her belt and there was a barely audible crackle of someone gabbling urgent instructions at the other end.

'I'll have to go,' she said to Emily. 'There's a problem in D wing.'

'But – I was told – not to be alone with—'

'It's all right. She's never any trouble,' said the attendant, sending a quick look at Pippa. 'But they only sound the alarm if there's a serious incident – a riot or somebody trying to make a run for it. In that situation it's all hands to the pump. I'll come straight back, or I'll send one of the others.'

'Yes, but what do I do—'

'You'll be OK,' said the attendant, crossing to the door. 'Pippa won't be any trouble, she never is. You won't be any trouble, will you, Pippa?' she said in the too-bright, too-loud voice of someone talking to an idiot or a subnormal child.

'You said a problem—' began Emily, and the attendant, who was halfway through the door by this time, turned back and said, 'I don't know what it is until I get there. It might be a storm in a teacup.' In a resigned way, she added, 'But I'll bet my pension that if real trouble's broken out, that demure-eyed bitch Mary Maskelyne will be at the bottom of it.' And she was gone, banging the door behind her.

Emily turned back to Pippa, and saw with sudden fear that Pippa was staring at the door, her hands gripping the arms of her chair so tightly that her knuckles were white. There was a look half of fear, half of puzzlement on her face.

Emily had no idea what she ought to do, but, trying to speak calmly, she said, 'Pippa – it's OK. Don't look so frightened. It's just that one of the other—' God, what did they call them in here? 'One of the other patients has probably got a bit upset and caused a row,' said Emily, hoping this sounded all right. 'It's nothing to be worried about.'

Pippa was trembling by this time, and without thinking Emily went to sit next to her. 'Does the idea of a row upset you?' she said. 'It always upsets me: I hate people fighting or shouting. But what we'll do, we'll sit here until somebody comes back, and we'll try one of the cakes the children baked for you. I was hoping we could have a cup of tea as well. Do you have a cup of tea in the afternoons, Pippa? It's a very English habit, tea, isn't it?' She foraged in the haversack again. It took a few minutes to unearth the lunch-box – it had slipped down the side which served her right for toting so much rubbish about. She hauled it out and put it on the little low table between their two chairs. It was a brightly coloured plastic-lidded box, with a picture of Stornforth's bird sanctuary on it. They sold things like that at Stornforth – posters and tea towels and notepaper – mostly to help with the upkeep of the sanctuary. Emily had got a T-shirt with a gorgeous golden eagle on it.

The box had a golden eagle on it as well; a huge, beautifully clear photograph showing the eagle's massive wingspan and powerful shoulders. Emily reached out to prise off the lid, and it was then that Pippa's hand darted out and closed around her wrist. Like a claw. Like a snake uncoiling. Emily tried to jerk back, and saw that the poor mutilated face was wearing a look of stark and absolute horror. Emily said, 'Pippa, what's wrong? Has something frightened you?' Because this was how you would look if you had suddenly been confronted with your absolute, all-time worst nightmare. She hastily reviewed what she had said in the last few minutes. Something about the children? Something to do with drinking tea? And then she saw that Pippa was staring down at the vivid eagle photograph on the plastic lunch-box.

Whatever you do, Patrick Irvine had said, don't talk to her about animals in any form . . .

'Is it the picture of the eagle that upset you?' said Emily, trying to speak very gently. 'It's only a photograph, you know.' She tried to pull her hand free, tensing her muscles for a quick dash across the room to the door or to the alarm bell but Pippa's fingers were like steel clamps and stark blazing terror was pouring into the room, filling it up like thick, choking silt. At the back of her mind Emily knew the attendant was going to come back but she had no idea how soon that would be, and she was starting to feel very frightened indeed. Cracked minds, that's what I'll remember. I'll remember she's sick, poor thing. But the smothering feeling of madness was so strong that she found herself remembering that it was not so long ago that people like Pippa would have been regarded as possessed by devils or demons, and she remembered that clawed-out eye—

No reference to animals when you talk to Pippa, Emily . . . She's potentially very dangerous indeed . . .

And, *If we knew why she never speaks we might make sense of some of the things she's done . . .*

Patrick's warnings bounced back and forth across Emily's mind, and then Pippa jerked Emily out of the chair and pulled her backwards, hooking one arm around her neck. Emily yelled with surprise and the sudden pain as her legs smashed against the edge of the table, and then struggled wildly. But Pippa's free hand came round to imprison her wrists and the hold on her throat tightened. Emily fought to get free, but the vice-like grip on her throat increased. There was a very bad moment when she felt a sickening, throbbing pressure against her eyeballs, and for a moment her vision darkened and a crimson-veined blackness swam before her eyes. Then the grip lessened slightly and Emily's vision cleared, and she gasped, and said, 'Let me go! Pippa, for heaven's sake, let me go!' And oh God, oh God, let someone come back and put an end to this!

And then two things happened almost exactly at the same instant.

Patrick Irvine, two attendants behind him, burst into the room.

And Pippa said, in a harsh, difficult voice, 'Keep the birds away.'

The sound of her voice so close to Emily's ear was a shock. It was a dreadful voice – thick and grating and slow, like old, old machinery that had rusted with disuse and was struggling to move again. Emily saw Patrick stop dead, and she saw him indicate impatiently to the attendants to keep back. His eyes went to Emily, as if to briefly assure himself she was all right, and then he looked at Pippa, and in his gentlest voice, he said, 'Pippa, my dear child, what is all this about?' and Emily thought that if she had not loved him before she would have loved him then because of the infinite compassion in his face and in his voice.

The terrible voice said, 'You must – keep the birds – away. The children—'

Patrick came swiftly across the room. 'What is it about the birds, Pippa?' he said. 'Tell me what it is about the birds and the children, Pippa. Then I might be able to help you.'

Pippa was still holding Emily, but Emily thought she had forgotten why. She could feel that Pippa was trembling violently, but at Patrick's words there was a feeling of mental withdrawal. She's going back into the silence, thought Emily. She's retreating, and the door's closing. We've missed something, and she's going to be lost again.

And then Patrick said, 'You aren't Pippa at all really, are you? Who are you?' and Emily knew at once that this was the key, that if only they could know Pippa's real name they might reach her.

Yes, but never forget that she's potentially very, very dangerous, Emily . . . Keep remembering that, my dear . . .

The words brushed against her mind like a breath of cool sweet air, like the scent of rain in autumn, and Emily's eyes flew to Patrick's face. He was not looking at her, he was concentrating on Pippa with the whole force of his mind. But Emily thought she had not imagined that moment – no more than the space of a heart-beat – when he had seemed to send out a silent message of reassurance.

'Pippa, who are you really?' said Patrick again, and for a moment Emily thought the door that had started to open in Pippa's darkened mind had slammed shut again. He'll fail, she thought, staring at Patrick in an agony of suspense. Don't let him fail, *please* don't let him fail. She's dangerous and she's certainly not sane – I can *feel* that she isn't sane! – but she's so dreadfully sad and pitiful—

'Tell me your name, Pippa,' said Patrick, and this time there was a sharper note in his voice. And it's the third time he's asked her, thought Emily wildly, and there's an old magical belief that if you ask a question three times, you have to be given the answer— Oh God, now I'm becoming hysterical!

And then Pippa said, in a voice that made the hair prickle on the back of Emily's neck, 'I'm not Pippa. I'm Christy.' A pause. Then, in the voice of a carefully schooled child giving its credentials to a stranger, she said, 'My name is Christabel Philippa Maskelyne.'

CHAPTER TWENTY-TWO

———◆◆◆———

For what felt like a long time there was absolute silence in the room.

Patrick was still kneeling down in front of Pippa, and although he had not moved light was streaming from his eyes as if they were lit from behind. He reached out and removed Pippa's hands from round Emily's neck, and as Emily half fell in a jumble into a chair he said, very softly, 'I know who you are. You're Mary's elder sister, aren't you? You heard her name when they rang the alarm, didn't you? Mary Maskelyne. And hearing that made you remember. That's right, isn't it? Christabel?'

Pippa was shuddering violently, rocking backwards and forwards, her arms wrapped around herself. 'Christabel,' she said, nodding slowly. 'Christy,' and Emily heard with a cold thrill that she spoke as if she was referring to a separate person.

Patrick heard it as well. He said, with force, 'No. *You're* Christabel. You've tried to keep Christabel hidden away all these years – because you're afraid of something, isn't that right? Because Christabel was once very afraid of something. But it's safe now. You can let Christabel come out now.' He paused, and then, with a note of such absolute authority that Emily felt a shiver trace its way down her spine, he said, 'Christabel – Christy – come out into the light.'

Tears were streaming down Christabel Maskelyne's face – one-sided, thought Emily with helpless pity – and once she tried to brush them away, like an animal pawing at a wound. But Patrick's voice held absolute and compelling authority. She won't be able to resist him, thought Emily.

In a gentler voice, Patrick said, 'It's all right. Christy, it's all right. But now you must tell me where you are. So that I can help you. Tell me, Christy.'

There was another of the long silences. But she'll give in, thought Emily. I know she'll give in. When Christy began to speak, she was not at all surprised.

'Night,' she said. 'Dark everywhere.' It was not quite the voice of a scared child, but it very nearly was. Emily had the impression that two completely different people were fusing, and one of the people was a poor bewildered woman in her mid fifties, and the other was a small determined child, trying to outwit a dreadful menace. She glanced at the attendants and saw that they were still standing just inside the doorway. Neither of them had moved, and both of them were watching the figure in the chair.

'We were all so frightened . . .'

'What were you frightened of? The dark?'

'They were going to shoot us,' said the not-quite-child's voice. 'All of us. The men were going to shoot us, one by one, because our parents hadn't done what they asked. I never understood that properly.'

One of the attendants murmured the word 'hostages'.

'I hid,' said Christy. 'I didn't want to get shot. It was dreadful. You can't think how dreadful it was.' She covered her face with her hands.

'Tell me,' said Patrick's voice insistently. 'Tell me how dreadful it was.' He reached up to pull her hands away from her face, but she flinched and cowered back in the chair. 'Christabel,' said Patrick. 'Listen now, you must tell me. Then we'll understand why you stopped speaking all those years ago, and why you did all those other things—' There was a brief, perceptible pause, and then he went on again. 'Tell me everything you remember,' he said, and Emily heard again the hard insistence beneath the gentleness. He isn't quite hypnotising her, she thought in fascination. But he nearly is. That's why he keeps calling her by her real name. Christabel Maskelyne, that's her name. Christy. I don't understand this yet, but it's as if he's calling her out of the years of the dark silence where she's been hiding.

After a moment, from behind her hands, Christabel said, 'I found a place to hide. No one knew I was there, and I stayed there while the birds ate everyone up. I couldn't fight them off – the birds. There were so many of them. I thought they'd eat me as well.' Again there was the flailing of her hands as if to beat off some unseen assailant. 'So I hid and I stayed very still and very quiet until they went away. It was a long time before they went away, but I stayed there all the time.'

'Where?' said Patrick. 'Christy, tell me where it was that you hid.'

'Inside the tower,' she said, and Patrick sat back on his heels.

'The Dakhma,' he said very softly. 'The Parsi funerary Tower of Silence. That's what you mean, isn't it?'

'When the others were lined up to be shot I dodged back in the shadows all round the tower,' said Christy. 'They were thick shadows. They were black, like blood. Blood turns black in the moonlight, did you know that?' She looked at Patrick from between her fingers, and Emily had to suppress a gasp because there had been something unutterably sinister about that look. Just for a moment it had been as if something evil and grinning had peeped, goblin-like, out of Christabel Maskelyne's face.

'I know about the blood turning black,' said the voice. 'I know how it feels, as well, when the blood spills over your hands. Like warm silk. It's the best feeling in the world.' The cruel secret look stayed there for a moment. As if she's considering each of us in turn, thought Emily, suppressing a shiver. And then it vanished abruptly, and the frightened child was back. 'I could hear their wings beating,' said Christy. 'They flew backwards and forwards, over and over the tower, waiting to come swooping down on me. But I fooled them. I went up the iron stairway inside the tower—' Again there was the involuntary gesture as if she was trying to push something away from her face. 'It was horrid. It smelled so bad. Selina was sick on the floor – it went all over her shoes.'

'Selina?'

'She hid there as well. And then she tried to escape. But she went outside too soon, and I think they shot her. She thought it was safe to go outside, you see, but I knew it wasn't. I think the bad men caught her and shot her, that's what I think happened to Selina.'

'Are you sure?'

'They shot everyone,' said Christabel. 'Douglas and Selina and the others. I heard them be shot. I cried about it for a long time. I cried about Selina being shot. I loved Selina. I loved all my friends.'

Selina, thought Emily. Selina *March*? No, it's just coincidence. Selina isn't a very common name, but it isn't all that uncommon. Yes, but Selina March was in India as a child – she told me she was. And the dates would be about right.

'The tower's where they put dead people in India,' said Christy. 'And they leave them for the vultures to eat.' She looked at Patrick. 'You knew that, didn't you?'

'Yes. It was very brave of you to hide in there, Christy.'

'When you're dead in India, you're sacred. That's like being holy in England. So when the men tried to find me – after Selina went outside – I stayed in the tower. They came to look for me, but I hid where they couldn't find me.'

'You hid with the dead,' said Patrick, half questioning.

'The dead people were all on shelves,' said Christy. Her voice sounded very nearly normal now. 'Right at the top of the Tower. They have a shelf for the men and one for the women, and another for the children.' Her voice faltered, and then she said, 'There were a lot of children. They get sick very easily in Alwar, and they die, and their mummies and daddies take them there. But I didn't hide there because it was too near to the birds. I saw that the birds would get me, so I came down again.' She stopped for a moment, and then said, 'In the middle of the tower there was a hole. A pit. Like a well you have in the gardens of very old houses. That was where the bones went when the vultures finished eating up the bodies. The bones dropped down into the well. There were lots and lots of bones there, dozens and hundreds.'

'You hid there,' said Patrick. 'In the bone-pit.' His voice was devoid of all expression, but Emily heard one of the attendants smother a gasp of horror.

'I had to tread on heads and bits of jaws and things. They crunched under my feet. But I went to the very centre of the bone-pit, and I pulled all the bones over my head so that the bad men wouldn't see me. Some of the bones had bits of skin still on them, like bits of leather.'

Emily could not have taken her eyes from Christabel if her life had depended on it. She thought: that all happened to her when she was a little girl. Seven or eight.

Christy said, 'We knew a lot of things about those birds. Things that grown-ups didn't know. Selina called them ogre-birds. She said they were like the ogres in the fairy stories. Ogres eat children, did you know that? They shout, Fee-fi-fo-fum, those ogres, and they run across the countryside and they can run faster than anyone because they have special boots. And they like to make bread from human bones, and they like to have their dinner from human children.'

'Only in stories,' said Patrick. 'Not in real life.'

'You don't know that. You have to be careful,' said Christabel, and again the flicker of something that was neither childlike nor scared showed in her face. 'There're ogres in the real world – lots of them. Only you can't tell who they are because they wear human disguises, and they're very, very good disguises. But I know about the disguises,' she said, and, bizarrely, the child's voice came through again. 'I know because I'm clever as clever, my daddy always said I was clever as clever, like in the poem. "Now that I'm six, I'm clever as clever, and I think I'll stay six for ever and ever." My daddy used to say that to me. But he didn't know about the ogre-birds who pretend to be people. Selina didn't know either, although she knew a lot of things.' She looked at Emily suddenly. 'You know about them, don't you? About the ogres who pretend to be people.'

'Yes,' said Emily, who had absolutely no idea if this was the right thing to say. A distant memory from her own childhood stirred for a moment, and a half-forgotten childish belief came back to her. She said, 'They hide inside nightmares sometimes.'

'Yes. *Yes*. How clever of you, Emily. Your name *is* Emily, isn't it?'

'Um, yes.'

300

'They hide, those old ogres,' said Christy, and again it was the child speaking: the long-ago child who had possessed the gift of most children for accepting the bizarre or the macabre and the fantastical without question.

Patrick said cautiously, 'In houses?'

'In *people*. It's quite hard to know who they are sometimes; you have to look extra hard. They pretend to be your friend, and they say, Oh, what a pretty little girl. Come into my house and have tea, little girl. But after a bit, you can see what they really are. You can see the claws and the beaks, and when you see those,' she said, 'that's when you know. That's when you have to kill them.'

This time the silence went on for much longer. Then Patrick said, very gently, 'As you did, Christabel.'

There was a long silence, and then the struggling-to-be-born voice said, with terrible obedience, 'Yes. As I did.'

CHAPTER TWENTY-THREE

If they had been characters in a film, the scene in the day-room would have ended with Patrick clutching Emily to him, and saying something like, 'Oh God, I thought she was going to kill you, and then I'd have lost you,' and Emily sobbing into his shoulder like the worst kind of wimpish Victorian heroine, until the violins swept in and there was a soft-focus fade-out.

What actually happened was that Christabel simply stopped speaking, not abruptly, but in diminishing trickles like a tap being gradually turned off, and sagged back in the chair, and then somebody handed Patrick a hypodermic, and Patrick said, 'Chlorpromazine? Good,' and bent over Christy.

Emily was left to untangle herself from the chair into which she had tumbled, and somebody brought her a cup of tea, strongly sweetened, and one of the attendants said she would drive her back to the cottage. There was some talk of how Emily had got to Moy earlier on, and Emily tried to remember if she had come on her motorbike or if she had walked, and could not, which made her feel like a stooge all over again. The attendant said it did not matter how she had got here anyway; she could not possibly be left to get home under her own steam after such an upsetting experience, and it seemed to be decided that Emily would be driven home in the attendant's car.

Once home, Emily went round the cottage switching on every electric heater and radiator, and building up the coal fire in the hearth. After this she dragged the ancient afghan rug that had been her mother's from the depths of dad's wardrobe and wrapped it round herself, subsiding into a chair by the sitting-room fire, her hands curled around another mug of scaldingly hot tea. Despite all of this she was still shivering with cold.

The rug reminded her of her mother. In the months after she died Emily had not been able to bear opening her mother's cupboards or the drawers where her clothes were, but it was suddenly nice to be wrapped in the afghan; it felt as if mum was not so far away after all, or as if she might be reminding Emily that she was still looking out for her. Whether you believed in that stuff about an afterlife or not it felt comforting.

The knock at the door made her jump, even though she had been listening for it, and a bit of the frozen chill melted.

Emily unwrapped herself from the afghan and went to the door to let Patrick in.

*   *   *

He sat in the slightly battered chair on the other side of the little hearth, and drank the tea that Emily made for him, although he looked as if a large whisky would have done him more good.

In case he did not want to talk about Pippa – Christabel – or in case to do so might be breaching medical confidentiality, she said, 'What was the alarm bell for? The one that rang just after I got there? I never found out. Was there a riot after all?'

'Oh, that.' He finished the tea and set the cup down. 'It was that disgusting little ruffian Logan.'

'Flashing again, was he?' said Emily who knew the stories about Logan, and Patrick grinned and for a moment looked about ten years younger.

'Floorshow for the benefit of a DrugWatch group who were being given the guided tour,' he said. 'Most of them took it in their stride, but unfortunately they had their new patroness with them – some stupid society female whose name looks good on the letterhead, but who has absolutely no idea— She screamed, which was the worst possible thing she could have done, the silly bitch,' said Patrick. 'And so Logan immediately went into the full cabaret act – I don't expect you need the details, do you? – and most of D wing started banging the tables and egging him on. At times like that the place turns into a powder keg and it wouldn't take much to start a real riot, so we have to use emergency procedures.'

He leaned his head back and stared into the fire. 'Emily, you were very good with her – with Pippa. I mean Christabel. I wanted to thank you and explain about that, if you'd like to hear.' He leaned his head back and stared into the fire. The flames painted red lights into his hair and deepened the shadows around his eyes.

Emily said, 'Of course I'd like to hear. It's a weird coincidence, isn't it? Both of them ending up at Moy.'

'Only on the face of it. Moy's a specialist place; it's meant for cases exactly like Mary and Christabel. Disturbed people with personality disorders and a history of violence. So looked at from that aspect, it's not so remarkable that they're both there. But we had no idea that there was any connection between them,' said Patrick. 'Pippa came to Moy years ago – long before my time. There's a note on her file that she was placed in a juvenile institution when she was ten, and we do know she was moved several times. But her parents must have used a false name at the start—'

'Philippa,' said Emily. 'It's her middle name – she said so.'

'She did, didn't she? And there's some very ordinary surname – I forget it now, but it's something like Jones or Edwards. Totally unremarkable. I should think it was probably her mother's maiden name, or her grandmother's.'

'And so her real identity was lost.'

'Yes. We'll have to set up an inquiry about that,' said Patrick. 'It'll be a long way back, but it'll have to be done.' He suddenly looked impossibly tired again.

'You know Mary's history, though? You knew there'd been an older sister?'

'Oh yes. That was part of what drove Mary to kill her parents. The story was that Christabel died in India, and that Mary's parents never got over it. They canonised her memory – enshrined it – to such a degree that Mary felt excluded.'

Enshrined ... Emily had a sudden vivid memory of the odd sad little collection of childhood objects in Selina March's bedroom. She frowned and said, 'Was Mary really neglected or excluded? Or did she just think it?'

'I'm not sure we know. It's not always easy to separate the truth from Mary's delusions. She wasn't neglected in the physical sense. And the case notes say her parents displayed no more than the normal degree of grief at the loss of a child and that Mary had a perfectly normal, perfectly stable and loving childhood.'

'But – would anyone have known that for sure?' Emily was finding this so interesting she was forgetting about feeling cold, and she was nearly forgetting about this being the godlike Dr Irvine, who had better be treated with respect on account of being dad's immediate boss, never mind how she might feel about him in private. 'The doctors and social workers and what not couldn't have known so very much about Mary's childhood,' she said. 'They certainly couldn't know how anyone behaved because they didn't come on the scene until after Mary's parents were dead. After she killed them. So their opinions would be based on what Mary told them, wouldn't they? Or maybe on what her teachers said, or what friends or family said – uh, was there any family?'

'No. They seem to have drawn a line under their old life after they got back from India. They bought a house in a part of England where they didn't know anyone.'

'Then a lot of that stuff about whether Mary was neglected or excluded is – what's that word they use in court?'

'Hearsay,' said Patrick. He was smiling at her with indulgent affection. As if a child had said something clever. Damn and blast.

'Hearsay isn't reliable evidence, is it? It isn't admissible in court.'

'No,' said Patrick. 'But the thing is that Mary herself believed she was excluded. She believed that Christabel took up most of her parents' affection and energy. She considered she was neglected and as a result she hated her mother and father and she decided they had to be punished. It's pretty much a classic behavioural pattern, although it's an extreme case.'

'Did Mary hate Christabel as well? Because that'd surely have been normal? I don't know about you,' said Emily, 'but I think I might get a bit irritated if my parents had kept shoving a kind of Saint Christabel in my face every day. Anyone might go a bit peculiar after years of that. I don't mean you'd go on the rampage with the breadknife.'

'Yes, I'll give you the Saint Christabel touch,' said Patrick. 'I think that was probably what did happen.' He seemed to have forgotten that he was only talking to Don Frost's daughter, and he seemed to have forgotten about being tired, as well. He was leaning forward in the chair, his eyes brilliant, his face alight with energy and enthusiasm. He loves her, thought Emily. He loves all his poor mad murderers and rapists. He's passionate about them all. I don't suppose he has much passion left over for anything else.

He said, 'But the really odd thing is that each time Mary killed – and she killed at least twice more after her parents – she apparently said that Christabel was with her when she did it – that Christabel was urging her on and giving her strength – empowering her, that's the word I want. She thought Christabel was dead, of course, and in a bizarre way she thought her dead sister's spirit was speaking to her.'

'But Christabel wasn't dead at all,' said Emily thoughtfully. 'And when Mary came to Moy, Christabel was a whole lot nearer than anyone imagined.'

'Yes.' He considered for a moment, and then said, 'Christabel's case-notes are very scrappy indeed, but I've tried to piece things together. Knowing who she is – knowing her real name – helps immensely. I can fill in some of the details from what I know about Mary, and I'll be able to check back in the records. And I think there's probably a gap: a period – say a year or so – after the family came back to England with Christabel, when they lived in a different part of the country. Christabel would have been severely traumatised from what had happened in India and they probably tried to get help for her, although it was still only the late 1940s and the facilities wouldn't have been very good. But by the time she was ten, she had been placed in a juvenile asylum.'

'And that's when her parents moved away. Leaving her behind. I'll bet they pretended they were only just back from India,' said Emily. 'And they told people that Christy had died out there.'

'Yes. And you know, Emily, on the face of it, it was an entirely understandable way to behave. A fresh start. No painful associations. Mary was born round about then, and afterwards they built up their fantasy about the perfect child who had been taken from them. It might have been the only way they could deal with what had happened.'

'More likely they were ashamed of Christabel,' said Emily tartly.

'What a cynic you are.' Patrick's tone was indulgent and Emily scowled.

'It's very sad though, isn't it? Christy's story, I mean.'

'All their stories are sad if you look at them from one angle, Emily. But if I'd known the truth about Christabel I could probably have done more to help her.' A spark of anger showed briefly.

'Patrick—' The name came out before she realised it, but he did not seem to notice. 'You said they put Christy in a juvenile asylum. Why?'

'Because she was a child-murderess,' said Patrick. 'Like her sister. But where Mary only killed four or five times, Christabel killed seven people.'

'Oh God,' said Emily, staring at him. 'Seven.'

'Seven that we know of. Two were teachers at her

school – the notes aren't very clear, and the place has long since closed down. But I think it was what we'd call now a school for children with special needs.'

'Because she had stopped speaking?'

'Yes. While she was there she killed two of the teachers, and one of the older pupils as well. There was some story about a music teacher trying to befriend her; she was being given piano lessons, and the music teacher became fond of her. She used to invite Christy to her house.'

Emily said, '"Come into my house and have tea, little girl."'

'It sounds as if that's how she saw it. I don't recall the precise details of the other killings, but they were the same kind of thing. The juvenile asylum was probably seen as only a temporary measure.'

'But it wasn't temporary,' said Emily thoughtfully. 'They came to realise that it wasn't temporary at all. She couldn't be let out into the world. D'you think that was when her parents made the decision to pretend she was dead?'

'Yes, I do. It would have been reasonably easy for them, as well; it was only about 1949 or 1950, remember: there wouldn't have been the media coverage there is today, so the murders wouldn't have been very widely known.' He frowned, and said, 'I'm still trying to match Christabel up with what I know of Mary's background. I think the father worked for the British government in India, and I think they were modestly affluent. Mary was born when he was about forty-one or two.'

Emily was not much liking the sound of those two people who had consigned poor, flawed Christabel to an asylum and then announced her death. She said, 'And when Mary was born, they told her that she had had an older sister who was dead.'

'They did. They talked and acted as if Christabel was dead, and I don't think they ever diverged from that. Mary's referred to memorial services on the anniversary of Christabel's death each year, and to photographs in silver frames and a vase of flowers on her birthday.'

Emily found this slightly macabre but it was what people did. Like dad keeping that photo of mum by his bedside, and sometimes playing records they had listened to before they were married. Late Sixties and Seventies stuff, mostly. It was pretty naff music, but it was what mum and dad had shared and if it made mum live again, good for dad. And earlier on, Emily herself had dug out mum's afghan, as much for comfort as for warmth. You clung to memories because they were a link back to the person you had loved.

She said, 'But wouldn't it all have been dragged out at Mary's trial? If she killed her parents because she was jealous of her dead sister, wouldn't it have come out that the sister wasn't dead at all?'

'It didn't come out. And again it was pre-paparazzi, Emily. The mid Sixties. Christabel had been shut away from the world for fourteen years, and her parents had probably destroyed everything that might have given a clue to the truth. Even to giving her a different name.'

'If her father worked for the government he might have pulled a few strings over that,' said Emily.

'Yes, that's possible. Whatever he did, the truth died with him.'

'Until I let Christabel see a picture of a golden eagle on a lunch-box, and an attendant blurted out the name "Maskelyne" by chance,' said Emily. 'Oh, Patrick, I'm so sorry I did that. You said don't talk about animals, but I never thought that a photograph of a bird—'

'None of it was your fault,' he said at once. 'It's the law of something-or-other – something metaphysical. Cause and effect. A butterfly beats its wings in Japan, and because of it an earthquake occurs on the west coast of America.'

And because a poor mad creature beat the wings of her own insanity against the walls of her own prison, you're here with me now . . .

As Patrick stopped speaking Emily had the sudden feeling that a different atmosphere had crept into the warm sitting room. It was very quiet. There was a faint, rather comforting crackle from the fire, but other than that nothing stirred. And yet the impression that there had been a shift in the atmosphere – even that a third, unseen presence had walked in and sat quietly down with them – persisted.

It was early evening, the hour of dusk, which you hardly noticed in a city or a town, but which had a personality all its own out here. At times in Inchcape, Emily had sometimes felt very close to the invisible powers that had once roamed the earth; she had had the odd feeling that it would not be so very difficult to reach out and scoop up some of those powers, and use them to make things happen . . .

But even if I knew how to do that, I don't think I'd dare, and all I can do is keep him talking about what's just happened.

In an entirely ordinary voice, she said, 'How did Christabel kill those people? That music teacher and the others? What did she do to them?' Because there's that scarred face, that torn-out eye—

Patrick said slowly, 'I always knew how, but until today I never fully understood why.'

He looked across at Emily as if trying to assess how much to tell her, and Emily said impatiently, 'If you don't tell me I'll have nightmares anyway and they'll probably be worse for not knowing.'

'OK. Well, then, before the chlorpromazine kicked in, Christabel said, "They were ogres, those people I killed. I recognised them. I know all about ogres and I knew I had to kill them. First I had to cut off their feet so that they couldn't run after me, and then I had to cut off their hands as well, so that they couldn't snatch me up. And then they were dead and I was safe. And if I hadn't done that they'd have eaten me up."'

'Oh God, that's dreadful,' said Emily, horrified. 'She really did that? Hands and feet—'

'Yes.'

'What – what about her damaged face?'

Patrick appeared to think about this for a moment, and then he said gently, 'One of her victims fought

313

very fiercely. She clawed and bit. And Christabel was – injured.'

Emily stared at him and then said, 'Oh. Oh, yes, I see. Not an animal at all? A human,' and tried to think if this was better or worse. 'I'm desperately sorry for the people she killed,' she said, after a moment. 'And for their families if they had families. But I can't find any blame for Christy.'

He looked at her with a kind of affectionate exasperation. 'Oh, Emily,' he said, and there was a soft note in his voice that Emily had never heard him use before. 'What a nice child you are,' he said, and Emily could have hit him. 'You think the best of everyone, don't you?'

'Well, but the thing is that Christy never forgot what happened to her, did she?' said Emily. 'She never forgot how she lay among all those poor mangled bones, with the vultures – the other girl called them ogre-birds – swooping around her. Waiting to eat her up.'

'No.'

'Could she have been helped? When she was young – before she started killing people?'

'I don't know,' he said. 'Perhaps. We've come a long way in understanding the mind over the last fifty years. But the odd thing here is that there are two sisters who have never met one another, and although Mary knew about Christabel she thought Christabel was dead—'

'And Christabel didn't even know of Mary's existence—'

'Precisely. But both were childhood killers,' said Patrick. '*Vicious* childhood killers. That's the curious part.'

'They inherited something from the parents? Some weakness?'

'Sometimes there are tendencies within a family to certain mental conditions,' he said. 'Schizophrenia can certainly run in families, although it's unusual for it to present in children. Christabel was only nine when she first killed. It'll make some interesting research, now that we know who Pippa really is. And they're both delusional, that's another thing linking them. In fact, in Mary's case, the paranoia symptoms are classic. She thought her dead sister was encouraging her to kill first their parents and then other people she thought had injured her.'

Emily waited again, hoping he would go on, but he did not. He stood up and said, 'My poor child, I'm doing it again, aren't I? Boring you with my work.'

'I'm not bored.' But he doesn't really believe that, she thought bleakly. I've lost him. We shared an intimacy for the last half-hour – he talked to me and listened to me – but it's gone because he's remembering that I'm just Don Frost's girl. Emily, who visits one of his patients, and has offbeat hairstyles. In a minute he'll say something agonisingly polite, and I'll very nearly hate him. No. I won't.

As she stood up to go with him to the door, the afghan slipped from her shoulders and dropped to the floor. Patrick bent down to pick it up.

'It's beautifully warm, this,' he said.

'Yes. It was my mother's.'

'You looked so cosy in it, curled into the chair. I expect you were cold with the shock of everything, weren't you? Did you take that sedative I gave you?'

'I'll take it when I go to bed.'

'Don't forget.' He put the afghan across her shoulders, pulling it around her neck, doing it in the manner of an indulgent parent or uncle wrapping an untidy child into its warm coat before sending it out to play in the snow. It meant that his arm went round her shoulders. Emily bit her lip and stared at the floor, because his touch was so absolutely electrifying and she must not let him see, she utterly and completely must *not*—

But why not? whispered the sneaky little voice, and something inside Emily suddenly said, Oh, sod all this pretence! and she stepped forward, into the curve of his arm, at the exact moment that his arm came more tightly round her.

Something flared in his eyes, and he gave a kind of helpless groan and pulled her hard against him, and if she had ever had any ideas about the gentleness extending to other areas of his personality she had been wrong, because he was kissing her as if this was an emotion that had been banked down for years and centuries, and he was taking her face in his hands as if he wanted to learn her, because it might be all he could ever have, all he ever dared have, of her . . .

When at last he released her Emily gave a half-sob, and stepped back until she was level with the sofa and held out her hands to him.

Come onto the sofa with me now, Patrick, or come upstairs to bed with me . . .

He did neither. That small act broke the spell. It

bloody, sodding-well shattered the miracle, and it splintered the spiralling passion, and Emily could not *believe* she had been so fucking stupid, she absolutely could not believe it—

'Jesus God, Emily,' he said, and the faint trace of Irish was more strongly marked than she had ever heard it. 'Oh God, Em, I'm so sorry—'

'But I wanted—'

'No, you didn't want, and even if I did—' He took her hands. 'Of course I want you,' he said. 'I want you so much it's torture. It's killing me. I want all of you – you're sweet and lovely and funny and clever, and I love your mind and I love everything about you, but – you're Don's daughter—'

Emily lost her temper. 'I'm not a fucking child!' she yelled. 'I'm twenty-sodding-one, and I'm nearly twenty-bloody-two, and I was at Durham University for two years until my mother died and dad was in bits all over the place so that I had to take a sabbatical to put him back together – you didn't know that, did you? No, I didn't think you did! And I do want you, I want you in bed, *now*, or on the floor or anywhere you like, I don't much mind, and I've been trying not to say any of this for weeks, and now I *have* said it, and you'll probably hate me and avoid me for the rest of my life, and I wish I could say I don't care, but I do, I care so much it hurts, and I can't help any of it!'

She ended on a half-gasp, and they both stood in bewildered silence, staring at each other. Patrick was breathing hard, as if he had been running, and there was a blank, stunned look in his eyes as if someone had hit him and Emily loved him so much she wanted to fold her arms round him and take away the blankness, and shut out the world for ever.

He said, with a kind of helpless irrelevance, 'I didn't know you were at Durham.'

'Well, I was.' Emily sat down on the settee where, three minutes earlier, she had thought they would be together. 'I expect I'll go back to finish off next year.' She would not look at him again, she simply would not. 'I suppose you'd better go, hadn't you?' she said at last. 'I don't expect there's anything more to be said, really.'

'It wouldn't do, you know, Em.' He thrust the fingers of his hand through his hair in the familiar, impatient gesture. 'I'm not believing this is happening,' he said. 'I can't begin to think how I'm going to walk away from you— But you must believe that it would never work.'

'Yes, I see that,' said Emily. 'And it's all right, truly it is.' Focus on practicalities. 'Dad will be home soon,' she said. 'It'd have been awful if he'd caught us together, wouldn't it? French farce stuff.' That was better, that was lighter. Very nearly flippant.

It seemed to strike the right note, because Patrick said, 'Yes, of course. I'll phone you, though. Later this evening.'

'There's really no need.' This was terrible. They were talking like awkward strangers, just as if they had not, a few minutes earlier, been pressed so tightly together that they had both been able to feel one another's hearts and bodies and longings . . . She said, 'Will you be all right?'

'No,' he said, and then, very softly, 'Because – now I'm in a place where light is muted, and where the opposing winds batter, and the hellish hurricane never rests.'

'The *Inferno*,' said Emily, after a moment. 'You remembered it.'

'Yes. And I'll phone you anyway, Emily.'

'Yes, do,' said Emily politely, and waited until he had gone before she burrowed under the afghan rug and howled her heart out.

As Patrick went back to Moy, he was struggling to bank down the memory of the moment when he had pulled Emily against him, and when he had tasted her mouth and when he had wanted her so overwhelmingly that it had been a physical agony to detach himself from her.

But it would not do. There were seventeen years between them, and it would not do. She would go back to Durham University as she had said – he ought to have guessed that, of course; he thought he had hurt her by not doing so. He wondered what she had been reading. But she would go back and she would graduate, and Don Frost would show everyone the graduation photograph because he would be so proud of her, and Patrick might send a letter of congratulation or a card. And whatever she did afterwards, there would be scores of young men around who would want to go to bed with her because she was an original, she was *sui generis*, and although none of the young men would ever completely appreciate her, she would probably sleep with some of them, and then she would end up marrying one of them, and there would be more photographs to be shown – wedding ones this time – and Patrick would send a gift, and in the end life would go quietly on.

Except that he had meant it about the light muting and the opposing winds battering. He had gone down into the modern-day equivalent of Dante's hell, and there would never be any colour or any light or any joy in the world ever again.

CHAPTER TWENTY-FOUR

Krzystof waited until Selina March was out before making a further search of Joanna's things in the hope of finding a clue to her whereabouts. He thought this might be due to some deeply buried subconscious instinct at work – something that was warning him not to trust anyone, and reminding him that it was from this house – Miss March's own house – that Joanna had vanished.

'The mythical Hungarian sixth sense being dusted down and trotted out for an airing?' Joanna would have said, but Krzystof thought it was nothing to do with sixth sense: it was more to do with common sense. And maybe it was a little to do with the fact that he wanted to look into all the other rooms in Teind House, as well. For what? said his mind. Halfwit members of the March family, kept chained in the attics, Mrs Rochester fashion, for the last forty years? Low-browed gentlemen with courtly manners and unfortunate habits when there's a full moon? Now you really *are* becoming Hungarian.

Miss March did not seem to go out very much at all, but this morning she was apparently going on a little shopping expedition with her friend the schoolmistress – incredibly people up here still used expressions like 'schoolmistress' – and Emily-the-elf would be coming later on to help with the ironing. 'Monday is wash day, of course, and so Tuesday is always what I call *linen* day. Ironing, of course, and checking the laundry inventory, and then folding everything away in the airing cupboards.'

'Yes, of course,' said Krzystof, who was used to either himself or Joanna flinging washing into the machine whenever the linen basket was full, turning the dial to a vaguely appropriate setting, and forgetting about it.

'And I do hope, Mr Kent, that you won't think me discourteous for leaving you alone, but I promised to help with the setting up of a little local history project for the schoolchildren.'

'Of course not,' said Krzystof. 'That sounds rather an interesting thing to be doing. Are you an expert on local history, Miss March?'

But Miss March, it seemed, had only the most amateurish of knowledge. It had been Great-uncle Matthew who had been the real scholar. He had been very interested in local history during his life, and after his death Miss March had donated some of his notes and manuscripts to Stornforth library.

'There is a very good library in Stornforth, and also

a bookshop that stocks books and leaflets about the area. And the thing is that Miss Laughlin would like to study them and make notes, and this is the only day that both she and the librarian can be free. They have asked me to be there as well, because I am familiar with my uncle's work. We made the arrangement two weeks ago, you see.'

Clearly she felt that some enormous social transgression was being committed, and Krzystof said, 'Please don't worry about leaving me on my own. I was thinking of going into Stornforth later today, in fact. I could give you and your friend a lift if you want.'

But Miss Laughlin apparently had her own car, although it was extremely kind of Mr Kent to offer. Er – was there any news of Mrs Kent?

'No, nothing,' said Krzystof. 'I drew more or less a blank at Moy, but I thought I'd talk to the Stornforth police again. I think they're still treating Joanna's disappearance as just another runaway wife, and I'd like to put a few squibs under their— Under their chairs,' he amended.

This was not very well received. Miss March asked, worriedly, whether Mr Kent was sure it was advisable to harry the police who would certainly be doing all they could. Great-uncle Matthew had always said, and Aunt Rosa and Aunt Flora had agreed, that the police were a fine body of men. 'And I believe the Stornforth police are *very* conscientious. I'm sure they will be doing all they can to find your wife.'

'Yes, but it won't hurt to just give them a nudge,'

said Krzystof. 'You go off on your expedition, Miss March.'

'We shall be back by lunchtime,' said Selina. 'Unless Miss Laughlin suggests we have some lunch in Stornforth. She might very well do that, you know.'

This was said with such careful off-handedness that it was immediately clear to Krzystof that lunch in Stornforth with Miss Laughlin represented quite a spree. He wondered whether to suggest he meet up with them and treat them to a meal somewhere – the odd, mild little lady had been very kind, and it would be a small thank you – but decided that the prospect of lunch with a man might panic her and spoil her morning. Still, Stornforth was only a small market town; he might bump into them, and the thing might arrange itself naturally.

So he said, 'I'll be fine. Enjoy your morning. I'll be back sometime this afternoon.'

He waited until she had finally left the house, carefully wrapped up against the autumn weather – 'so chilly at this time of year, and my friend likes to drive with her car windows open' – and had disentangled an umbrella from the old-fashioned stand near the door. 'And *do* take one if you go out in the rain, Mr Kent, there are several always here. I usually take the *red* one, so cheering to have a red umbrella in the rain, I think.'

'You'd better take it today,' Krzystof said, reaching down and handing it to her. 'It looks as if it's going to pour down.'

At last Miss March had gone, in a dither of scarves and red brolly and exhortations to make sure he had his front-door key with him in case they missed one another later. Krzystof stood for a moment, feeling Teind House sink back into its silence, but as he crossed the hall to the stairs he was aware once more of the house's unquiet atmosphere swirling around him. It was as if Selina March's absence had released the ghosts; as if, once she had gone, those ghosts took the opportunity to creep from their shadows, and check that their erstwhile charge was being faithful to her upbringing. Ah yes, the two great-aunts might be saying, drawing inquisitive housewifely fingers across ledges and surfaces to check for dust, and peering into store cupboards and larders; ah yes, she is not neglecting her stewardship of the old place. All is well. Great-uncle Matthew probably sneaked into the little room that Miss March called the study, and leafed through housekeeping accounts, the desiccated old miser. Krzystof had not much liked the sound of Great-uncle Matthew.

As he went past the smugly ticking grandfather clock in the hall, he wondered if Joanna had picked up the lingering echoes of Miss March's lonely childhood and the shades of the omni-powerful triad of Great-uncle Matthew and Great-aunts Rosa and Flora, and whether she would use them in a book sometime or other. There was a good deal of the vampire about most writers; an inbuilt compulsion to assess or dissect newly met people in case they could be made use of. Before they were married Joanna had explained about this trait, half humorously, half apologetically, and had said that there was not much she could do about it; it was an inescapable

by-product of writing fiction, and it was to be hoped
Krzystof understood and did not mind. Krzystof had
replied that he entirely understood, and that he would
not mind living with a vampire in the least; in fact quite
the reverse, because there might be times when it would
prove intriguing.

And yes, Joanna would certainly have heard the echoes
inside Teind House.

There was nothing in the least suspicious to be found
inside any of the rooms, and if Joanna had left any clues
for Krzystof to find they had long since been cleared
away. Krzystof, his heart beating guiltily, peered into all
of the bedrooms and opened cupboard doors, and found
nothing, except evidence of Miss March's conscientious
housekeeping.

That left the laptop. Emily had said, on that first
morning, that she did not think Joanna would have gone
away and left the laptop behind, and she was perfectly
right, of course. Joanna might just conceivably leave the
other things behind, but she would never, not if she was
eloping with the richest lover in five continents, not
if hell froze and Armageddon was imminent, have left
Teind House without taking the laptop with her.

He set it on the bed and lifted the cover, his hands
unsteady. He flipped the boot-up key, and the screen
flickered into life, and he scanned the file headings.
After a moment, he keyed into the folder that Joanna
had labelled 'Preliminary Notes'.

If looking through Joanna's clothes had felt intrusive,

this was a million times worse. It was like eavesdropping on her innermost thoughts. I'm sorry, my love, said Krzystof silently to his wife's photograph. But if this is the way of finding out what happened to you, it's got to be done.

The notes were short and a bit scrappy, but the theme was more or less formed, and he saw at once that Joanna had abandoned her usual format of murder/inquiry/suspects/detective. It looked as if she had even abandoned her beloved Inspector Jack Tallent, whose private life was a complexity of slinky females, and his sidekick the stolid Sergeant Prinkworth, who had no private life outside the Metropolitan Police Force at all.

Instead she seemed to be drafting a synopsis for a rather dark, rather brooding story with, at its centre, a flawed and haunted heroine who had suffered some kind of loss or tragedy in her life, and must uncover the truth about that loss and confront the ghosts who clawed at her mind before she could find some peace. This was puzzling, because so far as Krzystof knew Joanna had a contract to deliver a new Jack Tallent book in six months' time.

But here, in what seemed to be a draft for the opening chapter, she had written: *Never having been told the truth was a great part of the problem, because the truth festered beneath the pretence, and any child would have sensed something out of kilter within the family. Most children would probably have sensed, as well, that there were parts of the past that had been sealed away, and might have come to see those years as dark forbidden chasms which must never be approached for fear of falling over the rim. 'There are some eyes that can eat your soul,' one of the younger and more fanciful of the aunts said once, and the phrase, in all its surreal horror, stuck. It was the stuff that nightmares were made on, and in the end it was pointless because the secrecy defeated and distorted its own ends ...*

It was a reasonable opening, with a hook in the first sentence to snag the reader's imagination and draw him or her in. What slightly puzzled Krzystof was that it read as if Joanna was planning a 'dark journey to the centre of the soul' type of book, and while she would probably make a competent job of it – if the use of the word 'competent' was not to damn with faint praise – it was by no means her usual style. Krzystof read on.

For a child to have stumbled on that small, largely incomprehensible fragment of the story was at best unfortunate, at worst, damaging. The trouble was that there was no one who could be asked for the truth – there was no one who could be approached, and even if there had been it was doubtful if the truth would have been told. And so the barely understood secret became woven into childhood nightmares and childhood fears, and in the end it called the poor mangled ghosts out of their uneasy resting places ... At times, the pretence spilled over into ordinary life ...

There was a rough synopsis of events – Joanna seemed to be intending her heroine to tell her story from early childhood onwards, describing key incidents along the way. There were scrappy references to whispers and to the pursed-lipped conversations of older family members when she was six and seven – there was a note about the child listening unseen to a conversation at some family gathering, which she had not, at the time, understood, but which, Krzystof supposed, was intended to indicate to the reader a little of what lay ahead.

There are some eyes that can eat your soul ... Yes, a child, overhearing that, would interpret it literally; not understanding that it was intended to convey a specific character trait or one of the hungers that sometimes erodes the human psyche.

He scrolled the screen down. There was the discovery of a scrapbook of press cuttings when the heroine was ten; Krzystof understood that this would be the girl's stumbling on the fragment of the old tragedy, whatever the tragedy might be. He considered it doubtfully, because this finding of old newspaper articles smacked of the 'device', the too-slick, too-convenient trick to further a plot or engineer a situation. It was not like Joanna to make use of that. But perhaps in the context— She's arguing out her plot, thought Krzystof. She's talking into the computer to see if she can reach a credible story.

The notes ended abruptly, with the heroine deciding to ferret out the truth about her family's past. No, it was not Joanna's normal stuff by a very long way, in fact it was verging on Gothic romance. Krzystof exited the file and logged off thoughtfully, closing the laptop's lid and putting it back in place.

It was interesting and vaguely thought-provoking, but it did not seem to provide any clue to Joanna's state of mind before she disappeared, or to what might have happened to her.

Or did it? As Krzystof donned a jacket and hunted

for his car keys, something was tugging at the back of his mind, and he had the feeling that there had been something in the roughed-out notes that he had missed. Some kind of sub-text that he should have been able to read.

But even if he was right about that, would it have led him to where Joanna was now?

He drove away from Teind House, his mind still sorting through what he had read, but he could not fasten onto anything of any significance. The best thing to do was to put the whole thing to one side and see if his subconscious could make something of it. He concentrated on looking for the Stornforth sign, which was three-quarters hidden from view by an overhanging tree. He had missed it on his first journey, and had had to retrace his steps. No, here it was. Sharp turn right.

He glimpsed the Round Tower's brooding shape in the driving mirror as he turned. Mary Maskelyne had mentioned the tower: she had said Joanna had seemed interested in it. That was probably true. Joanna would have been attracted by the place; she would have absorbed its faintly eerie atmosphere delightedly through every one of her senses and she would probably have tracked down a few local legends about it.

Would she have latched onto the tower as a base for a plot? Had it been at the heart of that curious, uncharacteristic synopsis? It would be quite atmospheric to have a murder in a place like that, of course. Mystery writers were always looking for unusual venues where corpses could take up residence.

But this line of thought brought Krzystof back to the curious fact that Joanna, who had made her name by writing jigsaw-puzzle whodunnits, and who was committed to delivering a new Jack Tallent novel in time for publication next November, seemed to have been setting out not a straightforward detective story, but something quite different.

An introverted child who believed that there were people with eyes that could eat your soul, who suspected that there were dark chasms within her family, and that within those chasms were the mangled ghosts of the past.

He drove on towards Stornforth, his mind working.

CHAPTER TWENTY-FIVE

——⋙◆⋘——

Selina had a very pleasant and very useful morning in Stornforth.

First, there had been the library, where she had been received with flattering deference. The McAvoy papers, said the librarian, producing the box for Selina and Lorna Laughlin to sift, were regarded as an extremely good source for students of the area. They were always happy to make them available to genuine enquirers.

The McAvoy papers. Great-uncle Matthew would have liked to hear his work called by so scholarly a name. He would have been pleased to think of the fruits of his work filed in the library's reference section, labelled and docketed in such seemly fashion, and even, it seemed, now destined for immortality on computer.

Lorna Laughlin was pleased with the results of their morning's work. They had found some interesting snippets of little-known legends about Inchcape which the children could trace back – things like the ancient record of Henry the Minstrel – 'Blind Harry' – visiting Inchcape's monastery and being paid the sum of two shillings for singing to the community on Twelfth Night in 1485. Great-uncle Matthew, conscientious as always, had added a note to say that the entry for this payment could be seen in the monastery rolls which were preserved in the museum.

And there was the tale of how the famous Stone of Destiny – the *Lia Fail* – had come through Stornforth on its way to Scone in AD 840, nearly five hundred years before the English stole it and took it to Westminster Abbey. Lorna thought this would be a very good inclusion in the project, since it would bring in several aspects of history. Great-uncle Matthew, a stickler for accuracy, had pointed out the improbability of the Stone's ever having rested at Stornforth, but even he had gone on to note down the prophecy supposedly affixed to the Stone, and translated by Sir Walter Scott as,

> *Unless the fates be faulty grown*
> *And prophet's voice be vain*
> *Where'er is found this sacred stone*
> *The Scottish race shall reign.*

'Nice,' Lorna said, pleased. 'The brats can take in some seventeenth- and eighteenth-century border ballads along the way; in fact we might even make it the basis for a little end-of-term play. I'll bet Emily Frost would help with that. She's amazingly good with the children, and she was reading history at Durham until her mother died.'

This came as something of a shock to Selina, who had been assuming that Emily had simply left school the instant it was legally permissible and had drifted around doing nothing ever since. It was rather upsetting to find she had so misjudged the child; she would try to find a tactful way of making it up to her. But Lorna's idea about the children's play was a good one, and Selina offered to help in any way she could. Costumes, perhaps; she had always been a reasonable needlewoman.

They did stay out for lunch, so it was as well Selina had mentioned the possibility to Krzystof Kent. Lorna insisted on taking them to the Stornforth Arms, where Selina had something called Coronation Chicken which sounded fairly traditional, and turned out to be chicken pieces in a tomato-flavoured sauce, flanked with a jacket potato and some sprigs of broccoli. There was apple tart and ice-cream to follow, and then a cup of coffee. It was nice to be out like this, watching all the people coming and going, although it was a pity the Stornforth Arms played pop music so loudly all the time.

It was quite late when they set off again, and they were a little delayed by Selina's having left her umbrella in the Stornforth Arms and having to go back for it. And then Lorna took a wrong turning which was something to do with a new one-way system and delayed them even more, since it involved driving round Stornforth three times more than they had expected, and then taking a road that wound around the northern outskirts.

'Magical mystery tour,' said Lorna, frowning at the road-signs. 'I do wish they'd give you better warning when they change the road systems. Oh, wait though, isn't that the road that goes out to the old infirmary? Yes, it is. Oh good, then I know where I am now.' She swung the car ruthlessly into a different lane, and said, 'Now we're on our way home.'

'Now we're on our way home,' Great-uncle Matthew used to say, on the rare occasions when Selina was allowed to accompany him into Stornforth. This was not something that happened very often, but after both the aunts were dead and Selina had left school, there were sometimes calls to be made at the various stores in Stornforth which delivered provisions to Inchcape.

Selina kept an inventory of the store cupboards because Aunt Flora had said it was the correct way to run a house. Even though the interfering old trout was dead it did not mean that Selina had to disobey her training, and three or four times a year she went into Stornforth with Great-uncle Matthew when he attended his hospital governors' meetings. He was very conscientious about the meetings, and arranged his activities around the dates because he said people depended on him.

They did not drive to the little market town because Great-uncle Matthew had never learned to drive and did not approve of cars anyway, so they caught a bumbly country bus that left Inchcape at half past eleven, and rattled and bounced across the moors and finally disgorged its passengers at Stornforth bus station forty-five minutes later. Uncle Matthew usually waited for a lift from one of the other governors which he had arranged beforehand, and Selina was free to sample the muted delights of Stornforth's hectic metropolis by herself. These consisted of a cup of tea and a poached egg on toast at the little coffee shop near the bus station, which Great-uncle Matthew said was ample nourishment at lunchtime, and then the delivery of the quarterly order for what Aunt Flora had called dried goods to Mr Mackenzie, whose shop smelt pleasantly of tea and coffee beans and raisins, and who had huge tubs containing flour and sugar and sago and pudding rice.

Twice a year a visit to O'Donnell's drapery was incorporated into the expedition as well. O'Donnell's smelt of bales of cloth that prickled Selina's eyes, and it was where she bought new tea cloths or sheets for the house, and knitting wool and patterns for her winter jumpers, and sometimes a new summer outfit. It was nice to go into the shops like this, and it was always a busy day when the orders were delivered to Teind House the following week, what with waiting for Mackenzie's van to come. Mr Mackenzie's nephew drove the van and helped to carry the things in; he was learning the business from the bottom up and one day he would be Neil Mackenzie of Mackenzie's. Selina always gave him a cup of coffee, and they talked while he drank it; he told her how he was learning about profit-and-loss accounts, and how to distinguish between good quality tea and what used to be called floor-sweepings, and how he hoped to go to Kenya next year, to see the coffee plantations. Next time she was in the shop he would show her the different coffee beans and how they were ground up in a little machine.

Great-uncle Matthew thought it was a waste of milk and sugar to be feeding tradesmen cups of coffee, and he was annoyed when, one month, Selina washed her hair on the night before Neil Mackenzie's visit and he could not get into the bathroom to pare his corns, but Selina went on making the coffee and hearing about the profit-and-loss and the coffee beans.

Great-uncle Matthew did not come with Selina to Mackenzie's or O'Donnell's, of course. He went straight off to the hospital, where he had his lunch with the other governors, which would be considerably more than poached egg on toast. But he did not like going in shops, although he occasionally bought shirts and collars at Stornforth's Gentlemen's Outfitters, and twice a year he went to the wine merchants. He would not permit Selina to buy alcohol, just as he had never permitted the aunts to buy it. He made a lengthy business of choosing sherry and port, sampling the wine merchant's stock in the tiny taster glasses provided, and tsk-ing over the shocking way prices went up every year.

Selina was just seventeen when she discovered that Great-uncle Matthew had been sampling other things than wine on his monthly visits to Stornforth.

It happened by the purest chance, and if it had not been for Selina's having turned her ankle on a bit of uneven paving stone, and being helped to hobble into a chemist's shop in Malt Street by a concerned passer-by, she might never have known about the tall thin house standing in the alley.

The chemist's shop was not Timothy White's in Market Street, which was where Selina usually bought aspirin and bismuth and the senna pods without which Great-uncle Matthew's life, viscerally speaking, would have been unendurable. It was a small, rather dark little place with huge glass bottles filled with coloured water taking up the windows, and a dusty sign saying that prescriptions were dispensed here. But the chemist was helpful and concerned; he applied arnica to the ankle and bound it with a crêpe bandage, and after a little while Selina tested it and thought she could walk as far as the bus station. She had done all her errands, and she was due to meet her uncle, she said. It would not do to be late.

'If you turn left as you go out of my shop and keep going along Malt Street,' said the chemist, 'and then go through Farthing Alley, you'll come to the bus station in five minutes. It'll be a sight quicker than going all round through Market Street.'

Selina had not known about this short cut. She thanked the chemist for his kindness, and wondered if she was expected to pay for the arnica and the crêpe bandage. It was a situation where the wrong thing might easily offend. So she said, 'While I'm here, could I buy some really nice men's shaving soap? For a Christmas present.' The soap would do for the vicar; Selina never knew what to buy for him.

The chemist was pleased at the request. He helped Selina to choose a box of gentlemen's soap called Spruce which smelt like a pine forest in winter, and wrapped it up in a neat little parcel for her. When Selina paid for it the arnica and the bandage were not mentioned, so she thought she had balanced things out nicely.

She made her way to the bus station, taking the short cut the chemist had described, and it was just as she was halfway along Farthing Alley, which was not quite an alley but not quite a street either, that she saw Great-uncle Matthew. He was coming out of a tall, slightly seedy-looking house with furtively curtained windows and he was in company with another man whom Selina recognised as the other governor who usually gave Uncle Matthew a lift to the hospital meetings. They both looked a bit flushed of face and bright of eye and they were laughing together in a sly way that was so completely unlike Great-uncle Matthew that Selina had to look twice to make sure it was not his double.

But it was not. He was wearing his dark overcoat and the paisley scarf he had put on that morning, and carrying the rolled-up umbrella with the horse's head handle. As she watched, the other man said something, fruitily, jokingly, and pointed, and Great-uncle Matthew looked down, and fumbled with a button on his trousers, and they both laughed again.

Selina was not entirely clear what the house with the peeling façade might be, but whatever else it was, it was certainly not the boardroom of Stornforth's Hospital governors.

She thought about the house and Great-uncle Matthew's curious behaviour all the way home on the jolting bus, staring through the window so that she would not have to look at him, so that she would not keep seeing that sly gleam and that furtive buttoning of his trousers.

Great-uncle Matthew did not think that Selina had balanced things out nicely by buying the Spruce soap from the unknown chemist's shop at all.

Once they were home and Selina had made a pot of tea, he asked to see a list of her purchases and the receipts, just as he always did. He took them off to his study to check, and was shocked to his toes at the cost of the Spruce soap. He came into the kitchen where Selina was seeing to the fish they were having for supper, because Great-uncle Matthew could never stomach a large supper after eating lunch in the hospital dining room. While Selina was trimming runner beans to go with the fish, he told her she had wasted good money buying such rubbish.

'I thought I ought to buy something in the shop as a thank you. I thought it would do as a Christmas present for the vicar. And the chemist was so nice, and so helpful. There was the arnica and the crêpe bandage as well. He didn't charge me for either of those.'

Great-uncle Matthew hoped not indeed. If Selina must needs go stravaiging about Stornforth, falling down in the street, it was only Christian for her to be helped. He would call at the man's shop the next time he was in Stornforth and thank him personally. That was all that was required, and there had been no need for Selina to go spending money like a drunken sailor.

As he went out of the kitchen, he said, apparently as an afterthought, that it was to be hoped that Selina was not making herself cheap by running after the vicar, as her Great-aunt Flora used to do.

When it was the Stornforth day again, he went off on the eleven-thirty bus as he always did, carrying the leather briefcase he always carried, dressed in his familiar overcoat and the paisley scarf. (Preparing to unbutton his trousers inside that slummy-looking house . . . ?)

There was some cold lamb left over from Sunday's lunch, so Selina minced it for shepherd's pie. The dish could stand on the marble slab in the larder, and the potatoes could be added and crisped in the oven for supper later on. Great-uncle Matthew liked shepherd's pie.

She made herself an early lunch, and washed up afterwards, and then she went upstairs and put on her school mackintosh and a felt hat with a deep brim. The Stornforth buses came through Inchcape several times a day: she would easily catch the two o'clock one.

It felt exciting in a peculiar and slightly disturbing way to be doing this: to be going secretly into Stornforth, and to be wondering what she was going to find inside the seedy old house in Farthing Alley. She kept her mackintosh well buttoned up and her hat pulled down, but even if anyone she knew saw her there was no reason why she should not be in Stornforth.

Farthing Alley was exactly as she remembered it: narrow, slightly run-down old houses that might once have belonged to quite prosperous merchants, but had now fallen into forlorn disrepair. Most of the buildings had grimy windows and doors which needed painting, and several of them had obviously been turned into lodging houses. The house where Selina had seen Great-uncle Matthew was halfway along, and it was larger than she had realised; there were three storeys and the upper windows were all firmly curtained. The vaguely uncomfortable excitement returned. What was going on behind those curtains? Was her uncle in one of those rooms?

There were not many people abroad in Farthing Alley; Selina thought it was not a place where you would linger. You would only come here if you had business of some kind – perhaps in one of the dark, dismal little offices on the ground floor of several of the buildings – and once you had conducted your business you would leave as quickly as possible. Or you would come here if you were unfortunate enough to live in one of the lodging houses with the dusty fig-leaf plants in the windows and the grey net curtains. Or, of course, if you were bound for the large three-storeyed house whose windows had drawn curtains at three o'clock in the afternoon . . .

No one was around as she went towards it, and the only movement was from a discarded newspaper, flapping in the gutter. Selina kept her eyes on the house. Her heart was still beating too fast, and she felt sticky with sweat under her arms. Did Great-uncle Matthew feel excited like this when he came here? It was difficult to imagine him feeling any emotion other than disapproval.

There was an empty building on the other side of the road with an inset doorway; it smelt of public lavatories and cats but it would provide reasonable concealment. Selina stepped into the doorway, trying not to notice the smell, and waited. She was not sure what she was going to do, but surely at some point someone was going to come out of the house or go into it? And providing she was careful, it ought to be possible to stand forward a bit so that she could see in. As long as it was not Great-uncle Matthew himself who came out, it might even be possible to walk briskly past the house and sneak a good look inside.

But it was a very long time before this happened, and Selina was beginning to think she would have to go back home, because she had got to catch an earlier bus than Great-uncle Matthew's usual five o'clock one. She had to be back in Teind House when he got home, and look as if she had been there all day.

And then, just as she was thinking she would have to start walking along to the bus station, the door of the house was thrown open, and a group of men stood there talking and laughing. One of them looked like Great-uncle Matthew. Selina pressed back into the empty doorway, her mackintosh collar turned well up. She dared not lean too far forward in case she was noticed, but it would be infuriating if, after all this, she did not see anything.

But she did. The men were not looking into the street at all, and she was able to see straight into the wide hall beyond the open door. There were not only men in the hall; there were females as well. (But hadn't she expected that?)

Three women were standing in the hall, clearly bidding farewell to Great-uncle Matthew and the two men with him. They wore silk dressing gowns – vivid scarlet or brilliant turquoise – sketchily tied at the waist so that their thighs showed when they walked, and their bosoms were half spilling out. The dressing gowns were nothing like any dressing gown Selina had ever seen: they were thin and clingy, and so revealing the females might almost as well not have bothered to wear them.

It was Great-uncle Matthew, of course; Selina could see him quite clearly. The woman in the scarlet silk gown was standing with him, and she was laughing in what Great-aunt Rosa would have said was a very common way, and even from here Selina could see that she had bright red lipstick on and blue stuff on her eyelids. It made her face look sharp and predatory.

She was smoking a cigarette – Great-uncle Matthew had always said he hated to see a woman smoking; he said it was a sign of very low breeding. He did not like lipstick, either; he said it was vulgar and only fit for street women, but he did not seem to mind about the cigarette held between the woman's thin fingers. Her fingernails were enamelled bright red. They looked like claws.

Claws ... A shred of deep-buried memory uncurled itself. Thin hungry claws swooping out of a night sky, tearing at soft flesh, digging out eyes ... Like a harpy. Selina knew about harpies; they were mythological creatures with the faces of women and the bodies of birds.

Great-uncle Matthew was bending his head to the scarlet-clawed, lipsticked harpy creature, laughing at

344

something she said, and then looking at his watch and tapping it in the way he did when he said that time was getting on. Selina pressed back into the doorway because if he should look up and see her—

He did not look up. The harpy had wound her left arm around his neck, and her other hand slid under his overcoat and down between his legs. There was a burst of laughter from the other men and a shriek of mirth from one of the women, and the harpy said to Great-uncle Matthew, 'Well, ye're a randy auld devil,' in an ugly Glaswegian accent.

None of them noticed Selina scuttling back down Farthing Alley, to catch the four o'clock bus back to Inchcape so that she would be safely home in time to cook the shepherd's pie for supper.

CHAPTER TWENTY-SIX

❖

For several days after the furtive visit to Stornforth Selina felt quite ill every time she looked at her uncle. It was not that he seemed any different; in fact one of the grotesque things about the whole affair was that he looked and acted precisely as he always did.

The difference was within Selina herself. She kept seeing the falling-open scarlet silk dressing gown of the blowsy, sleazy woman, and she kept seeing the red-tipped hand that was really a claw sliding in between her uncle's thighs.

She kept seeing the two of them together in a bed as well, Great-uncle Matthew's trousers folded over a chair, his mouth smeary with lipstick from where he had kissed the woman's jam-coloured mouth, his scrawny legs embarrassingly naked as he pressed his body up against her . . .

It was still only the late 1950s, and enlightened sex education was a thing of the future. The girls at Inchcape's little school had been given the basic details about menstruation by an embarrassed but determined district nurse whose task it was to travel from school to school to talk to thirteen-year-olds, and then to return to tell the fifteen-year-olds how babies were conceived. It was not the nurse's fault that by that time most of her audience had gleaned the necessary information from older sisters or cousins anyway, and passed it on to their friends, and it was certainly not her fault that the information she imparted was often surprisingly different from the whispered, giggled-over details exchanged in the playground or on the edge of the hockey field.

Selina had listened to the nurse's talks along with the others, keeping her eyes fixed on the ground because it was dreadful, it was the most embarrassing thing in the world, to have to hear words and descriptions like that. 'First the man has to be aroused . . .' 'Here is a diagram . . .' 'Here is what happens at the moment of conception . . .'

The woman in Farthing Alley had called Great-uncle Matthew a randy auld devil. Had he done *that* with her? It was worlds and light years away from the act described by the impassive-faced nurse and depicted by the carefully characterless diagrams, but when you boiled it down it was exactly the same thing. *First, the man has to be aroused . . . Here is a diagram . . . This is what her body looks like . . . This is what his body looks like . . .*

It was horridly easy to see the enamelled claws stroking

that body, and to imagine the harpy crouching over Great-uncle Matthew, waiting for the moment when she would tear into his flesh with her claws. And all the while, the common voice whispering coaxingly that he was a randy auld devil . . .

Great-uncle Matthew, who drank a brew of senna pods twice a week to help his recalcitrant bowels, and who frowned if the clock in the hall lost time and tsk-ed if Selina tuned the wireless to the Light Programme— This was the man who was a randy auld devil who went to bed with prostitutes and harpies – who *paid* them to let him do those things to them. (*First the man has to be aroused . . .*)

He *paid*. After a while, it was this aspect of the whole thing that stuck in Selina's mind, and kept nibbling at her. Great-uncle Matthew, who complained if the grocery bill was a shilling too much, and insisted that every scrap of leftover food was used up in hash and fishcakes and mulligatawny soup, had *paid* that woman to go to bed with him. The aunts always used to say that Matthew was careful with money, but in the aunts' time he had not been as – as *obsessional* about saving money as he was now. Because he wanted to spend all his money on the harpy-woman? Was that why?

Selina looked up the word 'harpy' in the encyclopaedia in her uncle's study after that extraordinary afternoon. He was in the bathroom and it had been a senna pod night, which meant he would be up there for a while, so it was safe to sneak into his study and find what she wanted. Selina rifled the pages, her heart racing with apprehension in case he came in and caught her, because she was not supposed to touch anything in this room. But she would hear him coming back downstairs; she would hear the creak of the fourth stair where the boards were worn. She flipped the pages over. Surely there would be something— Ah, here it was.

Harpies, said the entry, were monsters from ancient mythology. They had the faces of hags and the bodies and claws of birds. They tormented blind people, snatching their food away or even defecating on it, and cackling delightedly. In some of the myths they lived inside the storm-winds, and helped the storm-winds to sweep mortal travellers down to the underworld. There was an artist's impression of a harpy; Selina thought you would only have to clothe it in a scarlet gown and paint its claws red for it to look like the woman in Farthing Alley. And if you placed it against a darkling sky on the top of an old black tower on an Indian hillside, would the harpy look any different from the ogre-birds who had eaten dead bodies . . . ?

Directly under the entry was a description of harpy eagles. It explained about the harpy eagle's predilection for killing animals much larger than itself: young deer, monkeys, sloths. Humans? There was a photograph of a harpy eagle; you could practically interchange it with the drawing of a female harpy in the entry above.

Selina closed the book and returned it to its place on the shelf. Harpies. Great-uncle Matthew was in the clutches of a harpy. Scarlet claws and talons. Greedy harpy-mentality. Not quite one of the ogre-birds who came swooping out of the dark sky and tore at flesh and bone, but near enough to it to be dangerous. That woman would not claw out his eyes or dig out his heart and lungs, but she would bleed him dry of his money.

Selina had never really thought much about money, but she thought about it now. She thought about what might happen if Great-uncle Matthew spent all of his money on the harpy, and about what might happen to Selina herself in that case. Might they have to sell Teind House? And move to another place entirely? Selina was seized with panic at the prospect. Teind had been a haunted place when she was small, it had been haunted by the terrible shades of her parents, but she had found a way to deal with those ghosts; she had created a shrine for them, and it had kept them safely at bay all these years. It did not precisely accord with the Religious Knowledge lessons Selina had learned at Inchcape's school, but it was not so very different. The important thing was that the shrine seemed to have helped her parents to make their way into the afterlife, and it had stopped them from sneaking and creeping into the house under cover of darkness.

But what if Selina had to live in another house, where she could no longer walk across to the Round Tower and its secret room whenever she wanted, or put flowers in the little crystal vase for her mother, and take a newspaper cutting of foreign events for her father, and what if she had to live somewhere where it would not be so easy to set up another shrine? What if they even went to live in Stornforth itself so that Great-uncle Matthew could be nearer to the harpy?

For a few days Selina considered getting rid of the silly

boring old man, but every time she tried to formulate a plan to do so, she came up against problems. The aunts had both died when Selina was very young, and their deaths had been thought accidental; it had not occurred to anyone that Selina had had anything to do with them.

But for Matthew to die in an 'accident' might make people look at her askance. It might make them start to ask questions. A *third* accidental death? they might say. Bit of a coincidence, isn't it? And what about Teind House and the money? Selina thought that any money the aunts might have had would have gone to Great-uncle Matthew, and if anything happened to him it would come to Selina herself. She was not very well up on inheritances and wills, but she was reasonably sure that she would not be allowed to inherit anything in her own right until she was twenty-one. She thought some kind of guardian or trustee might have to be appointed, and the last thing she wanted was someone snooping and prying and telling her what to do, and perhaps even finding the shrine. It was not to be thought of, and neither was murdering Great-uncle Matthew; or, to be precise, it was not to be thought of for the next four years, until Selina was safely twenty-one.

But something had got to be done.

Selina went over and over the problem in her mind, but it was several weeks before she found the answer.

In the way of such things, the solution came to her when her mind was concentrating on something else altogether, and by a quirk of coincidence it happened on the day of a delivery from Mackenzie's.

It was only six weeks after the astonishing, disgusting afternoon in Farthing Alley, but there were only three weeks to Christmas, and normally Selina would have gone along on the Stornforth trip because there were extra things to order for the holiday, along with the normal tea and coffee and sago and porridge oats. She would have enjoyed seeing Stornforth with the festive lights in the shops and the decorated tree in the little market square. She would have eaten her modest lunch in the friendly little café, and she might have spoken to Neil Mackenzie if he was in the shop and heard how the plans for the Kenyan trip were going.

But none of this could happen, because there was now a complete ban on Selina's going into Stornforth. Shortly after the Farthing Alley episode Great-uncle Matthew had told Selina that he had never really been happy about letting her roam around by herself while he was conducting business, and that he had been giving the matter some thought. He did not see why the orders for provisions could not be posted to Mackenzie and O'Donnell, he said. A twopenny ha'penny stamp would in fact be considerably cheaper than the bus fare, to say nothing of the lunch that Selina had to buy for herself in Stornforth.

Selina said, 'I only have poached egg on toast and a cup of tea. It doesn't cost much at all.'

This was not the point. If you added everything up it came to quite a sum. They were not made of money, did Selina understand that?

'Yes, I understand,' said Selina.

*　　*　　*

And so the Christmas orders had been written for Mackenzie's and O'Donnell's, with a little explanatory note enclosed with each, and both letters had been posted in the village. When Neil delivered the provisions that morning, he expressed regret at having missed Selina last week.

But oddly, it was no longer possible to enjoy making the cup of coffee in Teind's kitchen and offering Neil the biscuits, carefully baked the previous day. It was no longer possible to take a mild pleasure in washing her hair the night before and setting it in wavy clips, and brushing it out until it shone. It was only possible to remember the diagrams – *First the man has to be aroused* ... – and to see scarlet-tipped talons fumbling at trouser fastenings, and hear sly laughter. *Ye're a randy auld devil* ... And to wonder, all in the same breath, whether Neil could behave in that way. Sly. Fumbling and groping. Furtive and hot-eyed.

Dreadful. *Disgusting.* Selina thought that Neil probably could behave in that way, because very likely all men could. Best to keep clear of all men, in that case.

After Neil had gone, there was quite a lot to be done. The newly-delivered provisions had to be stored away, and new labels with dates on them had to be written out and pasted onto jars and packets. An up-to-date inventory had to be prepared, and a list tacked onto the larder door, in the way that Aunt Flora had taught Selina.

She was not especially thinking about the house in Farthing Alley, and she was not particularly thinking about how to deal with Great-uncle Matthew and safe-guard her own inheritance. And then – between tipping the tea into the little tea chest and setting the tins of sardines in their place – the idea slid into her mind, and it was so abrupt and so unexpected that for a moment the cool, north-facing larder blurred and wavered all around her. Selina took several deep breaths and held on to the edge of a shelf, and after a minute she was able to go on with what she was doing. But her mind was no longer on labelling tins; her mind was scurrying back and forth across the extraordinary plan that had dropped into her brain, and the more she studied it, and the more her mind padded cautiously around it, the more she saw it was the only thing to do.

Annoyingly, it had to wait until Christmas was over.

Because of the prohibition on Stornforth, Selina had bought her small gifts from the village store. She had a tiny, grudgingly given sum for pocket money, and she had saved it up to buy woollen gloves and a matching muffler for Great-uncle Matthew, a calendar for the vicar's sister who housekept for him, and Yardley's lavender bath salts for two of the ladies in the Church Ladies' Guild.

When the aunts were alive there had always been roast turkey or roast goose for Christmas dinner, and the vicar and some of the Church Ladies came to lunch on Boxing Day. Since the aunts had died, Great-uncle Matthew had decreed that Selina could not cope with cooking food for other folks to eat, and so they just had a roast chicken for their own Christmas dinner, and sandwiches and trifle in the evening. On Boxing Day they were asked to supper at the vicarage, and Selina wore her best blouse with the embroidered collar. The next Stornforth hospital meeting – what Great-uncle Matthew *said* was the next Stornforth hospital meeting! – was set for 15 January. He wrote it down on the calendar.

'Oh, what a coincidence,' said Selina at once. 'That's the day I have to be at Dr Munroe's surgery.'

Doctor? Munroe?

'He's in Stornforth. I've got to be there at twelve o'clock. I thought I could catch the ten-thirty bus, and come home straight afterwards – that needn't disrupt you at all, need it? I'll be home well before you, and I'll have supper ready as usual.'

He could not decide whether it was disruptive or not. He did not quite ask why Selina could not see old Dr Leckie in the village, but he nearly did. Selina, picking this up, said, vaguely, 'Oh, it's only to get a routine check. Dr Leckie thought it would be a good idea. A female thing.'

Great-uncle Matthew said, oh, a female thing, was it? and h'rrmphed himself out of the kitchen and into the unembarrassing safety of his study. Selina smiled and went on peeling potatoes. Everything was working out beautifully, and when you thought about it from another angle it would be a very good thing to save Great-uncle Matthew from that scarlet-fanged creature. He was committing the sin of fornication with her, of course – Selina was not absolutely clear about fornication, despite the brisk talks by the nurse – but the Bible said it was a sin. So if the harpy could be removed, Great-uncle Matthew would not be tempted to fornicate with her.

On 15 January she went off punctually to catch the ten-thirty bus, wearing her camel coat and brown beret, carrying a small shopping bag. After she had been to Dr Munroe's surgery she might look in at O'Donnell's, she said. Someone had told her they had an after-Christmas sale there, and she could look for buttons for the cardigan she was knitting, and perhaps some new tea cloths. And with reasonable luck she would catch the one o'clock bus back to Stornforth and have a late lunch at home.

She waited until the bus had trundled back across the square, and then pulled her mackintosh out of her shopping bag and put it on over her coat. She tied a headscarf over her hair, and tucked her hair under it. The beret was laid carefully in the shopping bag. Good enough? Yes. In the reflection from a shop window she looked so insignificant as to be nearly invisible. So far so good, in fact so far more than good. She smoothed the thin leather gloves over her hands, making sure they would not slide off. The aunts had said you could always tell a lady by her gloves. Selina would not have dreamed of going out without gloves.

It felt peculiar to walk down Farthing Alley once more, but it also felt exciting again, in the secret, heart-pounding way. Selina stood in front of the tall old house and looked at the tightly drawn curtains at all the windows. Was she in there now, that harpy? It was a little after twelve o'clock. Great-uncle Matthew, if he followed his normal pattern and if the eleven-thirty bus was on time, ought to get here in just over half an hour. Was that sufficient for what she had to do? Selina thought it was.

Taking several deep breaths, she crossed the road, continually glancing about her to make sure she was not observed. If someone came along, she would take it as a sign to abandon everything. But Farthing Alley was sunk in its usual deserted quiet, and no one appeared. It was not really a fair test, though. If the door of the house was locked, that would be the real sign, the one she would obey. But the door would not be locked; Selina knew that.

She was right. The handle turned softly and easily, and the door swung inwards. Selina looked up and down the alleyway once more, and then stepped inside.

CHAPTER TWENTY-SEVEN

＞＜

She had not been able to form any mental image of the inside of the house, because nothing in her life until now had prepared her for such a place. She supposed, vaguely, that there would be a degree of comfort, and obviously there would be beds to lie on (did Great Uncle Matthew get undressed and lie on one of those beds, pulling his shirt up, the harpy helping him . . . ?); but weighed bewilderingly against all that was the run-down appearance of the house itself and the sordid seediness of Farthing Alley.

What she was totally unprepared for was the grubby splendour of the interior, and its curious smell, which, although Selina did not realise it, was the smell of years of cheap perfume, ingrained cigarette smoke, and sexual intercourse.

She stood looking about her. The hall was larger than

she had expected; doors opened off on each side and directly ahead was a staircase. The walls were papered in thick crimson flock paper with a fleur-de-lys pattern – Great-aunt Flora had been very fond of the fleur-de-lys pattern; the dining room at Teind House had wallpaper with that design, although it was as well that Aunt Flora could not see it here.

There was a desk littered with papers and a telephone, and there were pink-shaded lights, and pink chairs with crimson satin cushions. Horrid, thought Selina. Cheap and gaudy and altogether horrid.

The doors on the left and right were both ajar, but as far as she could see neither was a bedroom. There were heavy mahogany tables in both the rooms, with bottles of whisky and brandy, and glasses on silver trays. The glasses did not look very clean and the ashtrays did not look as if they were emptied often enough. At the other end of the hall, beyond the stairs, was an archway, and beyond that was what was clearly a door into the kitchen quarters. Selina could hear, very faintly, the clatter of crockery, and voices. Would there be servants here? Would they be preparing a midday meal? She had no idea, but she must not stand here and risk discovery. If anyone did come out and see her she was going to say that she was looking for Number 23 where her cousin was staying. Number 23 was the larger of the two lodging houses in Farthing Alley; Selina had made a mental note of the number before coming in.

But no one came out, and after a moment she began to stealthily ascend the stairs. Every nerve in her body was jumping with apprehension by this time, because if someone found her now the story of the cousin at Number 23 would sound a bit thin. But nothing stirred, and she reached the first floor without mishap.

She had had no idea how she was to find the harpy, and she had had no idea how many other harpies there might be inside the house either. There had been three of them on that never-forgotten afternoon, but this was quite a large house and for all Selina knew there might easily be half a dozen of them. There was also the problem about whether they actually lived here, or whether they just came here to go to bed with men, but Selina thought it more likely that they lived here.

It was now quarter past twelve, and unless Great-uncle Matthew ate his lunch somewhere in Stornforth and then came on here, he would arrive in about fifteen minutes. Selina's heart began to race, because this was cutting it finer than she had hoped. But it had taken longer than she had thought to get her bearings, and it might take even longer to find the right bedroom.

The right bedroom. There, at the end of the first-floor landing, was an open door, and inside the room was a satin-covered bed with a familiar scarlet silk dressing gown lying on it, like a glossy pool of blood. Selina's heartbeat accelerated, but with it came a heightened excitement. It's all right. I'm meant to do this, that's why it's being made easy for me. I've found the right room straight away.

There was no one in the room. It would not have mattered very much if there had been, because by now

Selina was strung up to a pitch of such high tension that she knew she could have done what she had planned to do. But the room was empty, and Selina looked round carefully, and then took up a position behind the door. She set the shopping basket on the floor next to her, taking from beneath the rolled up beret the long-bladed knife, carefully sharpened in Teind House's kitchen that morning. The handle felt familiar in her hand, even through the thin gloves. It gave her confidence, not that she really needed it, because she knew this was the absolute right thing to do. She was saving her uncle from the predator who had dug her claws into him, and she was saving her own inheritance.

Twelve twenty. Come on, Great-uncle Matthew. And come on, scarlet-taloned harpy. A hideous doubt skittered across her mind. Supposing he *was* having his lunch somewhere else? Selina had assumed he came straight here from the eleven-thirty bus, but she might have been wrong. If he did not come soon, the entire plan would collapse. Oh God, oh God, let him come, don't let him be delayed. But did people who came to this kind of house expect to eat lunch here as well as going to bed? Selina dug the fingernails of her left hand into her palm in mingled anger and panic. Stay calm. Think of alternatives. Think of what to do if the scarlet harpy brings someone else here. Might that happen? Did these females go to bed with more than one man in the day?

And then there was the sound of the main door downstairs opening, and a man's voice. Was it him? Yes, there was the throat-clearing sound he sometimes made. Oh thank you, thank you! And now she could hear the shrill Glaswegian voice greeting him, saying, Oh, here you are again, and saying, Oh, we'll have a fine auld afternoon together. There was the chink of crockery, and Selina caught, very faintly, the aroma of hot food. She held her breath, because if people were going to start coming into the room with trays—

But again it was all right. Great-uncle Matthew's voice said, 'Perhaps a little whisky right away, my dear. But lunch later on, I think.' There was a wet suggestiveness in his voice when he said that which rasped across Selina's mind like a pin catching on silk, but the harpy gave its screeching laugh and said, Och, you'll be in need of the sustenance later an' all, ye horny auld ram. Selina felt the bitter anger well up at that, because the bitch was pretending, she was *pretending* to want to take her clothes off for him. Nobody could possibly want to be in bed with Great-uncle Matthew, and she was deceiving him so that she could suck out all his money.

They were coming up the stairs now; here came the harpy's light skittering footfall, with, behind it, Great-uncle Matthew's clumping tread. Selina took a firmer grip on the knife's handle, because it was important, it was absolutely vital, that she took the harpy by surprise.

They were on the landing – there was the rustle of clothes, and Great-uncle Matthew's voice mumbled something that Selina could not hear, but then the harpy screeched with horrid glee again, and said, Get away wi' ye, canna ye even wait 'til we're in the bedroom, ye old devil! and Selina's heart did its flip-flop again because if they both came in together— Help me! she cried silently. Whoever you are who's been guiding me, help me now! Keep him out of the room just for those few minutes!

'Go back down now, and get the whisky,' said the harpy. 'An' pour a glass of gin for me while ye're about it,' and Selina heard him go back down the stairs. This was it, then. Everything had fallen exactly and precisely into place, and this was it, this was the moment to act—

The harpy came into the room. She was wearing a slightly too tight black skirt and a vivid green blouse with frills. It was cut low so that her bosom showed. Her hair was a brassy colour; it was arranged in elaborate curls, and her mouth was a wet slash of colour. Selina thought it looked awful. Common, Aunt Rosa would have said, but in fact it was much worse than common. It looked as if she had drunk somebody's blood and the blood was still dribbling out of her mouth. So I was right! thought Selina. She really *is* a harpy! Well, the creature would not be feeding on Great-uncle Matthew's blood or anybody else's after today, that was for sure!

The harpy did not immediately realise there was someone in the room. She crossed to the bed, and reached for the red silk robe, humming a little tune to herself. Selina stood very still, but every muscle was tensed. In another two seconds she would spring—

And then the harpy did realise. She turned sharply round, and saw Selina, and her eyes widened. Her gluey red mouth dropped open in a silent 'O' of surprise, and she started to say, 'Who are you?' but she only got as far as the 'Wh—' because that was the moment when Selina moved.

She knocked the creature back across the bed, clapping a hand over the sticky-jam mouth so that the harpy could not shriek for help. She had the advantage of surprise, and she also had the advantage of being younger and fitter than her victim, and although the harpy was fighting back Selina was too strong for her. It was horrid almost beyond bearing to be pressed down on the creature's body like this – she could smell the cigarette smoke in its hair and on its breath and she could feel the soft flabbiness of its body struggling to get free. Selina had thought it might be exciting and exalting to be doing this, but it was not. But you won't get free, you evil greedy thing! she thought determinedly.

Making sure to keep her hand firmly over the creature's mouth, she lifted the knife above her head, and brought it slicing down hard on the plump white throat. The harpy jerked and flailed wildly at the air, and as Selina dug the knife in as deep as she could, from a great distance she heard that someone in the room was sobbing with dry heaving sobs. Whoever it was must be quite a young child, because it was gulping and whispering something about saving mummy, oh please, *please* save mummy—

But the sobbing child could not be paid any attention. Selina dragged the knife free, causing blood to well up and soak into her good leather gloves and the cuffs of her mackintosh. The harpy made a choking bubbling sound, and fell back on the bed, and Selina straightened up, looking down at her. There was blood everywhere

– it was on the grubby satin coverlet and the pillows and it smelt disgusting. It made you think about a dark, bad-smelling stone tower, with a black yawning well at the centre . . .

But the harpy was dead. Her eyes were wide and staring, slimy trails of saliva running from the corners of her mouth. For a minute Selina thought she was bleeding from the mouth as well, but then she realised that it was the creature's lipstick that had been smeared when Selina had her hand over its mouth. She glanced down at her left hand and saw the lipsticky marks on the leather glove.

She was just wondering, a bit dizzily, whether she could wipe the knife a bit clean on the bedcover when there was a creak of floorboards outside, and she heard Great-uncle Matthew's h'rrmphing little cough as he came up the stairs. Perfect timing.

As if the half-nervous, half-catarrhal throat-clearing was a signal or a catalyst jerking her back on course, the plan, in all its beautiful symmetry, snapped back into Selina's mind. She put the knife down alongside the harpy's body, and then stepped behind the door once again.

He came into the bedroom with a stupid leery smile, and he was carrying two glasses, one of whisky, one of gin.

But when he saw what lay on the bed he turned white and stopped dead just inside the doorway. Selina, in the sketchy concealment of the door's shadow, saw him put the two glasses down, and approach the bed; he walked unevenly, like a man in a dream or someone who was very drunk. For a dreadful moment Selina thought he was going to go back out of the room and call for help, but he did not. He bent over the bed, his hands going to the harpy's throat, feeling for a pulse. The cuffs of his shirt dabbled in the blood, just as Selina's mackintosh cuffs had done. *Good.* Get as much blood on your clothes as you can. But pick up the knife, you foolish old man, *pick it up*, because if you don't my beautiful plan won't work nearly as well—

But he did pick it up. He did so with a bewildered expression, as if he was not quite sure what it was, and he looked at it, turning it over and over as if it might hold some secret that he could unlock. He looked back at the harpy, and that was when Selina said, 'She's quite dead. There's no point in trying to revive her, or trying to call for help.'

He spun round at that, his face flabbery and patchy with fear and shock, and Selina took a step forward.

'Her blood is all over your sleeve,' she said, and then, speaking very deliberately, she said, 'And your fingerprints are all over the knife that killed her.'

It was the business with the fingerprints that broke him. Selina had known there would be something that would do that – she had known there would be just one single thing that would tip the scales in her own favour, and in the end it was the ineradicability of his fingerprints on the knife.

For a few minutes he tried to bluster; he used his righteous, I-am-your-guardian voice and said he would not be defied or blackmailed, and they would call the police here and now and Selina would be taken off and very likely shut away inside an institution for the rest of her life. She was a monster, a maniac, said Great-uncle Matthew blowing out his cheeks and glaring, and he would not hesitate to see that she received her just deserts.

But he did hesitate. He still stood there, between Selina and the thing lying in its own congealing blood, and he kept looking down at the knife and at his stained coat-sleeve, and he kept looking at Selina herself with an odd furtive sideways look, and Selina knew that he was sufficiently unsure of himself to risk calling the police, and also that he was sufficiently unsure of Selina herself. In the quiet room she could hear his thoughts as if they had been printed on the air: *She's killed once already, and for no reason at all . . . If I oppose her, might she kill me as well . . . ?*

Selina moved to close the door so that no one would come in, and then she sat down on one of the silly frilly chairs, and said, 'It's all perfectly simple. I've got it all worked out, and if you want to avoid being questioned by the police you've got to do precisely what I tell you. And it's no use blustering or whining, because if you do I shall go out into the street and scream for help. I shall say I saw you come in here and followed you, and that I found you standing over a murdered female. With,' said Selina, softly, 'a knife in your hand.'

And the knife has your fingerprints on it, uncle dear . . . Neither of them said the words because neither of them needed to: the inference lay thickly on the silence. He heard it at once, of course; he was no fool when it came to reasoning. He was only a fool when it came to greedy females. So he swallowed a few times, and looked at the bed again, and even dashed a tear from his eye, the stupid sentimental old idiot, and asked what was to be done and what Selina wanted.

'It's simple, really,' said Selina. 'I just want a little more money now, and I want to be sure that the money my parents left me is going to be intact when I finally get it. That's when I'm twenty-one, isn't it? Yes, I thought it was. You see, I couldn't risk you frittering all the money away – your own and my parents' money – on – on this kind of thing.' She made a brief gesture at the room. 'I want the money for myself after you die,' she said. 'And I want to go on living at Teind House. I don't want it to have to be sold because you've spent it all.' She paused, her mind brushing against the knowledge of why she must never ever leave Teind House.

'And also,' said Selina, 'I was saving you from the harpy's greed. Once I discovered what you were really doing in Stornforth, I knew I had to save you, although I have to say that wasn't the main reason.'

A little frown of puzzlement creased his brow at that, as if he could not quite work this out, but before he could speak Selina said, 'And so that's all the explanations. What we must do now is leave this house immediately. If we could be sure no one saw you on the bus we could go back to Teind House and pretend we had been there all along. But we can't be sure. And so we'll go into

shops together for an hour or so – we'll buy some
new cushion covers in O'Donnell's sale – and we'll act
very normally indeed. If ever we're asked any awkward
questions about this afternoon – if ever you're traced
through your fingerprints in this room – I'll swear on the
Bible that we were together all the time. I'll say I was on
the bus with you – it's always crowded, that eleven-thirty
bus, isn't it? – and people will believe me because I'm so
young and I've led such a sheltered life. And I can put
on a very good act if I have to.'

He nodded, dumbly, as if he understood.

'And so,' said Selina briskly, 'you can put on your
overcoat – I expect it's downstairs on the hallstand, isn't
it? – and then the blood on your cuffs won't show.'

He looked at Selina's own cuffs rather pointedly, and
Selina laughed. 'Once we're downstairs all I've got to do
is take off my mackintosh and fold it into the shopping
basket. When we get home it can be burned. Your
jacket can be burned, as well, but the knife we'll wash.
It would be awfully wasteful to throw away a perfectly
good meat knife, wouldn't it? You'd hate me to be
wasteful, wouldn't you?' She picked up the shopping
basket, and held it out. 'Do what I tell you,' she said.
'I've got it all worked out. I expect you think I'm cal-
lous and hard, don't you? But I had to safeguard my
future, you see. I really did.' I had to make sure I
would never be forced to leave Teind House and the
shrine . . .

'So just drop the knife in here. And now we'll walk
down the stairs – you'd better tell me if there's anyone

likely to be around at this time— No? Good. But we'll be ready to dodge back in here, just in case.'

It was a little like guiding a life-size doll down the stairs and through the front door. Selina took his arm, which felt stiff and strange, and together they walked out into Farthing Alley, and turned right past the helpful chemist's shop, and along to O'Donnell's. They chose new cushion covers – a nice warm rust colour – and Selina took some fabric swatches for new curtains as well. Great-uncle Matthew made some suggestions as to patterns and colours. They had a cup of tea and a buttered scone in the little café where Selina had once had her poached-egg lunch, and then they caught the bus home.

Selina cooked pork chops for supper, with apple sauce, and creamed potatoes and peas. It was one of Great-uncle Matthew's favourite meals. It was nice to be giving it him after the events of the day. After he had eaten it and drunk a cup of tea, he sat down in his favourite chair with the newspaper. Halfway through the evening he made a gasping, gargling sound, and when Selina looked up from her knitting his face had turned the colour of a ripe plum about to burst and his eyes were staring at nothing. The left side of his face had slipped down so that it no longer matched the right.

Everyone said that Selina was wonderful after her uncle's stroke. Everyone said she was absolutely devoted and selfless, and that no one could possibly have done more.

Even when the vicar's sister tried to arrange for poor
Mr McAvoy to stay in a very nice nursing home just
outside Stornforth for a couple of weeks, in order to
give Selina a little rest from the constant feeding and
changing and washing, Selina would not permit it. She
did not need a rest, she said, and she did not in the least
mind looking after her uncle. He was really no trouble
at all; he could not speak, of course, but she managed
to anticipate most of his needs pretty well. She enjoyed
cooking tempting little dishes and spooning them into
his mouth, and the washing of the sheets when he had
what she politely termed an accident in the bed was no
trouble, because Jeannie came up twice a week from the
village, and Teind had its own little wash-house with the
big copper boiler. And he liked her to read to him – there
was the morning newspaper with all the current events
and politics, and there was the evening paper which was
chattier and less serious. She had bought a second wireless
for his room, so that he could listen to the Home Service.
He had never been over-fond of music, but he liked the
Home Service.

And as for getting out and about, said Selina in answer
to people's concerned queries, she actually got out quite a
lot. There was the Church Ladies' Guild, and the Flower
Rota, and her little shopping trips in Stornforth. And she
very much enjoyed what she called her nature walks –
they might sometimes have seen her walking around
Teind, perhaps? There were so many interesting places
to explore – oh yes, the old Round Tower was certainly
one of them. Yes, she often walked in that direction, said

Selina serenely. Poor dear Great-uncle Matthew's illness did not hinder any of her activities really, she said, and people told one another how brave she was, and how selfless. The vicar's sister made it a rule to invite the dear good girl to lunch on Mondays when Jeannie from the village went to Teind, and could be left to give Mr McAvoy his midday meal.

Everyone was extremely kind and sympathetic to Selina when, shortly after her twenty-first birthday, Matthew McAvoy died quietly in his bed. There could be no reproaches whatsoever, they said; it was a thing that might have happened at any time, and Dr Leckie had no hesitation in writing out a death certificate.

No one thought it was odd or strangely coincidental that Mr McAvoy had died just one month after Selina came into her inheritance.

CHAPTER TWENTY-EIGHT

Emily had cried for quite a large part of the night after Patrick left, and she had cried again when she woke up next morning. What she had really wanted to do was burrow back under the warm safety of the bedclothes and shut the world out, and to go back to sleep until all the pain of so nearly having Patrick and then of losing him so completely had gone.

It *will* go, said Emily to Emily. You know it will. You'll leave Inchcape, of course – yes, that would be best – and you'll finish your degree, and you'll meet somebody else. Oh yes, of course I will. And what would I have done in Inchcape anyway? Something at Moy, said her mind with sneaky and surprising promptitude. Taken some further training of some kind so that you could really understand people like Christabel, and do something to help them. This was suddenly a very alluring prospect indeed. Emily considered it, and then quenched it firmly, because ten to one it was only a side-product of having fallen for Patrick.

And it would be great, really, to be back at Durham, finishing her course, picking up the threads of friendships. She had shared a house with two girls and a boy, and they had had a lot of fun. She might phone one of the girls later today, in fact, to see if there was still a room available for her. She would probably be able to go back next year – her head of department had suggested the spring term, and Finals in June. It would be a tragedy not to at least try after getting so close, the head of department had said.

Emily thought she would phone the head of department later as well, to see whether this was still on. Dad was pretty much back on course after mum's death by now, not that he would ever be completely over it, of course, any more than Emily would ever be completely over it. But he could probably be left on his own now.

And she could not stay in bed today, or any other day really, because that would be giving in, and she absolutely refused to give in. But today was especially awkward for giving in and staying in bed because it was Tuesday, when she was due to go down to Teind House later on. Monday was wash day at Teind, and Tuesday was what was called linen day, which meant ironing everything in sight and checking it off on a list before consigning it to the airing cupboard. They had agreed to do this later than usual, because Miss March was going into Stornforth with Lorna Laughlin this morning, which was a long-standing arrangement with the Stornforth library, but when Emily had suggested they have their linen day tomorrow it seemed this was not to be considered. If the world had been forecast to end on Wednesday, with the Four Horsemen of the Apocalypse due to ride into town any minute, Selina would still have Monday's wash day and Tuesday's linen day, and she would still expect Emily to help.

Emily stared up at the ceiling, and considered phoning to say she was too ill to turn up, but the prospect of Selina's ditherings at this disruption to her routine was simply too exhausting to contemplate and anyway life had to be faced.

She stood drearily under the shower, and then she thought she might as well wash her hair while she was there, and then she thought she might as well change its colour while she was about it.

Black. Pitch-dark, raven's-wing black. She had a spray-on, wash-out tint labelled Ebony. Exactly right. Once on, her hair dry, it looked startling. It made her look like Morticia Addams, or Shakespeare's Dark Lady the morning after a night on the town. Emily glared at her reflection, and put on a dark purple sweater and a black knitted skirt, because since life had to be faced, she might as well face it looking the way she felt.

After that astonishing episode with Emily, Patrick had gone back to his own rooms in Moy, and had divided the rest of the evening between the whisky bottle and work.

Work was the panacea for everything, of course; there was the old tag about Nature's abhorring a vacuum, and there was the undoubted fact that if you filled your mind up with something – anything – the forbidden memories could not slip through the defences. The whisky, viewed as an analgesic, would not hurt, either.

The forbidden memories would get through the defences, of course, whatever he did, and they would probably do so at night, returning to taunt him in dreams. Because you could have had her right there on that sofa, or on the carpet in front of the fire, said his mind bitterly. And afterwards? Afterwards she might have been with you for a little while – even a year or two – but inevitably at some point the gap of the years would have widened, and there would have been other, younger, men.

He reminded himself that he was thirty-eight to her twenty-one. Seventeen years. Verging on the indecent, really. Svengali was a dirty old man anyway, if you thought about it from one angle. Emily would meet a younger man, and she would remember that brief incident in the cottage – if she remembered it at all – as a strange, slightly bizarre, slightly flattering adventure. Yes, it was better to let her go now. But go *quickly*, my dear love, thought Patrick, because I don't think I can stand feeling like this for very long!

He forced himself to focus on the immediate. On poor mad Christabel Maskelyne's extraordinary story and its repercussions. Yes, that was the way normality lay. Think how she's lived for nearly fifty years with those appalling memories; how she's constantly seen things that were invisible and inaudible to most people. The wings of ogre-birds beating ceaselessly on the air, for instance . . .

There was an air of Gothic darkness about Christabel's insanity: a flavour of blood-dripping cobwebs and slavering, human-hunting giants; of black windowless towers. And which of us, thought Patrick, is not haunted by some deeply buried childhood fear that we never admit? Yes, but how severe must those gibbering phantoms have been to make Christy kill, and with such viciousness that one of her victims had clawed out one of her eyes ... ?

He tipped the whisky bottle into the glass again, and slumped back in his chair. His hair was tumbled and uncombed, and he had loosened his shirt collar and thrown his tie into a corner of the room. When he caught sight of his reflection in the glass front of a bookcase he thought he looked like a tramp. It did not matter.

He rose the next morning with a skewering pain above one eye, and the impression that something dark and dreary beyond bearing was pressing down on his shoulders. He drank two cups of tea and took three aspirin, and then forced down a slice of dry toast. Better? No, but it will have to do. And I'm as good as I'm likely to be for some time.

He spent the morning closeted in his office, reading Christabel's case notes, looking for leads as to what might have happened to her previous records, and telephoning various health authorities. Later today he would talk to her, but Don Frost had already reported that she was still dazed and unfocused from the chlorpromazine.

'Thanks,' said Patrick, speaking a bit curtly because it was suddenly awkward to speak to Don in the old, ordinary way. To soften this, he said, 'I've no idea yet how I'm going to approach her,' and Don had merely nodded and gone away.

It was midway through the afternoon, and from the darkness beyond his office windows it looked as if Inchcape was in for another of its spectacular storms. Patrick was just reaching out to switch on his desk lamp, when from somewhere within Moy's jumble of buildings issued a deep, muffled sound.

It shivered through the darkening afternoon, and it was so unfamiliar and so abruptly invasive a sound that for several minutes Patrick simply sat there, trying to make sense of it. Whatever it was, it was coming from within Moy, of course, and in a minute he would recognise what it was, and he would know what he was supposed to do about it.

It came again, then, a massive rhythmic clanging, iron beating inexorably against iron, a sound that might have been dredged up from the bowels of the earth or that might equally well have been pulled down from the highest of the heavens to assault the senses of men. Iron, its tongue dripping with blood—

And then Patrick's mind clicked back on track, and he knew what the sound was.

Iron tongue. Moy's great bell being tolled.

One of the inmates had escaped.

Emily was on the first-floor landing of Teind House, putting freshly ironed pillowcases on the appointed shelf in the linen cupboard while Miss March diligently ticked them off on a list. She had just knelt down to stow away a blanket when she heard the sound.

To begin with she was only puzzled. It was vaguely like the chiming of the church bell on Sundays, except that this was deeper and more menacing and there was an urgency about it. A little pulse of fear started up, and she half turned to look out of the window in the direction of the sound, trying to identify it.

And then memory doubled back, and she was walking through Moy with Robbie Glennon, and he was telling her about Moy's huge alarm bell in its own tower, and how it had been put there to warn the surrounding countryside if any of Moy's inmates escaped.

Oh God, thought Emily in horror, someone's escaped. And they're sounding the bell to warn us all, and that must mean it's somebody really dangerous— Oh, for goodness' sake, they're *all* dangerous in Moy. Even Christy? Yes, especially Christy. She remembered how Christy had said there were ogres in the world, disguised as humans, and how, after a bit, you could see the claws and the slavering teeth . . . You have to kill them, then, she had said. You have to cut off their feet so that they can't run after you, and then you have to cut off their hands, so that they can't snatch you up and eat you.

Was Christabel Maskelyne out there now, prowling through the storm-laden afternoon, seeing fantastical nightmare creatures that had to be killed . . . ? She can't help it, thought Emily. She truly *can't*! But would that be any consolation if you were to meet up with her in some lonely place?

Emily looked across to Miss March, and started to say something about locking all the doors and checking where Mr Kent was, but before she could speak Selina said, in a voice so totally unlike her normal one that Emily's skin crawled, 'They're sounding the bell, aren't they? That means a raid, doesn't it? It means they're going to raid the village – my father said they might. He's always right, my father.'

Emily had no idea what she meant, but she got carefully to her feet because you could not deal properly with crises or hysteria when you were kneeling down at the bottom of a linen cupboard.

She said, 'Miss March, it isn't a raid – it's the alarm bell at Moy. It means one of the prisoners has tried to escape. But we'll be perfectly all right here, only I think we ought to lock all the doors—'

'Oh no,' said Selina at once. 'Oh no, locking the doors won't be enough. We mustn't stay here. They'll find us if we stay here and they've got guns. We've got to hide.'

'Well, maybe just until it's all over—' Emily had no idea whether she should go along with any of this.

'Come with me,' said Selina, and her hand came out to close round Emily's wrist. 'We must hide inside the tower, that's what we must do.'

Her eyes were wide and unfocused, and Emily was aware of another beat of fear, because just for a moment Selina's face had worn the exact same look as Christabel's. She remembered Christy's difficult voice saying, *We were all so frightened . . . Douglas and Selina and the others*. Selina went outside before it was safe and the bad men caught her and shot her, Christy had said.

It can't be the same Selina, thought Emily. It's stretching coincidence way beyond credulity. Yes, but she said that about hiding inside the tower, and about hiding from people with guns . . .

Selina was already pulling Emily across the landing in the direction of the stairs. 'We must hide,' she said. 'We really must.'

'I truly don't think it's necessary—'

'It is necessary,' said Selina at once. 'We must cheat them, those men. Only once we're inside, we'll have to be careful,' she said, and again there was the echo.

You have to be careful . . . Christabel had said, the sly goblin-eyes peering out through the eyes of the middle-aged woman. But Christabel, poor flawed Christy, had believed that it was the ogres she had to be careful of – she had thought they hid inside ordinary people. When Selina March said they would have to be careful she was surely only referring to the dangers of a prisoner, escaped from Moy.

But who is it who has escaped? said Emily's mind, chillingly.

Krzystof had drawn a blank in Stornforth. He had spent most of the morning talking to the detective sergeant who had been in charge of investigating Joanna's disappearance, and had learned precisely nothing. They had followed all the leads, the sergeant had said, and they had discovered nothing at all. There were no signs of violence, no signs that Mrs Kent had been taken anywhere against her will – Krzystof might see the reports if he wished?

'Yes, I do wish,' said Krzystof rather grimly, and spent the next hour reading the careful transcripts of interviews conducted with Selina March, Emily Frost, Lorna Laughlin, and – this last was a surprise – Patrick Irvine. He rather grudgingly admitted that the Stornforth police had been thorough; they had talked to everyone who had had any contact at all with Joanna while she was here.

The hire car had been checked for traces of anything that might indicate violence, but the forensic department had reported nothing in the way of blood or fragments of skin or nails. A few stray hairs had been picked up on the driver's side – chestnut brown, the report said, and Krzystof had remembered Joanna's habit of thrusting the fingers of her left hand impatiently through her hair when she was concentrating. She would probably have had to concentrate quite hard on the unfamiliar roads between Aberdeen and Inchcape.

After this frustratingly fruitless morning, he had eaten some lunch in an anonymous pub, and then had drifted into the local library, half wondering whether he would meet up with Selina March and her friend. But either he had missed them or they were closeted in some inner sanctum, and so Krzystof had a general look round the shelves for politeness's sake before leaving. Two of Joanna's books were in stock; one was her most recent one in which she had allowed Jack Tallent a quite serious love affair, ending with a rather powerful renunciation scene. Did that indicate that even then she had been turning over in her mind the idea of a much darker, more serious book?

. . . the barely understood secret became woven into childhood nightmares and childhood fears . . . her notes had said. *And in the end, it called the poor mangled ghosts out of their uneasy resting places . . . At times, the pretence spilled over into ordinary life . . .*

A child, stumbling on a barely understood secret. Something shameful, something criminal, even? Something in Joanna's own childhood that she had kept a secret, even from Krzystof himself? Something she was intending to draw on for a new book? She always said you drew on snippets of experiences, just as you drew on snippets of people's personalities. Vampire-stuff again, she had said, grinning.

As he drove back down the road leading to Inchcape, his mind was still gnawing away at those scraps of plot, and the feeling that he was missing something was still strongly with him. Come *on*, said his mind angrily. If ever you possessed that semi-apocryphal Hungarian sixth sense, this is the time to be using it!

It was getting dark, which meant he must have spent longer than he had intended in Stornforth. He glanced at the dashboard clock, but it was only just on four, so the gathering darkness must be another of the wild thunderstorms in which this part of Scotland seemed to specialise. It was odd and rather disturbing the way that a storm could change the entire landscape. Everywhere became slowly soaked in brooding violet light, and there was a feeling of immense and powerful menace that you could not quite pin down, so that you found yourself remembering all those old doomsday prophecies. You found yourself wondering about ancient buried secrets that might lie at the heart of your wife's disappearance—

Rot, said Krzystof's mind crossly. Yes, but if the fabled twilight of the gods ever did descend on the world it would very likely start with this sick, depressing gloaming, although if Joanna was dead Krzystof did not care if mankind was facing the final apocalypse of all the religions of the world rolled into one.

Halfway home the rain began, lashing down from the heavens and hurling itself against the windscreen so fiercely that the wipers could barely keep up with it. The road was already awash, and with the thickening light all around it Krzystof felt as if he was driving along the bottom of a murky green ocean. Once he thought he had missed the turning, but then he caught sight of the ancient tower stark and black against the storm clouds, and knew he had not. He drove on through the storm, relieved to think he was nearing Teind House.

Whatever its history might be, it made a good landmark, the Round Tower.

CHAPTER TWENTY-NINE

Moy's huge bell was still sounding as Emily and Selina crossed the gardens. Emily thought it was a terrible thing to hear, a huge muffled booming sound that made you think of all those massive tons of solid iron and bronze, clanging to and fro within the depths of the belfry. Beware! the iron tongue was saying. There's a murderer on the prowl! Beware the murderer!

As they went towards the small orchard behind the house, Emily wondered what Patrick would be doing. Would he be dashing to and fro at Moy, organising search parties and things? Everyone would jump to his command, of course, because they always did. Emily would have jumped to it as well if she had had the chance. No, she was not going to think like that. She would not jump to anyone's command. She was a free spirit and a staunch feminist, and if she cried into her pillow for the next five years over Patrick it was nobody's affair but her own.

She glanced a bit uneasily at Selina March who could never have cried into her pillow for a man, or wanted to be made love to, shamelessly and rapturously in front of a fire, in the way Emily had wanted to make love with Patrick.

'Miss March – where are we going?'

The words came out a bit more abruptly than Emily had intended, but Selina looked round in surprise. As if it ought to have been obvious, she said, 'To the tower, of course. I've already told you that. The tower's the one place they might not look for us. It's where I hid last time, and they didn't find me. They won't find me again. So we'll be quite all right. We've gone back, you see – surely you know that by now. We've been given a second chance, and this time we're all going to escape. You don't need to be afraid.'

Emily was uneasy, but she was not really very much afraid, because it was impossible to equate Miss March – prim, twittery little Selina – with anything violent or harmful. But as they walked through the already darkening afternoon, a little voice in her mind whispered, But supposing Selina *was* the child who hid with Christy in the bone-pit? Well, so what if she was? It doesn't make her an outcast. No, but it might have made her mad, said the voice, warningly. Oh, shut up.

Whoever Selina was, or was not, it would clearly be kinder to fall in with what she wanted, and if she really had been there on that horrific night Christy had described, it was small wonder that she had spent the rest of her life sheltering in the boring, peaceful safety of Inchcape.

She was still clutching Emily's wrist and her fingers were unexpectedly and rather worryingly strong. As an errant spear of lightning flickered somewhere over to the east, heralding one of Inchcape's fierce storms, Emily saw that Selina's eyes were too wide open, and that there was a rather horrid stary look to them.

But I'd better go along with her, thought Emily. It won't be very nice, hiding out in the tower, but I don't suppose it'll be for very long. Most likely it'll just be a question of staying there until the bell stops tolling and she comes out of her panic, poor old Selina. She wished she had not lit on the word *toll*, which was a bit too reminiscent of all those snippets of poetry you picked up about death knells. Never send to know for whom the bell tolls, because it tolls for thee . . . That had been John Donne, hadn't it? writing about the universality of death. There was some gorgeous sexily romantic passion among his work. People did not quote poetry much these days; in Emily's experience they just wanted to get you into bed, and afterwards they were more inclined to send out for a pizza than to quote beautiful poetry to you. Patrick might quote poetry in bed though— Except that she had stopped thinking about Patrick in any guise whatsoever, and most of all she had stopped thinking about being in bed with him.

As they went through Teind House's little orchard she could feel the thrumming vibrations of the great bell disturbing the air and making the trees shiver, and it brought back the mad, confused fantasies that Christabel Maskelyne had poured out the day before. There are ogres in the world, Christy had said, her poor, cracked mind no longer able to distinguish dark fairy tale from reality; her perceptions clouded and distorted by the memories.

Ogres. Ever since that appalling experience in India Christy had seen ogres everywhere – she had believed they hid behind masks of human flesh and human bone and skin, and she had been continually on the watch for them. Ogres, thought Emily, feeling round the word. Giants, who might come pounding across the landscape when you least expected it, shaking the earth with their huge, fee-fi-fo-fum tread, slyly timing their movements to coincide with the booming clamour of a tolling bell so that you would not hear their approach; all you would feel would be the shuddering of the bell's brazen clanging . . .

The thought: I hope Christy can't hear Moy's bell from her room! formed in Emily's mind, and then she remembered that it might be Christy who had escaped anyway.

They had reached the edge of Teind's gardens, and Selina was drawing her through a small gate at the bottom of the orchard. When Emily had gone out to the tower last time she had not come this way, she had used the uneven road that branched off the highway. She had not known about this gate: it was so overgrown on both sides by bramble hedge that if you did not know it was there you would have walked past it. The storm was gathering momentum, and there was the feeling of pressure from overhead, as if the sick twilight was pouring downwards, smothering the puny humans who walked their little world . . . Oh, don't be so ridiculous!

And then there ahead of them, rearing up against the lowering skies, with the scudding storm clouds as its backdrop, was the tower, and no matter how confidently Emily had thought she had banished her own private ghosts by going inside the place that day, approaching it now, with the sound of Moy's bell shivering on the air and a storm blowing in from the east, it was still the windowless tower of the nightmares.

As they crossed the uneven ground, Miss March's hand still looped tightly around Emily's wrist, Emily said, as calmly as she could manage, 'You know, I think we could go back to the house now. I think they've stopped sounding the bell, don't you? Let's go back and I'll make a cup of tea.'

But even as Emily was speaking Selina was pulling her forward, and as they moved into the shadow of the tower she gave a mad ladylike little chuckle that was the most horrid thing yet.

'Oh, we can't stop,' she said. 'We must hide. If we don't, they'll drag us out and shoot us. I watched it all, you see. I saw them all shot. Douglas and the little ones – and Christy. Dear brave Christy, she was the best of them all, you know. I thought she got away – I thought she hid with me in the tower – I heard her speaking and I felt her hold my hand. But she was dead by then, so after all it was a ghost.'

The lowering skies splintered into shards that spun crazily around Emily's head. She thought: so I *was* right! She really is the child who escaped – the one who called the birds ogre-birds. Selina March and Christabel Maskelyne were together in that place – that place in India whose name I can't remember— It all fits and what's happening now fits as well. They hid in that tower with the bodies and the vultures, and now Selina's going to hide in this tower where the birds from the Stornforth sanctuary sometimes come. She's confusing the two places; she's gone back – she said something about being given a second chance to escape. Oh, *poor* Miss March, thought Emily in dreadful compassion, and as the storm closed down in earnest she allowed herself to be taken forward towards the tower's small door.

Emily flinched as the first major crackle of lightning sizzled across the skies, and then thought that if you had to be entering nightmare places you might as well do so with the full complement of sound effects and atmospheric lighting. I won't mind about any of it, she thought determinedly. I certainly won't mind about the thunder, and now that I understand what's behind Miss March's peculiarness, I won't mind that either. I'll be perfectly able to cope and I needn't even be frightened.

It was not until Selina opened the door and pushed Emily inside the tower, stepping in after her and slamming the door shut, that Emily finally saw that the Selina March she had known – the Selina March that probably everyone in Inchcape had known – was no longer there. It was as if her face was dissolving and bits were peeling off and falling onto the ground, so that you kept getting brief, horrifying glimpses of the real person beneath.

It was exactly as poor, crazed Christabel Maskelyne had said: there were people in the world who could put on disguises – not velvet or fabric or paper disguises, but ones made out of human flesh and skin and eyes and lips. And they were *good*, Christy had said. The disguises were so good you would never know the truth. Until the mask fell away . . .

Selina March was not one of poor Christy's ogres in disguise, but she had been wearing a mask, Emily could see that now. She could see that under the persona of an old-fashioned spinsterish lady, Selina March was in fact very, very insane and very, very dangerous.

It was at this point that Emily finally admitted that she was very frightened indeed.

Teind House, when Krzystof finally reached it, was shrouded in darkness. Miss March was probably sheltering from the storm with her friend, Miss Laughlin, because only a fool or a maniac would have driven through that downpour, and Krzystof was thankful to remember the key she had given him at lunch which was clipped onto his keyring. He drove the car as near to the house as he could, skewing it so that the headlights fell on the front door. It was only a few steps away, but by the time he reached it his hair was plastered to his head, and his jacket was drenched. He unlocked the door and looked inside. The cold stormlight cast grey moving shadows across the oak floor of the hall, and Krzystof called out,

'Miss March? Are you here? It's me – I'm just parking the car.'

Nothing. Silence. And the house had the feel that empty houses did have. Krzystof felt for the light switch, and reassuring yellow light flooded the hall. At least the storm had not killed the electricity yet. He ran back to the car to switch off the headlights, and then thought he had better park it more tidily so that if Lorna Laughlin drove up with Selina later on she would have room to manoeuvre. This time when he ran back to the house his shoes made squelching noises on the gravel. Krzystof swore and stepped inside, closing the door against the driving rain.

The storm was crashing overhead and the lights were already flickering ominously. Krzystof glanced uneasily up at the ceiling, wondering where the storm lanterns would be. It might be a good idea to have one to hand, along with a box of matches. He would have a look in the kitchen in a minute. He dragged off his sodden jacket and hung it on the hatstand. He might as well step out of his shoes as well; there was no need to leave wet, gravelly marks all over Selina March's polished floors. He could scoot upstairs in stockinged feet, and dry his hair in the bathroom.

He bent down to take off his shoes, and it was then, his sightline nearer to floor level, that he saw something that sent a little scud of nervous fear across his skin. He straightened up slowly, his eyes on the old-fashioned black-and-white tiles. The electric light was still flickering, but it was more than enough to show the wet footprints crossing the hall. Krzystof stared at them. Footprints – *wet* footprints left by someone who must have come in from the storm a very short time ago. Someone who had gone across the hall and had not bothered about marking the nicely polished floor.

Miss March? It must be. But the house had been in darkness when he arrived, and there was no indication that she had returned from Stornforth. And be logical, said Krzystof's mind: would Selina, who polishes everything to within an inch of its life, really have walked across that floor in wet shoes?

He remembered she had taken an umbrella, and turned to check the umbrella stand. Red because a red umbrella was cheerful in the rain, she had said, and Krzystof had reached into the stand for the red umbrella and handed it to her himself. It was not there now. It was not propped against the outside of the door to dry, either. Don't be absurd, said his mind. She's not here. You know she's not here. Then who is it who came in here and walked across that floor? His heart began to beat more rapidly, but he went to the foot of the stairs and called out again. 'Miss March? It's me – I'm back from the storm. Are you up there?'

Still that same silence. Or was it the same? Had the atmosphere of Teind House suddenly shifted, so that there was no longer the feeling of an empty house? Wasn't there now the indefinable, unmistakable feeling of someone listening? He looked back at the footprints, and remembered that he had left the front door unlocked and partly open while he went back to the car. Had there been enough time for someone to get inside and hide? Oh God, yes, more than enough.

He's in the house, thought Krzystof. I can feel that he is. He's lying in wait for me somewhere. Oh, don't be ridiculous, that's the urban legend of an intruder luring the unsuspecting householder outside, and then sneaking into the house to hide. I'm not falling for that hoary old one! he thought crossly. But Hungarian extra sense or not, he knew that there *was* someone inside Teind House, and he knew it was not Selina March.

Just then, with their unnerving habit of dramatic timing, Teind House's lights went out, plunging the hall into pitch darkness.

It took Krzystof longer than he had thought to grope his way to the kitchen, and rummage in cupboards for the storm lamps, or, at the very least, a torch.

The storm was reaching its zenith and as far as Krzystof could make out it had decided to do so directly above Teind House's chimneys. He winced as lightning sizzled blindingly across the dark skies beyond the windows, thunder exploding at the same time by way of accompaniment. Donner and Blitzen again, whooping it up over northern Scotland.

The lamps were neatly stored in a cupboard, with several boxes of matches next to them. It took a few minutes to get one lit, but Krzystof was used to field trips where lighting could be even more primitive than this, and he managed fairly well. He went back into the hall, carrying the lamp carefully, and looked about him, trying to decide what to do next. Nothing moved. The few bits of furniture stood exactly where they always stood: the carved dower chest was on the right of the door, and the narrow hall table that its maker had intended to hold an elegant salver for visiting cards, or a genteel arrangement of flowers, was next to the chest. Great-uncle Matthew's clock was ticking away, and the hatstand was still partly covered by Krzystof's rain-drenched jacket – a dark tumble of blackness. Krzystof glanced at it, and tried not to imagine that it might suddenly twist itself into a threatening bogeyman shape . . .

The footprints were already starting to dry out, in the way that wet footprints inside a house did. They faded halfway across the hall, so that it was impossible to know where the intruder had gone. Krzystof hesitated, wondering if there mightn't be some quite ordinary, innocent explanation. What? demanded his mind. Because it certainly isn't Selina March who made those prints, and if it's some amiably disposed neighbour sheltering from the storm, why didn't he – or she – answer when I called?

And surely it was incredible that some sinisterly intentioned person had been hiding in Teind's grounds – perhaps in the little outbuildings that had once been a wash-house and disused earth closet – and had taken advantage of those few minutes when Krzystof had left the door open while he parked his car? Still, for all he knew, an entire network of burglars might be swarming all over Inchcape at this very minute. Itinerant serial killers might regard the place as a stopping-off point. Itinerant killers ... How about an escapee from Moy? Now there was a chilling idea.

Oh hell, thought Krzystof, I'm on my own in the middle of nowhere and I'm visualising homicidal maniacs creeping around all over the place. Yes, but I might be about to confront a murderous thug after the silver, he thought. Had I better call the police, I wonder? But when he went across to where the sit-up-and-beg telephone was discreetly housed under the stairs, there was no dial tone and no amount of jiggling the receiver produced one. The thunder crashed overhead again, and Krzystof recalled Selina March saying placidly that the phone lines had a way of disconnecting themselves in thunderstorms. And perhaps it was better not to start up a scare on such flimsy evidence, because it was always possible that Krzystof's imagination had got the bit between its teeth and bolted into the realms of outright fantasy. But Joanna had vanished from this house several days earlier, and anything sinister, anything out of the ordinary, ought surely to be investigated. His heart was still jumping, but the idea that this intruder might provide a clue to Joanna's whereabouts made the adrenalin kick in with what felt like a million volts. Krzystof thought he was no braver than the next man – in fact he suspected he was probably a lot less brave than the next man – but he would give a great deal for ten minutes with anyone who might have hurt his wife.

He closed all the doors that led off the hall so that nothing could fool him by hiding or sneaking outside while he was searching the rest of the house, and then, gripping the oil lamp firmly, he set off up the stairs.

It was a nightmare journey. At intervals the lightning tore through the old house, illuminating everything with livid clarity, but between times dense shadows huddled in the corners of the half-landing, hunched outlines that might have been crouching intruders waiting to spring. There were black pools of darkness everywhere, which might contain anyone or anything, and several times the sparse branches of the trees leaned down to tap against the windows like skeletal ghost-fingers.

Oh God, for electric light to see properly, and a phone to summon help! thought Krzystof, but he went doggedly forward. This was certainly turning out to be the classic walk through the storm-ridden house by flickering lamplight. Joanna would make a good tale of this when it was all over, and when he had finally found her. He clung to the thought of finding Joanna alive and well, and hearing her embroidering the whole thing for friends, burlesquing it in the telling. 'And he wandered through the spooky old house like a Gothic hero, my dears, hunting for the ghosts who were all hiding under the beds like a game of Sardines.'

Krzystof was not a Gothic hero at all, of course, any more than this was a ghost-hunt. For one thing, ghosts did not leave footprints.

He paused at the centre of the first landing, looking about him. Several bedrooms, including Selina's own, opened off the landing, as well as the antiquated bath-room. At the far end the stairs went up to the second floor, where his own half-attic room was, and where the water tanks lived in a grisly little half-room under the roof. OK, bedrooms first. One at a time. He was grateful for the heaviness of the oil lamp; if it came to a fight it would make a reasonable weapon. He looked warily into each of the bedrooms, slamming the door back against the wall each time, checking walls, windows— By this time his heart was beating so loudly that it felt as if it might burst out of his chest at any minute.

In one of the unused bedrooms the curtains stirred gently, as if someone might be standing behind them. Krzystof tensed his muscles and whipped one curtain back, but there was nothing save the cold window panes, still spattered with rain from the storm, and a faint draught of air in one corner where the window did not fit very well. He drew the curtain across again, and went up to his own room, pushing the door back to the wall, and standing at the centre of the room, moving the oil lamp around to show up the dark corners. *Was* there someone here with him? Someone crouching in a corner, breathing very quietly? He moved the lamp round trying to see more clearly, and overhead the thunder growled threateningly again. Like a giant drawing in its breath, ready to bellow for a victim . . .

A movement from within the green depths of the looking-glass over the dressing-table made his heart skip several beats before he realised that it was only his own reflection. He crossed to the window, and it was then that he saw what he had missed before. Beyond the glass, silhouetted blackly against the storm clouds massing over Inchcape, was the outline of the Round Tower.

And within its depths, a light was flickering.

There were only two courses of action, and only one of them was really sensible. That was for Krzystof to beat it down the stairs and out into the storm, locking the door on the way if he remembered, and then to drive like a bat escaping hell down to the Black Boar, to summon help.

The other option, which was not, of course, to be seriously considered, was to go through the darkling orchard, across the patch of wasteland and along the disused little road, to find out what the hell was going in inside the tower.

Krzystof stared at the elusive light for another thirty seconds or so, and then went quickly back down the stairs and out into the night.

Through the darkling orchard and across the patch of wasteland to the disused road that led to the tower.

CHAPTER THIRTY

———◆———

Robbie Glennon had been on an early turn of duty when Moy's bell started to sound – seven a.m. to three p.m. it was – and only minutes earlier he had been thinking with relief that it was nearly the end of the shift.

He had been planning on having his meal in Moy's canteen, rather than at the cottage he was sharing with a couple of the other warders. The canteen usually served a fry-up around mid-afternoon: high tea for people coming off the seven o'clock shift, breakfast for people going on early evening duty. Coronary on a plate, people said, but when you had got up at six, and spent a day coping with Flasher Logan's antics and one or two more, you were in a mood to say, Oh, sod the cholesterol levels, and pig out.

He piled eggs and bacon and mushrooms onto his plate, accepted a mug of tea from one of the servers, and sat down to eat. The food was very good here; it was mostly local farm produce, delivered to Moy's little cottage community every week. You could always tell really fresh stuff from mass-produced supermarket fodder.

He was just taking his tray up to the serving hatch, and asking for a second cup of tea, when something seemed to shiver on the air – almost like a minor earth tremor – and after a moment he realised that somebody was sounding the huge old alarm bell. Almost at once a tremor of something seemed to ripple through Moy – in part fear, in part consternation, but in part a guilty excitement.

Who is it? Who's tried to get out? The murmur crackled like a forest fire through the different wings and blocks, and people started turning anxiously to one another and asking what the drill was for this. Did anyone know what they were supposed to do, for God's sake?

'Go to your own wings and wait in the main hall for instructions,' said Don Frost harassedly. 'For heaven's sake, don't any of you ever read the training manuals these days!'

'Bur Mr Frost – sir – who is it who's escaped?'

'Don't you know that yet?'

'No—'

'It's Mary Maskelyne,' said Don Frost tersely. 'She's strangled one of the doctors and disappeared.'

If Mary had realised how easy it would be to outwit her gaolers and get out of prison she might have done it years ago. But years ago there had not been any particular incentive to escape, and in those days her face would have been too well known for her to pass in the world unrecognised. It had only been when she had heard about the woman living in Inchcape – the woman who knew about the towers of silence in India – that she had known what she must do.

The first thing had been to establish that the woman in whose house Krzystof Kent was staying really was the bitch who had been in Alwar with Christabel and the other children. There was no point in upsetting the unblemished record of the last thirty-odd years if it was not the right person after all. A certain amount of cunning and stealth would be needed here, but Mary could be very cunning and very stealthy indeed when she had to. That was one of her strengths and it was one of her gaolers' weaknesses: none of them had ever really known just how very cunning and clever she could be. Certainly none of them at Moy knew.

And so she had asked her carefully off-hand questions of the warders who had been at Moy the longest, and she had listened with apparently casual attention to the answers. She had appeared to be interested in local history and local personalities after that – she had even taken a book called *Folklore of Inchcape* out of Moy's small library. The talk by Joanna Savile last week had fired her enthusiasm to try her hand at one or two essays, she said. She thought she might start with something local, since there would probably be first-hand sources available for her researches. It made her laugh inside to see the approval on all the stupid flabbery faces.

Folklore of Inchcape was a locally printed book by some boring old fart called Matthew McAvoy and Mary had no intention whatsoever of wading through its tedious pages. But borrowing it had opened up a conversation with the librarian, and within a very few minutes she had a name. Selina March.

And Selina March, it seemed, was the great-niece of this Matthew McAvoy who had written about Inchcape, and had, from the look of the book, succeeded in suppressing any interest that might have existed in his subject.

'He was one of our local scholars,' said the librarian, who had been at Moy for several centuries as far as Mary could make out. 'His niece still lives here as a matter of fact. A very respected lady in Inchcape, Selina March. Orphaned young, of course – I believe the parents died in India when she was very small – some kind of uprising in the late nineteen forties I think – and Mr McAvoy and his sisters arranged for her to come back to England, and they brought her up between them.'

'How interesting.'

Selina March, said Mary's mind. *Selina March.* It sang through her brain like an incantation, like a spell. And it all fitted, everything about it fitted, and she knew now that that first, gut-jabbing instinct had not betrayed her. The woman at Inchcape called Selina March was the child who had escaped from the tower all those years ago.

So. So, the hated one was here: living perhaps as near as a mile from Moy. The information was so huge and so colossally satisfying that Mary wanted to run about and shout. She did not, of course. She sat very quietly in her room, and let the knowledge pour inwards, until it had filled up her entire mind and heart and body.

She had the extraordinary feeling that she had been given this knowledge for a reason. Revenge? Was that the reason? Yes, of course, it was; revenge was what this was all about. It was about redressing the balance, and it was about retribution against the bitch who had let Christabel die and ruined Mary's life as a result.

If Christabel had still been whispering into Mary's mind, Mary might have evolved a different kind of plan, but Christabel had turned out to be a traitor. Just when Mary needed that extra strength from Christabel, the selfish cow had vanished. But probably Mary did not need Christabel any longer; in fact when you looked at this sensibly, Mary was doing very nicely by herself these days, thank you.

She thought very deeply and very carefully about Selina March, not sleeping at all that night, just lying on her bed and staring out of the small oblong of window. Skies were good things to watch when you needed to think: you could often see faces in the clouds, and the faces gave you ideas. And when the bell sounded for washing and breakfast at seven fifteen that morning, she had the plan all worked out. She felt a bit light-headed from not having slept and she felt a bit detached from everything as if she was separated from the world by glass. But she was not so detached and she was not so light-headed that she could not carry out her plan.

Delight welled up – she had forgotten how fiercely good it was to feel like this – and this time it was all her own delight and all her own excitement, because that unreliable bitch Christabel had not played any part in this.

When the warder came along to wake people, rapping on the doors and sliding back the spyholes, Mary got up as usual. She washed and dressed in the ugly white-tiled showers, and then she ate breakfast in the dining room just as if it was an ordinary day. Early morning would not be a good time to set the plan in motion; there were too many people coming and going: change-overs of shifts, breakfasts being prepared for staff and inmates. She would wait for the before-lunch period, when it was generally a bit quiet.

She was scheduled to attend a group therapy session at ten o'clock – something boring and utterly futile about expressing your emotions through photography, and if Flasher Logan was part of the group it would give the therapist a bit of a shock because everyone knew what emotions the Flasher liked expressing – but she asked if she could be excused from it.

'I feel sick,' she said to the on-duty warder.

'How sick? D'you need an infirmary check?'

'Oh, not that sick,' said Mary. 'I think it was the kedgeree at breakfast. I'll just lie flat for a while in my room. I can do that, can't I?'

'I'll get you some magnesia or something,' said the warder, completely unsuspicious, and within half an hour Mary was left on her own in her room. The warder would check back in an hour, she said. Would Mary be all right for an hour?

'Yes, I'll just lie quietly. Thanks for the magnesia.'

OK, the foundations had been laid. Now to the practicalities. She had one hour.

Anyone who had been inside any kind of institution for more than a couple of months knew how easy it was to induce a bout of vomiting in order to be carted off to the infirmary wing for a couple of days. You sneaked a packet of salt or a tin of mustard from the kitchens – bribing or threatening one of the kitchen workers if necessary – and then you drank down two or three pints of heavily salted, or mustard-laden, water. Or you did what the bulimics did; you learned how to jab a finger at the back of your throat or use the end of a feather from your pillow to make yourself retch. Mary would use this last method, because she was not going to trust anyone with even a fragment of her plan.

The being-sick part would be relatively easy, but she had had to think quite hard to sort out the next part of the plan, which was to get blood – as much blood as possible – into the vomit, so that they would not just think she was suffering from a brief bilious attack. At the Young Offenders' Hostel the girls had sometimes put menstrual blood in the vomit, which looked very convincing, but Mary had not had a menstrual period for over a year, and in any case, this had to be done *now*.

None of the inmates were allowed scissors or knives, of course, and nor were they allowed nail files or needles or tweezers. Nothing that could be broken to create a sharp edge was allowed in any of the rooms. Two photographs were permitted, but the frames and covers had to be plastic or perspex. The rooms and lockers were all searched once a week, on random days. Mary had already realised, rather grudgingly, that Moy's security was very good indeed. Even combs were plastic rather than metal, and the mirrors over the washbasins were fixed so firmly to the wall that it would have taken an electric drill to get them off.

And then she had it. The under-wiring from a bra. Unpicking the seam was awkward but she used her teeth and her nails, and in the end she managed to draw out the semicircle of thin springy wire. She had put it in the little plastic wastebin, so that even if there was a spot-search of her room while she was at breakfast it would look as if the thing had snapped and Mary had put it to be thrown out.

But it was all right; no one had been in, and the wire was still there. Keeping her ears alert, she finally managed to snap the wire halfway along. It was quite difficult because each end was padded, but she did it. Now for the unpleasant part.

She used the finger-down-throat method, and after several attempts she was sick in the washbasin in the corner. She managed to let some of it go onto the floor. So far so good. Still listening intently for footsteps coming along the corridor outside, she dug the jagged end hard into the fleshy part of her underarm, holding it over the washbasin as she did it.

This took three attempts – it was harder than you realised to inflict real hurt on yourself – but Mary set her teeth doggedly and jabbed the wire deep into the wound twice more, until the blood really flowed. Drip-drip into the smeary washbasin. Horrid. But necessary. And there was quite a lot of blood now. She made sure that some dripped into the little scooped-out part for the soap where it would not dry out.

They would realise what she had done at some point, of course, but they would not suspect anything for quite a while, because she had no history of this kind of deception. She had been a model prisoner, really. Anyway, providing nobody found the bra-wire until she was out of their reach, it did not matter. She pressed a wadded handkerchief against the wound to stop the bleeding, and then bound her arm up with strips of a cotton pillowcase. It was still bleeding quite a lot so she pulled two thick sweaters on, in case it bled through the bandage.

Her timing was absolutely dead-on. She had just finished hiding the broken wire under her bed when she heard the warder coming along the corridor again. Mary scooped up the still-wet blood from the soap dish and smeared it inside her mouth and over her chin. In the oblong of mirror and in the dull morning light it looked pretty fearsome, but it looked extremely convincing. She slumped against the washbasin, and waited for the warder to reach her door.

When she heard the sound of the key being turned, she called out in a shaky and frightened voice, 'Please, I need help . . . I need a doctor. I've been dreadfully sick. And there's blood in it – quite a lot of blood.'

The infirmary was a brightly lit, antiseptic-smelling place.

Mary was not allowed to walk there; two of the warders brought a wheelchair and a blanket, and they even brought a stainless steel kidney-dish in case she was sick again on the way. If only.

The warders wheeled her into a little examination cubicle off the main ward. There was a glass panel set into the door leading onto the corridor, and there was another glass panel in the wall looking out over the ward, but Mary saw that despite this it would be fairly easy to stay out of sight. Several of the infirmary beds were occupied, but from the look of it nobody was paying much attention to what was happening in here.

The doctor who came in was a large four-square female with a no-nonsense haircut and a brisk manner. She said, 'Onto the bed, please,' and Mary had a moment of panic, because surely the warders would not have to stay in here while the doctor examined her? But the doctor was nodding dismissively to the two warders, and both of them went back into the corridor. Mary watched them through the glass panel, and saw that one returned to the wing but that the other remained outside the door. Damn. But to be expected, really.

'Any pain?' said the doctor as Mary clambered onto the examination couch, doing so awkwardly as if it hurt her to move.

'Yes. Stomach. Quite bad. But I don't want people fussing around me—'

'We don't fuss around anyone in here.'

Mary waited until the brisk doctor turned away to pull on the thin surgical gloves, preparatory to making an

examination, and then sprang up from the bed in one
swift movement, and brought the kidney dish smashing
down on the woman's skull. The dish was not as heavy as
she would have liked but improvisation was the name of
the game, and even if it did not actually knock the doctor
out it would surely be enough to daze her.

She was right. The doctor staggered back, one hand
groping instinctively for the alarm button set into the
wall. Mary lifted the stainless steel dish again, and dealt
a second blow, and this time the woman slumped to the
floor. Mary sent a quick look through the glass panel.
Had anyone noticed? No. How about the door? No, the
remaining warder was still there, still staring into space.
Deal with her in a minute.

She knelt on the floor and curled her hands around
the doctor's flabby neck. She would have liked to stab the
creature – stabbing was satisfying – but it was important
not to get blood anywhere, and speed was of the essence
now. Strangling would be fine – even half strangling
would give her the time she wanted. She had not actually
strangled before, so it would be a new thing to try. It was
slightly annoying that the first time she tried it she was
hampered by having an injured arm.

But even with the injury it was easy. It was far easier
than she had thought. Yes, but you're protected and
guided, Mary, remember . . . ? She thought there was
a whisper from Christabel at that point, and then she
thought it was not Christabel at all, but her own mind.
But when she straightened up from the inert body of
the doctor there was a moment when she saw, as she

had seen on the night she cut off Darren Clark's penis, a shadowy ghost-outline watching her. Christabel? Her heart lurched and then resumed its normal pace, because of course it was not Christabel, the faithless bitch-cunt, it was Mary's own reflection she was seeing. Still, it was a reminder that she needed to move quickly.

She had expected to have to drag off the doctor's white coat at this stage, but in fact there were a couple of the coats hanging behind the door of the examination cubicle, and so Mary simply reached up and took one. Her arm was throbbing quite painfully now, and it felt as if it was bleeding through the handkerchief as well. She opened several drawers and in the fourth one found packs of surgical dressings. Good! She put two into the pocket of the white coat for later, and then she was ready. No – a couple more things to do. She wrapped a crêpe bandage around her right wrist, making sure that it was visible beneath her cuff, and dropped a further bandage in her other pocket. Then she bent over the doctor once more – she thought the woman was not quite dead, but she was unconscious which was all that mattered – and removed the spectacles. When she put them on they distorted her vision, but she could let them slip down her nose a bit and peer over the top to see. They altered her appearance quite a lot. Last of all she took the bunch of keys from the unconscious doctor's belt.

She walked across to the door, to where the warder was still stationed outside, stupid slab-faced creature, and opened it. The warder half turned and saw Mary, and Mary saw the confusion and bewilderment in her face.

Before the creature could work out what had happened she lifted the stainless steel dish yet again, and although the warder made a swift instinctive gesture of defence Mary was too quick for her. This time she used both hands and the blow was heavier and better. There was a satisfying bone-bruising sound as she crunched the dish's edge hard against the woman's skull, and the woman dropped to the ground with barely a grunt. Good. Getting better at this. It was a shame there was not time to actually kill this one – there were several methods Mary had not tried yet – but at any minute someone might come along, and she could not risk that. With a swift look up and down the empty corridor, she dragged the stupid creature into the cubicle, and to delay her from raising the alarm she pushed one of the wadded crêpe bandages into her mouth. It might in fact suffocate her – she was lying on her back, so there was quite a good chance. Mary pushed it as hard in as she could.

It was this next part that would be really nerve-racking. She set off along the corridor, forcing herself to be calm, because this was where she needed coolness. Panache.

She was counting heavily on the fact that she had not been at Moy for long enough for all of the warders and doctors and attendants to recognise her. She had certainly never been in the infirmary wing. But despite the dangers her heart was thumping with excitement because this was new territory, just as strangling had been new territory. Just as she had never strangled anyone before, she had never tried to escape before either.

It seemed that the luck was staying with her. She had

only the sketchiest idea of Moy's layout and she dared not go anywhere near her own D wing, but she had noted the way here very carefully, and if she could get to the central section without being challenged—

It worked like a charm. It worked as if the plan had been oiled and polished, and smoothed to a seamless finish. The white coat and the spectacles had been a stroke of genius; no one questioned her as she walked confidently through the corridors and most of the warders hardly gave her a second glance. She was just another doctor going along to see a patient or attend a group therapy session.

The infirmary wing joined the main central portion of Moy's cluster of buildings by means of a small guardhouse that gave onto a courtyard. Beyond the courtyard Mary could see other guardhouses, each one manned by a warder, each one the entrance to one of Moy's other wings. She paused unhurriedly at the guardhouse and held out the keys, making sure to let the warder see her bandaged wrist.

'Hi – I'm Dr Brooker's new assistant.' Dr Brooker had been the name clipped to the breast pocket of the doctor she had strangled. 'I'm needing to fetch some case notes from her car for her, is that OK?' Had that sounded casual enough? Modern enough? You got out of the way of modern expressions when you had lived inside institutions for so many years. And what if she had got the car-parking arrangement wrong? She said, 'I haven't been here very long, so I don't know all the procedures yet.'

'That's all right,' said the warder, glancing up. 'I expect she's parked on the Bell Tower car park – she usually parks there.'

'Yes, she is,' said Mary, picking this up at once. 'Uh – could you do the unlocking for me, d'you think? I've sprained my wrist, and it's awkward to turn these big keys.' She held out the bunch of keys to him. See? said her mind. I really am who I'm saying I am. And my wrist is bandaged.

'No problem,' said the man. 'But you'll be quicker to go through the east gate, you know.'

Mary gave him her best smile. 'I told you I was still getting used to this place,' she said. 'It's an absolute maze, isn't it?'

'I'll walk you across,' he said. 'Don't want you getting lost.'

'I should think not! I'd never live that one down, would I?'

They chatted quite companionably about the weather as they went across the inner courtyard, and as the man unlocked Moy's great outer door. He even sketched a little mock-salute as Mary went through.

Ten minutes later she was standing on the Bell Tower car park, and Moy's bulk was behind her, and she was *out*.

CHAPTER THIRTY-ONE

Patrick had spent most of the hours since Mary's escape was discovered in helping to organise search parties.

Stornforth police were in command of the actual search – 'We couldn't have coped by ourselves,' Don Frost had said – and the area around Moy had been divided into sections, with some of the men assigned house-to-house investigations and questionings. But there was still a lot for the staff to sort out in addition to the search. There were press releases to prepare, and various governmental departments to contact. Radio and television stations would carry the story with their early evening news programmes, and up-to-date photographs of Mary were being photocopied. This last was very important indeed, said the chief superintendent from Stornforth. Mention the name *Mary Maskelyne*, and most of the population instantly visualised that famous Sixties shot, but at least

95 per cent of people would not recognise Mary as she looked now, said the superintendent ponderously. Mid forties, ordinary and unremarkable.

Ordinary, thought Patrick going back to his own office. She would never be ordinary, that one. Yes, but she could don ordinariness at will, almost like a cloak, and she could pass unnoticed in a crowd if she wanted to.

'And by anybody's reckoning it's five, if not six, hours since she got out,' he said to Don. 'They took her to the infirmary shortly after ten this morning, and it wasn't until nearly midday that they found poor old Brooker's body.'

'I know.' Don sat down in the chair facing Patrick's desk.

'Is that warder all right? The one she knocked out?'

'Dazed and a bit concussed, but they say she'll recover.'

'That's something, I suppose.' Patrick glanced at the darkness beyond his office windows. It was almost five o'clock. 'Maskelyne could be halfway to anywhere by this time,' he said.

'We had to search Moy before we gave the main alarm and called in the police,' said Don defensively. 'We had to be sure she wasn't hiding somewhere.'

'Don, I'm not criticising anyone,' said Patrick, who wasn't. The probability had been that Mary was still inside Moy's complex; it had only been when they began the systematic questioning of the staff that they had realised what had happened, and the governor-in-chief had taken the decision to sound Moy's great bell to warn the surrounding villages. 'But,' Patrick went on, 'I think we should try to work out why she escaped in the first place. That might get us one step ahead of her.'

'Presumably she escaped because she wanted to be free.'

'No,' said Patrick. 'There's more to it than that. Think about it, Don. She's been shut away for more than thirty years, and she's never tried to escape before. Not from any of the institutions where she's been. Exemplary behaviour, day to day.'

'Except for the small matter of killing two people in Broadacre, and a question mark over that matron's death in the Young Offenders' Hostel,' observed Don, and Patrick caught the faintly caustic note that Don's daughter occasionally used.

'You're such an old cynic,' he said, and Don grinned rather half-heartedly. 'But listen now, my point is that Maskelyne has got more than enough intelligence to have concocted a reasonably workable escape plan long before this. Moy's security system is very good, but no security system in the world is foolproof. Well, maybe Devil's Island or Alcatraz might be. But Broadacre wasn't nearly as good as Moy, and the youth place was laughable from the security angle. So, why did she never try to escape from either of those places?'

'She wouldn't have wanted to risk failing,' suggested Don after a moment, and Patrick pounced on this.

'That's very shrewd of you, and you're right, of course. But it needs taking a step farther. I think it's more that she doesn't want to risk being *seen* to fail.' He frowned, and then said, 'I don't understand her, and I don't think anyone ever will understand her. But I do know that under all that false humility and that deliberate colourlessness she's overwhelmingly vain and mind-blowingly arrogant. So *why* in the name of all the gods at once has she taken the risk now?'

'Something she wants that's outside Moy?' hazarded Don Frost, who could not always keep up with Patrick's swift twists of mind when he was in this mood, but who was following him at the moment.

'Exactly,' said Patrick. 'But it must be something so compelling that she was prepared to take the risk of failure.'

'Like what?'

'I don't know. That's why I need to reread her case notes.' He had been rifling his desk drawer to find the last batch of notes on Mary Maskelyne, because he had not got round to sending them for typing and entering on the computer system. 'I'm hoping I can fathom out what she might be after. Something recent it'd need to be – even something from the last two days.'

'I'll leave you to your fathomings,' said Don, getting up. 'They're preparing a press release and I need to make sure it doesn't make us sound like total incompetents. Oh, and I want to phone Emily—'

'Emily?' Patrick looked up sharply. 'What about Emily?'

'She was going to Teind House after lunch,' said Don. 'If she's still there I'm going to ask her to stay put and lock all the doors. Miss March won't mind, in fact she'll probably be grateful for the company if she heard Moy's bell. But I don't want Emily coming back from Teind by herself with Maskelyne prowling the undergrowth.'

Patrick had only an approximate knowledge of Teind House's whereabouts, but he did know it occupied a rather remote situation on the outskirts of Inchcape, and he knew that the roads between Teind and Don's cottage were lonely and unlit. He said, more sharply than he had intended, 'Don, for Christ's sake ring her now! Here, use my phone! Wherever Emily is, tell her to stay put. We'll get someone out to her— Young Glennon or someone.'

Don stared at him, and Patrick said, trying to beat down his impatience, 'Maskelyne's a multiple killer, Don! She isn't a quiet, middle-aged lady who's a bit eccentric, she's a full-blown schizophrenic and she's wildly delusional! She'll kill anything that tries to get in the way of – well, whatever it is that she's gone to find! She always does! Remember that three of her victims were killed within call of any number of people? Remember poor old Brooker, strangled in this very building this morning, within yards of at least thirty people? If Maskelyne meets anyone on those lonely moorland roads—' And if anything happens to Emily— He snapped off the rest of the thought because it was too appalling to contemplate, and it was then that he saw something of his own panic mirrored in Don's eyes. He remembered too late that Don's wife had died barely a year earlier. (And Emily came back from university to be with him, said his mind).

He understood that if Don lost Emily so soon after his wife's death, he would not be able to bear it. He understood this all too well, because if anything happened to Emily Patrick would not be able to bear it either. In a gentler voice, he said, 'I'm sorry. I expect I'm over-reacting. But ring anyway. Tell her to stay put.'

As Don reached for the phone, Patrick went back to the filing drawer, this time finding the handwritten notes detailing his interviews with Mary. Something so compelling that she was prepared to take the risk of failure . . .

What would compel Mary Maskelyne to break out of Moy? He flipped over two or three pages. Something to do with Joanna Savile, could it be? Yes, that struck an immediate chord. Joanna had unquestionably been interested in Mary: there had been that subtle probing on Joanna's first visit here. And there had been that look in Mary's eyes when she had first seen Joanna on the afternoon of the talk. The flicker of the serpent's tongue and the smile of the Saxon – Patrick remembered how the simile had formed in his mind.

And now Joanna was missing. But that was four – no, five – days ago, surely? Mary could not possibly be involved in that. Then what else? *Think*, Patrick. What's happened that's been out of routine? Krzystof Kent's visit to Mary? And with the framing of the thought he knew, quite definitely and quite unarguably, that that was where the clue lay. Something had been said that afternoon – something said by Kent to Mary – something that Patrick ought to have picked up.

What?

And then he knew what it was. It was the look on Mary's

face when Krzystof Kent had said – quite casually – that he was staying with someone who had been in Alwar as a child. Selina March. Krzystof was staying with Selina March. Patrick stared at the three things in his mind. Mary Maskelyne. Selina March. And an Indian village. It's there, he thought. The clue is there. He rearranged them, to see if a different pattern emerged. An Indian village, Mary Maskelyne, and Selina March. Like a child's game where you built up brightly coloured blocks to make a pattern. *Think*, Patrick – for Christ's sake, man, look at it the right way up, because the answer's got to be there!

And then he saw that the answer was there, and he saw that it had been there all along, that in fact it was bloody staring him in the face, and so vividly and so glaringly that he could not imagine why he had not seen it straight away.

As Don put the phone down, Patrick stood up and reached for his car keys. 'I know where Mary's gone,' he said. 'And we've got to get after her. No, there's no time to summon the police. We'll ring them on the way – you've got your mobile with you, haven't you? Yes, good. Oh, but wait now, see if you can get Robbie Glennon, will you? Ask him to meet us on the car park. He can think on his feet, that one.'

Don dialled a number, and then started to say, 'Where are we—?'

'I know where Mary's gone,' said Patrick, who was at the door by this time. 'She's gone to find Selina March.'

'*Selina March?*'

'Listen,' said Patrick when Don caught him up in the

central wing. 'Mary Maskelyne has spent the whole of her life hating one person, and that's the one who escaped from the Tower of Silence in Alwar fifty years ago.' He waited with barely concealed impatience as one of the duty warders unlocked the gates leading to the central courtyard. 'The child who got away, leaving Mary's older sister to die,' he said, as they crossed the paved yard together and approached Moy's main gates. 'Oh – did you get Glennon?'

'Yes, he's on his way. Patrick, you said the child who got away—'

'That child,' said Patrick, 'was always the focus of black bitter hatred, first by Mary's parents, and then from Mary herself.' He broke off, the memory of Pippa – Christabel Maskelyne – flooding into his mind. But Mary did not know about Christabel; she still believed that Christabel had died in that grisly tower all those years ago. Would it have made any difference if she had known the truth? I can't tell, he thought, gesturing to the officer on the main gates to let them out.

As they went across to where his car was parked, he said, 'Two days ago Mary found out – and I've only just realised it – that that child who escaped that night is here. Living in Inchcape.'

'Selina March,' said Don. 'That's what you meant, wasn't it? Dear God, Patrick, are you sure?'

'Not entirely. But Mary is. She believes it. And so we've got to get to Teind House before she gets there ahead of us. In fact—' He stopped, seeing the other man's face. 'Don, what is it?'

'There was no reply from my cottage,' said Don. 'So I tried Teind House.'

'And?'

'There was no reply from there, either.' He opened the passenger door, as Robbie Glennon galloped towards them, his tow-coloured hair blown into disarray by the wind.

'Does Emily have a mobile?'

'Yes. I tried that as well. It's switched off. That probably means she didn't bother to take it with her. She often forgets it.'

'So,' said Patrick, switching on the ignition, 'either no one's in at Teind House—'

'Which isn't likely, if Emily was booked to go down there—'

'Or if she's at Teind, she can't answer,' said Patrick, horror washing over him.

It was completely dark by now, with the thick soupy night that descended on this part of Scotland in late October. As they drove down the road leading to Inchcape Patrick could hear a faint growl of thunder, as if, deep within the turgid skies, the storm was still seething and threatening. He had noticed the storm from within Moy, but only as part of the confusion and panic.

'Mary escaped so that she could get to Selina March,' he said, as they neared the cluster of buildings that made up the village. 'That's the thing that compelled her, Don. That's why she took all those risks to get out. And that's why we've got to get to Teind House before she does.'

'She's five hours ahead of us, Patrick—'

'I know.'

'And it looks as if Emily's with Selina.'

'I know that as well.' Patrick glanced at Don who was seated next to him, and then in the driving mirror at young Glennon, white-faced and fearful in the back. I suppose he'll go dashing to the rescue, white knight on a charger fashion, and she'll fall into his arms, he thought. Very suitable, of course. He's an ambitious intelligent boy; he'll do well in life.

'The police are coming,' said Don, after a moment, switching off his mobile phone. 'They said they'd catch us up.'

'Good.' Patrick was concentrating on the road, which was awash with rain from the storm, and trying to shut out images of Emily in Mary Maskelyne's hands. As he turned onto the bumpy track that led up to Teind House, he said, 'I don't know if either of you believe in any kind of God. But if you do, this is the time to start praying that we've beaten Maskelyne to it.'

'I can't see any lights in the house,' said Don after a moment. 'But that might be the storm again.'

'Let's hope so.'

'Uh – Dr Irvine – you really do think Mary might – hurt Emily?' said Robbie.

'Maskelyne's waited nearly thirty years to find the child who survived in Alwar,' said Patrick. 'She's wanted to kill her for all of those years. Tonight she won't let anyone get in the way of that.'

CHAPTER THIRTY-TWO

Krzystof had unearthed a torch from the glove compartment of the hire car, and this made him feel a bit better equipped for storming the dark citadel.

The rain had stopped but as he went through the orchard the trees were dripping with moisture, and the damp night soaked into his jacket and spangled his hair. Several times he paused to listen, thinking he had caught the sound of furtive footsteps coming after him, and once he whipped round, flicking on the torch to scan the darkness. But there was nothing to be seen save the skeletal outlines of the trees, and if anything moved in the darkness it did so under a cloak of invisibility.

Even Joanna would have had to acknowledge that this was a situation where embroidering was not necessary. Having done the classic prowl through the dark old house, Krzystof was now preparing to storm the ancient, legend-drenched tower. Gothic hero stuff after all. He walked cautiously because the road was deeply rutted, and the last thing he needed on a night like this was to stumble on the uneven surface and sprain his ankle.

As he neared the tower, his heart began to beat uncomfortably fast. I'm not good at this hero-stuff, he thought. I'm not designed for it. Yes, but supposing this leads you to Joanna. Supposing it was her mythical lover who made those footprints inside Teind House and caused those lights in the Round Tower? But there isn't a lover, thought Krzystof fiercely. I *know* there isn't.

But if Joanna had not had a lover – and of course she had not! – might she have had a murderer? The thought struck chillingly against Krzystof's mind, but he knew it had been there for some time. Oh, get on with it, you nerd!

He was no longer entirely sure about the light he had seen inside the tower. He could not see it now, and he was starting to suspect that it had only been a vagrant spear of moonlight, perhaps catching a gleam of something. Moonlight in the midst of a thunderstorm? You're trying to duck out of this!

But he was not trying to duck out at all. It was just that the closer he got to the tower, the less likely he thought it that there would be anything to investigate. Or would there? The Stornforth police had checked the tower; they had assured Krzystof that it had been one of the first places they had looked, and there was no reason to disbelieve them or doubt their efficiency. But he would check anyway.

The palpable age of the tower did not especially daunt him; in fact, in other circumstances he would have been extremely interested in the place, and would have been wondering what fragments of history might be found inside, and whether the Rosendale might mount a small exhibition under the banner of warlike Christianity. Eighth- and ninth-century monks guarding their small religious treasures from the marauding Vikings who had frequently made raids to grab anything that was going in the way of females and possessions . . . Sixteenth-century abbots burying Mass vessels in the garden to fool Henry VIII's commissioners. Yes, it was a good idea. Krzystof went on thinking about it because it helped him to ignore the feeling that the nearer he got, the more clearly he could be seen by the eyes that watched him from the slitted windows.

(And there are some eyes that can eat your soul, remember . . .)

Whatever the eighth- or ninth-century monks who had built this tower had done about marauding Vikings, they had built this stronghold firmly and well. It was amazing that it was still in such good repair a thousand years on. Krzystof walked round it until he found the small door set deep into the black stones.

The door swung inwards easily and smoothly when he pushed it open, with only the faintest whisper of sound, and a faint warning note jabbed at his mind. Did this mean the hinges had recently been oiled? No, it was more likely that the recent police search had loosened any rust.

The darkness came at him like a thick stifling cloak,

and he pulled the torch from his jacket pocket and flicked it on, fully prepared for dirt and decay and for scuttlings from mice or rats or birds. But the little round room was far cleaner than he had expected, in fact it was far cleaner than it had any right to be. It's been swept, thought Krzystof incredulously. Quite recently as well – there's no dust or dirt anywhere. Was that the police search? But as he moved the torch slowly around, he thought it was not. The little room had the look of constant care – of dust and cobwebs kept ruthlessly in check, even of ledges in the stone walls carefully wiped clean. There might be some perfectly ordinary explanation for this, however; the place was bound to be a landmark and there might be a local history society or a preservation group who kept it in reasonable condition for tourists and students.

Other than the surprising cleanliness there was nothing to be seen, except, of course, for the steps directly in front of him, which would wind up inside the tower, probably to the very top. Krzystof shone the torch onto the ground. Footprints in the dust this time? jeered his mind. Well, why not? But there were no footprints, because there was no dust. The only prints were the invisible ones left on the atmosphere by centuries of history.

After a moment Krzystof went back to prop the door open, using a stone from outside, and, taking a firmer grip on the torch, he began to ascend the stair.

And now it felt as if the ancient tower was coming alive all around him. The steps were solid stone, a little worn at the centre, and Krzystof's feet made no sound on them as he went cautiously upwards. The light he had seen from Teind House – if light there had been – had seemed to come from the slit-like windows, halfway up. Could it have been the light of a torch – of someone going slowly up and up these steps, and round and round, until the very top was reached?

The higher he went, the more he was aware of the past all around him, as if the tower's history was waking, and projecting itself, palimpsest-like, onto the present. The beleaguered monks, after all? Bustling worriedly up and down these very stairs, squirrelling away religious artefacts in the face of a raid? But Krzystof thought what he was sensing was far more recent: he thought it was more as if something violent and shattering had happened here, so that the early memories of the tower's origins and its creators had been smothered and dimmed.

Joanna's death? Would that be violent and shattering enough? For goodness' sake, man, you've been in enough peculiar places to know about unquiet spirits and the lingering echoes of extreme violence. But she can't be here; they searched this place from top to toe. She can't even have been kept here, or they'd have found signs. But supposing whoever took her cleaned up afterwards? Swept and tidied everything away, and swabbed down the decks? But this was so preposterous an idea that Krzystof dismissed it instantly, and went on up the stairs.

The steepness and the sharp twist of the steps made his leg muscles ache before he had gone even a quarter of the way up, but the higher he went, the more he was aware of real sounds: of tiny scufflings and murmurings that might only be the wind groaning in the gaps of the ancient structure or mice scuttling to and fro, but might as easily be the sound of soft footsteps creeping up the stairs after him, or the groaning of someone held prisoner somewhere in the sour darkness . . .

He swung round, trying to see back down the steps, but they wound too sharply round and he could not. Oh hell, this was turning into outright melodrama. But I'm blowed if I'm going to retreat now, he thought. And of course there's no one in here. Onwards and upwards. But every slight sound tore at his already stretched nerve-endings, and every twist of the stair sent his heart pounding with nervous dread. There *is* someone in here with me, he thought. I'm not imagining it: I can *feel* that there's someone else in here, just as I could feel it in Teind House. Someone crouching just above him, waiting on the next twist of the stair, perhaps? Was that the sound of someone breathing very quietly, or just the wind scudding through the ancient stones again?

A faint spill of light was visible ahead of him, which must mean he was reaching the halfway point and one of the narrow windows. Yes, the stairs widened briefly into a tiny stone room, five or six feet square, with a narrow window set into the stone walls. A resting place, probably; a tower this high would probably have several. Krzystof paused, and turned to shine the torch back down the stairs.

His heart leapt in the most complete terror he had ever known. Standing just below him was a woman whose hair hung in rain-sodden tangles over her face, and whose eyes were mad and glaring, and empty of all sanity. It was the woman he had interviewed three days earlier at Moy.

Mary Maskelyne.

And in her right hand she was holding a glinting knife.

For a brief, bizarre moment, the two of them were enclosed in the cold blue triangle of light from Krzystof's torch, as if they were standing on a lit stage. Krzystof had no idea how Mary came to be there, or what she wanted, but all that mattered was getting away from her and raising the alarm. How? demanded his mind. Because in case you hadn't noticed, she's standing between you and the stair leading down and to get to the ground you've got to go past her—

He stared into the mad eyes, aware that he was seeing the real person who lived behind the demure, polite woman he had met at Moy. This was the girl who had butchered her parents when she was fourteen, and who had gone on to kill two people in prison years afterwards.

And in a minute she's going to kill me, he thought. I'm in her way – I've seen that she's got out of Moy, and she'll need to get rid of me. It'll be a question of survival for her. He took a firmer grip on the torch, which could be used as a weapon, but his mind was darting ahead, flinching from the crunch of bone as he smashed it down on her skull. Yes, but if it's her or me . . .

But Mary did not move, although Krzystof had the impression of tightly coiled nerves and muscles that would spring into action at the smallest touch. He forced himself not to look at the knife, and he tried not to look at the wild eyes. But once you had looked at them – really looked – it was very hard to look away. Panic-stricken half-memories of primitive beliefs – of how the evil eye of a murderer could hypnotise – tumbled through his mind, and to dispel these he said, 'Mary? It *is* Mary, isn't it?' By this time he was so wrought up that he would not really have been surprised to discover that he was seeing a chimaera or a ghost, or even just some weird thought-projection of the creature still locked inside Moy.

She said, in a voice so laden with madness that Krzystof's skin crawled, 'Yes, of course it's Mary.'

'I thought it was. We met a couple of days ago. I'm Krzystof Kent. Do you remember?'

'Oh, I remember, Krzystof.'

'Why are you here?' said Krzystof. 'What do you want?' And what will you do if she says, in that wet gloating voice, *I want you, my dear* . . . ? Oh, for pity's sake.

'I want *her*,' said the mad voice. 'The one who lives at Teind House.'

'Selina March?' said Krzystof, uncomprehendingly, and then thought: damn and blast, I shouldn't have said her name, because if this mad creature didn't know it before, she does now.

'Selina March,' said Mary softly, making it sound like an obscenity. 'Yes, that's the one. The one who should have died all those years ago in India. But she didn't die; she escaped and my sister died instead.'

'Your – I didn't know you had a sister.' First I'm asking if she remembers meeting me, and *now* I'm enquiring politely about her relations as if we're at a social gathering, for heaven's sake! Yes, but if I can keep her talking like this I might manage to lull her into a false sense of security. And then what? You've still got to get past her. And she's mad. Not just disturbed or eccentric, she's *really* mad.

'Yes, I had a sister,' said the terrible thing on the stair. 'Only she died before I was born, and my parents never got over it. They never loved me because there wasn't room for me in their minds. She was perfect, you see, my dead sister. Perfect and unspoiled. She never grew up, so she couldn't ever be anything *but* perfect and unspoiled, and that's why they were able to turn her into a saint.'

'That's immensely sad. But—'

'There was a group of children who were taken hostage in a village in India,' she said, as if he had not spoken. 'Alwar. Years and years ago. Before I was born. Another world. Except it's lived on, that world. It's here with us now – can't you feel that it's here now? They all died, those children. All except one.' She was edging up the steps towards him, and Krzystof could very nearly smell the madness. Like stale sweat. Like old, dried blood. And I'm trapped on this narrow stair with her.

'My parents used to say, If one child had to escape that night, why was it not our child?' said Mary. 'Why was it that other one? they said. They hated her, that other child,' said Mary. 'I hated her too.' She tightened her hold on the knife; Krzystof saw it glitter. 'I always knew that if I found her I'd kill her,' she said. 'And now I have found her. Selina March. Prissy little Miss March, never going anywhere or doing anything. Living here all her life, going to church, helping local charities. I've listened to them talking about her inside Moy. And that writer woman – she's your wife, isn't she? – she knew who Selina was as well.'

Joanna! Krzystof's mind snapped to attention. But Joanna had not known about Alwar and the fifty-year-old tragedy. Or had she? How about those notes on the laptop? *There were parts of the past that had been sealed away ... she had written. Dark forbidden chasms which must never be approached, and for a child to have stumbled on that small, largely incomprehensible fragment of the story was at best unfortunate, at worst, damaging. The trouble was that there was no one who could be asked for the truth ...*

Krzystof suddenly saw that he might have been looking at those notes from the wrong angle. Was it possible that Joanna had not been setting out a fictional plot at all, but writing of her own childhood? But how could Joanna, born nearly a quarter of a century later, be involved in something that happened in the late 1940s? Look at that one later, Krzystof. Focus on the immediate danger. He said, 'And so you – escaped from Moy? In order to find Selina – is that right?'

'It's easy to escape from a place like Moy,' she said. 'They're all so stupid in there; I fooled them easily.' A glint of something artful and pleased with itself showed, and Krzystof felt a fresh jab of fear. She's clever and cunning and devious, Patrick Irvine had said. And when she appears sane, that's when she's at her most mad and her most dangerous.

'I went to Teind House first,' she said. 'It took me a little while to find it, but in the end I did. It's signposted from the road, isn't it? Easy. But when I got there it was empty, and I couldn't get in because all the doors were locked. So I was going to wait in the outhouse until *she* came home, so that I could kill her. I cut the phone wires while I waited – it's very easy to do that, did you know? Snip-snip, and it's done, and the person in the house is completely isolated from the world. I didn't want Selina to be able to get help, you see. I wanted her to myself. Isolated from the world.'

'Alone and in the sea of life enisl'd,' said Krzystof, softly.

'Yes. *Yes.* That's poetry, isn't it? You'd know about poetry, wouldn't you? Your wife – Joanna – knew as well. She knew about being alone and enisl'd.'

'What do you mean?'

'*You* know what I mean,' said Mary. 'Of course you do. I didn't know, not at first, but later on I worked it out.'

And barely understood secrets become woven into childhood nightmares and childhood fears, and sometimes they call the poor mangled ghosts out of their uneasy resting places . . .

'I saw you drive up to Teind House,' she said, 'and I waited until you unlocked the door and went back to your car. That's when I went into the house and took the knife from the kitchen drawer. You knew I was there all along, didn't you? I hid behind the kitchen door and watched you. I watched you go upstairs, and when you came down again, I followed you here. I took a jacket from the hall stand – I knew I needed to be wearing something dark and anonymous so that no one would see me – and then I crept through the orchard. I followed you all the way, Krzystof, and you didn't know that, did you?'

But he had known it, of course. He had felt the watching eyes, and he had felt the trickling menace as he went between the trees.

'Why did you follow me?' he said. But he knew already. She was simply removing everyone who came between her and Selina March. The thought: then she hasn't yet got to Selina, formed briefly.

Mary seemed to catch this. 'I haven't killed Selina yet,' she said. 'I'm still waiting for her. But I'll have to kill you; you do understand that, don't you? I knew I'd have to kill you when I realised that you knew someone had got into Teind House. You saw the footprints – I hadn't thought about leaving footprints. Careless, that. I'm not usually so careless. So I knew I'd have to get rid of you.' She held up the knife again. 'This is what I'll be using. I took it from the kitchen drawer. It's a good knife, isn't it? It's sharp.'

She moved up two more steps as she said this, so that she was almost level with him. Krzystof glanced over his shoulder, to where the stair wound the rest of the way up. Could he make a quick sprint up there? Yes, but to what? said his mind. It's a one-way street, this tower. It's just a stairway and a half-landing. Several half-landings, probably. And if you reached the top you'd be trapped there. He remembered that people in the grip of genuine mania were supposed to possess the strength of at least three. And if she kills me, I'll never find Joanna, he thought, and there was a renewed jab of bleak and bitter despair, and then a wild surge of anger. I *won't* let this evil, inhuman creature kill me, he thought. I'll get away somehow.

'I didn't plan on killing you,' said Mary regretfully. 'And in some ways it's a nuisance. But you do see that I can't let you go free, don't you? And I've been quite clever about it all – I've closed the door downstairs so that we shan't be interrupted. You propped it open, didn't you, but I closed it when I followed you in. You didn't hear me do that, did you?'

'Mary, you need help. Dr Irvine—'

'Oh, fuck Dr Irvine,' she said, and Krzystof stared, because just for a moment it was as if a nice, middle-aged lady had used the word. 'He's no use at all,' said Mary. 'None of them are any use, because none of them understand.'

'Do you think I might understand?'

'Oh no,' she said at once.

'You could try. We could talk—'

'No, I couldn't try and no, we couldn't talk.'

'But if you kill Selina and if you kill me, they'll catch you eventually,' said Krzystof. 'And you'll be—' He broke off.

'Punished?' she said, and incredibly there was amusement now. 'What else can they do to me that hasn't already been done? They don't hang people any longer.

And in this country they don't give them a lethal injection or send them to the electric chair. In any case I might get away with it. I might be able to get out of Inchcape and find somewhere to live where I won't be recognised. There are shelters, hostels for homeless, these days, aren't there? Places where questions aren't asked. I might even find work and earn some money.'

'You'd never do it,' said Krzystof at once. 'You've been away from the world almost all your life.'

For the first time he saw hesitation in her face. 'That's true,' she said. 'And I'd forgotten how huge the world is, and how the sky stretches on and on and how it sometimes seems to press down on you when it gets dark—'

She broke off, and Krzystof said cautiously, 'It's a huge place, the world, Mary. Frightening. Would you really cope, after all these years?'

'I coped with getting out of Moy,' she said, and the hesitation vanished at once. 'I coped with finding Teind House.' The mad face suddenly swam nearer. 'I'm here, aren't I?' she said in the thick treacly whisper. And the hand clutching the knife was suddenly raised, and then brought swooping down.

Krzystof half fell backwards in an attempt to avoid that evilly sharp blade, hitting out with the heavy torch, no longer caring where the blow fell, intent only on defending himself. But the torch flailed uselessly on the air, and she was already half sprawling on top of him. There was a nightmare moment when he felt the feminine crush of breasts against his chest, and the softness of feminine thighs straddling his body – dreadful! Her breath, dry and

438

slightly sour, gusted into his face, and he turned his head to one side, struggling to bring the torch up once more, because if he could smash it into her cheekbone— He made a grab for her hand, but she snatched it back, and lifted the knife a second time, grinning horridly down at him. A snail-trail of saliva trickled from the corner of her mouth. Disgusting! Revolting beyond bearing! Damn you, thought Krzystof furiously, I *won't* let you kill me before I've found Joanna, I *won't*—

He was just managing to raise the heavy torch high enough to swing it into Mary's face when two things happened almost simultaneously.

A car drove past the tower, on the private, little-used road below, its engine snarling through the quiet darkness.

And Mary dug the knife into him.

The pain was instant and intense, but incredibly there was a spiral of surprise. She's done it! thought Krzystof. The bitch really has stabbed me!

For several nightmare moments his senses were so confused that he could not tell where the pain came from. The torch had rolled out of his hand and into a corner, and the light had gone out. Krzystof was dimly aware of Mary, straightening up, the knife still in her hand – dripping blood? Yes, and it's your blood, it's *your blood*— He felt as if he was being sucked down into a dizzying black whirling tunnel – down and down and down – only he dare not let himself reach the bottom of the tunnel because if he did that he would die—

There was the sound of a moan that he did not at first realise was his own, and he managed to claw back up the spinning darkness, and back into the dimly lit stone tower, and it was then that he realised that the knife had gone in not to his body, which presumably she had aimed for, but to the upper part of his thigh. There was a jumble of panic, interspersed with fragments of half-knowledge about severed arteries and tourniquets, and then his senses righted themselves, and he thought that if he could manage to get something – his handkerchief? – tightly enough over the wound at least he would not bleed to death here in the darkness.

His whole leg was a mass of wet, grinding agony, but by dint of exerting every shred of will-power he managed to fold his handkerchief into a thick pad, which he pressed over the wound. He thought the bleeding slowed a little, although it was difficult to tell in the darkness. Could he put on a tourniquet? What could he use for it? He was not wearing a tie, only a sweater with an open-necked shirt under it. Could he use a sock? One for you there, Joanna – 'My dears, there he was, bleeding like a pig the poor darling, and he managed to tie a woolly sock round his leg to stop it.' Krzystof would happily have given five years of his life if he could have believed that he and Joanna would be sharing the joke of that one in the future.

He had no idea who had driven along the disused road, except that clearly it was not the Fifth Cavalry riding to the rescue, but there had been a swift, nightmare image of Mary going back down the steps, her shadow falling eerily on the stone walls, the hand that still held the knife raised over her head.

Following her was clearly impossible. Krzystof tried to stand and found he could not. He might have dragged himself across the small landing, but in his present condition the stairs would have taken about a year to negotiate. How about the window? If he could get onto the ledge, he might manage to shout a warning to whoever was below. Everything was still spinning sickeningly around him but he was managing to hang on to consciousness by a thread. He set his teeth, and by half crawling, half dragging himself across the floor, he made it. He was drenched in sweat by this time, and the pain from the stab wound was sheer bloody torture, but he managed to grasp the ledge surrounding the window, and haul himself up until he could see out. The narrow slit was open to the elements, and the cold night air blew into his face, drying the sweat on his face. He drew in several deep lungfuls of it, and felt his head clear slightly.

Leaning forward as far as he dared, he looked down, and there, far below him, was Mary's figure emerging from the tower. Even from up here, Krzystof could see that she had smoothed her hair back, and turned up the collar of the jacket she wore. She looked a bit dishevelled, but she looked normal. Yes, but her right hand is thrust deep into the jacket pocket, said his mind. She's still got the knife.

The car was moving slowly, clearly trying to avoid the deep ruts in the road's surface. Krzystof did not recognise the car, but it was a small one and he thought there was only the driver inside. He saw Mary pause and look about her, as if unable to get her bearings beyond the tower's confines, and he remembered that curious moment when she had seemed afraid, and talked about the world's vastness. And then she ran along behind the car, waving, and the car's brake lights came on, as if the driver had seen the figure in the mirror. Mary went to the driver's side, and appeared to speak for a moment. And then, to Krzystof's horror, she went round to the passenger side and got in.

The car drove away.

CHAPTER THIRTY-THREE

Emily did not know the precise moment when the last remnants of the mask fell away from Selina March, and the dreadful mad creature beneath was finally exposed, but she thought it might have been the moment when they actually stepped inside the Round Tower. The place was sufficiently nightmarish on its own account, of course; it did not really need mad people masquerading as prim fifty-something spinsters to add to its atmosphere.

What Emily did know, however, was that by the time Selina grabbed her arm, and said, 'Don't go up the stairs – not until we know the men have gone,' the mask had vanished completely, and the situation had gone beyond all logic or reality.

She tried logic anyhow. 'Miss March, there are no men. Truly there aren't. Someone's escaped from Moy – that's what the alarm bell was for. So wouldn't it be much better to just go back to Teind House and – and lock the doors, and wait until they've recaptured whoever it is?'

'Oh no,' said Selina at once. 'Oh no, that's just what they want us to do. They'll be waiting outside the tower for us. They'll be there now – you won't see them and you won't hear them, but they're there for sure.'

So strong was the conviction in her voice that for a moment Emily really did believe that men were hiding outside, waiting to snatch them up.

'They're very cunning,' said Selina softly. 'That's what you have to remember. They were so cunning and so sly last time, but I was slyer. I hid inside the tower and I cheated them all.'

The tower . . . She means that other tower, thought Emily. That dreadful place that Christy talked about. The burial pit, and the poor drying bodies on the shelves – one shelf for men and one for women, and another for children. That's where she thinks we are. We've gone back, thought Emily. We've fallen backwards into that long-ago Indian village, with a group of doomed and terrified children trying to escape from terrorists. And it's no wonder that Christy has been mad all these years, and it's no wonder that Selina is mad as well. You could surely only feel extreme pity for someone who had been through that kind of childhood trauma.

So she said, in a bright, practical voice, 'OK, then, what we'll do, we'll hide in here for as long as we have to. I'll stay with you, and we'll be quite safe.'

'We mustn't go up the stair, though,' said Selina, and the glance she cast towards the winding stone steps sent a shiver of purest terror down Emily's spine. 'That's where *they* are, you see.'

'"They"?' This was sounding like the most way-out dialogue ever written. 'Miss March, there's nothing up there except maybe a lot of dust and dirt—'

'The ogre-birds are there,' said Selina, and this time Emily heard, as she had heard in Christabel Maskelyne's voice, the terrified child speaking through the woman. I don't know how to handle this, she thought in renewed panic. I haven't a clue about what to do and what not to do.

'They're waiting,' whispered Selina. 'They're crouching on the ledge up there, and they'll pounce. You don't even have to be dead, you know. My mother wasn't dead, but they tore her into little pieces. I watched them do it.'

'Oh, God, that's terrible—'

'Yes, it was. It was terrible. So this time we've got to outwit them,' said Selina. 'The men are outside and the ogre-birds are up there, and we've got to outwit them both. We've gone back, you see, and if only we're careful and plan ahead we might escape this time. And then they'll all be alive in the world again – Douglas and the others, and dear Christy. I've missed them so much all these years, you know. We were such wonderful friends, and I loved them so very much,' she said wistfully, and her voice was suddenly filled with such sadness, and such aching loneliness, that Emily wanted to put her arms round the poor bewildered little creature and tell her that yes, this time they would escape, and her friends would all be here with her once again.

'So we'll go down, not up,' said Selina, suddenly brisk again.

'Where—'

'Didn't you know about the secret room?' said Selina, half turning to regard Emily. 'No, I keep forgetting, you don't; you wouldn't know because you've never been here before, have you?' There was the faint childish superiority now – the tone of I-know-something-you-don't. 'It's a good secret,' she said eagerly. 'I only found out about it when my Great-uncle Matthew died. He knew a lot about Inchcape and all the old buildings. He wrote a book about it, you know.'

'I didn't know.' At least, thought Emily gratefully, they seemed to be back in the present day.

'He didn't put about the secret room in his book, but he mentioned it in his private notes,' said Selina. 'I read them all. And one of the things he wrote was that he thought the Round Tower would have had a hidden store-room; a place where the early monks could put their Mass vessels when there was a raid. Chalices and crucifixes and plates, you know.'

'Buried treasure,' said Emily, wondering if this would strike a chord with the child-persona that kept coming so macabrely to the surface.

'Yes, but when I found the room, all the vessels had *long* since gone. It took me a little while to work out exactly where the room was, because those monks were very clever. And they had to face a great many dangers for their faith, the early Christians. So brave, I always thought them, although my aunts said it was a lot of hysteria. They thought religion was about going to church on Sunday and helping with fund-raising events, and asking the vicar to tea on Sundays.' As she spoke she was kneeling down and scratching around on the stone floor. Emily watched helplessly, not having the least idea whether the secret room really existed or was just another mad fantasy.

'When I found the monks' hideout, I was *so* pleased,' said Selina. 'I knew, you see, that there might be a time when I would have to hide again, and I knew that if only I could get it right this time—'

Emily said, gently, 'Then you would be with your friends again.'

'Yes.' It was said gratefully and humbly, and Emily felt the pity of it close around her throat. Then Selina said, eagerly, 'This is where we have to go,' and Emily saw that she was pulling up a kind of square trapdoor set into the stone floor, its surface so exactly flush with the stones surrounding it that you would never know it was there. Narrow steps led down into a gaping darkness.

Selina gestured impatiently and Emily thought: well, I dare say this is the maddest thing yet. But she's not armed and I truly don't think she means me any harm. I think she's just sad and lonely, and I think the best thing is for me to go along with what she wants.

She glanced at the trapdoor's underside as she stepped onto the stone stairs, and was relieved to see a hefty-looking handle sunk into the surface.

'It's very easy to get back out,' said Selina. 'You just

447

push the trapdoor up from the centre, using that handle. When it's closed, you can see a faint line around the edges, so you know where it is.' And, anticipating Emily's next thought almost before it had formed, she said, 'And it won't be pitch dark down there; there are candles and oil lamps. I brought them ages ago, in case I ever had to hide again. It's a good thing I did that, isn't it? Put lights down here?'

'Yes,' said Emily, and then, because there seemed to be no reason to resist, she began to descend the steps.

There was a dull scraping sound as Selina pulled the trapdoor back into place over their heads, and as the dim light from above slowly disappeared Emily paused and looked back, panic threatening to engulf her again. I'm shut in with her! No, it's all right; I can push the trapdoor back up quite easily.

But the dream-quality was returning with every step they took: it was not precisely a nightmare, but it was a curious, out-of-the-world feeling. We're going down into the bowels of the earth, she thought. Down below an old, old tower where people fought for their religious beliefs and hid from Vikings and Danes, and we're going underneath a place whose stones have stood here, silent and grim, for a thousand years. She could not see the ghosts, but she could feel them all around her, and she knew that this was a place where the echoes of the past and the echoes of the future lingered, and perhaps even met and melded. And I expect I shall wake up quite soon, she thought, striving for reality. What's really happened here is that I fell asleep, and I'm dreaming all this.

Selina must have been down here very recently, and she must have left one of her oil lamps burning, because as they descended Emily could see a gentle glow coming from below. Then she didn't tell me everything, she thought, with a fresh jab of unease. Unless, of course, the light had been made by someone else who was down here already . . .

Someone else down here. The stairs ended abruptly, widening into a small dungeon-like room, the floor and walls lined with black stone. Two thick iron pillars were embedded in the floor, and they stretched up into the low stone ceiling; Emily had the unpleasant thought that these iron columns were all that was supporting the immense black weight of the tower overhead. Two oil lamps, standing in opposite corners, cast twin pools of soft light.

The little room was the strangest place she had ever seen. It was furnished neatly and carefully; there was a little low table, polished to a silky sheen, with several silver-framed photographs on it. Emily half recognised the photographs as being of Selina's parents. A silver bud vase containing a tiny spray of something green and purply stood next to them. Lavender? No, not lavender, rosemary, because rosemary's for remembrance, and remembrance was what this was about. With the photographs was a powder compact with the initials *EM* engraved on it. How long was it since people had used powder compacts? There was a small scattering of rather old-fashioned jewellery as well – the kind of pearls that ladies had worn in the Forties – and there was another of the between-glass sheets of newspaper that Emily had seen in Selina's bedroom. John Mallory March again? Yes, of course it would be.

But Emily gave these things only the most cursory of glances, because set next to the table was a small fireside chair, and seated in it—

'Hello, Emily,' said Joanna. 'Have you come to share my captivity?'

Her hair was dishevelled and there was an ugly bruise on the side of her forehead. She was so pale that for a dreadful moment Emily thought she was one of the ghosts she had sensed earlier, and then she saw the chains circling Joanna's wrists and the small padlock holding them in place, and she saw that the other end of the chain was looped around the nearer of the iron pillars.

'You're a prisoner,' said Emily, and thought that was probably just about the stupidest thing she could have said. 'You've been down here all along?'

'Yes,' said Joanna, her eyes on Selina March. 'Miss March will explain it to you, I expect.'

'She's been kept quite comfortable,' said Selina at once. 'Food and drink – every need attended to.' With bizarre delicacy she indicated a small chair-like structure against the wall, and half lifted the hinged wooden lid of the seat.

'It's a very ladylike captivity, you see,' said Joanna, and although her voice sounded tired and strained Emily saw the glint of irony that had been such a vivid part of Joanna.

She said, 'I don't understand any of this—'

'I found the shrine,' said Joanna. 'That's what it's all about. Miss March had made a – a shrine to her parents' memory, and she kept it down here where it was secret and private. That's right, isn't it, Miss March?'

'It was necessary,' said Selina. 'Right from the start it was necessary, because when they died there was no one to pronounce the repentance-prayer over them. The *patet* it's called in India. So there was nothing to help them take the three steps across the old and holy Bridge into paradise. Humata, Hukhta, and Hvarshta, the three steps are called.'

It sounded like an early Sixties pop song. Three Steps to Heaven. I'm becoming hysterical, thought Emily. Concentrate, you stooge.

'Until I made the shrine,' Selina was saying, her eyes glazed and stary again, 'they used to come into my bedroom every night. They were mutilated, because of the ogre-birds. Half eaten. My mummy was the worst,' she said, and Emily glanced at Joanna and saw the dreadful comprehending pity in Joanna's eyes, and knew that Joanna understood.

'My mummy wasn't dead when they started to eat her,' said Selina. 'But they clawed her eyes out – they like eyes, those bad old ogre-birds. So when she came into my bedroom after she was dead, she had to be brought by my daddy, on account of being blind, you see.'

She paused, and Emily, hardly daring to speak, said, 'So you made a shrine to their memories.'

'Yes.' Selina turned to look at Emily, and incredibly it was the familiar, briskly efficient Miss March again. 'It kept them away. So I could never risk anyone's finding it and destroying it. It was found once, a long time ago, and I was made to dismantle it—' Her face twisted in a second or two of anger, but after a moment she went on. 'But I hoped it would be all right. I thought that they would be sure to be across the Bridge after several years. You would think they would have been, wouldn't you?' This last was directed at Joanna, who said, 'Yes, you would have thought so.'

'But they weren't. The very night the shrine was dismantled they came into my bedroom. The very same night. And it was dreadful. You have no idea how they looked— So I made a vow that no matter what I had to do, I would preserve the shrine for always. And I did. For a long time I kept it out here – in the little room just inside the door – but after my Great-uncle Matthew died I took it back to Teind House. I was there on my own, you see; there was no possibility of anyone's finding it – of not understanding how vital it was. But then . . .' She paused, and then, as if forcing herself to go on, said, 'There was not enough money. So unpleasant to say it – I was brought up to consider it ill bred to discuss money – but it is the truth. Investments were no longer paying the dividends – I didn't fully understand that, but I understood when there was not enough money to meet the bills every quarter.'

'So you started the little paying-guest set-up,' said Joanna, softly, and Selina turned to her eagerly, as if grateful for this prompt.

'Yes. *Such* a good way to make ends meet. It was Gillian's idea – my god-daughter. She was so helpful. And once I got used to it, I really rather enjoyed it.'

'But it meant you couldn't have the shrine in the house any longer,' said Emily.

'Anyone might have stumbled upon it by chance, you see,' said Selina. 'It was too risky. So I brought it back here.'

'And I found it,' said Joanna. 'I was curious about this place, and I found the hidden room entirely by chance. My husband had visited round towers in Ireland – some of them had concealed rooms under the ground, and he had described them.' She glanced at Emily. 'So I thought I'd see if there was one here. It would have made a terrific basis for a plot.'

'Yes, of course.'

'But I would never have come down here if I'd known about your shrine,' said Joanna, looking back at Selina. 'And in any case, I wouldn't have touched it or – or spoiled it. I told you that. I would have honoured it, just as you did.' A pause. 'I do understand,' said Joanna in a rather odd voice, 'about honouring the memories of the dead.'

'Yes, but I couldn't be sure that you told me the truth,' said Selina. 'People are such liars. Fire and brimstone shall be the portion of all liars, did you know that?'

'Fire and brimstone or not,' said Joanna, 'you can't keep

me here indefinitely. People will be looking for me— My husband—'

'He's here already,' said Emily, and Joanna turned to her eagerly.

'Krzystof? Is he really? But he's meant to be in Spain— Oh, but I should have known he'd come.'

When she says his name, it's as if a light comes on behind her eyes, thought Emily, and she felt suddenly and dreadfully lonely, because that was how she wanted to look when she said Patrick's name, and it was how she suspected she did look really, except that she had tried to hide it—

She said, 'He's been here for a couple of days and he's been frantic with trying to find you. I should think he'd find this place pretty soon, as well, wouldn't you? Because if he knew about the secret rooms in the Irish round towers, he'll realise there might be one here.'

'Yes, of course he will,' said Joanna, and Emily saw that Selina was watching Joanna and listening to what Joanna had said about Krzystof. The lonely envy in the little woman's eyes was almost more than Emily could bear.

She said, 'Miss March – Selina – you'll have to let Joanna go. No one will make a fuss. People will understand.' I could grab her and knock her down quite easily, thought Emily. I'm much younger and far stronger than she is. And then I could sprint back up the stairs and get help. But something in her flinched from it: Selina was so vulnerable and so pitiable. It would be like hitting a small child or an animal, thought Emily. She's quite mad, of course, the poor creature, but I don't think she's evil. I think we might be able to reason with her.

And then Selina said, in a perfectly ordinary, completely sane voice, 'I usually kill people who find my shrine. That's what I usually do. I haven't killed you, Joanna, because I liked you. I didn't expect to, but when you came to Teind House that day, I liked you right from the start. You were so friendly, so nice to me. That's made it quite difficult to find the resolve to kill you.' She looked from one to the other. 'I've covered my tracks very well,' she said. 'Reporting your disappearance, Joanna, and helping the police and your husband. And everyone's been very sympathetic – Gillian even offered to come up here to stay with me until it was all sorted out.' She paused, and then said, in a brisker voice, 'Of course, I had worked everything out first. All the things I had to do to stop people from suspecting. But I really do think I'll have to kill you,' she said. 'And now Emily will have to be killed as well. It's a pity, because I like Emily, too. But she's seen the shrine, so it can't be helped.' She paused. No one spoke. 'In the past,' said Selina, 'I've always disliked the people I've killed. That's made it easier. So I don't know how it's going to feel this time.'

It was then that Emily knew that she had been wrong, that there was nothing in the least defenceless or pitiable about this woman, and it was then that she bounded forward and knocked Selina to the ground.

CHAPTER THIRTY-FOUR

When Mary came out of the Round Tower there was another of those frightening moments when the world felt as if it was expanding all around her, and as if it might be opening up onto other worlds. For several dreadful seconds she had no idea where she was.

And then she saw the Round Tower's bulk, and she remembered about the car that had driven down the narrow, barely visible road, and she remembered that the driver might have seen activity within its dark fastness and her mind zipped back into top gear. The car was still there; it was going along the road that branched off the main highroad and meandered around a bit before ending up at Teind House – Mary had noted that on her way here.

Was it likely that anyone would use that road, other than someone who lived at Teind House? Selina March?

Presumably Selina had a car, as most people had nowadays, and presumably she would take the little road as a short cut to her own front door. Mary's heart began to thump with excitement and apprehension. Selina. I'm about to confront you at last. I'm about to redress the balance for all those years.

Krzystof Kent was not dead but he was bleeding so badly that he did not pose any immediate threat. He could safely be left up in the tower, where he would most likely bleed slowly to death, although if necessary Mary would go back to finish him off. She had better go back to check on him anyway. She considered briefly whether he might be able to call out a warning, but that was patently impossible. He was on the little landing by the window twenty feet up, and the tower was solid stone so that any mewling cry he might make could not possibly be heard outside.

The car was going slowly – slowly enough for Mary to run after it, and wave both arms. Adrenalin was flooding her body in huge torrents and the vast menacing darkness had ceased to matter. It was no surprise when the car's brake lights came on, and it stopped. I can do anything. I can make anything in the world happen.

She walked swiftly up to the driver's side, and waited for the window to be wound down. The driver was a young woman, and even in the uncertain light Mary saw she was too young to be Selina March.

But the unknown female was saying in a friendly way, 'Hello? Is something wrong? I'm just going up to Teind House,' and Mary recovered herself at once, because this was another of those situations where you had to think on your feet. Whoever this was, she clearly had not heard any television or radio bulletins about the escape of the infamous Mary Maskelyne. She glanced into the car's interior; no, the radio was not switched on. It was unlikely that this woman would have stopped for a lone female if she knew about the escape. 'Be wary of hitch-hikers' was what the news reports would say.

Even so, she would be cunning, and remember about being one jump ahead of everyone else. So she said, 'I'm sorry to flag you down – I don't know if you've heard yet, but one of the prisoners has escaped from Moy, and there're search parties out.'

The response was instant. 'Oh, how dreadful,' said the woman. 'No, I didn't know. I've been driving for the last three hours and I haven't had the radio on, I've been playing tapes. Who's escaped?'

'Mary Maskelyne,' said Mary, hugging herself inside at the brilliance of this. 'We're scouring the countryside for her, and I'm with the group that's using that old tower as headquarters.' Had that sounded convincing? Yes, the woman seemed unsuspicious. 'And we're trying to warn everyone to keep a very sharp look-out,' she said. 'Did you say you were going to Teind House?'

'Yes. Selina – Miss March – is my godmother. My name's Gillian Campbell, by the way.'

'I called at Teind House a while ago,' said Mary with perfect truth. 'To tell her what's happened. The phone lines are down because of the storm. Only she wasn't in. She lives on her own, doesn't she?' It was not as long a shot as it might sound; the librarian at Moy had given a pretty good thumbnail sketch of Selina's life.

'Yes, she does,' said the woman. 'She must be out somewhere. But I've got a key, so I can get in. I'll tell her about the escape when she gets back.' And then, as Mary appeared to hesitate, the woman said, 'Or you can come back with me now, if you like.'

'I suppose your aunt – did you say aunt? Godmother, sorry. I suppose she ought to be properly warned,' said Mary, appearing to consider this. 'There's a system of procedures we like people to adopt in this situation. Doors locked and so on. And if you're two ladies on your own— Yes, it might be better if I go through it with you both. Leave you an emergency number to ring, and so on.'

Too late she remembered that she had already said the phone lines were down, but Gillian Campbell did not seem to notice. She said her godmother was probably back home by now. 'She almost never goes out after dark. Get in and I'll take you up to the house.'

'Thank you very much,' said Mary. 'I think that's what I ought to do.'

She felt better in the car's enclosed space: she felt shielded from the menacing darkness, and the knowledge that by joining forces with Gillian Campbell she would be outwitting the real search parties brought a shaft of pure pleasure. Everything was falling into place for her, even to the extent of being invited into Selina March's home. You're doing pretty well, Mary. You're on your own – you don't really need Christabel at all, because you're dealing with the world and its people as smoothly as if you hadn't been inside institutions since you were fourteen.

'Selina isn't precisely expecting me,' said Gillian Campbell, as they pulled up in front of the house. 'But someone who was staying with her has apparently vanished rather mysteriously. I thought the old dear might be in a bit of a flap about it – she worries about everything in the world and she sounded quite agitated on the phone – so I drove up to give her a bit of moral support.'

As she parked and switched off the engine, she looked half questioningly at Mary, and Mary understood that this was the point at which she was expected to make her own introduction. She said, 'I'm Leila Edwards.' Leila Edwards had been her mother's maiden name, and it was the only one that came into her mind. 'I'm one of the wing governors at Moy.' At least she could give a reasonable portrayal of that.

'Have you been there long?' Gillian Campbell reached into the back of the car for her handbag, and Mary looked at her sharply. Had there been a sudden questioning sideways look then? As if the woman was suddenly suspicious? Mary slid a hand unobtrusively into the pocket of the jacket snatched, more or less at random, from the hall stand in Teind House earlier on. Was she going to have to produce the knife and make threats? Get out of the car, and if you try any tricks I'll kill you . . . ? How cumbersome would it be to take Gillian Campbell hostage?

She said, 'I've only just been transferred here. So I don't know the countryside yet.'

'It's a very restful place,' said Gillian. 'I like coming up here.' She stood up and surveyed the house. 'It doesn't look as if Selina's back yet. But let's go in, anyway. Mind your step – it's a bit dark, isn't it? There's usually a light over the porch, but the electricity's a bit erratic and if there's been a storm it probably knocked the power off. Thank goodness that awful rain's stopped at last.'

The feeling of slightly panicky distortion and menace nudged her mind again as they went into Teind House, but Mary pushed it down determinedly. It's only a house, for goodness' sake!

She had not decided yet what she would do with Gillian Campbell; she did not especially want to kill her, but she would do so if it became necessary. She would see what happened.

Gillian was taking off her coat and hanging it on the hall stand with the ease of long familiarity. 'I'll just nip up to the loo and have a wash, if you don't mind,' she said. 'I've been driving for nearly three hours without a break. It looks as if the electricity is off, doesn't it? I thought it would be. Wait a minute, I'll see if I can find the oil lamps—' There was a brief pause and Mary heard Gillian moving around the hall. 'I've got them,' she said after a moment. '*And* the matches next to them – Selina prepares for just about every eventuality you can think of. Hold on, and I'll light a couple; it's like the black hole of Calcutta in here . . . That's better.' Soft golden light

461

spilled into the darkness. 'Go through to the kitchen, will you?' said Gillian. 'Straight at the end of the hall. It'll be warm in there because of the range. I'll make us some tea or coffee.'

It was a great many years since Mary had been in this kind of casual domestic situation and there was a prickle of confusion again, because she had no idea how people behaved these days. She did not know, for instance, whether Gillian would expect her to fill the kettle and set it to boil while she was upstairs. Mary's mother, all those years back, would have considered it very impolite to do such a thing in a stranger's house, but people were far more relaxed these days, Mary knew that. The confusion was replaced by a surge of resentment because she ought not to have been kept away from ordinary things like this.

She looked about her. The kitchen, seen in the oil lamp's light, was larger than she had thought on her earlier visit. There was a massive old dresser against one wall, and a range, and there was the big scrubbed-top table at the centre. A couple of doors opened off the room; Mary checked to see what was beyond them because you should always know your terrain. But one was just a large, walk-in larder, and the other one, which seemed to lead out to the garden, was locked and bolted. She had still not made up her mind what she was going to do about this Gillian Campbell. She had been intending to focus her entire energy on Selina, and killing people used up a lot of energy. Each time you killed someone you gave away a little of yourself. That was one of the things the stupid sheep-creatures in Moy and Broadacre had never understood.

Gillian was coming back down the stairs; Mary could hear her footsteps on the polished oak of the floor. They coincided exactly with Mary's pounding heart. Beat-beat, pad-pad. Have-to-kill, have-to-kill. But as she came across the hall they were faster, so that the synchronisation was lost. Mary found this vaguely irritating. Like a fly buzzing against a window pane; a minor annoyance, only you could not ignore it.

And then Gillian came through the door and set the second oil lamp on the table, and turned round. Mary thought she started to say something about a cup of coffee, but then for the first time she saw Mary properly, and her eyes widened in sudden alarm. For a moment Mary did not understand this, and then Gillian said on a note of puzzlement, 'That's my godmother's jacket you're wearing.'

'No, it—' This was crazy. And for pity's sake, why shouldn't two people own an identical jacket!

'It *is* Selina's,' said Gillian, still staring. 'That's the gold lapel pin she got from the local Red Cross Society for her charity work. She always wears it on that jacket. Why would you be wearing her jacket—' She broke off, and then said, in a different voice, 'There's blood on your arm. There's a bandage.'

Mary looked down, and realised that the bandage she had transferred from her wrist to the wound on her arm earlier on had unravelled, and that one bloodied end was dangling below the jacket's cuff. Visible. Clear as a curse.

In a voice of absolute horror, Gillian said, 'You're not from Moy's staff at all, are you? You're the escaped prisoner.'

The escaped prisoner.

The words ought not to have stung so sharply, but they did. They labelled Mary but in an odd way, and at the same time they rendered her anonymous. Just another inmate of a prison. A reference on a file. She stared at Gillian and thought: but I'm not just any escaped prisoner! I'm famous! I was the Sixties icon who made banner headlines, not once but several times over! Everything I did was seized on and reported. I was *important*! And now I'm out of prison and I'm going to stay out, and nobody's going to get in the way of that! She slid her hand into the jacket pocket, her fingers closing around the knife once more. This person who was Selina March's god-daughter was certainly not going to get in the way of Mary's escape.

Selina March. With the name, the hatred came again, filling her up with a black choking bile of fury and anger. *Selina March*. The creature who had brought about all Mary's tragedies. And now, it seemed, there was something else. Selina had had a god-daughter. A god-daughter. All these years Selina had been able to enjoy a cosy godmotherly rôle – virtually that of a surrogate mother – while Mary, shut away inside Broadacre, had been deprived of her own daughter within minutes of the child's birth. Another unfairness to add to all the other unfairnesses. The realisation of this smacked into

Mary's mind, churning up a fresh wave of resentment and jealousy.

The strength came roaring in again, flooding her entire body, and she lunged forward, raising the knife, ready to deal with this creature who was Selina March's god-daughter, but Gillian was already scrambling out of the way, grabbing the edge of the big pine-topped table and pushing it forwards so that it toppled over, crashing onto the floor, inches from Mary's feet. The oil lamp rolled across the floor, and went out, plunging the room into darkness, and in the darkness Mary heard Gillian run across the room, and push past her. There was the sound of the outside door opening and then of the little car's engine starting up.

Mary thrust the knife back into her pocket, and went out through the door, and into the dark night beyond it.

CHAPTER THIRTY-FIVE

Emily had expected to be able to overpower Selina March with ease, but Selina fought back like a wild thing, her hands scrabbling at Emily's neck. The feel of the thin dry fingers was so repulsive that Emily jerked back, half falling into a corner of the stone room.

She was aware of Joanna shouting to her to grab the oil lamp and use it as a cosh, but she was dizzy and disoriented. She drew in a shaky breath, and saw Selina dart across the room towards the steps.

'She's going back up into the tower!' shouted Joanna. 'Oh, hell's teeth, why can't I get out of this bloody chair!' She dragged uselessly at the snaking chains.

'It's all right,' gasped Emily, clambering to her feet. 'I'll go after her—' She stood uncertainly for a moment, the room still a bit fuzzy, and then her vision cleared, and she realised that Selina had already vanished back up the stairs. There was the sound of the stone trapdoor being pushed back, and then of scampering feet. 'She's going up inside the tower,' said Emily. 'But at least I can go for help now— Oh shit, no, I can't, can I, because the minute I try to get to a phone she'll be back down here to finish you off—'

'You're sounding like a Victorian melodrama,' said Joanna. 'But you're right. You'll have to follow her, Emily – but for pity's sake take one of the lamps—'

'Yes. Oh, bugger it, I left my mobile phone at home.'

'Well, at least you're sounding as if you've come out of the Victorian melodrama,' said Joanna, and grinned. 'Never mind the phone, just go.'

'Yes.' Emily paused to snatch up the lamp, and then pushed the second one to where Joanna could reach it. 'Whack her over the head if she comes back,' she said. 'It'll be horrid, but if it's her or you . . .'

'I've already worked that one out,' said Joanna dryly. 'For goodness' sake get after her, and see where she's gone. If you can safely get to a phone, do so.'

'OK,' said Emily, and went back up the stairs.

The trouble was that once beyond the hidden room, there was no knowing where Selina had gone. She might be anywhere, thought Emily in trepidation, standing in the stone-floored room just inside the tower's entrance, and looking about her. She might have gone back to Teind House or she might still be hiding in the tower somewhere. Her instinct was to beat it down to the main road and the phone box on the corner, but that might be to leave Joanna at Selina's mercy. And there was no way of knowing how easy it would be for Joanna, chained in a chair, to fight Selina off. I can't risk it, thought Emily. I'll have to find her first – I'll have to go up to the tower's top and make sure she isn't up there. She thought she would hear if Selina went sneaking back into the hidden room, and she thought she could be back down the stairs quickly enough to get her away from Joanna.

She hesitated at the foot of the twisting stairs, holding up the lamp and trying to see upwards. But the stair wound sharply around to the right, and after the first few steps there was only a thick blackness. Emily drew in another deep breath, and, steadying herself against the wall with one hand, began to climb.

Even with the oil lamp's thin light it was a spooky experience. The higher you went, the colder it felt, and the more you were aware of leaving the safe familiar ground behind. Emily tried not to remember how narrow the tower was, and how it might sway a little in a high wind. She tried not to remember that Selina March was almost certainly hiding up here, waiting to spring out and strangle her.

She could hear the wind keening in and out of the narrow windows now, which presumably meant she was nearing the halfway mark. If you were fanciful, you might almost think the wind sounded like somebody moaning, very softly, in the dark. Selina, mourning her murdered childhood friends? Don't listen. Just keep going, said Emily firmly to herself. If she's up here you'll just have to knock her out with the lamp, and then belt back down the stairs to get help.

There *was* someone crying up here. There was someone crouching in the dark, sobbing dismally with loneliness and fear. The sound tore at Emily's heart, but she set her teeth and went on, because this was something that absolutely had to be done, and it was no good hoping that rescue was at hand – in the shape of Patrick, dashing in and scooping her up in his arms? don't be ridiculous! – because there was not going to be any rescue apart from what Emily could contrive for herself.

And then she saw the thin ingress of light just ahead of her, and she came up onto the cramped half-landing, and saw Krzystof lying huddled in a corner, a messy, bloodied handkerchief tied around one leg.

And Selina March standing over him, moaning.

The madness had faded from her eyes; Emily saw that at once, although she did not know whether she could trust it. But her expression was bewildered, and as Emily came onto the last step Selina put both hands over her eyes, as if to shield them. Emily saw that she was trembling, and was aware of a dreadful pity for the poor creature. Yes, but she's *mad*, remember? She tried to strangle you? She's *killed* people for goodness' sake! She said so.

From his huddled-over corner, Krzystof said, 'Emily – thank God to see you! Are you all right?'

'Yes, and so's Joanna – she's downstairs in a secret room,' said Emily because this was the one thing he would be wanting to hear. Even in the dimness she saw his eyes flood with delight, exactly as Joanna's had flooded with delight when Emily had said Krzystof was in

Inchcape. Marvellous to know you could make someone look like that.

She said, rapidly, 'We'll sort her out in a minute, and we'll sort you out in a minute as well. Uh – are you much hurt?' It looked pretty gory, but it might not be too bad.

'It's bloody painful,' he said. 'But I'll live.'

'Did Selina—'

'Selina? God, no! It was that bitch, Mary Maskelyne. Emily, listen, she's gone off in a car somewhere with some lone driver, and we've got to get the police or somebody after her—'

There was a bad moment when Emily thought: but I can't possibly cope with all this! I can't cope with Selina and Mary Maskelyne, and with Krzystof injured and Joanna chained up— It's too much. I don't know what to do. And then her mind snapped back on course, because of course she had got to cope with it, and of course she would think of something to do. And Krzystof was here, which was a remarkable comfort.

He was speaking to Selina now, saying with extraordinary gentleness, 'Selina – I think we should all go back down to the ground, and get you home. Don't you think we should do that?'

'We'll both come with you,' said Emily. 'I'll make us some tea – you'll like that. Remember how you said I made a nice cup of tea?'

She was just wondering if she dared reach out to touch Selina when Selina lowered her hands from her face and said, 'I can't go home yet. I've got to reach the others.'

Turning, she went up the remaining stairs, towards the very top of the tower.

Emily said, 'Oh shit,' and started up the stairs after her.

The Round Tower's summit was the most frightening place in the world. As Emily reached the top of the stairs she saw with panic that it was open to the skies at the centre, and then she saw that there were gaping holes in the surrounding wall where, at various times, the stones had crumbled and fallen to the ground. The wind was icy; it whistled through the jagged holes, and the tiny platform was perilously uneven. Here and there were the ghost-shapes of bird skeletons, heaped forlornly on the stones.

Emily felt sick and dizzy from the sheer height and because of the jagged holes through which she could see the countryside spread out far below them. Her stomach was turning over and over with vertigo, but she kept tight hold of the oil lamp, and she tried not to think how extremely high up they were, and above all she prayed to anything that might be listening that she would not have to fight with Selina March up here. Because we'd both be over the side and smashed to a pulp on the ground below within seconds, she thought.

Selina was pressed back against the wall facing Emily; the stonework immediately behind her looked fairly sound, but there was a large gap in the wall on her left.

Emily said, 'Selina – for pity's sake, come back down, and let's go home and get warm.'

'No—' It came out in the high-pitched frightened wail of a child, and it made the hairs prickle on the back of Emily's neck. 'No, I must wait for the others,' said Selina. 'They're so close to me now, you see. I told you, didn't I, that we had gone back – that this was our second chance. And we've cheated the men so far, haven't we?' The eager, trusting voice of the child was blotting everything out now. 'We've hidden from them, and we've only got to be quiet a very little longer now. Mouse-quiet, we've got to be – that's my daddy's word. Be mouse-quiet, Selina, he says. He'll be proud of me when he sees I've got away this time.' She stretched out a hand. 'You can be with us as well,' she said. 'You can meet all my friends – Douglas and the rest. He's Canadian, Douglas, and he's very clever. When he grows up he'll be rich. I might marry him when he's grown-up. And there's Christy, of course. Oh, you'll like Christy. She's so pretty and she's such fun. She thinks up such good games for us all. She's the leader of the group, really.'

Emily said, very gently, 'You've missed them very much, haven't you?'

'Oh yes. I never said, because the aunts and Great-uncle Matthew wouldn't have understood. But it doesn't matter any longer, because they're all very close to us now – can't you feel that they're close? Listen—' She lifted her head, her eyes bright, and just for a moment the wind whipped at her hair and it was no longer a mousy, rather drab, middle-aged woman who stood there; it was a pretty, bright-eyed little girl, eager to be off with her friends. 'That's Douglas calling now, I'm sure of it,' she said, and whirled round to lean out through the gap in the stones.

Emily started forward at once. 'Selina, don't lean out—'

She heard Selina call out, 'I'm up here! Can you see me! We've escaped this time! Oh, do wait for me—'

There was a soft cracking sound, and the old stonework seemed to sigh and groan. And then it fell away, and as Selina fell forward in a jumble of flailing arms and legs Emily had the incredible impression that she heard a pleased laugh inside the wind, and several childish voices calling delightedly, 'Selina! Selina, run to catch us up! Hurry! Oh, do hurry! We've been waiting so long for you . . . waiting so long for you, Selina . . .'

And then the sounds vanished, and there was only the wind sobbing in and out of the old stones, and Emily was alone on the platform.

By the time Mary got outside Teind House, Gillian Campbell's car had already reached the main road. She could hear the engine, very faintly, roaring into the distance.

She stood for a moment, uncertain what to do. It was completely dark now and Gillian Campbell would presumably be going off to tell people that the escaped prisoner had been hiding out in Teind House. I'll have to move on, thought Mary. I'll come back later and deal with Selina March, of course, but I can't risk doing it tonight. But where do I go now?

She walked down the narrow path that wound away from the house, the lost feeling increasing. She was so used to the structured days inside Broadacre and Moy, where people constantly told you what to do and where to go, that it was bewildering being on her own. Wait, though, how about returning to the tower? Yes, she had to go back there to check on Krzystof Kent; she had almost forgotten that. For a moment this was worrying, because she had never forgotten anything so vitally important before. Was it because she was concerned about Gillian's bringing police and Moy people out here, or was it because she was so completely on her own, now that Christabel had left her? But she did not need Christabel, the faithless cow; she had managed perfectly well by herself.

Yes, but Gillian had got away, and then Mary had almost forgotten about Krzystof Kent. Not good to have done that. Best to go back up into the tower, and deal with Krzystof. In any case, the tower might be a good place to go. The police would go to Teind House first; they would not immediately search the tower. And Krzystof might as well be finished off in case he gave the police any more information. Mary tried to remember what she had told him. Nothing much, really. Nothing important.

But now the night had a purpose to it again – Mary had not liked those moments of aimlessness, of not knowing where she should go or what she should do. There had been a dangerously off-balance feel about everything: as if the ground might be moving, or as if there were flaws in the dark skies, and the darkness might suddenly tear open and dreadful faces leer down at her. As if the world might be enclosed in a crust, and sometimes, when you were at your most afraid or most angry or most powerful, the very force of your emotions could break through that crust, so that you saw other worlds and other existences.

As she went back through the little orchard and approached the tower, she wondered what she would see tonight if the crust really did split. Would she see her mother and father, locked grotesquely in that last embrace, her father with the knitting needle dug into his brain, her mother half asphyxiated with the chopped-off fingers thrust down her throat . . . ? Or would it be Darren Clark drained of blood, looking like a white slug, squirming on the ground . . . ? Or the child they had taken from her all those years ago – Darren Clark's daughter. How odd that she had not thought about that child for years, and now she was thinking about her quite strongly. It might even be Ingrid she would see within that chasm; Ingrid, drugged and helpless, her cheating deceitful lips cut off her face . . .

Ingrid. Yes, if anyone was close to her tonight, it was Ingrid. Was that possible? Just as Christabel had once walked with Mary, might Ingrid now be doing so? Where did the murdered go after they were dead? Christabel had been murdered by Indian separatists fifty years ago, and Ingrid had been murdered as well – Mary had done that herself.

But the skies remained dark and smooth, and Mary reminded herself that she was strong and invincible and there were no cracks in the world, and she remembered as well that she had got to remain free because of the headlines they would put out in tomorrow's newspapers, and reports on tonight's television.

Sixties killer Mary Maskelyne escapes from Moy . . . Police combing the countryside . . . Daring break-out foils prison governors . . . Yes, it would be a pity to be cheated of those headlines.

The headlines might even say, *Another death to Maskelyne's credit . . .* Krzystof Kent. She padded back to the tower, and went in through the old door.

She knew at once that something had happened here. The whole aura of the place had shifted. There was movement – Mary took a moment to pinpoint it, and then knew the movement was not in the tower's top, but beneath it. She saw then the faint oblong of light in the floor, and, within it, shallow steps leading down into the bowels of the earth.

And the panic was roaring back now, and with it the feeling that the world's crust might be bursting open after all, and that things might be climbing through—

Because from out of the oblong of light, moving slowly up what looked like narrow stone steps, were two men – Mary saw they were Dr Irvine and Mr Frost from Moy. But she spared them only the briefest of glances, because between them, being helped to walk, was a thin, dishevelled figure, and it could not be, it simply could not—

'You're supposed to be dead,' said Mary, staring. And then, her voice rising to a scream, 'You're dead, you bitch, you bitch-cunt, you cheating cow, you're dead, I know you're dead because I killed you—'

She did not see Patrick Irvine dart forward across the stone floor, and she barely felt the hypodermic go into her arm before the real darkness closed down.

CHAPTER THIRTY-SIX

They sat in the little cottage on Moy's outskirts, Joanna and Krzystof, Emily and Patrick, Gillian, and Emily's father.

Krzystof's leg had been stitched and bandaged in Moy's emergency room, but afterwards he had asked to be driven back down to the cottage; Emily thought he had booked himself and Joanna into the Black Boar for what was left of the night, but she understood that for the moment the six of them were clinging together. There was a kind of camaraderie about it; a feeling of not being quite ready to face the rest of the world yet. Emily and Gillian had cooked a huge fry-up for everyone: sausages, bacon, eggs and mushrooms, and Patrick had made coffee.

Krzystof had not said very much since they had carried him down from the Round Tower, and Joanna had not said very much either. She had bitten her lip when she saw him, as if to stop herself crying, and then had said, 'Hello, Krzystof darling. What kept you?' And then she had bent over Krzystof's supine body on the makeshift stretcher, and there had been a moment when they stayed like that, not speaking, Joanna's beech-leaf hair falling over Krzystof's face, his arms round her. Everyone had turned tactfully away, and Emily had felt stupid tears sting her eyes.

Krzystof was seated on the slightly battered window seat, where he could stretch out his injured leg. He was white and a bit dishevelled, but had eaten hugely of the fry-up. Joanna was sitting by him, her hands wrapped around a mug of coffee. This was a good arrangement because it left the settee and the two armchairs for the others. It was a bit of a squeeze having so many in the little sitting room all at once, but it was not as bad as it might have been, and anyhow Emily did not in the least mind curling up on a cushion on the floor, next to the chimney. Also, she could see Patrick from here. He looked practically transparent with fatigue; there were dark smudges under his eyes, and his hair flopped untidily over his forehead. Emily loved him so much that she could hardly bear it.

They had given their statements to the police, and someone – Emily thought it had been Patrick – had arranged for Selina March's body to be taken away. There would have to be a post-mortem and an inquest, of course; Emily supposed she would have to give evidence. She also supposed she would start feeling something sooner or later, although she was not sure whether that would be better or worse than this present frozen state. But when Patrick said, 'Let me give you a mild sedative, Em – something to help you sleep tonight, at least,' Emily had instantly said, 'No, I won't have anything, thanks.'

Someone – Emily thought it had been her father – had banked up the fire and drawn the curtains against the night. The little room was warm and brightly lit, and the coffee pot was keeping warm in the hearth. The whisky bottle had gone round three times already.

It was Don Frost who said, 'Patrick – about Mary—'

'Sedated to the gunnels at the moment,' said Patrick, looking up. 'We'll have to confront the problem in a day or two, of course. But I ought to have realised as soon as she escaped that she was going after Selina.'

'I ought to have realised who Mary was when she got into the car,' said Gillian. 'If I had done—'

'You couldn't possibly have known who she was,' said Don, and Emily, who was liking Gillian and feeling sorry for her because of all the stuff that had come out about her godmother, said, 'In any case, you didn't even know that anyone had escaped.'

'No, that's true. And it was dark, and she was so plausible about being part of the search party.'

'She always was plausible,' said Patrick. He sipped the whisky in his glass, and then said, 'But I still wish I'd realised sooner that Selina March was the child who escaped in Alwar all those years ago.'

'Mary's hate-figure,' said Joanna, softly.

'Yes.' Patrick glanced at Gillian, who said, 'Selina

never got over what happened in Alwar. She was an odd, difficult creature. I used to try to ginger her up into doing things – having a wider life – but I never managed it. And she would never leave Inchcape, not even for a weekend. I understand that a bit better now.'

'It was where she felt safe,' said Emily.

'Yes.'

'And yet,' said Joanna thoughtfully, 'it was a dreadfully precarious safety, because only a mile or two from her house was a woman who was hell-bent on killing her.'

'If it comes to blame,' said Krzystof, 'I was the one who told Mary that I was staying with a lady who had lived in Alwar as a child. I even said that Selina knew about the Tower of Silence.'

'Any one of us might have told her that at any given moment,' said Patrick at once. 'You can't possibly be blamed for that. None of us can.'

'But – it was finding out that Selina was living in Inchcape that tipped Mary back into the mania, wasn't it?' said Krzystof.

'Believe me, Maskelyne never needed tipping,' said Patrick. 'The mania never left her.'

For a moment no one spoke, and then Emily said, 'But when Mary finally got to Selina's house, she found out that Selina had had a god-daughter, while Mary had had to give up her own child—'

'Yes, that might well have fuelled the fire.'

'It did,' said Gillian, shuddering. 'I saw it happen, and it was dreadful. But pitiful, as well. Mary went for me, but I managed to dodge out of her way and get back into my car. She followed me, of course – I saw her in the driving mirror.'

'That was when she went back to the tower,' said Don.

'Yes. And saw us bringing Joanna up from the hidden room.' Patrick looked across to where Joanna was listening quietly.

Krzystof looked down at Joanna. 'And that, Joanna,' he said, 'is the part that none of us understands.'

'Well, no.' Joanna was not looking at any of them.

'Mary said something to you like, "You're supposed to be dead,"' said Patrick. 'She saw you and she just seemed to suddenly – explode.'

Krystof looked down at Joanna's bent head. 'Well? Who did she think you were?'

Joanna hesitated, and Krzystof said, 'You might as well tell us, my love. It's a night for telling things.'

Joanna made a oh-what-the-hell gesture, and said, 'I'm supposed, in certain lights, to look like a sister I once had. A sister who was much older than me.'

Patrick and Don Frost turned to stare at her, and Patrick said, in a questioning voice, 'A sister who died nearly thirty years ago?'

'Yes.'

'Ingrid,' said Patrick, softly. 'Dear God, of course. Ingrid.'

'We couldn't have guessed it,' said Patrick, at last. 'And yet the clues were all there.' He looked at Joanna. 'It's why you came here – to Inchcape and Moy, isn't it? You could have gone anywhere for your research, but you chose to come here.'

'I wanted to see her,' said Joanna. She was leaning forward, her arms curled around her bent knees, staring into the depths of the fire. 'I wanted to see the woman who killed Ingrid.' She glanced round the room. 'The murder happened before I was born, but the – the shock-waves of it went on for years and years. It was as if I was born into those shock-waves. My family was shattered by Ingrid's death – well, you'll realize that: it was a particularly brutal murder, wasn't it? But as well as that, they were ashamed. They were very conventional people, and what had upset them almost as much as the murder was learning about the relationship between Ingrid and Mary. It was the Sixties by then, but being gay wasn't really accepted, you see. Not by older people at any rate. My parents didn't understand about Ingrid, and they didn't really want to understand. So they clamped a lid down on it and tried to pretend it hadn't happened. I can see that now, although I couldn't work it out at the time.'

'And your parents wouldn't have forgotten what had happened,' said Krzystof. 'It isn't the kind of thing anyone ever could forget.'

'No. From time to time, little bits of the truth got out, like steam hissing out from a boiling saucepan. It was a peculiar atmosphere to live in. And when I was born my parents were both well into their forties, so I grew up in – well, in the atmosphere of an older generation. Almost the aura of the Forties and Fifties. There were whispers behind hands, and warning looks between aunts and cousins.' She gave a half-smile. 'I don't mean to go all Brontë about it, but for years I sort of sensed there was something wrong somewhere. Something in the family history that people were very carefully not talking about. I used to have the most appalling nightmares.'

Krzystof said, half to himself, '*The barely understood secret became woven into childhood nightmares and childhood fears, and in the end, it called the poor mangled ghosts out of their uneasy resting places . . .*'

'And at times,' said Joanna, turning to look up at him, 'the pretence spilled over into ordinary life. You read my notes.'

'Yes. I had to, in case there was a clue in them that would help me to find you. And there was a clue,' he said. 'Only I was too dense to see it. You were writing about your own childhood, weren't you?'

'Yes. Writing it out, maybe. Catharsis,' she said, looking across at Patrick. 'Confronting the nightmare, isn't that what you'd recommend?'

'Possibly.'

'What happened?' asked Don.

'When I was ten I finally found out about Ingrid – about what had happened to her. My father died, and I was helping to sort out some of his things. There was an old newspaper cutting: I read it in the attic – it was about the only place where I could ever be private.' She paused again, and then said, 'Afterwards I always associated the whole thing about Ingrid with the scent of the attic – dust and discarded books, and old furniture. Anyway, I

484

made a vow the way Selina March made a vow – only hers was to keep a shrine to her parents. My vow was to one day confront the monster who had killed my sister and spoiled my family's life.'

'And?' This was Patrick again.

'And,' said Joanna, speaking very deliberately, 'when I did see her, that afternoon at Moy, I saw a poor, mad, middle-aged woman, who was determinedly trying to cling to a grisly notoriety from the past. At first I simply couldn't equate her with the creature I'd visualised for so many years.' She paused, and then said, very softly, 'And then she looked straight at me, and it was – it was the most extraordinary feeling. I felt as if I was being dragged down into a pit of icy black water. I never actually hated her, not directly, because I never knew Ingrid. So there wasn't very much emotion about the meeting.'

She paused, and Emily, listening intently, thought: I bet there was, though.

'But,' said Joanna thoughtfully, 'I don't think I've ever felt so spooked by anyone in my whole life.'

'She's a very remarkable creature,' said Patrick gently. 'If that intelligence and that strength could have been directed into more positive channels, she might have done anything, become anything.'

'But it went wrong.'

'Yes. She's very very sick, of course.'

'Has she ever had any happiness?' Emily asked the question hesitantly, and Patrick did not immediately reply. She said, a bit defensively, 'Listen, I'm not being stupid or bleeding-heart about it. It's just that I'd like to think she wasn't always in that black icy pit that Joanna referred to just now.'

Patrick said, 'Descriptive prose would be more Joanna's thing than mine. But Mary's life has been a – a very dark life. It's been filled up with hatred and anger for a long long time. But occasionally, in that darkness, I think there have been moments of happiness.'

Joanna said, 'Like unexpected splashes of sunshine in a dark old house.'

Patrick smiled at her. 'I said the descriptions were your job, didn't I? But, yes. For most of her life Mary has lived in the shadows. But—'

Joanna said softly, 'But even someone who lives in a shadow-world occasionally steps into an unexpected patch of happiness.'

A patch of happiness . . .

Joanna was brushing her hair at the dressing-table in the Black Boar's large double bedroom, and Krzystof was seated in the chair by the bed, watching her. He thought he would never want to take his eyes off her.

Joanna had put Mozart's Clarinet Concerto on the portable tape recorder that Krzystof had brought from Teind House, and had taken a long hot bath with every drop of scented oil and bath essence she could find tipped in. Krzystof had opened a bottle of the Black Boar's champagne, which they were now drinking. Neither of them had spoken much, because they had not needed to by that time. But when Joanna smiled at him in the mirror, Krzystof was so consumed by happiness that there was a feeling of pressure inside his chest, as if his heart might burst. Fine thing if I succumb to a heart attack, he thought. Yes, but I never thought I'd get the chance to feel like this again.

Joanna said, a bit hesitantly, 'How is your leg feeling?'

'Bloody painful.' He limped across the room to close the curtains. It was dark outside; Krzystof saw, with vague surprise, that it was well after midnight. 'I expect you could sleep for a fortnight,' he said.

'Sleep be blowed,' said Joanna, setting down her champagne glass, and coming towards him.

A patch of happiness . . .

Emily had been clearing up the plates and coffee cups, and she was just dunking everything in the sink in the cottage's little kitchen when she heard the door open, and Patrick came quietly in.

He said, 'Don's driving Gillian down to the village to get her car. It's still parked there, apparently.'

'Oh.' Emily squirted washing-up liquid into the bowl.

'He's offered her the spare bedroom here, for tonight. The police are still crawling all over Teind House.'

'Yes, I know.' In a minute she would have to turn round and face him in the knowledge, not of the nightmare that had just happened to them all, but of that other, earlier nightmare that had been between just the two of them.

I love your mind and I love everything about you . . . he had said. *I can't begin to think how I'm going to walk away from you, but you must believe that it would never work . . .*

And he had walked away, just as if they had never clung

together for those dizzying few moments, just as if their bodies had not fused, and – what was more important and far rarer – as if their minds had not met and blended and flowed seamlessly into one—

'Are you going back to Durham?'

'I expect so. Yes, of course I am. If I go all out for it, I might manage to take my Finals in the summer.'

'And then?'

'Don't know,' mumbled Emily, bending over the washing up.

'Come back here, Em. Would you?'

'To this cottage?'

'To me,' he said, and Emily turned round, the stupid tears half blinding her so that she could hardly see him, but finding that it did not matter, because his arms were reaching out for her, and happiness – the real thing, the genuine piercing happiness that was so strong you could practically taste it – was filling up the entire kitchen.

In her narrow, hatefully familiar room inside Moy, Mary swam in and out of the drug-induced drowsiness. For most of the time her mind drifted aimlessly on a sea of uncaring half-consciousness, but there were moments when she was able to shake it off, and to consider the events of the last twenty-four hours, and wonder whether her break-out had been reported to the press yet, and, if so, what the press had made of it.

Remarkable bid for freedom by the famous Sixties killer, Mary Maskelyne . . . Mary Maskelyne today cheated her gaolers and was, for a few hours, a free woman . . .

What none of the press reports would say, of course, was that for those few hours when she had been free, the ghosts of her enemies and her victims had walked with her. Her parents. Darren Clark. Curious to think that although she could not remember what he looked like, Darren Clark's daughter was somewhere out there in the world, working, living her life, maybe with a boyfriend or a husband. Had she ever been told who her parents really were, that child who had had dark hair and blue eyes when she was born? A daughter . . . A new idea began to take shape in Mary's mind.

Supposing that one day the newspapers carried headlines that said things like, *Emotional reunion between Mary Maskelyne and the daughter she was forced to give up* . . . '*I never forgot her,*' *said Mary, a catch in her voice.* '*I always knew that one day I would find her.*'

It would make a very good story. She could do the emotional catch-in-the-voice thing pretty easily, and she could even write an account of it all if they wanted. Yes, she would rather like to do that. And finding, and meeting, the child would be something to plan for in the dreary years ahead. You had to have something to aim for, otherwise you would go mad in a place like this. She began to turn over various ideas in her mind, knowing she would think of something, knowing that whatever she thought of would be good. Never mind its being good, let's make it newsworthy.

And what of Selina March? They had told her that Selina had died tonight; Mary was still not sure if she believed this, because it would be like the conniving creatures who ran Moy to say it, purely to prevent Mary from trying to get out again. So she would have to listen and watch very carefully to find out the truth of that.

But even if Selina was dead, the bitch might find a way to come back. Christabel had done that over the years: she had whispered things into Mary's ear when no one was around. Ingrid, the faithless cow, had done it as well. Mary had seen Ingrid very clearly indeed tonight: she had seen her looking out through the eyes of that woman, Joanna Savile.

Ghosts. They never quite left you. They affected your whole life, and they stayed with you for ever. As Mary drifted into sleep again, she was once again feeling, quite strongly, that Christabel's ghost was very near.

Christabel Maskelyne did not sleep very well that night, because she did not sleep very well any night. You had to remain alert; you had to be constantly on the look-out for the creatures who lived inside the dreadful towers. They were cunning, those ogre-creatures; they donned their human masks and their human manners, but Christy knew them for what they were. She had known, the instant the great clanging bell started to boom its horrid warning, that the ogre-creatures would be involved somewhere, and she had known she must be more watchful than ever. The ogres were still out there in the world – the sonorous note of the bell might even be to warn people of them.

Eventually, she drifted into the light shallow sleep that was the only rest she had known for half a century.

* * *

Of the people whose lives had been affected by the tragedy of Alwar and the Tower of Silence, only one lay silent and unknowing tonight, and only one had gone beyond the pain and the fear and the ghosts.

Selina March, carefully laid out in Inchcape's little Chapel of Rest, awaited the good Christian funeral she would be given by the little community in which she had lived for almost her whole life. There would be a post-mortem, of course, and an inquest, but it had already been agreed that once those unpleasant formalities were over, it was only right that Selina be buried next to her two great-aunts and her great-uncle.

Everyone agreed it was what she would have wanted.

To whet your appetite for her next book,
here is an exclusive extract from

A DARK DIVIDING

By

Sarah Rayne

CHAPTER ONE

Writing an article on a newly opened art gallery in Bloomsbury was the very last kind of commission that Harry Fitzglen wanted.

Slosh down over-chilled wine and sandpapery savouries in company with a lot of smug females with too much money and not enough to do? It was hardly in keeping with the image, for God's sake! Harry observed, with some acerbity, that covering arty society parties was a female thing, and then was so pleased with the disagreeable nature of this remark that he repeated it in a louder voice to be sure no one in the editorial department missed hearing it.

'You're really just a sweet old-fashioned romantic at heart, aren't you?' said one of the sub-editors, at which point Harry threw a reference dictionary at the sub-editor, and went off to his editor's office to point out that he had not joined the staff of the *Bellman* to report on fluffy Bloomsbury parties.

'It's not until next month,' said Clifford Markovitch, ignoring this. 'The twenty-second. Six till eight stuff. The gallery's called Thorne's, and it's the latest fling of Angelica Thorne.'

'Oh God,' said Harry, and demanded to know where Angelica Thorne had got hold of the investment capital to be opening smart Bloomsbury galleries.

'I don't know, but it's one of the things I want you to look into,' said Markovitch.

'It's probably guilt money from some ex-lover.'

'Well, if he's a front-bench MP with a wife and children in the Home Counties, we'd like to know his name,' said Markovitch at once. 'The thing is that Angelica's reinvented herself as a purveyor of good taste and of Art with a capital A, and the gallery opening's worth a few columns on that alone. What I want is—'

'Names,' said Harry, morosely. 'Celebrity names. The more celebrity names the wider the circulation.'

'It's our golden rule.'

'I know it is. It's carved over your office door like the welcome to hell line in Dante's *Divine Comedy*.'

'You know, Harry, I sometimes wonder if you're quite suited to this place,' said Markovitch doubtfully.

'So do I. Let's get on with this, shall we? I suppose this gallery opening will be packed with the great and the good, will it? Angelica Thorne knows half of Debrett, in fact she's probably woken up in the beds of a good few of them.'

'Yes, but I don't want anything libellous,' said Markovitch at once. 'Gossip, but not libel. Oh, and you'd better have a look at the exhibits while you're about it. Up-and-coming paintings on the one hand, and futuristic photography on the other, apparently. The photography's the partner's side of things, by the way.'

'If they turn out to be exhibiting displays of dismembered sheep pickled in formaldehyde you can write the copy yourself.'

'You have *met* Angelica Thorne, have you?' demanded Markovitch. 'No, I thought not. Dismembered sheep and Angelica Thorne aren't words that occur in the same sentence.' He considered for a moment, and then quite suddenly leaned across the desk and in an entirely different voice, said, 'It's Thorne's partner I'm interested in, Harry. She's down on the PR hand-out as Simone Marriot, but I've been delving a bit.' Markovitch loved delving. 'Her real name is Simone Anderson.'

Silence. Markovitch sat back in his chair, eyeing Harry. 'Now do you see what this story's really about? And why I've given it to you so far ahead of the date?'

Harry said slowly, 'Simone Anderson. But that was more than twenty years ago— Are you sure you've got the right person?'

But Markovitch would have the right person, of course. He had a complicated card index system of events that might be worth saving up in order to disinter them in ten or twenty years' time. Harry would have bet next month's rent that the wily old sod had been gloating over these particular notes for at least a decade. The *Bellman*'s critics said, loftily, that reading it was like eating reconstituted leftovers, but Markovitch did not mind this in the least; he said the *Bellman* did everything in good taste and took no notice of people who said he would not recognize good taste if it bit him on the backside every morning for a fortnight.

'Simone Anderson,' said Harry again, thoughtfully.

'You do recognize the name, then?'

'Yes.' Harry said it with supreme disinterest. Never display enthusiasm for a job. Hard-bitten Fleet Street hack, that was the image. A reporter who had come up the hard way, and who rode with the knocks on the journey.

'We'll run the Thorne Gallery thing, of course,' said Markovitch. 'But what I really want you to do is delve back into the Anderson story. Properly delve. I don't just want a cobbled-together re-hash—'

Harry observed that this would make a change for the *Bellman*.

'—cobbled-together re-hash of the original facts,' said Markovitch firmly. 'I want some new angles. Now that Simone Anderson has turned up in the world again, so to speak, let's try to find out what she was doing while she was growing up – school, college, university if any. Boyfriends, girlfriends, lovers of either sex. How did she end up in photography? Is she any good? How did she come to link up with Angelica Thorne? I daresay you can manage all that, can you?'

'I might.' As well as never sounding enthusiastic, never sound optimistic, either. Always sound as if there's a bottle of Chivas Regal in your collar drawer, like a sleazy American private-eye. 'If I agree to do it, I suppose I might come up with one or two angles,' said Harry unenthusiastically. 'I'm not a bloody research assistant, though, you should remember I'm not a bloody research assistant.'

'I know you're not, but something odd happened within that family, Harry. I can remember the whispers, and I can remember three-quarters of Fleet Street trying to ferret it out. It was twenty years ago but I can remember the buzz. People died and people disappeared from that family, Harry, and although most of us suspected something odd had happened, no one ever got at the truth. There were rumours of murder covered up and whispers of collusion within the medical profession.'

'Collusion? Collusion over what?'

'I don't know. None of us could find out.'

'And you think I'll find out, twenty years on?'

'You might. But even if you don't, an update on Simone Anderson – Simone Marriot – will still make a nice human interest story.'

The *Bellman* specialized in nice human interest stories. It liked to tug at heartstrings and it liked publishing rowdily illustrated triple-page spreads about celebrity couples, and minor royalty. Sometimes it ferreted out an injustice and mounted a campaign to put it right, or petitioned for the release of some wrongly convicted criminal.

Harry suspected that Markovitch selected the injustices and the wrongly convicted criminals more or less at random, but he had never said this because he needed the job, in fact he needed any job, and so far he had managed to steer clear of drafting appeals to clear the names of old lags which was one mercy.

'Oh, and keep a note of all your contacts. I want them on the computer, *and* on the card-index.' Markovitch did not entirely trust computers. 'In another ten years' time there might be another follow-up on this one. I'll save it up.'

'Don't save it up for me. I won't be here in ten years, in fact I won't be here in five, in fact you'll be lucky if I'm around this time next week. Now that I think about it,' said Harry, disagreeably, 'you might as well give the whole thing to somebody else here and now.'

'I'm giving it to you.'

'Well, I don't want it.'

They often had this kind of discussion but it never got to the 'You're fired' stage, because Markovitch could not forget that Harry had worked in the upper echelons of Fleet Street before the messy and acrimonious divorce that had eventually led to him being sacked, and Harry could not forget that he needed the money after Amanda's perfidy over the joint bank account and the house.

'You can have a by-line.'

'I don't want a by-line,' said Harry. 'I don't want my good name attached to the drivel your paper serves up. But I'll tell you what I will have, I'll have a bonus if that week's circulation goes up.' He would not get one, of course, because nobody on the *Bellman* ever got bonuses. So he got up to go, but before he reached the door, Markovitch said, 'Harry.'

'Yes?'

'It's the mother I'm most interested in.'

'I thought it might be.'

'She might be dead by now,' said Markovitch. 'She vanished completely, and we could never find her.'

'Was she nice-looking?' Harry had no idea why he asked this.

'She had a quality. Something that made her stick in your mind.' For a moment Markovitch even sounded wistful.

'She'd be mid-forties now, presumably?'

'Maybe even a bit more. Melissa Anderson, that was her name. I would very much like to know what happened to her, Harry. What you need to do is find a pathway into the past, that's what you need to do.'

'You don't want a reporter on this job, you want an orienteer,' said Harry crossly, getting up.

'Where are you going?'

'To the pub to find the magnetic north,' said Harry.

Extract from Charlotte Quinton's diaries: 28th October 1899
Tonight during dinner, I suddenly wished there were pathways into the future so that one could know what lay ahead, and sidestep awkward situations.

But at least Edward v. pleased at confirmation that it's almost definitely to be twins in January as already suspected, and is already talking about moving to a bigger house after the birth. This house dark and gloomy – dark houses no place for children (don't I know it!), and anyway, there will have to be extra servants, have I thought of that? Surprisingly enough, I have.

Has told everyone we know that we are expecting twins (in fact has told some people several times over), and is expanding delightedly like a turkey cock all over London. Suppose he thinks that appearing to have sired twins emphasizes his virility.

Dr Austin has promised that I will be given something to help with the birth – expect that will be chloroform which they use for royal births nowadays, although Edward's mother, who came to dinner tonight, disapproves of the practice, and says it's God's will that children come into the world through pain and suffering. Pointed out medical science now strongly in favour of alleviating pain of childbirth – better for both mother and baby – at which she said I was being indelicate and supposed it came of mixing with writers and artists in Bloomsbury.

Suspect Edward of being of the same opinion as his mamma. He has a lot of opinions, Edward – most of them disagreeable. Wish I had known about all his opinions before marrying him.

10th November 1899
We have been discussing names for the babies, although Edward's mother says it tempts Providence, and that pride goeth before a fall.

Still, Edward thinks George and William will suit very nicely, since these both good English names, none of this foreign rubbish. Sounded exactly like Mrs Tigg when she orders in household supplies. A nice saddle of English lamb for Sunday, madam, I thought that would suit very nicely, she says.

At a pinch, Edward will concede George and Alice for the twins, since a daughter always a pleasant thing to have, and if the name Alice good enough for Her Majesty's daughter, good enough for a Quinton.

Asked him what about Georgina and Alice, to which he said, Oh nonsense, my dear, you're built for bearing boys, anyone can see that. Hate it when Edward is bluff and head-patting! Pointed out crossly that am actually quite slim-hipped and strongly object to being regarded as brood mare anyway, to which he wondered huffily what the world was coming to when a wife could make such a very unbecoming remark, and said his mother had been quite right when she said I was indelicate at times. Told him I thought it unbecoming and indelicate for husband to discuss wife with mother.

Sulky silence all through supper as result of this. Would not have thought it possible for anyone to sulk while eating steak and kidney pudding and steamed treacle sponge, but Edward managed it.

Question: What am I doing married to a selfish and self-centred turkey cock who sulks at supper?

Answer: Being revenged on Floy. (Who does not, I fear, give a damn what I'm doing any longer).

Answer adjudged correct in all particulars. And if there really were pathways into the future, I would never (underlined three times) have succumbed to Floy's silver-tongued seduction.

CHAPTER TWO

Except that the drinks were better than he had expected and the food more plentiful, the opening of Thorne's gallery was almost exactly as Harry had predicted. Expensively voiced people milling around and murmuring things about paintings. Females covertly pricing each other's outfits. Good lighting and nicely-grained wooden floorboards.

There were no dismembered sheep or flayed corpses, and no unseemly displays of avant-garde or existentialism, in fact some of the paintings were rather good.

Whatever the house had been in its previous incarnations it lent itself very well to its present existence. It was a tall narrow building and either Angelica Thorne's taste was more restrained than her legend suggested or the London Planners had wielded a heavy hand, because the outside had hardly been tampered with at all. The paintings appeared to be grouped on the ground floor with the photographs upstairs. Harry made a few suggestions to the photographer he had brought with him, and then left him to get on with it.

There were quite a few decorative females around – Harry spotted Angelica Thorne early on. She appeared to be embracing the Bloomsbury ambience with the fervour of a convert; either that or someone had recently told her she resembled a Burne-Jones painting, because the hair was unmistakably pre-Raphaelite – a corrugated riot of burnished copper – and the outfit was suggestive of flowing cravats and velvet tea-gowns.

Of Simone Marriot, or anyone who might conceivably be Simone Marriot, there was no sign. Harry propped himself up against a door-frame and scribbled down a few semi-famous names more or less at random to keep Markovitch sweet, and to let people know that he was press and might therefore be expected to behave erratically. After this he helped himself to another glass of Chablis and went up to the second floor.

There were not so many people at this level. That might be because it was still early in the evening and they had not yet permeated this far, or it might be that the wine was still flowing downstairs, or it might even be that the wine had flown a bit too well for most of them already and the narrow open stairway presented an awkward challenge. ('Break my neck by falling downstairs in front of Angelica Thorne's up-market cronies? Not likely,' most of them had probably said.)

But even after several glasses of wine Harry negotiated

the stairway easily enough. He came around the last tortuous spiral and stepped out on to the second floor which had the same pleasing Regency windows as downstairs. There was even a view of the British Museum through one of them. Nice. He began to move slowly along the line of framed prints.

There were two surprises.

The first was the photographs themselves. They were very good indeed and they were thought-provoking in rather a disturbing way. A lot of them used the device of illusion, so that at first glance an image appeared to be ordinary and unthreatening, but when you looked again it presented an entirely different image. Nothing's quite as it seems in any of them, thought Harry, pausing in front of a shot of a darkened room with brooding shapes that might have been shrouded furniture, but that might as easily be something more sinister. The outline of tree branches beyond a window formed themselves into prison-bars and one branch had broken away and hung down, giving the false image of a coiled rope, knotted into what might be a hanging noose. Harry stared at this last one for a long time, the noise of the party fading out.

'Do you like that one?' said a voice at his side. 'It isn't exactly my favourite, but it's not bad. Oh – I should explain that I'm not trying to pick you up or anything. I'm Simone Marriott and this is my bit of Thorne's Gallery so I'm meant to be circulating and making intelligent conversation to the guests.'

Simone Marriot was the second surprise of the evening.

*　　*　　*

'I thought you looked as if you might be easier to talk to than most of the others,' she said. 'I'm not sure why I thought that.'

They were sitting on one of the narrow windowsills by this time, with the sun setting somewhere beyond the sky-line and the scents of the old house warm all around them. The party downstairs seemed to be breaking up, and Angelica Thorne's voice could be heard organizing some of them into a sub-party for a late dinner somewhere.

Simone had longish dark brown hair with glinting red lights in it, cut in layers so that it curved round to frame her face. She wore an anonymous dark sweater over a plain, narrow-fitting skirt, with black lace-up boots, and the only touch of colour was a long tasselled silk scarf wound around her neck, in a vivid jade green. At first look there was nothing very outstanding about her; she was small and thin and Harry thought she was very nearly plain. But when she began to talk about the photographs he revised his opinion. Her eyes – which were the same colour as the silk scarf – glowed with enthusiasm, lighting up her whole face, and when she smiled it showed a tiny chip in her front tooth that made her look unexpectedly *gamine*. Harry found himself wanting to see her smile again.

'I like your work very much,' he said. 'Although some of it makes me feel uneasy.'

'Such as the barred window and the tree that might be a hangman's noose?'

'Yes. But I like the way you identify the darkness in things, and then let just a fragment of it show through.

In most of the shots you've disguised it as something else though. A tree branch, or a piece of furniture, or a shadow.'

Simone looked pleased but she only said, 'I like finding a subject and then seeing if there's a dark underside.'

'Isn't there a dark underside in most things?'

She looked at him as if unsure whether he was baiting her. But she seemed satisfied that he was not; she said, 'Yes, in almost everything, isn't there? That's the really interesting part for me: shooting the darkness.'

'Can I see the photographs again? With you as guide this time?'

'Yes, of course. Hold on, I'll refill your glass first.'

She hopped down from the windowsill. She was not especially graceful, but she was intensely watchable and Harry suddenly wondered if she had inherited the quality that had put that wistful note into Markovitch's voice when he spoke of her mother.

They moved along the line of framed photos together. 'I like comparing the kempt and the unkempt as well,' said Simone. 'When I was doing this sequence over here—'

'National Trust versus derelict squats.'

'Yes. Yes. When I was doing those I saved the really decrepit shots for the last. Like when you're a child and you eat the crust of a fruit pie first and save the squidgy fruit bit for last. This one's Powys Castle. It's one of the old border fortresses and parts of it have hardly changed since the thirteen-hundreds. It's beautiful, isn't it? Ruined but glossily ruined, and the ruins are being nicely preserved so there's a bit of the past that's caught and frozen for ever.'

'And then to balance it you've got this.'

He thought she hesitated for a second, but then she said, 'That's a seventeenth- or eighteenth-century mansion. It's meant to illustrate the past dying – the place has been neglected for years, in fact it's decaying where it stands. Actually, it's a vanity thing to have included that one – it's a shot I took when I was about twelve with my very first camera and I always felt a bit sentimental about it. But I thought it was just about good enough to include as contrast in this sequence.'

'It is good enough. Where is it?' said Harry, leaning closer to see the title.

'It's called Mortmain House,' said Simone. 'It's on the edge of Shropshire – the western boundary, just about where England crosses over into Wales. I lived there for a while as a child.'

'Mortmain. Dead hand?'

'Yes. Somewhere around the Middle Ages people used to transfer land to the Church so their children wouldn't have to pay feudal dues after they died. Then the heirs reclaimed the land afterwards. It was a pretty good scam until people tumbled to what was happening, so a law was drawn up to prevent it – the law of dead man's hand it's sometimes called and— Am I talking too much?'

'No, I'm interested. It looks,' said Harry, his eyes still on the place Simone had called Mortmain House, 'exactly like the classic nightmare mansion.'

'It does rather, doesn't it?' Her voice was just a bit too

casual. 'I haven't exaggerated its appearance, though. It really does look like that.'

'Filled with darkness? With nightmares?'

'Well, nightmares are subjective, aren't they? We've all got a private one.'

Harry looked down at her. The top of her head was about level with his shoulder. He said, '"I could be bounded in a nutshell and still count myself a king of infinite space, were it not that I have bad dreams."'

'Yes. *Yes.*' She smiled, as if pleased to find that he understood, and Harry wondered what she would do if he said, 'We all have a secret nightmare, but what you don't know, my dear, is that I'm here to see if I can wind back Time or find a pathway into the past ...'

He did not say it, of course. Never blow your cover unless it's a question of life or death.

He said, 'Is it a particular quality of yours to see the darknesses in life?'

Simone hoped she had not banged on for too long about darknesses and Mortmain House and everything, to the journalist from the *Bellman*. But he had seemed to understand – he had quoted that bit about nightmares – and he had appeared genuinely interested.

So it was vaguely daunting when Angelica, conducting a breathless post-mortem on the opening two days later, reported that Harry Fitzglen had phoned to ask her out to dinner.

'How nice.' Simone refused to be jealous of Angelica, who was giving her this terrific opportunity. People hardly ever mentioned Angelica without adding, 'She's *the* Angelica Thorne, you know – one of the real *It* girls in the Nineties. Dozens of lovers and scores of the most extraordinary parties. There's not much she hasn't tried,' they said. But one of the things that Angelica was trying now was being a patron of the arts, and one of the people she was patronizing was Simone, and for all Simone cared Angelica could have tried necromancy and cannibalism. She refused to be jealous because Harry Fitzglen was taking Angelica out to dinner, even when Angelica, smiling the smile that made her look like a mischievous cat, said they were going to Aubergine in Chelsea.

'If he can afford Aubergine, he must be pretty successful.'

'I like successful. In fact— Oh God, is this the electricity bill for the first quarter? Well, it can't possibly be right – look at the *total*! We can't have used all that heating, do they think we're *orchids* or something, for pity's sake!'

They were in the upstairs office in the Bloomsbury gallery. Simone loved this narrow sliver of a building, tucked away in a tiny London square, surrounded by small, smart PR companies, and hopeful new publishing houses, and unexpected bits of the University or the Museum that seemed to have become detached from their main buildings and taken up residence in convenient corners. The office was small because they had partitioned it off from the rest of the attic floor, wanting to keep as much gallery space as they could, but from up here you could see across rooftops and just glimpse a corner of the British Museum, a bit blurry because the windows of the house were the original ones and they had become wavy with age.

Simone liked the scents of the house as well, which despite the renovations were still the scents of an earlier era. In the late 1800s and early 1900s Bloomsbury had been the fashionable place for what people called intellectuals – writers and painters and poets. There were times when she had the feeling that it might be possible to look through a chink somewhere and glimpse the house's past, and see them all in their candlelit rooms, discussing and arguing and working— No, it would not have been candlelight by then, it would have been gaslight. Not quite so romantic.

Still, it would be nice to trace the house's history; Simone would love to know the kind of people who had lived here when it had been an ordinary private house. She and Angelica might set up a small display about it: they might even find some old photographs that could be restored. Would Harry Fitzglen have access to old newspaper archives and photographic agencies? Could Angelica be asked to sound him out about it? Angelica was enthusiastic about Thorne's but the enthusiasm might not stretch to discussing marketing strategies with a new man.

Simone studied Angelica covertly. Today she was wearing the newly acquired glasses with huge tortoiseshell-framed spectacles. She did not need them but they were part of her new image. Simone thought they made her look like a very sexy Oxford don; she thought only

Angelica could have managed to look both sexy and studious at the same time, and she suddenly wanted to make a portrait photograph of her, to see if she could show both moods at the same time. Would Harry Fitzglen see these two aspects of Angelica when he took her out, and if so which one would he prefer? He would prefer the sexy side, of course. Men always did.

Or would he? He had been far more intelligent than he had let on at the opening and much more perceptive; Simone had known that almost straight off. Even without that Shakespeare quote about bad dreams he had seen the darkness within Mortmain, although anyone with halfway normal eyesight would probably have done so. But that question he had put about Simone herself seeing the darkness had put him in another category altogether because as far as she knew no one else had ever sensed the presence of darkness in her own mind.

No one had ever known about the little girl who watched her.

She had been four years old when she became aware of this inner darkness, and she had been a bit over five when she began to understand where it came from.

The other little girl. The unseen, unheard child whom no one else could see or hear, but who lay coiled and invisible inside Simone's mind. Simone did not know her name so she just called her the little girl.

To begin with it had not been anything to be especially frightened or anxious about. Simone had not even known that other people did not have this invisible companion to talk to. And she quite liked having this other little girl around; she liked the sudden ruffling of her mind that meant the little girl was there, and she liked talking to her and listening to some of her stories which were really good. Simone liked stories; she liked people to read them out of books, although not everybody read them in the right way.

Mother always read them in the right way. Simone liked listening to Mother, and she liked watching her when she read. Her voice was rather soft and everyone thought she was quiet and gentle – people at school said, Gosh, what a great mother to have, isn't she a pushover for things? – but Simone's mother was not a pushover at all. She made rules about not watching too much television, and about homework and bedtime at seven o'clock every night, but everyone said this was what most mothers did. And Simone was pretty lucky not to have lots of boring relations because you had to be polite to them, and sometimes there were cousins who came to stay and you had to give up your bed, or uncles who had too much to drink and aunts who got cross. It was not so great having lots of family.

But Simone would have quite liked some family, and so when the little girl said, 'I'll be your family,' she was pleased.

The other little girl did not have to do the same things as Simone. She did not seem to go to school although she had lessons at a table and she had to learn a lot of things by heart. Simone did not get to know this all at once; it came in bits, like a series of pictures coming inside her head, or like the nights when she could not sleep and kept hearing snatches of the television from downstairs but not enough to know the programme or recognize the voices. She always knew when the little girl was there, because there was the feeling of something ruffling her mind, like when you blew on the surface of water and made it ripple.

Once she tried making a drawing of the little girl. This was a bit spooky because it turned out to be much easier than Simone had expected. As she drew, the girl's face got steadily clearer, like polishing the surface of a smoky, smeary old mirror until at last you saw your reflection.

The girl's face looked straight up out of the paper. Simone thought it was what people called a heart-shaped face, and she thought the girl ought to have been quite pretty. But she was not. She had a sly look, which made Simone feel uncomfortable and even a bit frightened. Until then she had been quite pleased with the drawing but when she saw the sly eyes she scrunched the paper up and threw it in the dustbin when Mother was not looking. But even then she had the feeling that the eyes were still watching her through the thrown-away bits of food and tea-leaves.

Extract from Charlotte Quinton's diaries: 30th November 1899
Edward points out that if calculations are all accurate, the twins may be born on 1st January 1900, and thinks this a good omen. Has even gone so far as to make a little joke about that night in March after your birthday dinner, my

dear, which is the kind of remark he normally regards as rather near. Clearly I'm being viewed with indulgence at the moment. It will be God's mercy if it lasts.

But a new year and a new century and two new lives, Edward says, pleased at having coined this neat phrase by himself. He adds, expansively, perhaps a new house, as well, what do I think? Some very nice villas out at Dulwich.

Saw copy of Floy's latest book in Hatchard's while shopping this morning. Horrid shock since dozens of them were displayed in the window, and especially a shock since photograph of Floy in middle of it all. He looked as if he had been dragged protesting into the photographer's studio for the likeness to be taken. Highly upsetting to come upon image of ex-lover staring angrily out of Hatchard's window.

Came straight home and went to bed, telling Edward I felt sick and dizzy. Felt dreadfully guilty when he insisted on calling Dr Austin out, since could hardly explain real reason for sickness and dizziness in first place.

Had to endure excruciating examination, although must admit Dr Austin v. gentlemanly and impersonal. It will teach me not to tell untruths, however. He prodded around and measured my hips, and asked some questions, then looked portentous, but said, oh nothing to worry about, Mrs Quinton, and he would send round a mixture for the sickness.

Edward's mother to dinner tonight (third time this month!), which meant one of Edward's mother's homilies. This one was to the effect that I am racketing about town too much, and rest is important in my condition. Told her high time science found a less inconvenient and messy method of reproducing after all these thousands of years, and was accused of being Darwinian and having peculiar reading habits – also of scamping on house-keeping since first course was eggs in sunlight, and the tomato sauce was pronounced too acidic. Not surprising I feel sick if this is the kind of dish I allow on my dinner table . . . And on and on.

Went to bed in bad temper. Will not buy Floy's book, absolutely will not . . .

Later
Sent out to Hatchard's for Floy's book on principle that better to read it and be prepared before anyone tries to discomfit me by telling me about it. Have always suspected that Wyvern-Smith female of trying to sink her claws into Floy on her own account, and do not trust her not to drop the subject into dinner-table conversation out of sheer malice. Edward's mother says she dyes her hair – Clara Wyvern-Smith that is, not Edward's mother. Would not be at all surprised, although wonder how Edward's mother knows.

6th December 1899
Think something may be wrong. Dr Austin downstairs in earnest conclave with Edward earlier, although when I asked if anything wrong, all Dr Austin would say was that he thought the twins were a little quiet, considering how near to the confinement we are.

However, Edward has gone off to his managers' meeting as usual, telling me not to wait up since he may be late. He may be as late as he likes for all I care.

9th December 1899

Floy's book brilliant. Have had to read it piecemeal and in secrecy in case anyone sees and wonders, and it is not the kind of book that should be read like that. Should be read in one glorious sweeping read, so that you shut the rest of the world out while you walk through the landscapes that Floy unfolds, all of which are like glowing jewel-studded tapestries unfurling silkily across your inner vision. It's about lost loves and relinquished passions, and a heroine who struggles between duty and love . . . Have not dared wonder, even for a second, if Floy wrote it after that last agonizing scene, when I told him I must stay with Edward and he called me a middle-class provincial-minded conformist, which is about the most stinging string of epithets Floy can bestow.

(I'm lying, of course. I spent the rest of the night wondering furiously if he wrote it after we parted.)

But whenever it was written, Floy has – and always will have, I think – a gift for making his readers feel that he has invited them into a soft, secret world, glowing with dappled afternoon sunlight or golden lamplight, with siren songs humming under old casement windows, and sexual stirrings and erotic whisperings everywhere. And that the reader is there alone with him, and that it's a wholly enchanted place to be . . .

Refuse to apologize for that burst of sentiment, since

if cannot be sentimental about a lost love, not much point to life.

12th December 1899
What a delight to have an excuse for handing over the Christmas and New Year preparations to Mrs Tigg and Maisie-the-daisie! Also to avoid unutterably tedious dinners with Edward's business colleagues – 'Dreadfully sorry, don't quite feel up to formal entertaining this year. What with the birth imminent – feeling wretchedly tired – sure you'll understand.'

'A quiet Christmas,' Edward has told everyone. 'Charlotte is not feeling quite the thing.'

Charlotte is feeling very much not the thing, especially when it comes to interminable dinner parties with eight courses and the conversation exclusively about politics, banking, or scandalous behaviour of Prince of Wales. Last Christmas one of Edward's managers stroked my thigh under the tablecloth.

Ridiculous and pointless to wonder how Floy will spend Christmas. Do people in Bloomsbury have Christmas, one wonders? Or do they sit around earnestly and paganly discussing life and love and art (or Art), like they did on the one occasion when Floy took me to someone's studio, and we all ate Italian food and drank Chianti, and somebody asked to paint me only Floy objected because he said the man was a bad leftover from the Pre-Raphaelites, and I was so beautiful no painter in the world could possibly capture my looks . . .

All flummery and soft soap, of course, I know that now.

Even so, spent most of the evening remembering Floy's house in Bloomsbury, with the scents of old timbers and the incense he burns when he is working because he says it stimulates his brain . . . And the night he lit dozens of candles in his bedroom and we made wild love there, with the sounds of London all around us and the distant view of the British Museum from the window.

Wonder if Floy will be stroking anyone's thigh under tablecloth at Christmas?

Later
Am increasingly worried about that remark of Dr Austin's that the twins are a little quiet. Do not want them leaping around like the Russian ballet, but would feel better if they were a bit more assertive.

If everyone's calculations right, only a couple of weeks left now.